Michele HAUF

and **Alexis Morgan**

BOUND

MILLS & BOON

Hooked on dark, dangerous seduction?

You can find more from Michele Hauf and Alexis Morgan
in Mills & Boon® Nocturne™

www.millsandboon.co.uk

Michele Hauf has been writing for over a decade and has published historical, fantasy and paranormal romances. A good strong heroine, action and adventure and a touch of romance make for her favourite kind of story. She lives with her family in Minnesota and loves the four seasons, even if one of them lasts six months and can be colder than a deep freeze. You can find out more about her at www.michelehauf.com.

Alexis Morgan grew up in St Louis, Missouri, graduating from the University of Missouri, St Louis, with a BA in English. She met her future husband sitting outside one of her classes in her freshman year. Eventually her husband's job took them to the Pacific Northwest where they've now lived for close to thirty years.

Author of more than nineteen full-length books, short stories and novellas, Alexis began her career writing contemporary romances and then moved on to Western historicals. However, beginning in 2006, she crossed over to the dark side. She really loves writing paranormal romances, finding the world-building and developing her own mythology for characters especially satisfying. She loves to hear from fans and can be reached at www.alexismorgan.com.

First published in Great Britain 2012
by Mills & Boon, an imprint of Harlequin (UK) Limited, Eton House,
18-24 Paradise Road, Richmond, Surrey TW9 1SR

BOUND © Harlequin Enterprises II B.V./S.à.r.l. 2012

The publisher acknowledges the copyright holders of the individual works as follows:

The Devil to Pay © Michele Hauf 2009
Vampire Vendetta © Patricia L. Pritchard 2010

ISBN: 978 0 263 90239 6

012-1012

Harlequin (UK) policy is to use papers that are natural, renewable and recyclable products and made from wood grown in sustainable forests. The logging and manufacturing processes conform to the legal environmental regulations of the country of origin.

Printed and bound by
CPI Group (UK) Ltd, Croydon, CR0 4YY

THE DEVIL
TO PAY

Michele
HAUF

Dear Reader,

I like to write books in a series. Once I take the time to research and create the 'world,' I then enjoy playing with all the characters who people it. Sometimes I even learn new things about the world after I've written two or three books in the series. *The Devil To Pay* is the final book in the BEWITCHING THE DARK series, which pits vampires against witches. Each story in the series stands alone. You can read it without having read a previous story and understand what is going on. But if you have read *Kiss Me Deadly* (which features in *Cursed*, available now) then you're probably wondering about Ravin and Nikolaus's child. It didn't end well for the poor thing, and he hadn't even been born yet!

So here is Ivan Drake's story. I almost feel I should apologise to the guy for giving him such a rough start, but as with any good hero, he rises to the challenge.

For a complete term list on the BEWITCHING THE DARK world, do check out my website at www.michele hauf.com. I also post frequent updates of my upcoming releases on my blog. Find that at www.dustedbywhimsy. blogspot.com.

Here's to love at first bite!

Michele

To: Pat White, because she understands about the tea and chocolate, and Christian and Clive, and 'What the hell does he want?!' and, finally, let's just let it all go and learn from it.

Prologue

Ivan Drake celebrated his twenty-first birthday by handing over his soul to the devil Himself. It wasn't a mutual agreement; the deal had been signed, sealed and delivered twenty-one years, eight months and five days earlier.

Ivan's parents had made the bargain only days after his conception.

From very early on, Ivan's parents had told him the truth. They had been young, in love and hadn't realized he had been conceived when they'd promised Himself their firstborn. Hell, Nikolaus Drake had despised Ravin Crosse at the time; as a vampire, the last thing he would have purposefully sought to do would be to father a child, let alone father one with the witch he'd once hated enough to wish dead.

A misdirected love spell had brought the two enemies together. They grew to genuinely love one another: Nikolaus, the phoenix vampire; and Ravin Crosse, a witch who once stalked vampires to their deaths. Their child had been born half witch and half vampire. The most powerful vampire/witch hybrid to walk this earth, they believed.

Ivan did possess unlimited power, yet with the added encumbrance of the devil riding his back.

Ivan had almost forgotten his fate as he'd entered his teen years. His parents had taught him to be moral and were ever trying to focus their son's attention on the future, and the goodness he could create in this world, instead of allowing him to wallow in his destiny.

Not being schooled in the public education system, Ivan had studied alongside his father until he was fifteen, then he'd gone on to Princeton at the ripe old age of sixteen. He had studied generals in college, not necessarily focused on any career but with a mind to understanding the world, its cultures and the people and politics that shaped it. He'd graduated with a bachelor's degree in sociology and history in his nineteenth year.

The most valuable lesson Ivan's parents had given him? Tolerance. He did not take sides in the ever-present war between vampires and witches, a war that currently threatened to destroy one side or even both.

Having toasted his birthday and opened a few gifts, Ivan now strode the dark alleyway in the city where his parents lived, Minneapolis. Ivan was a free spirit, and, due to a small trust fund and an excellent accountant, he owned houses all over the world. Nikolaus Drake's foresight had spread family residences about the world. Ivan put great merit in his father's business sense and wisdom.

Well into the small hours of morning, the night wasn't yet still. In the distance a car honked, and perhaps a taxi squealed to pick up the last of the bar crowd as booze-dizzied singles headed home in pairs to finish encounters begun with a wink and a dance.

The air, sticky humid, and the late August temperature, still in the nineties, melted Ivan's cotton T-shirt to his flesh like plastic wrap. He tugged it off and gave his back a stretch, flexing his arms and inhaling a cleansing breath.

He didn't immediately associate the strange smell with his fate. But he would soon regret not recognizing the sulfuric taint that had clung to him from the moment he'd stepped out from his parents' loft edging the Mississippi River.

Ivan stopped in the center of the alley. He sensed a presence behind him. Being a vampire made it easy to pick up the minutest of sounds, including spiders and mice scurrying through the cracked brick wall to his left.

But it was the scent that bothered him most. And though he'd not ever smelled it before, he could name it without question. Brimstone whispered upon the atmosphere, snaking, prodding. It suffused his very being.

Ivan's heart fell in his chest.

He'd known this was coming. But though he'd thought about its arrival, he'd never really anticipated the moment.

Bolstered by innate confidence, his resolve held firm. He stood there, fists curling and shoulders rolled back to bulk up the muscle honed by years of world-crossing adventure and defensive training.

Be calm, he cautioned inwardly. *Accept what you must.*

He would never forget the sound of hooves upon asphalt. One, and then another. Stepping into his psyche. A glass-breaking crunch pounded a basso thump up through Ivan's ankles and reverberated along his spine.

Himself had arrived to claim his soul.

"Ivan Everhart Drake," a deep, sepulchral voice commanded. "Turn and face your master."

Ivan had faced all sorts of dark denizens, demons and just

plain nasty vampires in his life—but for the first time, he felt sweat form in the creases of his palms and a reedy whine sought to escape the back of his throat. His limbs shook subtly.

Turning abruptly, Ivan cut off a choke of fear. His leg muscles loosened and felt as if they would snap out from under him, bringing him down—but by some miracle he maintained an upright stance.

Looming three or four heads taller than Ivan's six and a half feet, the creature before him occupied the very air with a dark eminence. Regal. Macabre. Heartrending. It owned the humid air, sick with a miasma of fetid refuse and chemicals. It commandeered the glittering eyes that crept in the shadows. It bled pain from the lost. It devoured mirth with a twist of limb, a slice of flesh.

It owned Ivan's very breath.

Horns black as jet curled out in top-heavy spirals from the skull. The beast's gaunt face was shellacked with the blackest flesh. Ebony talons clacked at the ends of humanlike fingers growing from near-as-mortal arms. The body appeared human, though distorted in musculature and all of black greasy flesh, like fresh tar steaming on the freeway. Strangely disjointed legs ended with thick, cloven hooves.

"Don't stare, boy. Only into my eyes is where I wish to feel you."

And Ivan met that challenge. Red irises teemed with liquid-black electricity. Swallowed whole by those eyes, Ivan felt his confidence sink.

"You have been told of your debt to me?"

Ivan nodded. And now his legs did give way. He couldn't prevent his reaction. Much as he wished to stand firm, he dropped to his knees.

So this is how it will be. The thought stirred bile in his gut.

"Good. You will show the appropriate respect to me from now on."

Himself leaned forward. A clacking talon shivered before Ivan's face. With a snap, the multijointed fingers stretched out in a hideous gesture of command.

Ivan's body jerked forward, his chest arching high and his ribs straining at the intense pull, as he was lifted from his knees. But his toes touched the ground. His arms whipped backward, stretching at the shoulder sockets sharply. Pain soughed through him. Incredible searing fire worked every muscle of his being, collecting in his extremities and working toward his center.

He cried out, but no sound left his throat. He wanted to slap at his chest to numb the havoc, but his body was not his to command.

And a brilliant light exploded from his chest, drawn toward the directing orchestration of Himself's talon. The light sparkled, so vast, fathomless.

A tear rolled down Ivan's cheek.

Gone. His soul. Raped from his body.

Landing on the gritty asphalt on all fours, Ivan rolled forward, coughing as he attempted to draw in air.

Give it back. But the sounds would not leave his mouth.

Taken. Claimed. He must now begin his slavery—a promise made without his consent. He wanted to crawl away into the darkness. Was it not where he now belonged?

But no, something inside of him would not surrender. *You are better than that. You will never succumb, not completely.* So instead, he pushed up with his hands, and knelt proudly before Himself.

The dark prince swept Ivan's gorgeous soul into a ball and opened his maw and shoved it inside. A glint of pure light appeared in each of Himself's obsidian eyes, and he grinned with the smile of a satisfied diner.

"Well kept, Drake. It is rare the soul of a vampire and a witch is so pure. You've drunk your blood and cast your spells, but it's all been done with good intention."

"I have never done a soul harm if I could prevent it."

"What a sorry half-breed creature you are."

The sudden strike across his jaw sent Ivan sprawling to the left. Blood oozed from his split cheek; he could feel the cut flesh with his tongue, so deep it had gone.

Himself chuckled. The humorless sound burbled up brimstone, and the buzz of a million insects swarmed Ivan's brain.

"From this day forth you are my fixer, boy. Your soul is mine. I command your nights. You will be my eyes, my ears and my vengeance upon this mortal ground. You will track those who seek to betray me and punish them swiftly so they will know my wrath. Welcome to hell, Ivan Drake."

Cloven hooves pranced around him as Ivan again pushed himself to his knees. Disoriented and shivering with the pining need for his stolen soul, he cringed when something icy touched him at the back of his neck.

Himself drew his long black tongue down from the base of Ivan's skull to the center of his bare back, relishing the slow, lascivious act. Like hoar frost on steel to wet flesh, and yet steam rose.

And in its wake, black tendrils dug into Ivan's flesh and spiked out, drawing themselves in darkness across his back. A shadow of Himself's reflection. It rooted down deep, wrapping barbed tips about Ivan's ribs and lungs and poking at the hard muscles of his heart.

"You are mine," declared the master of darkness.

Chapter 1

Seven years later...

Ivan Drake slapped his palm across the offender's reedy neck and shoved hard. Simon Grimm hacked out a groan as his spine and shoulders collided with a brick wall.

It was midnight. Ivan had tracked the mark from his legal office in downtown Berlin to this ritzy underground parking garage boasting rubber flooring and a heated car wash.

"You've been stealing souls, psychopomp," Ivan hissed.

He clamped both hands to the man's bony shoulders and pressed his fingertips until he felt the silk business suit tear— and then flesh popped. Blood perfumed the air, meaty and more than a little inviting.

"Let go of me! Who the hell are you?"

Ivan dug in deeper. "I'm your worst nightmare."

"Ha! You don't know nightmares until you've vomited up the sins of murderers. You don't scare me."

How the idiot managed such lack of reason—so many of his marks acted equally as belligerent—never ceased to amaze Ivan. This psychopomp had been moonlighting as a sin eater. Simon Grimm had been stealing souls for years, and Himself wanted it stopped.

Grimm kicked, his leather loafer landing on Ivan's thigh. Though the man was as tall as Ivan, he was slender and wasn't designed for defense. Or self-preservation.

Slapping the guy hard across the cheek sent him reeling to the ground. He landed ten feet from where Ivan stood, but inches from the license plate of a black BMW claiming SHESMINE.

Giving his head a discombobulating shake, Grimm then spat out blood. "Let me guess, Himself sent you. Are you the devil's fixer? Shouldn't you be less *GQ* and more *Demon's Quarterly?*"

"You're stealing his souls," Ivan reiterated.

Stretching his left arm out pumped a bicep beneath the fitted Italian leather jacket. So he liked style. Just because he was a badass didn't mean he couldn't look good doing it.

Stalking toward the fallen cretin, he fisted his hands. Neck tense, he strained to unmake those fists.

Just once. *Could I resist just once?* Turn away and run. Leave this wretched psychopomp to a hell of his own making.

But his fists remained. Ivan was the psychopomp's designated hell for the evening.

Every time Ivan tried to fight the coercion, it coiled tighter about his will. A boa constrictor wrapped about his very being. Anger over his life boiled in his gut, making escape from the invisible bonds impossible.

He was the devil Himself's fixer. And he hated every second of it.

"I'll never stop!" Grimm shouted as he shuffled along the wall, spider-long legs scrambling across the rubber-tiled floor, away from Ivan's relentless approach.

Grimm was a soul shepherd, a man who ferried souls after death, directing them, much like a traffic cop, either to heaven or hell. The official term was *psychopomp*. Lately, he'd been directing far too many of Himself's plunder in the other direction—that is, *after* he'd eaten away their sins.

While Ivan cheered for those unofficially pardoned souls, he also understood the universe functioned thanks to a system of checks and balances. If a soul was intended for Himself, it shifted the universal balance to send it elsewhere.

"There's nothing you can do to me that'll hurt worse than my life already does," Grimm slammed out. "Go ahead. Beat me bloody. If I can rescue a soul from the flames, then I will."

Ivan leaned over the shivering psychopomp. "There *are* no flames," he said calmly.

"How do you know? Every man conceives his own hell. *I* say there's flames!"

Lifting the man until his feet dangled above the rubber matting, Ivan held him beneath both armpits. Grimm didn't struggle because he was exhausted. So it was easy for Ivan to tap into the coercion—Himself's power—and conjure a summoning.

The shadow on the back of his neck pulsated with what Ivan had come to know as a sort of wickedly macabre pleasure. It acted as an entity apart from Ivan, and yet its roots were planted deep in his being.

Focusing his every sense to the psychopomp's spirit, his very essence, Ivan mined deep for those tendrils of darkness never completely purged after an eating. The man had been eating sins and then sending the newly cleansed sinner on to heaven. Even Ivan disapproved of that. Sinners should know better; no amount of money could buy their way to heaven, even after their deaths.

Ivan felt the heavy darkness rise to the man's surface, like molecules of sludge bubbling up through the fragile veil of humanity. Sour wickedness tapped at Ivan's palms, teasing, vying for entrance through the pores of his flesh, but he blocked it.

Instead, he released the summons, and it flowed from Grimm in a massive black cloud, which instantly surrounded the man, fixing to him like a hungry hive eager for blood. It buzzed over the twitching psychopomp as Ivan held him in the air. Legs kicking, and now shouting bloody murder, Grimm struggled against the vicious darkness he'd never known he'd harbored within.

Remnants of his client's stolen sins took their due.

When the inhuman shrieks grew hoarse and the man's body fell limp, Ivan deported the summons. It happened with a sigh from the psychopomp and a prick of icy pain to Ivan's shadow. He dropped Grimm on the ground and stepped away.

Fifty feet away, the exit to the garage opened to the night. Not a single city building blocked the view of the black summer sky. The moon perched high and gorgeous, pale and pocked with mysterious gouges and alien landmarks. Ivan wondered if she were as cold as she looked.

Concentrate on anything but the evil. Grab on to the good. Or you will know your hell, too.

If for a moment, he had to do it, draw his attention away from the task at hand, push out the anger, the coercion. If he did not, then he would be brought down completely, a willing supplicant to Himself.

"Never," Ivan murmured.

Punching a fist into his opposite palm, he turned and pressed a booted foot to Grimm's shoulder, holding him against the wall, for otherwise the man would slump forward and pass out.

"Change your mind?" Ivan asked.

Simon nodded.

"I didn't hear that. I've just visited all the sins you've eaten upon you. They wish to tear away your flesh and pluck out your eyeballs. Every day. I can set them loose again, and they will be bound to you for the rest of your days on this earth. And when you perish, they'll be waiting for you in hell." He leaned in and tipped up the man by the chin. "You cool with that?"

"No!" Grimm grasped out, but his hand fell weakly upon his stomach. "I'll stop," he muttered. "They all go where they belong from now on."

"Do you swear it?"

"On my mother's soul."

Ivan winced at the easy wager. Didn't the man understand the weight of his words? Should he slip up, Himself would snatch his mother's soul away in a blink.

"I'll be keeping an eye on you."

Ivan pushed away from the man's shoulder and stepped back. Fear emanated from Simon Grimm in a shivery gray mist. Probably he would never again send a soul the wrong direction. Some men were too weak to challenge a wicked fate.

Like you challenge yours during the dark hours?

Exactly.

Likely, Grimm had not asked for the job as a psychopomp. He'd been born into it, no doubt, or recruited. He was as much a victim of the world's whim as any other of the marks Ivan tracked. And for that reason, he could not leave him without one final comment.

"May your shadows be cursed."

Ivan strode out from the parking garage. His work was done. For this night.

* * *

The sun wouldn't rise for another four hours. Ivan had no other tasks for this evening. He headed home on foot. A small apartment overlooking the river Spree in Berlin offered solace. Perhaps he could manage an hour of sleep.

Not that he was tired. The work, it took a lot out of him, strained his body beyond the limits. And that was quite a lot. But the most devastating effects were mental.

The night was not his own. Whatever Himself wanted, Ivan did. Reluctantly. Always the compulsion to flee, to escape, was present. But he never could. Himself's powerful coercion held Ivan to the task, literally forcing him to it.

The more he resisted, the deeper the shadow at the back of his neck dug into his being. It pricked every nerve with an icy bite. Ivan would never become used to such pain. He embodied pain.

So he did what he was told. Because his mother's and father's souls were held over his head should he refuse.

Ivan tracked immortals and mortals alike, those who had made a deal with Himself and had then reneged on that deal. He fixed wrongs and fetched AWOL souls. He was Himself's fist. And he was feared.

But that was not who Ivan Drake was inside, deep in the pockets of spirit where his soul had once resided.

"I hate this," he muttered, as he stepped inside his building and took the four flights of stairs to his apartment in a dash.

The steel steps clanked under the thick rubber heels of his biker boots. Artificial lemon clung to the air; the landlady's attempt to freshen the stale smell of smoke after a rogue fire in the stairwell last month.

Some day he would be successful. With determination, he would push beyond Himself's control and finally be free.

Until then, Ivan led two separate lives. The night life and the one he walked during the day.

Knocking on the red apartment door next to his, Ivan waited until the door cracked open, then pushed it inside and slipped his hand around the man's neck. Pulling up the strong body of the thirty-something wrestler, he pierced the pulsing jugular with his teeth and drank. The man didn't fight. He expected this most nights. He was Ivan's supplicant, provided by Himself.

For with the immense release of physical and mental energy and his struggle against fate each night, he developed a desperate thirst. He had to feed the hunger, or die.

Dropping the man—whose name he refused to learn—at his feet, Ivan turned and backed out. "Curse your shadows."

It was the only sort of blessing he could offer.

Leaving the lights off as he entered his apartment, Ivan looked forward to a shower. But the wave of brimstone flowing out from his bedroom put up his hackles.

"I hate that smell," he muttered, and walked toward the intense odor. "You'd think the Old Lad would try a new cologne after a millennium or two."

The shadow on his back prickled with excited energy.

He should be used to these visits, though no more frequent than every other month or so. Himself's imps usually brought his assignments to him nightly.

Stalking into the bedroom, completely dark thanks to the electrochromic window shades, Ivan didn't need artificial light to see the distorted figure that lounged on his bed.

And he felt the immense pull in his muscles. The compulsion to submit. He didn't want to. He gripped the door frame, fighting the downward pull. But he could not win.

Not yet.

Wood splintering in his grasp, Ivan fell onto one knee and bowed his head. Jaw gritted tightly, he fought against the next move, but as usual, he yielded by spitting out, "Master."

"Always so insolent, Drake, even after all these years. Accept your fate."

"Never."

Himself sighed.

Though shadowed, Ivan saw the massive horns move before the window shades. Pinpoints of red glowed from the demon's eyes. The dull clack of hooves as he adjusted his position upon the bed sounded like two blocks of wood.

"You punish the psychopomp?"

"He's stolen his last soul."

"Splendid. Despite your reluctance, you must know how pleased I've been with your work. You never fail, as much as I know that kills you."

"My suffering serves you even greater satisfaction."

"Oh, indeed. But your complete surrender would finally accomplish my education of your reluctant and hapless spirit."

"Never happen."

"So you say. I recall your mother having a smart mouth as well. Look where that got you." He laughed loud and painfully, but cut off his demented mirth with an abrupt hiss. "So, I've a new task for you."

"I eagerly await your command."

"Sarcasm doesn't suit you, vampire. It *is* vampire tonight, right? I can smell the mortal's blood on you. A nice plump athlete to keep you well fed."

Ivan remained silent. Himself was aware of the fight Ivan put up against the coercion that always made him hungry for blood. To engage in conversation with Himself only served to further vex his spirit, and he knew the bastard always enjoyed that.

"I need you to bring me the book," Himself declared off-handedly, as if announcing a new imp to his legions. "It's in the United States. Along the coast of Maine. A witch guards it."

"The book?"

"Yes, *the* book. The *Grande Grimoire*. 'Nuf said. Details are not important to the jobs you perform. In fact, details only muddy the goal and slow you down. But I will give you an address."

Ivan did appreciate addresses.

"Bring it to me posthaste." Himself rose to stand before Ivan. The heat of his closeness waved off his greasy-slick body like sun off the sand dunes. He bent over Ivan's bowed head. "Don't dally, boy. I want it by tomorrow evening."

And the air in the room lightened, as if the humidity had been sucked away by a reverse fan.

Ivan used the iron frame at the end of the bed to push up and stand.

Another task?

"Just another day at the office. Thanks, Mom and Dad."

He loved his parents. And he did not.

"Why the hell did they do it?"

He clasped his arms across his chest and thought of his childhood. His parents had never made it a secret his soul belonged to Himself. They'd hoped to raise Ivan strong and powerful and resistant to Himself's influence.

That wasn't easy.

Had it been so easy for his parents to sell his soul before he had even been born?

Chapter 2

Ivan walked through the sleepy village of Willow Cove. It hugged the Atlantic Ocean along the southern coast in Maine. Granite cliffs and white sand beaches glinted temptingly. A whitewashed lighthouse, easily sighted from anywhere in the small town, transported the more imaginative back a century to a quieter, simpler time.

And Willow Cove was quiet and simple. Removed from the popular tourist destinations, this little village had managed to exist untainted by consumerism for centuries.

The breezy salted air reminded Ivan of Marseilles, on the coast of France. Much more touristy there, but there were a few secluded gems of beach to be had. He desired a place along the white coastline, with a private beach and a home high upon the rocky granite cliffs.

He generally went immediately to the mark, did the deed and got the hell out of Dodge. But for some reason, after the overseas flight and the insane taxi driver who would not turn down the Rasta music—and had been deaf to Ivan's subtle persuasion to do so—he felt the need to settle. To walk in the twilight, down the freshly whitewashed plank sidewalk that edged the beach. To use the last few moments of daylight to fill his body with all the fresh air and peace and goodness he could muster.

Since Himself had claimed his soul, wherever Ivan went, he saw them. And felt them like invisible insects crawling across his flesh. The demons, imps and familiars who answered to his dark master. Those wretched members of the lower rungs, the tainted, the vicious, the pure evil.

To which Ivan belonged. Not by choice, and not for lack of trying to rise up and overcome.

He also felt the angels.

Yes, they were everywhere, as myriad and legion as the ranks of darkness. Goodness and pure intent flooded from them. But though he sensed their company, he'd never *seen* an angel. Ivan had not earned the right to see them. He probably never would.

He was thankful enough he could feel their presence.

Mortals walked through life mostly unaware of the good and evil all around them. That was for the better, Ivan had decided.

When he reached the edge of town where a flower garden had been planted in the shape of the city's name, Ivan knew his destination was yet a few miles off.

The witch lived by the ocean. Himself had given a remarkable description of her house. But not so astonishing in that Himself always knew everything; he was all seeing.

"But not all powerful," Ivan said, and marched onward, down the packed dirt road.

Himself could not go near this particular witch because she

likely had fortified her home with devil traps and means to keep him away. It was possible to do so, but the magic required to keep back Himself, Ivan figured, must be colossal. This mark would prove a challenge.

Ivan grinned, pleased this trip would not be a bust. If there was no challenge to jump-start his adrenaline, then the coercion kicked in all the stronger. He preferred to act of his own accord, and fighting to maintain the upper hand fit that necessity nicely.

By the time Ivan gained the huge Victorian house, fireflies lighted in the grassy ditches. Crickets chirred at his feet. A fox, or some small creature, hid in a burrow near the culvert where the gravel driveway crossed the ditch. Its heartbeat quickened, sensing Ivan's presence.

The tinkle of tiny bells sounded. Some sort of yard decorations?

Painted a pale shade of green, and set upon a cliff, the house seemed to glow there at the edge of the world. The sea glimmered behind it, catching the last orange and silver rays of light before the sun disappeared completely for the night.

It wasn't as though Ivan could feel evil enter his veins come nightfall. But a sense of foreboding always struck at the exact moment day gave over to night. A clenched fist. A gritted jaw. Raw pain prickling at the shadow cleaved to his back.

Once again, he had become the devil's fixer.

A white picket fence fronted the property. Ivan stepped through the gate and onto a stone path, which crunched under his boots. It was something out of a fairy tale, replete with bright-faced flowers lining the path and thick, verdant vines climbing the front of the three-story house.

About thirty feet away from the steps that hugged the wood porch in front of the house, Ivan abruptly stopped. The salt-tainted air exhaled a luscious perfume.

"Roses," he murmured.

Taking advantage of the opportunity to infuse his being with goodness, Ivan drew in the odor. But his joy quickly turned to dread.

"Wild roses?" He squinted in the growing dark to examine the vines that crept along the ground and over the planks siding the house. Small flower heads burst with myriad petals. And thorns so bold and sharp he could see them glint. "Damn."

One of the few vampire deterrents that actually worked against Ivan was wild roses. But they had to be planted by a witch to prove a real danger.

Stepping cautiously forward, Ivan reached out, but not to touch. He wanted to feel out the atmosphere. He could tune his senses to the minutest scent, sound or movement. And he got a physical read, which surprised him.

Malevolent, he decided of the roses. And protective.

He straightened, setting back his shoulders. A scan of the house's facade revealed the roses covered sixty percent of the exterior.

Wild roses weren't supposed to kill a vampire, but—Ivan tapped into his vampire history, taught to him by his father— they did bestow agony. A wise vampire would walk away, not tempt the pain.

Because don't you get enough pain as it is?

A crack of his neck muscles, head snapping to the right, then the left, loosened Ivan's apprehension. This fixer never walked away from any challenge.

"No pain, no gain," he muttered.

Bracing for the inevitable, Ivan charged forward, pumping his arms and stomping the ground.

The first slice cut through his leather pant leg. A vine snaking along the ground whipped out, slashing him with thorns sharper than a samurai's katana. But the pain wasn't an instant piercing slice that made a man cry in shock. No, this pain dug into his nerves and electrified his entire system. The shock of it moved up into Ivan's head and tingled in the roots of his teeth. It was an extreme root canal. A vicious migraine. A leopard's bite to his flesh.

Crying out, Ivan took another nerve-slicing cut to his forearm. Again he could feel the cut travel his blood to his teeth. This time he couldn't even make a sound. It was too excruciating.

He stepped on the first creaking wooden step. Vines wrapped about his ankles. Thorns perforated the thick leather biker's boots and stabbed his flesh. He struggled. He growled and chomped his jaw.

If he turned back, rushed out to the road, the pain would stop.

"Never," he growled.

Lunging forward, he ripped away from the vines. Two long, struggling strides took him across the porch. He braced his hands to meet the door—when it opened. His palms hit the space where the door had been and connected hard, with nothing. Impact pushed him back to land on the porch, sprawled.

Bleeding everywhere, but thankful to be past the thorns, he took in the situation. And his eyes fell upon a figure standing in the impenetrable, yet open, doorway.

A flowing white negligee, thinner than air, caressed long legs and spilled about small bare feet. Ivan dragged his gaze up the narrow hips. The gossamer fabric revealed everything to him.

He spat to the side. He'd bitten his cheek while battling the vines. But his eyes did not waver from the heavy curves of her breasts, the nipples tight as rosebuds. A dream far removed from his current hell.

Dark blond hair sifted forward over a slender shoulder as she leaned down.

"I didn't invite you to cross my threshold, vampire," she

said in a confident voice edged with a smirk. "Stop bleeding on my porch."

"Can't," he managed to say.

Every nerve ending felt as if burnished raw by a disk sander. Each movement tugged at his bleeding flesh, and though he felt the skin closing to heal, he wanted to itch and scream from misery.

"I've come…," he began, huffing.

If he could stand, then he might get back a portion of the force he wished to convey. Too difficult. Needed more time to heal. And the attack roses slithered near the edge of the porch.

"I know what you've come for." She leaned against the door frame, a pale white curve of shoulder revealed as the fabric slid down to an elbow. Her hair was piled loosely upon her head, with delicate curls spilling upon that naked shoulder.

One leg was revealed amid the folds of silk and the fabric veed open high up to her hip. The most delirious aroma of— apricots?—carried over the rose perfume and Ivan's own thick blood scent.

Her blood. It was the first scent he always picked out on any person.

Ivan sucked in a breath. The moment tore him two ways. Pain lingered, boring at his need to act, to finish the task. Yet the bared flesh shimmering in the twilight and the blatant blood scent stirred his desires and made him swallow back his obsessive desire to complete the job.

"You might as well give it up right now," she said. "It's not going to happen."

"I bet you say that to all the guys, right before you invite them in."

What felt like a slap, might have been a slap, had Ivan been aware the witch hadn't even moved. Yet…yes, his cheek stung as if a firm hand had lashed across it.

If he were upright and at maximum capacity, he could send that air slap right back at her with his own magic. But right now…

"Himself tries this every decade or so," she said. A firm tone, yet tinged with a boredom Ivan found insulting. "Sends a so-called champion to get the book. That is what you're here for. I can smell the greed all about you."

"He's sent others?"

Tapping a finger against her lower lip, she looked him over. The shadows of the evening stirred in her eyes, but Ivan could distinctly see they were green. Witch green.

"Like I said. Just walk away, vampire. You're no match for me."

And the door slammed, leaving Ivan's head pounding with the dull echo of wood against wood.

He collapsed then, shoulders hitting the porch, and staring up at the rafters spaced beneath the awning. But two feet from him the rustle of moving vines warned him to beware.

The trip out of here was going to be a bitch.

"I'm not going anywhere." Whether he wanted to or not.

It would be a dream to traipse away, leave the witch alone and thumb his nose at Himself's stupid command. But dreams were not in Ivan's arsenal.

That greed she'd smelled? The coercion moving through his veins, an elixir formed of Himself and fed by the shadow.

Much as Ivan thought to lie there awhile longer would be the thing to do, his body began to move before his mind decided to go along for the ride. The coercion took hold.

He was not completely in control of his being at night, and never would be.

"I'm up, I'm up," Ivan muttered.

He'd developed an irritating habit of talking to that invisible part of him which reacted to Himself's desires.

"Now to gain an invite."

The door was flung wide open again. The witch stood there, brandishing a gold cross in her outstretched hand. She stood on the threshold, half of her inside the house, half out on the porch. The arm wielding the small religious icon was completely outside the house.

Ivan plucked the cross from her fingers and drew his tongue along the back of it, licking it slowly, defiant in his wicked glee.

"Not baptized, eh?" she said. "Then let's try this."

Tearing away the vial from around her neck, the witch removed a small cork stopper and then shook out the crimson substance onto Ivan's face.

He stood there, smirking at her efforts. The few drops of blood smelled like flowers, sweetened with earth and spice. And yes, that was definitely apricot. He dipped his tongue out to taste it.

And that was a mistake. Because she tasted incredible.

His fangs descended. Ivan stretched his mouth to resist the ache in his jaw.

"What under the stars?" Now panicked, the witch shook the vial at him again. "You *are* a vampire?"

"And half witch."

Ivan gripped her wrist and squeezed so she dropped the vial. It shattered upon his boot toe.

The vines stirred. Hungry for more than vampire blood?

"My father is a phoenix vampire, immune to witch's blood. Which makes me immune as well. Sorry to spoil your dramatic little show."

And he tugged her completely from the threshold and laced his arms around her back, drawing her slender limbs against his body.

This is not what you intend echoed at the back of his thoughts.

Yet Ivan reacted completely opposite of the manner the devil's fixer should.

It required immense determination, but he managed to will his fangs up. The embrace wouldn't work otherwise. Once in the throes of the blood hunger his focus would be shot.

Ivan bent and captured the witch's petal-soft mouth beneath his. Narrow fingers worked desperately against his unmoving shoulders. She'd never push him off. He was strong as a team of oxen, and she, a mere lamb in his embrace.

But she didn't fight him for more than the few seconds it took him to part her mouth and trace the underside of her upper lip with his tongue. Tasted like a shot of sunlight…like apricot wine.

A sigh slipped over Ivan's lips. Not his own. She yielded to him, and that subtle shift in compliance distorted his mission even further.

He'd come here to…

Kiss this gorgeous woman. To glide his hands down the bare, silken skin on her back, exposed by the low-cut negligee. To feel how she warmed to him, even going so far as to step into his embrace. Her breasts hugged his chest and her groin snugged hotly against his thigh.

No, that was not why he was here.

The book. You must get the book.

"I want to be inside you," Ivan murmured against her ear. "Now. No names. No regrets. No agendas. Me and you. Together. Let me come inside."

"Yes," she murmured. "Come inside."

And Ivan shoved her away from his body and stepped across the threshold.

Chapter 3

It had been centuries since a man had come close to owning her with a kiss.

Of all the nerve! The vampire tricked her. And he'd done it by appealing to her weakness for a well-served kiss.

Many men had kissed her soundly, seductively, knee-looseningly exact in their precision. But this kiss? Exactly as she'd imagined a kiss could be—fierce and commanding, yet with respect and the tease of giddy bliss.

So while Dez still reeled from the sensual assault to her better judgment, she tried to focus on reality. He'd tricked her to invite him inside, and now the vampire dashed up the stairway, heading toward the second floor.

"Not so fast, vampire!" Dez delivered an air punch that connected with his jaw.

He faltered on the stairs, slipping down one, but catching his forearm across the railing.

"A mere tap!" he bellowed. "Where do you hide it? Up here? I will find that book."

"Not tonight you won't. You thought that was a tap?" She stalked to the base of the stairway and flung out her arms wide to draw in her sacred energies. "Prepare for the wallop!"

Directing the force of her focus at the insolent intruder, Dez connected with her psychic and spiritual powers. The vampire's body splayed forward, as if hit across the shoulders with a baseball bat. Then his body soared through the air, over her head, and landed on the wall behind her with a sheetrock-pulverizing crunch.

Bits of white dust settled about him. He shook his head. And chuckled. "Nice try, witch, but I know that little parlor trick."

One thrust of his hand, fingers splayed wide, and Dez felt the energy a moment before it smacked into her chest. Lungs compressed, she wheezed as the force pushed her back against the wall. Her body moved up along the wide cedar paneling to the second-floor landing, where the invisible power released her. She landed, sprawled forward onto her elbows. Impact tweaked each funny bone smartly.

Dez blew at a thick strand of hair fallen over her left eye.

That's right, she thought. The thing had said he was half vampire *and* half witch. What kind of impossible mix was that? In all her centuries, she had never met the sort. And what a powerful witch he was, to be able to throw magic at her with such ease.

This particular fixer was formidable. One point to Himself. But this witch was far from out for the count.

Determined to banish the fiendish anomaly from her sanctuary, Dez scrambled to a partitioning wall and ducked behind it. She was out of the intruder's view, which should keep her out of his range of magic.

But she didn't need to see the vampire to set off an attack. The floorboards creaked, and she knew he neared the staircase. Stubborn. Directing her energy to the bottom step, she lifted the plank and sent it flying. A gruff "ouf" pleased her immensely.

The next step found its mark—or rather, set it off balance. And the next. And then there was silence.

Dez dared a look around the corner. The vampire dropped the last step with a clatter. Grinning deviously, he held up his hand, fingers separated, but—there was something between his fingers. Nails from the boards.

The deadly weapons shot through the room, aimed for Dez. She managed to dodge around the wall, yet felt the skim of one nail slice her bare shoulder. Three nails landed the wall opposite her, *plink, plink, plink.*

Tugging the loose night robe up her shoulders, she chuffed out a frustrated growl.

"I will not tear my precious home apart to fend off one miserable fixer. He's a stupid bounty hunter. Time to bring out the big magic."

He wanted parlor tricks? She'd give him a doozy.

"Feels like rain, vampire!" she called.

Focusing inward, Dez summoned her inner force. A cool violet electricity began at her core and illuminated out through her extremities.

Connecting to the seawater that crashed against the beach not two hundred yards from her back porch, Dez focused it to humidity and then to mist. Harnessing the power of the air and water elements, she summoned its energy through her spirit, altering it, refining it.

"I love a good storm," he called.

She heard him land another step. The wooden railing wobbled and creaked. She had to get that fixed.

Lightning, too? she wondered, gleefully thrilled he could have no comprehension of what was to come.

Power hummed in her being and the control felt exquisite. It stirred above her head. It had been a while since she had drawn on her water skills, but they hadn't depleted a bit.

Lightning crackled inside the house. The rockslidelike thunder of a downpour startled even Dez.

And then the rain began, right over the stairway, focused on the vampire. But no summer rain shower was going to keep back the vampire who had run shouting, yet determined, through her rose vines.

Stirring her hand before her, Dez conjured the increasingly heavy rain into a funnel. A shock of lightning snapped at the vampire, singeing his back. He cried out at the pain of it. His footing faltered. He slid down the stairs, slick with tsunami-force weather.

Dez guided the gale sheet of rain after the vampire, as, no matter how he tried, he could not press forward. Arms up before his face, he gasped at the water, and the tornadic swirl eventually swallowed him. Sweeping him from the room, the storm carried the vampire outside, down the porch and past the protective rose vines.

Water clung to the storm, leaving not a drop in its wake.

Dez stepped down the dry stairs. By the time the storm had taken the vampire to the picket fence, she relaxed her tight hold on the elements, and the entire sky over Willow Cove crackled with lightning. A great curtain of rain blanketed the village.

And the vampire was nowhere to be seen.

"Parlor trick? Right back at ya, fixer."

Dez slammed her front door shut. Hands to hips, she looked over the damage that stretched from the hallway up to the stairs. Minimal. A few stair boards would need to be pounded back in place.

But that fixer. Dez felt sure she hadn't seen the last of him.

He'd got in once. And now that the invitation had been violated to cross her threshold, it stood forever after. Dez would need to conjure new means to keep her home safe from vampires who were also witches who did the devil's bidding.

"I know why he's been sent," she said now, wistful in her sudden calm.

Surely he was not here on his own recognizance. Himself wanted the *Grande Grimoire*—and what a more perfect time to go after it?

Dez had nothing against vampires, so long as they didn't try to trick her, or kiss her without permission.

She traced a forefinger along her lip. The flesh was still warm, burnished by the intensity of the delicious lip-lock. He'd smelled equally as intense, focused and strong. His scent was unlike any of the hundreds of essential oils she concocted and used to create perfumes. Unique. And darkly sexy.

Dez shook the thought from her mind. Now was no time to go soft with the enemy once again in her camp. The war; that is what had reignited Himself's curiosity for the book.

For centuries vampires and witches had been at odds. It was because of the Protection spell cast long ago. Once vampires had enslaved witches by drinking their blood, which also infused them with the witch's magic. When finally the spell had been cast, it made the blood of all witches poison to vampires.

And ever since, both sides had been trying to kill one another.

"This needs to end," Dez said. "And I think Himself will do it. If he can get his talons on the *Grande Grimoire*."

Which would never happen. Not while she still lived.

"No, he can't have in mind to end the war. That would be

far too benevolent. What wicked games does that dark demon have planned?"

She shook off speculating on Himself's devious plot. Dez did not waste her energy focusing on evil. And to dwell overmuch on it only made said evil stronger, more able to pierce her fortressed home.

"I'm one lone woman," she said. "But I'm tough and wise. This fixer is strong. The strongest Himself has ever sent."

And the first ever to use sneaky seduction tactics.

"He won't win. He can't. Because if he does, then I will die."

Chapter 4

Ivan Drake, soaked to the veins, slapped down his Centurion credit card on the counter. The hotel receptionist, smirking, and commenting how the rain picked up so suddenly, processed his card and handed him a room key attached to a small piece of driftwood.

Poor girl.

Ivan reached across the counter, gripped her by the back of the neck, and drew her in for a long drink. There were no witnesses. And he was desperate to renew. Leaving her with a suggestion she'd gotten tired and fallen asleep on the counter, he licked the bite wounds, ensuring they would heal before she woke.

The room was down a walkway that sat directly on the beach. The ocean clattered with the heavy downpour. Ivan stomped through the rain, now oblivious to its force—because this stuff was nothing.

"A freakin' tsunami right in her house. That was some amazing magic."

He opened the door to his room and tossed the key aside onto an ancient television that looked like it belonged in the nineteen-sixties and was perched on top some olive-green shag carpet.

Shaking his head as if a dog dispersed water droplets about the room, he stripped away his wet shirt, took off his boots and then stepped out of the wet leather pants. The thorns had shredded both boots and pants.

Stalking into the bathroom, he retrieved a towel and patted himself as dry as he would get. He felt he would be wet for days.

Touching his shoulder, he jerked at the surprising tenderness of the wound. Right there, he'd been snapped by a lick of lightning. Burned flesh smelled awful, but it was almost healed, and no scar would remain.

"Why can't *I* do magic like that?" He tossed the towel to the tile bathroom floor. "I have water magic. *I* should be able to do that."

Whistling in appreciation for the witch's talents, he wandered out to the main room and flung himself across the double bed. Naked, pissed—yet strangely in awe—he reached back for the pillows and threw them across the room to land on the top of the desk. He shoved down the comforter because that was a piece of nasty. The thin sheets received his body and he managed to fit himself into the dent in the center of the mattress.

Was he exhausted? Hell yes. It wasn't every night a man got picked up by a hurricane and spat out like a chunk of debris.

Go back. Do the job. This is your life, man, you don't stop until you get it right. The insistent coercion tingled like words spoken in his veins.

He was too tired to do anything more than close his eyes and drift to sleep.

* * *

Ivan woke to the sound of water dripping. Droplets landed on his face. Was he still in that damned storm?

Snapping upright on the bed, he blinked at the pale light beaming through the window. Not yet sunrise, but dawn danced along the horizon. Realizing he was naked, he clutched the sheet to his lap but, well, there was no denying a morning erection.

Water droplets pinged his back.

And then he smelled the brimstone.

Since when did Himself make two visits for a job? The Old Lad must be keen on getting that book. A grimoire. All witches kept a grimoire. What was so special about this one?

"Nothing worth explaining to your naked ass" came the reply from the shadows in the corner. "You failed me, fixer."

"I never fail," Ivan growled.

And he did not. Yes, he was chained to the devil and forced to do his dirty work. But when given a job to do, Ivan always did it right. This vampire never did anything half-assed.

"I need more time. There were…obstacles."

Himself chuckled. Hooves scraped the floor.

Ivan did not turn around.

"I knew she would challenge you, but I must admit surprise at how masterful that challenge proved." Talons clinked against glass, and again the water spattered across Ivan's back. Himself was dipping into the pitcher on the bedside table. "A little rain scare you away, Drake?"

"This witch is…different."

That was no excuse. It was a cop-out, actually. Over the past seven years of servitude, he'd scared the hell out of wraiths, blood ghouls, werewolves and shaken-down war demons. One petite witch shouldn't even make him sweat.

"She's powerful," Ivan said.

"Indeed."

Drake felt the bed move, as if someone was sitting next to him. Not a comfortable position to be in, his bare ass facing— ah, hell. Ivan snapped up the sheet, and as he lunged off the bed, he winced to look over Himself seated so casually, legs crossed.

And then he felt the usual urge to supplicate move through his muscles, and before he knew it, he was on one knee, bowing and spluttering out, "Master."

"'Bout time you remembered your place, half-breed."

The term usually put up Ivan's ire, but coming from Himself, it gave him wonder. "A half-breed you were hungry to get your hands on."

"Touché." An obsidian talon tapped a tight black muscled jaw. "Failure is not an option with this mark," Himself said. "I'll give you all the time you need, Drake. That is how important this task is to me. And perhaps a suggestion. I know this witch. She has a weakness."

Like kisses?

For a few moments, standing on that porch with the stir of vicious vines creeping at their feet, she had been his. And he hadn't been considering it a trick. He'd dove forward, enjoying the moment—and then the coercion had kicked in and he'd shoved her off him and marched across the threshold.

Bastard.

It was what had to be done.

He could still recall the scent of her blood. Just a few minute drops. Apricots. Sweetly pungent.

"Her heart." Himself tapped his exposed ribs, which likely had never enclosed a pulsing, red heart. "She's known true love only once. And that was long ago. She pines for it. For connection." The words slid out on a prolonged slither.

"You're suggesting I seduce her?"

"Aren't you the quick one to pick up the ball? Good boy, Drake. I'll be checking in."

And Himself disappeared in a wisp of brimstone.

Released from his supplication, Ivan clutched for the baseboard of the bed. Pressing his forehead to the laminated wood, he closed his eyes and choked on the lingering acrid odor.

Seduction? That was certainly a new trick in his arsenal. Never had he used seduction to persuade, punish or annihilate any of his master's *problems* before.

"Seduction," he said resolutely. "I like the sound of that."

It was three in the afternoon, and not a single customer had stopped in to the shop. Elise Henderson had strolled by moments earlier, nose in the air and blue hair glistening in the sunlight.

"Like I expect that old coot to stop?"

Dez dusted the counter display of perfume oils for the tenth time. She'd finished filling the two dozen online orders in her e-mail box this morning. "Think I'll close up early today."

She'd opened the shop two years ago and called it Sweet Alchemy. Dez loved to craft unique perfumes from essential oils, and she had thought it would be a hit to open the store across the street from the city park.

Brian Smith had been hot for her when she'd first moved to town. It hadn't taken him long to lure her into bed. She was a grown woman; she could have sex whenever and with whomever she wished. But when Brian had asked about her irresistible allure, her offhanded comment, "Maybe I've bewitched you?" had been taken seriously and spread throughout the town.

They actually believed she could be a witch who lured innocent men into her cackling clutches. Add to that her propensity to dress eccentrically in velvets and laces, and an I-don't-give-a-damn attitude about how much flesh she showed, and, well, there you go.

It was a group attitude she was quite used to, for it had followed her for centuries. Did enlightenment really take longer than a dark age?

One thing to be thankful for was that they didn't burn witches anymore. Not the mortals. Nowadays she had only to keep an eye out for vampires wielding matches.

Dez didn't bewitch any of the perfumes she sold in the shop. Well, most of them remained unspelled. There were occasions when she knew the customer needed some extra help, so a touch of magic was warranted.

And there were days she wished she would have put a tongue-tying spell on Brian Smith. But she wasn't vindictive. Magic had a way of returning to the user the same force he or she put out.

Her online store was actually ragingly popular, and the few customers she did get in the brick-and-mortar store were usually fans who had traveled to seek the source. Made her feel good that people all over the world enjoyed her perfumes.

But for some reason she wouldn't be completely happy until she'd won over Willow Cove.

What was wrong with her? She wasn't a mean person. She rather liked chatting to strangers and getting to know them. But people in this town actually walked across the street to avoid her. It was bizarre. It hurt her feelings.

"For someone who's been around as long as I have, you'd think there'd be nothing left to hurt."

And yet, she *had* been around a long time. And most of those years had been spent keeping the world at a distance. She did that well. It was a requirement as keeper of the *Grande Grimoire*. But lately, the pining feeling for connection would not relent.

Dez wanted friends. And she was at a point in her life where she was ready to throw open her arms and welcome them in. But how to undo centuries of practicing exactly the opposite?

Patience, she coached inwardly. It will take time. And ole blue-haired Elise topped her must-befriend list.

Tossing her dust rag under the counter, Dez was startled when the bell above the door tinkled. It was high noon, and most of Willow Cove would be home eating or at one of half a dozen cozy cafés chatting and gossiping.

A man entered. The glare of sunlight behind his broad shoulders wouldn't allow Dez to see his face. Must be a long-distance customer. Or else he was lost, asking for directions. That happened a lot. Always got her hopes up.

Then she realized who it was—the vampire.

"Truce?"

"What are you doing in here? Didn't you get enough last night?"

He held his hands up in surrender.

Now she took a moment to look him over without having to cast a defensive spell. Not a particularly ugly man. For a vampire. Who was also a witch. Not that she had anything against vampires, but still she had to be careful, with the war and all.

Short, black, spiky hair raged about his head. Dark eyes set below straight brows took in her small shop, lined with white-washed walls and shelves of perfume vials. Broad shoulders and a physique tended more toward martial arts than witchcraft, impressed Dez only so much; she knew vampires were naturally athletic.

She restrained the urge to zap him with a gale wind. That would only set him back against the door, likely shattering the glass and knocking down half her stock in the process. She'd hear him out.

Besides, she didn't need to give the town more fodder for claiming she was a witch.

"Stay back by the door, fixer. You're not welcome in here."

"I thought not." He shoved his hands in the front pockets of his dark trousers. "Fortunately, I don't need an invitation. Public places are open to me."

"But how during the day?"

"Told you, my father is a phoenix. I inherited his immunity to sunlight."

The phoenix vampire was rare. Meant he'd survived a witch's blood attack. Dez had not heard of any survivors over the past decades. Not that she had an ear to the pulse of the vampire nation. She mostly did her thing and let the world pass her by. Until she'd decided having friends would be nice.

But this witch wasn't about to befriend a bloodsucker, even if he was only one by half.

"I can't believe your gall." Dez crossed her arms over her chest. "Didn't getting beat on by a girl do it for you?"

"You are no girl."

"Oh?" She walked around the counter and propped her hip against the curved end of the rose granite. Today she wore a snug, black calf-length skirt and a tight, low-necked black shirt. Beatnik stuff. She could dig it, but only with superspiked black heels.

"I'm no girl?" she repeated. "Then what am I?"

"You are a potent witch with an incredible arsenal. How did you do that? The tsunami thing. I've never been able to command the air and water like that. Can you teach me?"

"Back off, vampire. You may be half witch, but you'll never be able to do the things I do. Stick to your hi-tech conjures and bounty hunting."

He nodded, accepting. "Hi-tech not your thing?"

"I prefer simple spells." And that was all he was going to get regarding her spellcraft.

Turning, he examined a wooden display that featured dozens of perfume samples. He touched one, and Dez cringed. Not because she thought he'd drop the glass vial, but because the overmuscled trickster touching her things was not acceptable. She'd put her heart and soul into those perfumes.

"I'm quite sure you didn't come in here to buy perfume, and I was just closing up. So if you have a purpose—?"

"Everyone has a purpose, Desideriel."

"Don't call me that."

"Isn't that your name?"

"I prefer not to hear it coming from the devil's fixer. And since that *is* your purpose, you are not welcome anywhere near me."

"It's a night job," he offered. "Days are my own." Popping open the cork stopper on one of the samples, he then sniffed. "This is nice."

"It's called Blood Feud. Vanilla, bergamot, honey, and a touch of sour cherry and cream. Makes strange sense you would find it appealing."

"Because I bear the blood of both feuding nations in my body?" He smiled and sniffed again. "Appropriate. I love the creamy cherry afternote."

"Right. So you're a perfume connoisseur when it suits you? It doesn't suit me. What natural disaster do I have to conjure to get you to leave Willow Cove?"

"Can't leave until I've the book in hand."

"You're forthcoming with your evil intentions."

"I pride myself in being honest."

"Like that kiss last night was honest." She looked aside and rolled her eyes.

"It was damned honest."

"It was a trick!"

"Not to begin with. I couldn't resist you. You're so—" He clasped the perfume vial and fisted the air. Resolving some inner conflict, he sighed and shook his head. "Listen, Desideriel, I—"

"It's just Dez. Dez Merovech. And I'll thank you to get that right."

She was ready to summon an itching spell when the door tinkled open again. Another customer? This was an absolute rush. Dez recognized the woman immediately. Two trips by the store in one day?

"Mrs. Henderson." Dez went to greet her, but the old lady was too intent on checking out the vampire towering over her frail, thin body.

What was his name? He'd kissed her and she didn't even know his name.

"It's nice to see you in my shop, Mrs. Henderson."

Elise was the head of the Willow Cove Rose Club, which Dez pined to join. If only to be accepted into a group of women who had common interests. Friends.

"Are you looking for a gift?"

"Yes, er…" The woman, pushing seventy and a big fan of blue hair rinse, smiled up at the man. "Haven't seen you in town before. Saw you walking down the avenue to the shop. My name's Elise Henderson."

The vampire set down the perfume sample and accepted the hand Elise offered. He bent to kiss the back of it, and if Dez hadn't been standing to the woman's side, she would have fallen over in a swoon. As it was, the old woman's birdlike frame swayed against Dez, but she righted herself quick enough.

"My, but you're a handsome one." Without tearing her gaze from the man, Elise asked Dez, "Is he yours, dear?"

Before she could reply, the vampire said, "She's an old and

dear friend. I've never been to the shop, so thought I'd check it out. Such marvels Dez creates, eh?"

Fisting her fingers behind her back, Dez prepared a verbal volley, but Elise broke in.

"I didn't know you had friends, dear."

What to say when the old biddy knew darn well the entire town had put an avoid-for-dear-life tag on Dez?

Elise turned to the vampire. "You should bring your friend to the Rose Club's bash tonight. It's couples only. Willow Cove is celebrating all week, actually, with dances for various events to celebrate the end of summer. We dress up and dance in the town's gazebo. The scent of the night-blooming columbine is incredibly heady. So romantic."

"I'd love to."

"But he can't," Dez rushed out. "You're leaving town tonight on the train, remember?"

"Changed my ticket for an open-ended return," he snapped back.

His determined gaze flashed a glinting smirk at her. It was the first time Dez noticed the color of his eyes. Not so dark as a demonic fixer should possess. Perhaps whiskey brown, with glints of gold.

It was going to take a lot more than a sexy glower to charm her.

"What?" he entreated playfully. "You don't want to show the town how well we dance together? Remember Paris?"

Dez rolled her eyes.

"As I recall, it rained," she said. "And don't you remember the lightning?"

He eased a palm over his right shoulder where the lightning had snapped him. "We were soaked to the bone. I recall your dress was see-through."

Dez glanced away. Yet she couldn't deny the pining ache in

her chest to attend the gala. If all it took to be noticed by the townspeople was a handsome man, she would have hired a gigolo years ago.

But could she do that? Use Elise's interest in this vampire to gain entrance to the old lady's attentions?

"I'll take Miss Merovech's silence as a yes," Elise said, then pointed to the counter. "I need something for a teenager. My niece's daughter. She's a rebel. Lives in New York, poor thing. Something sweet, but I suppose a little spicy."

"I've just the thing," Dez said, and went to package up a bottle of Summer Heat. She made sure the vampire caught her rebuking glare over Elise's pouf of blue hair.

He smiled triumphantly.

"It's got cinnamon in it, so it might irritate the skin a bit. Make sure she does a spot test first."

Elise nodded and handed Dez her credit card. She didn't say a thing to Dez, but as she exited she grasped the vampire's hand and shook it, mooning blatantly.

If she only knew the man may very well be lurking around her porch later tonight, jonesing for her blood. Did he savor the older brews for their longevity and flavor?

The bell tinkled, leaving Dez alone with the grinning vampire.

"I'm surprised you took the bait. You must really want to dance with me."

"No, it's—" She wouldn't allow him to gloat over his win when her pride was at stake. "I'm interested in joining the Rose Club, so what better opportunity to get to know the members?"

"Haven't received an invite all the years you've lived here?"

"Haven't been interested until now." A lie.

"What time shall I pick you up?" he queried.

"This is war," she declared.

"War, I can do. I look forward to it."

"Glad to know where we stand. I can get there myself. And the rules are: no touching, no talking and no kissing."

"So I can do everything else?"

Not dignifying that one with a reply, Dez shuffled into the back room, and waited until the bell tinkled again.

What could *everything else* possibly imply? She worried her lower lip, pondering the possibilities.

"I'll have to look up a repellent spell before tonight. Something to keep back crazy, gorgeous vampire-witches."

Gorgeous? Yes, he was. And she'd faltered a bit when she'd demanded there be no kisses.

But everything else?

It could mean standing so close she could smell his essence and feel the pulse of his muscles. To tap into strength such as he possessed promised an intriguing foray. If he possessed a strange mix of vampire-witch magic, Dez wanted to learn more.

That's what she would tell herself. Accepting simply because she could still taste his kiss would never win any wars.

Chapter 5

Ivan was beginning to wonder if he'd been stood up as old lady Henderson put a third Shirley Temple cocktail into his hand and then dragged forward yet another biddy with fresh flowers clasped about her wrist to meet him.

"He's dating the owner of that shop," Elise said, as she smiled through her venomous introduction.

They really didn't care for Dez, Ivan deduced. Yet Dez had seemed eager to attend this event. So eager she had agreed to go on a date with the devil's fixer, when she knew he was after the *Grande Grimoire*.

Why did she want to be part of a group like this? For the camaraderie? The girl chats? There wasn't a female under the age of sixty here, and they all sported names like Olive, Daisy and Eveline.

Desideriel Merovech. Hmm. Sounded like another old-lady name. He was glad she preferred Dez. But, too, the longer version reminded him of the Latin *desiderata*, which means "desired things."

He bowed to a sighing Olive and planted a kiss on the back of her hand. Word must be getting around that the youngest guy at the gala was giving away hand kisses. Ivan smirked. It was a hell of a lot better than crushing skulls and capturing AWOL souls.

It was evening, though, and he had to grit his teeth every time the coercion pricked at his shadow. Certainly Himself understood seduction happened slowly. Ivan sensed the restraint in the coercion.

"Will you be in town for long, Mr...."

"Drake," Ivan offered. "As long as necessary."

"Will we be hearing wedding bells in the future?"

"Er..." That one blindsided him. Ivan twisted to catch a real drink from a passing waiter's tray. He put back a goblet of red wine in one gulp. "Wedding?"

"She's notoriously single," Elise whispered. "What that woman needs is a good man."

"Oh yes, a good man," the other biddy chimed.

Well, then he was definitely out of the running. Not that he needed to be *in* the running. Just dizzy up the girl, grab the book, and depart.

"Oh, here she is now," a geriatric proclaimed. "Oh my. Now isn't that an interesting color."

Ivan turned and now felt the heat from the alcohol rise in his cheeks. No, it wasn't the alcohol. It was the slinky red number that sashayed toward him down an aisle lined in worshipful violet pansies.

Desired things, indeed.

Since moving to Willow Cove a decade earlier, Dez had few reasons to don a party dress, fix up her hair and actually put on makeup. The makeup was spare: a little black eyeliner, though she did like to draw it out in a curl at the corners of her eyes, and some blush.

There were so few interesting men in this town. She'd exhausted her resources within two months of moving here. So why bother to fix oneself up when it wasn't worth it?

Same with clothes. Her wardrobe was huge, but she kept it concealed in a magical otherwhere. She'd conjured the slinky red number right onto her body.

Tonight, Dez had dug out the tigress. She wanted Ivan Drake to see exactly what he couldn't have.

All eyes followed her as she crossed the lawn before the gazebo. Lights had been strung about the various flowerbeds featuring designer roses and luscious clouds of baby's breath. The entire park looked a fairy revel—if the fairies happened to be aged horticulturists.

Tugging at a curl hanging from her upswept hair, Dez realized she'd never had quite so much attention before from the townspeople. It was a little unsettling. A woman accustomed to hiding away from the world perhaps shouldn't take so large a leap as this.

But she'd leapt. And she wasn't uncomfortable. Just ultra-sensitive to reactions and the vibration of emotions about her. She felt them all: curiosity, wonder, desire and even jealousy.

She had to look at this as if it were an interview for the Rose Club. She must hold her head high and dazzle the members with her wit and intelligence. It couldn't be that difficult. She had endured far worse trials than a mere social event. Witch floating, anyone? A popular pastime of a religious sect in the seventeenth century. She had not floated. But of course, being immortal, death hadn't come, either.

"I can so ace this inquisition," she murmured, then nodded to a few smiling faces.

"Miss Merovech." Harold Gorm stepped between her and her destination, which diverted her concentration. Dez had to mentally jerk herself out of the glare she knew she suddenly gave the man. "You're looking lovely this evening."

A wave of halitosis curbed her approach. She should have performed that repellent spell after all.

"Thanks, Harold. Why so friendly all of a sudden? You pass my shop every morning on the way to work at the butcher shop. You usually break your neck looking the other way."

"I, er…"

So she didn't have to shine on everyone.

Leaving the tongue-tied butcher to ponder her stunning lack of civility, Dez finally reached her *date*. Or, at least, his vicinity. He wasn't accessible for the crowd that had gathered about him. Elise and her gaggle of hens were gushing and beaming about the towering vampire's flanks. Didn't they know it was unbecoming for women of a certain age to gush?

Of course, Dez was of a certain age. Certainly she would never gush. Even if the man was impeccably attired in suit and tie, and looking not at all like a creature of the night who could very well send the entire gala screaming should he flash a little fang.

You have nothing against vampires.

Didn't mean she had to befriend the man intent on taking the grimoire from her.

This is war, she reminded herself.

Elise's giggle was followed by patting the vampire's arm and calling him Ivan.

So that was his name. Ivan. Sounded like some kind of warrior. Fittingly macho. Wonder what his nationality was? He looked European, possessed of unconventional charm that overwhelmed any physical flaws he might have. Said flaws she had yet to discover. Save an aversion to wild roses. To be expected.

It was Ivan's whiskey-dark gaze Dez focused on as she entered the press of admirers. Before she could acknowledge the ladies flittering about—fairies indeed—Ivan turned and swept up her hand. He pressed a kiss to the back of it, lingering, holding her hand as if it were a feather that might drift away. The heat of his mouth on her flesh traveled up her arm. The sudden surprising electricity of their contact tightened her nipples. The thin red silk revealed all.

Let them stare. Yeah, she was aroused. What of it?

"A woman named Dez dressed in red," he said, still holding her hand and looking up from the kiss. "I think I've never known the meaning of *beguilement* until now."

Dez tugged her hand away. She may be aroused, but that didn't mean she was easy. "Give it up, fixer. So where's the booze?"

"Would you like me to grab you a Shirley Temple, dear?"

Much as she wanted to ingratiate herself to the girls in the Rose Club, Dez couldn't stomach an evening spent chatting it up with the blue-haired geriatrics when it was very apparent her main concern should be on repelling the devil's fixer.

But then again, her purpose for being here was to gain friends. And if she could ditch the date sooner rather than later, well then. "Don't worry, Elise, Ivan will get something for—"

That was all he needed, an invitation to escape. But he didn't do it alone. Ivan hooked an arm in Dez's and strolled with her down the stone path toward the bar cart perched at the edge of the park.

"But I was going to talk to Elise," Dez protested.

"Really? I smell a lie."

"I want to join the Rose Club and—"

"You don't want to do that."

For the first time, Dez took a moment to really look at his face. Though young, his skin possessed the veneer of a long and hard life. She had seen farmers and blue-collar workers who had lines in their faces—not wrinkles of ages, but lines from strife. Those same lines traced the corners of Ivan's eyes; a mask of survival.

And then she really peered into his eyes. Yes, like whiskey glinting behind glass. They were kind. And not. Delving. He searched for something in her eyes she wasn't prepared to let him find.

Dez jerked her gaze out of what she knew could become persuasion—a little vampire trick—toward Elise and her posse.

"I had no idea the club insisted upon an age minimum of seventy. Do none of the younger people in town plant flowers?"

"Still want to join?" he wondered. He paid the bartender, then placed a goblet of white wine in her fingers. "This is definitely geriatric central."

Blowing away a loose strand of hair from her face, Dez asked, "What's wrong with an older woman?"

He tilted a gaze over her, eyes traveling the edges of her mouth and up to the corners of her eyes. Trying to figure her age? Dez would never tell, but he'd be surprised, even for an immortal vampire.

"You're too young to worry about that," he finally offered. "Care to dance?"

Something akin to a polka *om-pa-paa*ed out on the dance floor. The hair on Dez's arms prickled. "Actually I'd like to sit awhile. I can smell the heliotrope from here. I think I'll steal some petals for my oils when no one's looking."

A two-seater bench sat beneath a pergola laced with blooming honeysuckle. White heliotrope frothed around and behind the bench. The sweet scent attacked the air as Dez sat and slipped one shoe off to dangle on her toes. She preferred as much bare flesh as possible, and though she adored spike heels, the freedom of slipping out of the confining leather was a joy.

Ivan sat right next to her, so close their arms and legs brushed. He was an immense presence, and he made Dez feel rather small sitting next to him. But that didn't hurt her confidence. She'd once already mastered him with her magic.

"You know, this doesn't mean anything," she said. "I merely accepted your conniving invitation as a means to ingratiate myself into the club. You're nothing but a tool."

"A tool? I'm insulted."

"You know what I mean."

"I suppose I can live with that. Though I really hate to know I'm serving as a means to such utter boredom. But if it's what you desire."

He said the word *desire* on a murmur. It tickled at Dez's staunch determination. Easy to be here right now. Next to him. Close to him.

She softened her shoulders and smoothed a hand along her foot.

"Want me to rub it?"

"Huh? No. Don't touch me. And slide over. You're too close."

"There is but six inches on the other side of me to sit. And there's bird crap at that end."

"Make it disappear."

Ivan sighed. He hung his head, hands clasped between his knees.

Dez wasn't about to fall for the "poor pitiful me" act. She intended to keep her guard up and protect the grimoire to her very last breath. And it would be her last breath if she failed.

Keep one's enemy close? The theory sounded right, but the actual act disturbed her on a level she wasn't sure how to approach. Because right now *close* proved disconcerting. She wanted him; she didn't want him.

A trio of giggling elderly women waved at Dez and she waved back. A tilt of her wine goblet to acknowledge them was met with raised toasts.

"Wonder if they'll start coming into the shop now to ask me about my boyfriend? You're quite the hit. Bet those old ladies haven't seen prime USDA like you in decades."

"Doesn't matter what they think. What do *you* think? Tell me why a gorgeous woman like you is living in a lazy little place like Willow Cove? Without friends, or family or…"

"A man?"

He shrugged. "Smart, attractive women don't usually stay single for long."

"Sure they do. That's what makes them smart." A sip of wine rewarded her sweetly. "You forget my kind have a tendency to outlive our mortal mates. Having a relationship is never a wise thing."

"What if the man is immortal?"

"I think you're losing track of your goal, fixer. What you want from me cannot be obtained by seduction. Only sheer force of will and a stubborn sense of survival might see you a challenge. But never the victor."

"Relax, Dez. Do you find me threatening right now?"

Yes, but on a sensual level, not a magical-battle level. "You could never be a threat."

"You have no idea."

And if she truly were as smart as he claimed, she would be wise to heed that warning.

Sitting back, Dez's shoulder brushed Ivan's wool suit coat. Men fell into two categories for her: worth getting to know, and better just as friends.

The "better just as friends" kind attracted her on a mental level. They usually were smart and held an occupation that Dez wasn't familiar with, but that made them all the more interesting to listen to. They could be physically attractive, but she usually never felt the vibe from them, that intangible sense of wanting to come undone in the man's presence.

The "worth getting to know" ones attracted her physically and stirred that pining to fall to pieces, to come undone. An undoing she wanted to explore, go deeper into, to get lost in.

Right now she couldn't decide about Ivan.

All right, to be honest with herself, she knew exactly the kind of man he was. And denying it was the only safe option.

Ivan stood and said, "I came here to party. It's rare I'm allowed such freedom during the night, and I intend to take advantage of that. I'm going to find someone who wants to dance."

And he walked away. The suit was immaculately tailored; stylish fine gray pinstripes traced the deep navy color. The British cut, slender and close-fitted, emphasized his broad shoulders and sleek, long build. He looked as good from behind as he did from the front.

And Dez caught herself as she licked her lips. "Focus, girl. He's using persuasion. Has to be."

Quick enough, Ivan found a partner, and he started in on an impressive polka.

Dez crossed her arms and tapped the rim of the wine goblet against her teeth. The man actually knew how to polka.

"Wonder how long he's been around?"

A vampire could look as young as Ivan yet be centuries old. Surely Himself wouldn't pluck up a youngling as his fixer. And if his parents had been a phoenix and a witch, well, then he was truly a unique and powerful breed.

If he intended to seduce the book from her, then what if she switched her game of playing hard to get and, instead, seduced him first? Rendered him virtually incapable of wanting to harm or trick her, for he would wish only to serve as her sexual slave.

Dez smirked. The idea sounded far more intriguing than the execution did. Many a lover had rumpled her sheets, but this tigress had softened her mien of attack and conquer. She preferred to be conquered, actually.

Truth be told, she was vulnerable in the relationship department.

Was it because she so desperately pined for the attention? A simple hug. A lingering kiss? Waking each morning alongside a man who claimed love?

She shook her head and set the goblet on the bench. "I'm not a virgin. I have a few tricks up my sleeve."

Finishing the waltz with a spry-footed older woman dressed in violet chiffon, Ivan then bowed and led her off the dance floor to the waiting gaggle of hens. The entire crew giggled as he kissed her hand and begged off.

They were everywhere, the old ladies. Made him smile. He hadn't had such a good time in, well, seven years, to be sure.

With a threat of rain increasing the humidity in the air, the band immediately started to dismantle.

Just as well. A prickle at the back of Ivan's neck warned he had better get more serious about his task.

The coercion would never force him to do anything he wouldn't normally do. It wouldn't make him vamp out on a crowd of citizens. He could control his bloodlust. But it could make him brisk, focused and uncaring for anything that did not serve his ultimate goal.

Which was why he'd refused Elise another dance. He was

beginning to wish her home and tucked safely in her bed, and that the park was empty. Save he and Dez.

"You're making quite the impression," Dez said, as he joined her side at the edge of the dance floor.

"I am enjoying myself."

"You say that as if it's new to you."

"It is. Trust me, I'm still waiting for the wallop." A wistful smirk pulled his lips. The intensity of Dez's blood stretched beyond the mixture of floral aromas, and the humid air stirred it to a heady perfume inside his brain. His fangs tingled. Sinking them into her neck would be like stabbing a tooth into an apricot's flesh, juicy and sweet and dripping with deliciousness.

"I'm sorry to have left you alone for so long," he rushed out. "It was rude."

"On the contrary, I enjoyed watching you sweep those women off their feet much more than I would have cared to dance myself."

"We'll have our dance."

He clasped her hand. Sensing her initial need to pull away, he didn't hold tight, and was rewarded with a relaxed acceptance.

See, he could work with the coercion. It just took focus.

But his fangs were not listening to a mental command to retreat. They pricked the inside of his lower lip, wanting luscious fruit oozing over his tongue.

"What's that?" Ivan scanned the sky.

"The midnight bells." Dez pointed to the church half a mile down the main street. A flaking white spire jutted into the dark sky. "Willow Cove rings them every night and noon."

"Bet the townspeople love that."

"It's tradition. It gives me comfort. You know bells keep back the devil."

"Do they?"

Looking beyond her to the glint of moonlight on the sea, he

inhaled the salted air. It was enough to clear his head of her gorgeous scent. His fangs rose in their sockets. "Tell me one thing. If I were not a fixer after your book, would you find me attractive?"

She didn't even blink. "Yes."

Points for him! Obvious, because she hadn't tried to drown him or sweep him away in a tsunami. Yet. The night was young.

So the woman liked him. And he liked her. Which should cause him grief, knowing this was a job, but right now he wanted to ride the good feeling. Anything to keep back the insistent craving to gorge on her blood as if at a bacchanalian feast.

But he couldn't be obvious. There were diabolic forces that sensed his emotions and punished brutally should he veer from the task.

"Now that you mention my book…" she said.

He traced one dangling curl that touched her shoulder. A frenzy of browns and gold and even some red streaked through the strands.

"You don't even know what it is you're after, do you?"

"A grimoire. All you witches have them."

"'You witches'? Don't *you* have a grimoire?"

"My mother does somewhere. I've never felt the need to write down spells. My memory is quite good."

"You're not the least humble, are you?"

"Humility is for the weak. I can't afford weakness."

He leaned in, not so close she might flinch away, but near enough to her pale cheek to draw in the scent that sat above her skin, not below it. "What is that perfume you're wearing?"

"I never wear perfume."

"Liar. I can smell numerous scents whenever you are near. Must be from your shop, eh? I can pick out lavender and vanilla, and maybe clove. Difficult to avoid the apricot."

"Apricot? I never use—"

"The scent of your blood. It tastes marvelous."

When her palm pressed against his chest, Ivan wished his skin bared so she could feel his pounding heart. Yet even with the barrier of clothing, he felt her pulse. And behind the beat gushed the rich, sweet blood he'd tasted last night.

And his fangs descended again. He tilted his head, so she could not see him directly as he spoke.

"All blood smells different, from person to person. Some tastes metallic, others like meat or even dust. A rare few taste of herbs or flowers, or…fruit. A person's blood is infused with who they are, what they eat, what they desire, their passions."

She shoved him away. "It was just a drop. You can't possibly remember the taste."

"I'll never forget it."

Fighting the coercion was becoming more of a challenge— and the need to fight it dropped.

One hand wrapped about her neck. For the first time, Ivan saw she wasn't so bold. Good. A weakness. She wanted to know his bite, whether she realized that or not.

"I'm not going to vamp out and bite you in front of the townspeople, if that's what you think."

"Good, because I have a firm rule about no biting. Absolutely. No. Biting."

Like a hit to the groin, her *rule* stopped the craving for a bite. Ivan's fangs slipped away. "I'll remember that."

"Now about the book. The *grimoire*," she insisted, "is the *Grande Grimoire*. And again, you have no idea what you're after."

"Grand things, obviously." Nope, couldn't get the taste of her from his palate. "Grand things like…a kiss. Just one?"

He touched the porcelain line of her jaw, tilting her gaze up to his. A bit of defiance had returned, but softer, more open.

"I am beguiled by your scent and wanting to touch more than I dare."

"Sounds like the means to seduction. And isn't that what you intend? To seduce the book from my protection? If you bit me, you could persuade me to give it to you." A tilt of her shoulder shifted the red silk. Her small breasts rose in delicious mounds. "Am I right?"

Ivan licked his lips. "Eerily right."

She moved a step closer. A fine mist began to sprinkle their heads. All around them, people began to scatter.

"But as I told you from the start, I'll only give you the truth of me. You will know my intentions always. I don't want to scare you away."

"I should hope not, if you wish to be successful. But don't worry, I don't scare easily."

"I've noticed." He cocked a look skyward. Raindrops splattered his forehead. "Did you do that?"

"Not me," she said, and moved even closer.

A smirk tugged the corner of her mouth into an inverted comma. Ivan had to touch her. But he wasn't able to capture the curve of her expression, only stroke his finger along the finest flesh he'd ever known.

Now the rain began to fall with increasing intensity.

"You want to find cover?"

"I'm fine. You make a great umbrella." She traced a finger up the line of buttons on his confining dress shirt. And he felt every touch as a hot pulse, as if it were skin on skin.

Nothing could make him break contact with her now. Come lightning or tornado—even wild roses—he'd stand firm.

"Everyone is leaving," she said.

"Can I get that dance now?"

"You're very bad, Ivan." And she spread her arms up around his neck. "But I've never been particularly good myself."

Now this offer he could definitely get behind.

Drawing his hand down her back, his fingers dipped into her curves, gliding, lingering, imprinting. Ivan moaned, but the sound got lost in the thunder and rain. Soaked thoroughly, the weather did not dissuade his explorations. The red silk Dez wore was so wet he could trace the curve of her hip and the soft indents above her derriere through the thin fabric.

Let his fangs come out to play. He needed. He wanted.

But he wouldn't press his luck. Not yet.

They swayed there in the rain. The red-and-black-striped awning over the bar snapped shut with a clack. Band members shouted as they shuffled to load their instruments into the back of a waiting van. And at the periphery of his vision, Ivan saw a huddle of old ladies, observing from beneath the umbrella put up before the ice cream shop across the street.

"We've an audience," he said.

Dez sighed against his chest, and from that moment on, Ivan didn't care who watched. Even Himself. Sure, he had a task to complete. And he would do it without fail.

But just because he was focused on obtaining some book didn't mean he couldn't dance with a gorgeous witch in the pouring rain.

There were certain things a witch never did.

She avoided fire like the plague because that was her one bane.

She never cast a harmful spell unless she was fully prepared to accept the karmic counterattack the universe would slam back at her.

And she never consorted with a vampire—whether indifferent to his species or not.

Those had been Dez's rules for a lifetime. They'd gotten her through a lot. Though certainly she had broken the first two at some point—and had learned from it.

It was inevitable she would break the third.

Over her vast lifetime, Dez had collected a few regrets. But with each regret came a powerful lesson. So she plunged into this moment without looking over her shoulder or wondering what the hell she was doing. She was living. Simple as that.

The top of her head leveled at Ivan's shoulder. He was twice as wide as she and a behemoth to her petite form. It felt good, melting against his hard body, her rain-slickened clothing crushed up against his, and feeling his own warmth permeate the wetness.

She sized him up, finding he was lacking in no departments. Muscles. Check. Confidence. Check. A healthy bit of arrogance. Check. Charm to counteract the deceit. Check. And style to match a powerful knowledge of witchcraft.

No wonder Himself had chosen this one.

Crushing her hips against her dance partner put his erection at the apex of her mons. The solid hardness of him stirred thoughts of utter privacy, gasping moans and sweating bodies.

As if he were thinking parallel thoughts, Ivan drew her closer, tighter, until Dez thought she might become a part of him.

The embrace dizzied her. All her desire buttons had been switched on and now they rocketed to the top of the scale. Fingers digging into the wet fabric over his chest, she sighed, knowing he couldn't hear for the increasing rain.

All right, Dez, enough. Don't forget he could prove your death.

And she had meant it about the no biting. That was one rule she wasn't willing to stretch, twist or break. Never.

With a wistful last snug of her stomach against his hardness,

Dez stepped back, extricating herself with some difficulty from his grasp, but he relented.

"Thanks for tricks," she forced herself to say.

Then she turned and walked away. It was the longest walk she had ever taken. Feeling Ivan Drake's stare follow her to her car parked halfway down the block, Dez cautioned her steps so she wouldn't topple and bring him rushing to her side.

Because if he touched her again tonight, she wouldn't stop saying yes until morning.

Chapter 6

Ivan woke at 3:00 a.m. to the cell phone ringing. It was his mother's secretary. A Gray Council meeting was scheduled for this morning at nine. The private jet would be waiting at the Portland airport to whisk him away to Minneapolis.

Ivan dragged himself up and took a shower. He'd been rained on so much lately he wasn't sure it was necessary, but even vampires needed a good, brisk shower to shake away the remnants of Nod. He made the airport by five and arrived in Minneapolis before eight.

His parents staffed an amazing crew of people who chauffeured, designed and decorated, legally defended, massaged, bartended, kowtowed and even cleaned pools. Whenever Ivan visited, he rarely had to lift a finger. Made him feel like one of those rich and famous bachelors on TV, though he sensed those guys didn't have the devil breathing down their necks.

On the other hand…one never knew.

Thanks to his parents' savvy investments and his own financial choices, Ivan was rich, but he'd forgo the fame. If only he could.

Unfortunately—or fortunately, depending how one looked at it—his parents were grooming him to serve on the Gray Council, which combined a force of vampires and witches in a communications forum. They called themselves gray, since the witches had long ago labeled themselves "the light" and the vampires "the dark."

Since Ivan was both witch and vampire, he was an obvious choice to fill in any space vacated on the council. He had no alliances stronger to either side. He loved his father, who was a vampire. He adored his mother, who was a witch. He'd never grown up with the prejudice most witches and vampires felt toward one another.

And because of those prejudices and downright hatreds, the war between the two factions had pinnacled. If something wasn't done soon to end it, both sides would suffer immense loss. Even worse, the war was getting sloppy.

Sooner or later, the media would pick up on the strange magical rituals and blood sacrifices. It only took one paranormal theorist to label them witch- and vampire-related. Bring in a cryptozoologist to confirm the actual existence of said creatures, and *wham*, all hell would break loose.

The last thing the Gray Council needed was for the mortal world to get over their skepticism and start to believe vamps and witches really existed. Proof was all they required, and proof would be accidentally spilled sooner, rather than later, by one of their own.

No one in the council knew Ivan's soul belonged to Himself—they were not concerned with Himself; everyone knew He was firmly embedded in the mortal realm. It was no secret. Certainly the imps and demons and various marks knew who Ivan was, and feared him. As it should be. Himself didn't concern the council, nor should his fixer. And Ivan intended to keep it that way.

Hopping into the limo waiting on the airport tarmac, Ivan then plugged into his iPod and dialed to a classical music playlist. The operatic *Farinelli* soundtrack seeped into his brain. One of his favorite movies, it supposed the life of the famous castrato Farinelli and how he had become a virtual rock star to the eighteenth-century set.

A lilting opening arpeggio invaded his brain. He closed his eyes and let go of the night job and the forthcoming meeting. As the soprano's birdlike notes began, Ivan drifted into a memory of the previous night.

Holding Dez in his arms and breathing her in. Like some wild exotic flower, she put off so many wonderful scents. Each breath took in something new. A never-ending discovery, she. He was in for the journey. And he wouldn't stop until he tasted apricot blood across his tongue.

The rain had soaked Dez's dress to cling possessively to an amazing body. Aware they had an audience, he had strongly resisted stroking her hard nipples, though the agony of that decision had kept him more silent out of restraint.

And she'd pressed along his erection, knowing exactly what she was doing. He'd gotten so hard.

Had it been purposeful? To see if she could get a rise out of him? (Had she!) Or had it merely been reaction to standing in his arms?

Did the witch want him?

Maybe.

Nodding in appreciation, Ivan tapped his fingers to Porpora's *Polifermo* and imagined himself in a sweeping dance with the gorgeous witch in skin-clinging red silk.

The meeting room stretched across an expanse of white marble on the twenty-fifth floor of the Dain Rauscher building. Ivan arrived ten minutes early and, standing before the immense floor-to-ceiling windows, looked down over an exhibition tennis match going on below in the Marquette mall.

All along the street, a farmer's market was in full swing. Flowers and fresh vegetables and handcrafted items were abundantly displayed. Gaily colored umbrellas shaded the bounty. A street performer serenaded the passing crowd with a spoons rendition of a tune Ivan could not hear.

It felt good to return home. He traveled the globe as the fixer, and rarely stayed in any place more than a week at a time. But Minneapolis was home.

"Ivan!"

His father crossed the room and shook Ivan's hand. The vampiric shimmer tingled up Ivan's arm, a welcome feeling.

"Dad." He pulled his father in for a hug, noting he was a little taller than a man who was already quite tall. "Mom convince you to shave your head again?"

Nikolaus Drake smoothed a palm over his scalp, tattooed over all with arresting black tribal designs. "It's summer. I needed the change."

"Most imposing," Ivan noted.

His father had gotten the tattoos before becoming a vampire and after his own brain surgery, which, due to a slip of the knife, took away the dexterity that had once allowed him to operate. Yep, his father had once been a brain surgeon.

Ivan recalled tracing the heavy black tattoo as a kid and wanting his own.

But he'd never imagined his first foray into getting inked would be the shadow currently clinging to his spine.

"Yeah, well, you know I like to freak out the witches." Nikolaus smirked and lowered his voice as a trio of female witches entered the room. "You see that new witch? Anastasia? She's a gorgeous bit of magic, eh, son?"

Nikolaus Drake's affections never strayed from his wife. Ivan was uncomfortably aware of his dad's need to always fix him up with either a witch or a vampire. Ivan hadn't dated for years. He was too busy as a fixer. And did he really want to visit his nightmares on another soul, innocent or otherwise?

"Pretty," he commented of the slender blonde. "But, you know…things to do. Heads to bash. Wicked souls or imps to hunt."

"Right." Nikolaus's easy smile dropped. "But nothing wrong with taking some pleasure now and then, is there?"

"I do, Dad. Don't worry about me."

"I never do, not as much as your mother does, believe me."

His parents had stopped apologizing for their mistake years ago, but he could still see the grief in his mother's eyes. Ivan vacillated between blaming them for his situation and not. Because he had his own suspicions about the true events that had culminated in his being born. But every time he tried to bring up the subject with his mother she resorted to dissuasion, or outright tears.

A teary-eyed woman always put Ivan off his game. He didn't know how to deal with them. Did they need to be touched? To be reassured? Could he get himself as far away from the crier as possible without making her want to curse him an uncaring lout?

"You working on anything right now?" his dad asked.

"A new task. I've to claim some grand grimoire from a gorgeous number out in Maine."

"The *Grande Grimoire?*" Ivan's mother appeared from behind and hugged him. The top of her head stopped at his shoulders. Short, yet athletic, Ravin Crosse Drake had once stalked vampires with blood bullets and a take-no-prisoners attitude. If you looked up *imposing* in the dictionary, you'd find her picture in the margin. "What's this about the grimoire?"

"Just a book, mom."

"Not if it's the *Grande Grimoire*."

"Really?" Ivan turned and, aware the room was filling up, nudged his mother aside, closer to the windows. "Tell me about it. Himself wants me to fetch it for him."

A disgusted huff accompanied Ravin's sorry shake of her head. "That can't be good."

Ivan realized she was as petite as Dez, but where Ravin was dark and dangerous, Dez came off as more wise and sensual, yet still dangerous with the water magic.

"The *Grande Grimoire* is *the* grimoire, Ivan," she said, keeping her voice to a whisper. She clutched his hand and they turned their backs to the conference table. "The book of all spells. What the hell does Himself want with that? And now?"

"The book of *all* spells? So, you mean like—?"

"Every time a new spell is cast it gets recorded in the *Grande Grimoire*," Ravin explained. She glanced over a shoulder to make sure no one listened to the private conversation with her son. "Every spell that has ever been cast, conjured or summoned is listed in there. Should anything ever happen to the grimoire, any witch, and all immortals—and mortals—associated with any of the spells will suffer. It is the very binding of our craft. It keeps our species in balance, so to speak."

Ivan blew out a breath and shuffled fingers back through his hair. "I had no idea. So, the witch who keeps this book, does she record all those spells herself? I imagine she must be writing constantly."

Desideriel Merovech didn't look the sort who favored scribbling in a book all day. When did she find time to mix her perfumes or bewitch those damned roses?

"No, it's done automatically. Magically. But there's only one keeper of the book. And should she lose it, or someone steals it from her? Well."

That final word said it all.

Ivan paced away from his mother. Aware the room was settling and growing quiet, he turned and cast a look to the former vampire slayer.

Ravin shook her head and shrugged. They'd talk later. They must.

The meeting was called to order by Nikolaus, who served as the co-chair alongside the witch Abigail Rowan. As usual, Ivan stood off to the side and listened, but he was rarely invited to participate. He wasn't an official member of the Gray Council. And the only way to assume a position on the council was by an opening, which meant the death of a current member, all of whom were immortal. Though his parents had insisted he sit in on meetings so he could learn, and he'd been accepted, everyone knew vacancies were not frequent.

Though with the war raging, every day was another opportunity for such an opening.

Most immortals weren't really sure how to take Ivan. Half witch, half vampire? Which side did they relate to? The witches were generally repelled because he was a vampire. The vampires were curious because he could do magic.

All members of the council had no prejudices toward the others, but they still were reluctant about Ivan. He never pressed the issue that he was probably more powerful than the entire council combined. He merely wished an end to this war, as they all did.

"Last week, Eglantine's crew brought down the entire Zmaj tribe," Francois DeMere, former Nava leader and five-century-old unbaptized vampire, announced.

The council members seated around the oval mahogany table shook their heads. They kept tabs on all the vampire tribes and the various witch alliances. Eglantine Richards led one of the leading witch gangs. She had been around for centuries and was responsible for dozens of vampire deaths.

"They left the bodies in a dump yard," Francois reported. "Some were not completely burned to ash. The local news station reported on it as if it were a satanic ritual."

"Now that's fine," Nikolaus chimed in, "but we can't afford when mortals begin to label it witchcraft. We need a resolution, people."

"We're recruiting task forces daily," Francois said. "But there are simply not enough unallied vampires or witches willing to police their own. It's too dangerous. And thanks to the Stone corporation, the armored suits manufactured for vampires against witches puts them on the top right now. The witches are merely fighting for their lives."

"Not true," Gerard Langdouc, another vampire, said. "There exist organized cadres of witches hunting vampires in Europe, Russia and right here in the U.S. If we attempt to mark a victor in this war right now, it would come up a draw."

Abigail Rowan sighed heavily. Her utterance echoed the thoughts of them all, and for a moment everyone sat in silence.

A flash from down on the street captured Ivan's attention. He spied a young woman riding her bicycle through the farmer's market. Long hair captured the sun in many different shades of blond, chestnut and pale red. Like Dez's hair.

And there, a brilliant red flag, flickering above a stack of fresh vegetables, made Ivan lick his lips. That dress. It was almost as if she had not worn anything after the rain had soaked the thin fabric to her curves. His fingers had strayed low to the base of her back. There, where those sexy indents had teased him to trace out a design of his desire.

He wanted more. And this was not the fixer thinking he needed more to successfully complete a task. No, Ivan Drake wanted more.

"What if the Protection spell were reversed?"

The entire room looked to Ravin, who had suggested the bizarre idea.

Ivan shook off his straying thoughts. Reverse the Protection spell? Now that was an interesting idea. And for his mother, a witch, to have suggested it was remarkable.

"If the witches no longer held such incredible power over the vampires," Ravin said, "then perhaps both sides would step back and regroup. If the vampires are given no reason for defense, then they would not kill. Nor would the witches. We could go back to living peaceably among one another."

"Too simplistic," Francois challenged.

"We've never lived peaceably," Emmanuelle, a newer member, said. "And I for one have no desire to be enslaved by a vampire for my blood and magic."

"It wouldn't happen that way," Nikolaus said. "We've all learned from the past. Vampires have no more desire to enslave witches than witches do of drinking blood." He angled an eye at the witches who sat across the table from him.

The witches did drink blood, Ivan knew. Once every century, if they wished to maintain their immortality, a witch must drink the blood from a beating vampire's heart. *Sources,* the witches called the unfortunate vampires. *Ash,* was what the vamps called their fallen comrades.

"It's something to take under consideration. We need to act, people. Sooner rather than later." Ravin announced a break.

Nothing had been resolved, but it had been over two hours, and everyone was restless.

"Good idea," Ivan said to his mom, as they strolled out the room and headed toward the elevators. "Is the Protection spell in the *Grande Grimoire?*"

"Yes, I suppose so." Her dark eyes took in her son's neat appearance as she gave him a smirking smile. "What are you thinking, Ivan? Don't do anything rash. It would have to be voted on by the council first."

"Don't worry, Mom. I'm not sure I'll ever gain access to the grimoire. But I'm certainly enjoying the challenge."

"I knew it." Nikolaus Drake joined the two from behind and spread his arms around his son and wife. "The witch who guards the book has caught your eye?"

His father never let up. "Maybe."

Ravin suppressed a squeal. She didn't do things like squeal in delight; the woman was a leather-wearing, chopper-riding witch who'd once slain vampires for fun. But Ivan could see definite delight in her eyes.

"I'm ready for a grandchild," she suddenly announced.

That confession threw Ivan way out of reality. He didn't know what to say to that. What had become of his hard-as-nails mother?

"Me, too," his father added. "After you steal the book from her, are you going to sweep her off her feet and marry her?"

"Wait. Stop." Ivan pressed the elevator button and then spread out his hands before him. "I just met her. She's pretty, and yes, I'm attracted to her. But she's a job. Okay? And who said anything about marriage? I'm young. I've centuries in front of me. And Mom, you'll still be young when you finally get your grandchild, so don't push."

His parents appropriately bowed their heads, conceding.

The elevator opened and Ivan stepped inside.

Ravin thought she was whispering, but Ivan's ultrasensitive hearing picked up his mother's quiet remark. "This is the one," she whispered to her husband. "I can feel it."

Chapter 7

The radio was tuned to a local pop hits station. Dez liked the energy of the music and always played it softly when working in the still room.

Crushing pale violet heliotrope petals she'd stolen from the gala in her favorite marble mortar, she drew in the cherry scent. Cherry and vanilla were her absolute favorites.

She'd been brewing spells and ointments for centuries. For a time she'd been a healer, utilizing herbs and plants and spell-craft. She had taken a stab at alchemy in the seventeenth century, didn't like it; too messy and the metallic, chemical odors were oftentimes worse than roadkill.

The end of the nineteenth century had seen her extracting the poisonous wormwood oil to create the popular absinthe. But after she'd seen the results the wicked green fairy had on men—and real fairies—she destroyed that processing equipment and settled back to what she most enjoyed, creating perfumes.

Hmm, to think about fairies… "Wonder what Dominique is up to?"

She'd made a friend for life of Dominique San Juste during the Belle Epoque in Paris. He usually breezed through her life once every decade or so. Last she heard, he'd found himself another fairy, and that love might even be enough to break the curse of his broken heart. He'd once loved a real angel who had fallen to earth.

Life was never easy when an immortal fell in love with a mortal. Dez had loved mortals in her lifetime but had never allowed herself to grow attached to them.

"I do have friends," she muttered, as she selected a few vials of essential oil. "Okay, so friend." Singular. Not plural, as she'd like it to be.

But she was working on that.

Her perfume business had been a natural progression from something that was innate.

The year after she'd moved into this house, she'd expanded the porch out back, doubled it in size and made every wall a window. She trained the wild roses not to grow over the windows. The vampire repellent was necessary, because even though she did not fear them, their hunger to see her burn must not be ignored. Now this still room was where she concocted her perfumes and experimented with new spells.

The sunset on the ocean glinted. While she went through the mundane ritual of crushing and blending to make oils, her mind drifted to last night. Dancing in the rain with a handsome vampire-slash-witch.

A vampire *and* a witch? It was incredible, but nothing was out of the realm of possibility. She had lived long enough to learn that. Hell, when angels fell and learned to love changeling fairies, well then, anything was feasible.

She wanted to look into his parents, discover what Ivan Drake was about, but she knew to send out feelers would alert parties she didn't want to tip off. Not that Himself didn't already have a keen bead on her via his latest fixer.

"Maybe it's worth the risk? Himself is already aware of me."

Knowing one's enemy was never a bad thing. And such a multifaceted man as Ivan presented limitless challenges she must be prepared for.

"I'll scry on it later, at midnight." When her psychic energies were most clear. "Certainly can't hurt to know what I'm up against."

Because last night's attempts at seduction, while awkward, hadn't been awful. Nor had they been particularly devastating to the enemy. She'd welcomed Ivan's interest. So rarely did a man seek to spend time with her without then expecting a spell or ward against a spell in return. For some reason mortal men avoided Dez, even though she knew they hadn't a clue what it was about her that repelled him.

She had spent centuries perfecting a cloak of indifference, of protection, about herself and against those poor mortals who would foolishly become involved with her.

So Ivan's closeness assaulted her in ways she wasn't prepared for. The lack of companionship of late, of closeness and touching—hell, it had been months since she'd had sex— had allowed Ivan to easily peel away an outer layer from her. He'd seeped into her being, and he was still there. Making her wonder about him. Causing her to imagine scenarios such as furthering their embrace in the sanctity of a bedroom where she could study that erection up close.

Dez smirked. How quickly she could be reduced from stoic and distrustful to lusting.

"When you should be thinking of him as an opponent. By

the goddess, Dez, how desperate for a man are you? When you'd welcome Himself's fixer to touch you? Get your game face on, girl. Whatever that means."

Again she smiled. She never talked to herself. Heavens, but she needed a girlfriend, someone to share her secret thoughts about men with. Someone to offer her good old-fashioned advice about dating and lust and bad boys.

"He's about as bad as they come." And this time, Dez giggled.

Swiping a swath of hair from her face, she cast a glance outside. The sunset rippled orange across the silver water. A dark silhouette perched upon the rocks that edged her property and dropped to the beach.

"He would not. Is that—Ivan?"

Of course he would. She should expect nothing less.

Tugging off her apron and tossing it aside, Dez then marched outside. The breeze tinkled the bells she'd tied about the eaves of her house. Evening dew sprinkled her feet and somewhere close a bullfrog croaked.

She wore a loose black robe of stretchy rayon that hugged her curves and trailed behind her ankles across the grass. Ruffles spilled about the wide neckline and over her wrists and fingers. The satin frogs had long since fallen away, so she clutched the unfastenable opening of the robe at her stomach.

"You're trespassing!" she called as she neared the imposing silhouette.

Even clad in what looked like a business suit, he more resembled one of those high-class bodyguards the entertainers toted with them than something she'd expect to see shaking down demons and imps.

Ivan started toward her. "I couldn't ring the doorbell. Your attack roses sensed my first step through the front gate. I was hoping you'd notice me waiting outside."

Dez stopped near one of two fist-wide iron poles that she never did use to hang up wet clothes. It was apparent the man was going to walk right up to her. Did he have no sense of boundaries?

Why? You let them down last night. Naturally he feels entitled. Idiot witch.

Quickly, she summoned a white light to surround her.

Ivan put up his hands, like he would grab her by the shoulders, but his palms connected with the invisible shield, holding him back about a foot from her body.

"This isn't necessary, Dez."

"I don't take kindly to trespassers. And it *is* evening."

"Sun's still visible. I don't completely belong to Himself yet." He nodded toward the bells on the eaves, which tinkled out an offbeat tune. "What are those bells for?"

"They keep back the devil. I told you that."

"I'm no devil."

"That has yet to be determined."

Ivan bowed his head and closed his eyes. Concentrating?

Dez held her ground, keeping the white light strong. Yet she could sense he tapped at her energies, feeling about the edges of her spiritual aura.

"Did last night mean nothing to you?" he growled. He literally growled!

"Soaked to the bone and groped by a man intent on stealing from me? Hmm, let me think about that one." But not too long, because if she were honest with herself, yes, the night had been intriguing.

"You—"

Suddenly his palms penetrated the white light. Dez could feel the intrusion as an invading presence permeating her flesh.

Ivan's body lunged forward, and with nothing solid behind

her to stop his palms, his body crashed against hers. Wrapping his arms around her back, he held her gently, but firmly.

"—tempt me beyond all reason," he finished.

The robe barely covered her breasts. And the fabric had splayed high on her thighs so her pubic hairs tickled across the fly of his dark velvet pants. Velvet? The man dressed like some kind of vampiric rock star.

But this—this embrace—was not what she intended.

You're not being honest with yourself.

Right. But the lie was intended to put back the enemy, not conceal her own vacillating emotions.

Yet now he held her, Dez relaxed her compulsion to push him away. He'd growled at her. Right now his entire being stretched tight, ready to snap. She tempted fire.

And fire was never safe for witches.

Tugging back her arms, she didn't fight hard when it was apparent he did not want to release her. And to shake her shoulder back would drop the robe down to reveal more than was safe for propriety.

You don't subscribe to propriety, Dez. What the hell?

Never had a man so challenged her very sense of self so that she couldn't think straight, let alone grasp any of her truths.

"There's but a sliver of sun on the horizon. It is officially night, fixer. You promised me truth. So tell me, you're under his command, aren't you?"

"Of course I am." The growl in his voice, bruised with a deep hush, crept warmly over Dez's flesh. "Himself's shadow prickles up and down my spine as the sun slips away into the west. I belong to him. I will get that book."

He nudged his nose into her hair. A strange divergence from his violent claim to win. And yet, not. He had already confessed to use seduction against her.

"Tell me one thing, witch. Is the book in a tangible place? Can I dig, seek, or uncover it somewhere?"

"No."

"It's bespelled then? Only you can access it?"

"Exactly. Now you tell me one thing. And please, step back." She pressed against his chest, but he remained an unmoving statue. "Please?"

He relented, breaking their contact, but the shadows between them remained. He was close enough to bow his head forward and kiss her on the mouth.

Another kiss might completely undo her determination. Even in the darkness she could see his mouth, slightly parted. Not a mouth from which to refuse a kiss. And memory of its delicious dance across hers stirred a wanting ache at her breast.

But she had no intention of giving him the lead in this power play. Dez tugged the robe closed and swept the long skirt up around her legs. Right now she ached there, at her nipples and in her belly, but she wasn't wet for him. She wasn't *that* easy.

"What do you want to know?" he wondered. "Ask me anything."

Curling an arm behind her to wrap about the cool iron clothing-line pole, Dez spun a quarter turn away from the overwhelming presence of him. The sea winked at her.

Breathing room. That is what she required to keep a clear head.

And insight into the enemy's heart.

"What is it," she asked, "that compels a man to sell his soul to Himself?"

"Indeed?"

Ivan's footsteps crushed the dew-bejeweled grass. He stepped away from her, back to the rock where he'd originally been waiting.

Had she posed a question that made him uncomfortable?

Small surprise after she knew his manner was to cause discomfort in as sly and coy a manner as possible.

Bother, it was always the big lugs who clammed up whenever feelings were introduced. Introspection? Likely the fixer did not care to examine his own heart.

Dez walked over to him and stood at his side, fingers toying with the heavy fall of her skirt. The sensation of his discomfort compelled her closer. This enigma? He appeared so confident; this falter startled her.

"I didn't sell my soul," he finally said.

And he'd promised her only truths. Huh.

"I can't think of any other way for it to happen," Dez challenged. "Himself doesn't take unless it has been offered, sold, or otherwise contracted."

"Otherwise contracted." What should have been a chuckle sounded more like an abbreviated scoff. Ivan slammed his arms high across his chest. The air about him felt rigid, cold. "I was born into this world already promised to Himself."

The intensity of his confession took away Dez's breath. This powerful man? And he was obviously distressed to have made such a confession.

So there was another way of losing one's soul to the devil.

"Your parents?"

Ivan nodded. Before she could counter herself, Dez reached to stroke her hand along his arm. The tailored silk suit sleeve hid not a twitch of muscle nor the warmth of his being. Not dead, then.

Some vampires were dead, literally brought to a weird sort of life with blood, while others—the majority of them—were brought close to death during their transformations but never truly died.

For some reason, knowing he was alive made a world of difference to Dez.

"You must understand, I don't blame them," he said. "It was an accident. Mostly. My parents are repentant about it, and it gives them no joy to see me suffer. But I can't be sure it was an accident. I have my doubts."

He thought his parents had *purposefully* sold his soul to Himself? Yikes. Dez would hate to meet those two.

"So you've belonged to Himself since birth?"

"He didn't come for my soul until seven years ago. He waited until I'd grown, come into my full vampire strength and witch magic. The Old Lad wasn't going to waste time training me. My parents unknowingly did that. They thought to make me strong, a force to stand against Himself. But I've learned it's foolish to think anyone can stand against the prince of darkness."

"Yes," she muttered.

Suddenly uncomfortable with the conversation, Dez cast a gaze across the fading silver streaks wavering upon the ocean. A truly wicked knowing could only make her sympathize for Ivan.

"You have to know, Dez—" he took her hand and pressed the back of it to his mouth "—this man who comes to you at night begging for the book? *He's* the fixer. Ivan Drake is not him. But I can't fight the coercion."

She stroked a thick hunk of hair from his forehead. Himself must coerce Ivan into working for him. Rather, he owned the man's soul; there wasn't a lot Ivan could do to refuse a task, she felt sure.

"If you resisted?"

He stubbed the toe of his boot into a thicket of grass. Pebbles skittered down the cliff to the white sand beach below. "I won't. Or rather, I do, but I know I can only make the effort of resistance. I can never completely refuse. I know better than that. My parents' souls are the threat he holds over me. And the souls of any I should care about. It's not worth the risk. So I do what

I must. And I do it well. There's not a task you can set to me I won't complete or die trying."

"Because failure is not in your arsenal."

"Exactly. But I fight it even while I'm achieving the task. It's an incredible drain. Makes me crave blood something fierce. There's not a night following an encounter with a mark I don't need to drink blood to restore the energy I've expelled."

Dez suppressed a shudder. The blood drinking did not disgust her, but knowing Ivan was forced to feed to survive did. Normally a vampire could go for weeks without blood. Some, centuries old, fed but a few times a year.

Never would she allow a vampire to bite her.

"But you," his words whispered out in a sigh. "This job. It's like a freaky head-over-heels dream."

"Flirting with—"

"—a gorgeous witch. It doesn't eat at me like enforcing does. Beating skulls and forcing up nightmares? I have to drink heavily following such tasks. But seduction and dancing and slow, gentle kisses? I haven't needed blood since meeting you."

"Good for you."

"Though I have craved it."

His look crept down her face and to her neck. Dez could read his thoughts and they made her shiver.

"I can resist," he finally said. "If I wish. And I do. If it takes me forever to get that book, I'm all for it."

"I have a feeling Himself won't be keen with a leisurely approach."

"I fight the coercion as we speak. Half of me wants to stand here in the sunset, enjoying your presence, thinking of how many ways I can touch you to hear that sweet whimper you gave me last night while dancing in the rain. The other half wants to kiss you hard, seduce you relentlessly, weaken you until you fall to your knees before me pleading to take the book."

"Hmm, since I know the ultimate goal, I don't think seduction will have quite the result you desire."

"You never know what can happen, Dez. Himself said seduction was your weakness."

And Himself would know. Because he knew all.

"Why are you telling me all this?"

"So you will understand I'm not doing this because I want to. I have no choice."

But he was doing it. And even if he thought he was enjoying the seduction—and she in turn did, too—it could only ever lead them to one result.

She could fight Ivan off until the end of never. Yet Dez knew Himself would keep pushing his fixer back at her. Because this time it was different. For as many times as Himself had sent a lackluster fixer after the book before, this time she sensed it would be a fight to the finish.

"It's a lonely life," Ivan said.

And the chill of his loneliness shivered across Dez's shoulders. She could relate. And that softened her to his dilemma.

This was going to happen. The seduction. The fight for the book. The struggle inside herself against Ivan's attraction. She needed to be smart and control it from the get-go if she wanted leverage later on.

And so she would attempt to match his battle strategy.

"So kiss me," she said lightly. And she hoped this effort would not fall so flat as the night at the dance had.

"Really?"

She nodded and splayed out her arms in a sort of have-at-me gesture.

Ivan approached, ready to touch, but then paused. Even in

the growing darkness she spied his provocative smile. "Can I kiss you where I've been dying to kiss you?"

Dez lifted a brow.

"Be daring," he said with a hoarse rasp that spoke of craving and needing something more desperately than air. "Take a chance, Dez."

A dare? Dez never refused a dare. Or rather, the nerve of him! To imply she wasn't up to a challenge put up her ire. And then, as quickly, it fell away, to be replaced with the resolute lightness she required to not become mired in the darkness.

A kiss in the place of his choosing? "I keep all my clothing on?"

"For the kiss, certainly."

"Then have at me."

A curious smirk curved the vampire's lips. But why she considered him merely a vampire made Dez wonder. What *did* he call himself? A vamp-witch? A vitch? A wampire? Silly.

In the moments Dez had pondered the moniker, Ivan slipped around behind her. She wasn't sure what he was doing back there, but remained determined to stand firmly. Never let them see you falter.

The pebble-littered grass crunched. Had he fallen to his knees?

A stir of warmth coiled in Dez's belly, contradicting the shiver-raising goose bumps along her arms. The ocean air misted softly. Waves *schushed* the beach with a rhythm older than time.

A tug at the waist of her skirt made her briefly stiffen. Dez sucked in a breath. She let go of the robe openings. The soft fabric swished across her hip, though he held it up to cover her derriere. A wide hand spread across her bottom, cupping it, holding her as he wished.

Delicate touches from Ivan's fingers traced along her exposed lower back and tugged the robe farther to one side— not too far, but enough for the breeze to whisper across her flesh.

The chill of warning was quickly replaced by a hush of warm air. Breath. He breathed upon her skin.

Dez closed her eyes. There, at the rise of her derriere, where her flesh dented in two concave curves, he kissed her.

His lips barely traced the needy heat of her skin. It felt as if he would not complete the kiss, that he would suddenly retreat and step away, but he did not.

Dez swallowed. Her fingers curled as she clasped her hands to her chest. One of her breasts was exposed. She sucked in her bottom lip.

The scorching slash of his tongue frenzied her nerve endings. And the touch traveled her body, racing up her spine and tickling over her shoulders. Her nipples hardened, pressed against her wrist. Her belly tightened. Her loins hummed, seeking, praying for the sensation to linger, to never stop.

The barest scrape of teeth shocked her to gasp in a breath. Dez bit in the edge of her lower lip.

Arms falling out at her sides, her fingers grasped, wanting to touch him, to rake through his thick, dark hair. To hold something. To anchor herself to him. But she could touch nothing, and so she opened her palms to the cool air. And even the breath of the breeze worked as if a lover's tongue upon her palms.

This was as close to undone as she could dream to be. But it wasn't quite there. Complete surrender must never come.

And when she stumbled, losing her balance, Ivan wrapped an arm across her stomach and stood up behind her, drawing her close. His fingers threaded through hers and he brought it around to clasp under her chest.

"Dimples of Venus," he whispered aside her ear. "There at the base of your spine and the rise of your gorgeous ass. I felt them last night when your soaked dress clung to you. Turned me on. Tasted like a dream. Haven't been able to think of anything else all day."

The tickle of a kiss beneath her earlobe caused Dez to tilt her head.

"Didn't even have to remove your clothing." She heard a teasing chuckle in his tone. "Just a little rearranging."

She'd never heard those strange little indents at the base of her spine called that before. Sounded exquisite, like something that belonged to a goddess. And standing in Ivan's arms brought her close to such status.

I could fly, she thought. *Right now. So free. Even wrapped in his arms, I feel as if I could lift off.*

And she had never mastered flying in her magic. So the feeling was quite remarkable.

"Invite me inside?"

Initially she processed his plea as inviting him inside…her. But foolish thoughts scattered, and Dez realized he wanted to go inside her house.

"You no longer need an invitation to cross my threshold." She pulled away from the intense heat of him and walked toward the back porch.

"But the roses!"

"Not my problem," she called back. "If you can make it inside, I'll have tea waiting."

"Make it brandy, and I'll tear through those damned thorns for another kiss."

"Where next?" she wondered seductively. "Behind my knees? On the inside of my elbow?"

"Wherever you command me to touch you, I will."

Chapter 8

Dez hesitated over the simmering teapot on the stove. Ivan had mentioned brandy. She didn't keep alcohol in the house. Liquor, save the occasional glass of wine, didn't appeal to her.

"Maybe some chamomile will settle him down. Counteract the coercion?"

Doubtful. There was nothing that would work against a direct order from Himself, Dez knew. And though it sounded clichéd, resistance was futile.

"Poor guy." And then she caught herself. "What are you saying?"

Because the coercion was making him horny and call out promises to kiss her wherever she commanded. Behind the knees? What woman was going to turn down that offer?

"A woman who knows better."

A *clunk* up above redirected Dez's attention. The clatter was followed by his groan. "Must have found the open attic window."

She'd been keeping it open to air out after eradicating a family of bats a few weeks ago. Bats kept the yard free of insects, but she didn't want them nesting in her house. They hadn't known what had hit them when she'd zapped them with a death spell. One never knew when a spell might require eye of bat. All her spells were simple ancient works that required stuff like that.

Turning the burner to low, she collected teacups from the cupboard and set one across the counter before a stool and one before her. The chinoiserie porcelain cups were the only personal touch in the kitchen. She didn't collect keepsakes or mementoes. She'd given up on sentimentality centuries earlier.

As protector of the *Grande Grimoire*, she was required to keep the receptacle for the book open. No personal objects must clutter the atmosphere. Nothing must block the magic that constantly entered on a supernatural stream of energy. She no longer felt the cacophony of spells that had once bombarded her mentally and physically. The centuries had taught her to ignore it, and perhaps she'd even built up a magical hazmat suit of sorts to it all.

Footsteps crossed overhead.

It was funny, her allowing her natural enemy into her home without a fight. They'd done the fight, and while she knew she could again win, the effort didn't feel necessary tonight. This challenge had switched channels to something more intimate.

"Your house is cozy when it's not raining inside," Ivan commented, as he trundled down the stairs. "What's this color on all the walls, like a moss?"

"Yes, a pale sea green. I did the whole house in the white-washed shade. It's very soothing. Also it doesn't block magic like some more vibrant colors have a tendency to do."

"No decorations. Not a single knickknack. Very simple. Unlike you."

Dez smiled. Most men wouldn't comment on decorations. Ivan was a surprising contradiction of gentle giant, vicious fixer, and charming seducer. And he was exceptionally right-on regarding his judgment of her.

"So what's this room?" He twisted to look over the still room just off the kitchen. The high glass ceiling filtered in cool moonlight. "Eye of newt? Hair of dog? You're kidding me. You have a shelf full of clichés."

"These days modern witches would do to add a few clichés to their arsenal."

Ivan tapped a glass jar sitting on a shelf near the entrance. "What's this?"

"What does it look like?"

"I don't know. A frog heart?"

"Fairy heart."

"It's still beating."

"Yep. Had it for decades. S'pose I should use it before it expires."

"You're crazy," he said, and walked into the kitchen.

"Says the man who sips warm blood from the necks of mortals to survive."

"Touché."

"I see you found the attic window."

"Cleared most of the vines on the first leap." He tugged up a pant leg to reveal a slash through his thick leather biker boots. Dez could smell his blood. "Those things hurt like hell. What makes a woman plant them all around her house like that?"

"For the very reason they disturb you."

"You hate vampires that much?"

"On the contrary. I've nothing against the vampire race. I

don't appreciate my property being trespassed on by a blood hunter who's looking to take out a witch. The war makes it difficult to be open to others."

"I have a sense you're not easily open to anyone, vampire or not."

She shrugged. "Again, I have my reasons."

"We feel much the same about the war. I've never had a prejudice toward witches, but I'll be damned if I haven't had a few encounters with a wild-eyed witch looking to take down a vampire. You do have the upper hand, you know."

"Yes, we can take out a vampire with a splash of our blood. But you're resistant, so what do you care?"

"I do care," he said on a somber tone. "About my fellow vampire nation. And the witch nation. I wish there was a way to make it all stop. To bring peace to the two races."

"You don't favor one side over the other? Consider yourself more vampire than witch?"

"If you need to label me, I usually grab the term *vampire*. The 'drinking blood' part is more visible, commanding, than the need to cast spells. But neither side is more prominent. I actually feel like I've been a witch longer than a vampire because the blood hunger didn't manifest until I was sixteen."

"So what can one lone vampire, who is also a witch, do? For that matter, what can one lone witch do to bring about a change?"

The teapot began to whistle and Dez turned to pour steaming water into her cup and then Ivan's. She plopped a jasmine pearl into each cup. Impressed, Ivan observed as the tight ball opened into a gorgeous bloom at the bottom of his cup.

He hadn't sat across the counter, as Dez had hoped. Instead, he stood right beside her, one hip propped against the counter, distracting her in a way only six and a half feet of sexy vampire could do.

Did he study her backside? Wonder about that kiss? The base of her spine tingled for another touch.

"The council is at a loss what to do about this war," Ivan said. "If we don't come up with something soon, the media are going to catch on."

"That would devastate the two nations if mortals had proof of our existence. So you attend the Gray Council?"

"Only as an observer." He prodded the tea blossom with a fingertip. "Do I take this out? It looks like a big hairy spider."

"Let it brew for a few more minutes."

Ivan stood between her and the stove. Not much room to move around. And she wasn't going to pull a slip-out move and show him she was uncomfortable with him so close. Because again her body struggled between wanting to push him away and needing to pull him in for a good grope.

"You smell good."

Dez turned into his personal space. He smelled good, too. Dark, intense, kissed by the sea air.

"So!" It's his job to disturb you, she reminded herself. And what a fine job he was doing. "You divide your time between being a fixer and attending the Gray Council? Bet that pisses off Himself."

"He doesn't command my days. I'm being trained—groomed, so to speak—by my parents. They both sit on the council right now. I'm invited along to watch. It's good for me to learn."

He toyed with a curl of her hair. Even that small touch flustered her, made the heat seep up her neck. Dez lifted her tea for a sip. It hadn't brewed long enough, and it tasted like hot water with very weak flavoring.

"I suppose having a half vampire/half witch on the council would be a boon," she said. "So what do you call yourself? Vitch? Wampire?"

He delivered her a wonky look. "Try Ivan."

"All right, Ivan." A tilt of her head drew her hair from his fingers. Safe, for the moment. "Funny I've never heard about you until now. I usually know the names of all the council members. Though I suppose it has been decades since I last cared. How old did you say you are?"

"Twenty-eight."

She choked on another sip. "Just twenty-eight? Years? Not…decades?"

He grinned at her over the steaming rim of his teacup.

"Wow, you're just a baby."

"I may be, but I've seen enough for a thousand years, surely."

"I bet." She could fathom what he had witnessed serving Himself. And it was too horrible.

But only twenty-eight years old? Talk about robbing the cradle.

"How old are you?"

Dez plucked the blossom out of Ivan's teacup. "Didn't anyone ever teach you it's not nice to ask a woman her age?"

"Sorry. I was, well, you know, with our kind…you can never know."

"A few more centuries than you've tasted," she offered. "Let's leave it at that."

"Deal."

He prodded the wet jasmine blossom she'd set on a plate. The man's curiosity surprised her. One moment he could be staunch, the next, he could render her boneless with a kiss. And then he could dazzle with his sensitivity.

"So, about the book," he started.

And then there was the businessman. The fixer. A ruthless hunter of souls, who punished, maimed, and—well, she didn't want to think too far beyond that.

"Listen, Ivan. Let's get this straight, once and for all. I know you're here for a job. You have orders."

"Orders I don't intend to fail."

"Yes, you've said. But I have a task as well. I've protected the *Grande Grimoire* for a—" His eyebrows rose in expectation, but she wouldn't serve him that treat. "—a very long time. And I don't intend to let it out of my charge anytime soon. Such results could prove more devastating than even you could imagine. So seduce all you want. There's no amount of kissing or touching or even screaming orgasms that'll make me give up that book."

"Could we try that?" He set down the teacup with a *clink*. Swept up, Dez found herself in his embrace. "The 'screaming orgasm' part?"

Oh yeah?

His nose nuzzled at her hair, breathing her in. Wide, strong hands moved across her back, drawing her up close to his body. The heat of him exuded a virile power. "Which part next?" he murmured.

"Which part?"

"Behind the knee or the underside of your elbow?"

Mercy.

"Ivan, you're doing this because you have to."

"I'm glad you realize that."

She sneered at him. And stepped back—okay, shoved out of his wanting embrace. It was either that or succumb. And the succumbing part felt entirely too easy at the moment. "Maybe that's not so cool anymore."

"You don't think I'd really want you if this weren't a job?"

"How can you?" Anger vied to fend off Dez's ever-present desire that seemed to surface whenever he stood close. "You don't even know me."

"I know you are contradictory. One minute you're all about meeting the challenge, the next you're pushing me away."

"A woman's prerogative."

"I also know you're very smart. You care deeply about the world and how others look at you. Elise and the shop. And the war. We're on the same side, Dez. Don't push me away."

"Push you— if I don't push, I'll pull. There, are you happy? That's what I really want. To pull you closer. To have another one of those render-me-undone kisses. To, to… I'd love to have sex with you."

She paused to allow him to swallow the breath he'd surely choked on.

"But come back during the day. I'm not about to get naked with anyone under Himself's coercion. Got that?"

"Loud and clear."

"Prove to me that you want me more than to complete the task."

"I can do that. I should probably be going."

"So soon?"

"You've given me the rules. I know how to follow them. I'll be back with the first ray of daylight."

"I hope not. I like to sleep in."

He nodded and headed toward the front door, then swung around and jogged toward the staircase. "Better leave the way I entered. Safer. Thanks for the tea. Bye!"

"Well." Dez listened as he clumped up the stairs and leapt off the roof. "If that's all it takes to clear out a vampire…"

But he would be back.

And if it were during the day—and she could trust his intentions—she looked forward to it.

It was a good thing he had a side job to tend tonight. Something to divert the coercion into violence instead of pleasure. Dez had said she'd have sex with him during the day. He could wait that long. And he wasn't about to forgo the offer.

But *why* did she want to have sex?

Hell, don't think about it, man. You'll only drive yourself nuts with the contradiction that is Desideriel Merovech.

Seventy miles north of Willow Cove in the capital city of Bangor, Ivan tracked an imp down a dark alley behind a row of warehouses. Rotting fish and seaweed hung in the air.

"Trafficking in bargained souls is not smart," Ivan hissed. He shoved the three-hundred-pound imp against the wall.

The term *imp* implied something small and wily, but Ivan had learned differently. *Imp* meant "the devil's minion," in the broadest terms. They came in all shapes, sizes, colors and smells. This one was death-gray, and its sharp teeth were red as its eyes.

The thing stood as tall as Ivan, but it had perhaps seventy-five pounds on him, and it was strong. It shoved and sent Ivan stumbling backward. He didn't fall. Every muscle resisted weakness, and he charged back into the imp's chest. Contact sounded like stones slapping wet cement.

The thing roared like a hyena. As if Ivan's efforts were a mere fly to its scaly hide.

"So it's going to go this way, huh?"

Ivan stepped away and turned, knowing the thing wouldn't flee. It wanted the fight, and would toss around its weight until Ivan tired, and then it would take off before he could lift another punch.

Ivan wasn't stupid enough to entertain fools.

Summoning a chant that began silently in his brain, he tapped the air with his fingers, finding the rhythm of the spell as if a musician holding a beat. It was a trick his mother had taught him, since focusing completely on his magic had always been difficult with the vampire half of him to resist.

The vampire wanted the violence, to smell the blood.

So Ivan tapped and began to recite the nonsense tones out loud.

The imp stopped laughing, briefly tuning into the spell, then, realizing what was happening, it started to resist.

Too late.

The imp's jaw stretched wide. Its gelatinous bulk convulsed. A toad sprang out of its mouth. Followed by another huge bullfrog, and another. Quickly the ground became littered with hopping, croaking amphibians. The imp grasped at its throat, trying to close them off, but he would toss up the frogs all night so long as Ivan chanted.

Allotriophagy. It was an ancient practice that caused the victim to vomit up strange, foul objects. Ivan preferred toads, but he'd done snakes, stones, bees and even butterflies. It could bring down the most formidable opponent out of utter fear.

Soon enough the imp sank to its knees, squeezing toads blindly in its hands, and begging in a gurgled, croaking voice to grant it mercy. It would stop trafficking in souls.

"Cross your heart?" Ivan wondered over a shoulder.

The imp smashed a toad against its chest, right over the heart. It burbled what sounded like a *promise,* had another bullfrog not leapt from its distended jaws.

Ivan instantly dropped the spell. Relief flooded his muscles and the coercion stopped pricking his shadow. He'd completed another job.

Now he was thirsty.

What did it take to put back a man like Ivan Drake? Could she defeat him with tainted blood? It could possibly work. No, his father was a phoenix vampire. Ivan had already mentioned that his resistance to witch's blood carried through to the son.

There were spells against the devil, which Dez had mastered. Would they be effective against Himself's fixer? Her home was surrounded with devil pots, ancient pottery crocks that contained spells to keep back the devil. They didn't appear to have any effect on Ivan. Bewitched bells at the corners of her house tinkled with the wind.

Obviously the fixer was immune to devil-repelling wards.

What of an impotence spell? If he intended to seduce her, well then…

Dez shook her head.

The idea of rendering such a handsome, virile man impotent seemed criminal. And she'd been serious about wanting to have sex with him. Some touch time. And more kisses. Wherever he wanted to put them.

For, to infiltrate his armored exterior, she must put herself on the same playing field as he. Did she think she could seduce him to do her bidding?

"Anything is possible," she mused.

Chapter 9

Dez stood in the doorway with the Amazon.com box she'd collected from her porch. She loved learning new things, and books were the way to do it. The Internet was a bit of magic she truly enjoyed.

She spied a hunched-over figure in pink to the left side of the yard, examining the rose vines. The pink was blindingly bright and clashed horribly with the blue hair.

"Elise?"

"Ah, Miss Merovech! I hope you don't mind. I was passing by on my way to visit the grandkids. It's a marvel, these rose vines of yours. They're so thick and abundant. Do you use Miracle-Gro?"

No, she used magic.

"Something like that. Would you like to come in for some tea? I've apricot shortbread cooling."

"No, I'm just stopping by. Wouldn't want to intrude." The

woman tugged a stray lock of hair, taming it behind one ear. "Is your handsome man inside?"

Dez tucked the box under an arm and leaned against the door frame. Ivan was right; they weren't interested in her. And she had to stop fooling herself. "Nope. He's not keen on daylight."

That little lie gave the woman something to chew on.

"Hmm, well, I did come by with an offer, really. The Willow Cove Rose Club would like to invite you to join us. We meet every Monday afternoon at a different member's house each time."

"Really?"

Containing a sudden giddy rise of enthusiasm, Dez said to heck with it, and just beamed. "I'd like that. Is there a membership fee?"

"Just the sharing of secrets, dear," Elise said with a coy smile. She patted her pink pocketbook, hung about her wrist. She actually wore white gloves. "And seeds or cuttings, of course. Can you make it to Janice Blaine's house next Monday?"

"I'll be there. Should I bring treats?"

"Treats, dear? Oh no, leave the baking to the prof—er, no, we wouldn't expect a new member to bake for us. Just yourself. And your secrets. And, er…"

The pursed frown and nervous fingers were Elise's tells. Something troubled Elise more than how to get her hands on Dez's rose secrets.

"Was there something else, Mrs. Henderson?"

"Well, dear, I'm not quite sure how to say this. Oh, I'll just say it. There are rumors. Silly whispers, but, well… Are you…really a witch?"

Bother. Those old rumors again? The people of Willow Cove had no imagination whatsoever.

"Elise, you don't really believe in witches, do you?"

"Oh, of course not. Well, not the 'twitch their noses and

make things happen like Samantha Stevens' kind of witches. But those Wiccans." She shuddered noticeably. "And then there are the ones who dance about great bonfires. Naked!"

"Elise! That's incredible." What was so wrong with skyclad? "Don't worry, you'll never catch me chanting naked around a bonfire." Because Dez was very careful about things like that.

"Good, then. Sorry to have brought it up, but the other ladies were wondering."

Of course. It was always the *other* guy.

"You know how nasty rumors get started. We'll forget I brought it up, shall we? We'll see you in a few days. Ta!"

Aware she'd just been dissed by a woman with artificially dyed-blue hair and not enough meat on her bones to satisfy the hungriest of stray dogs, Dez still waved happily as Elise scuttled off and climbed into her boat of a brown Lincoln Continental.

What had Ivan called Elise? *An old biddy.* Yeah, well, technically, Dez figured she was at least one of those descriptive words herself.

"You're not old, you're wise."

Sure. Wise.

And so hungry for friendship she'd join a gang of geriatrics who had no interest in her beyond what she could help them grow. So long as she didn't twitch her nose at them.

"Don't do it, Dez," she chided. "If you go to the meeting it will be like surrendering to the status quo. Ivan would have a good laugh if I joined the club. Just surrendered to this desperate craving for connection."

Parts of surrender appealed to her. And another part of her toyed with the idea of showing up naked at Janice Blaine's house and inviting them all to call down the moon.

"Ha!"

She ripped the tape off the box, and the contents spilled out onto the porch. Three books, each of them a Dover edition of da Vinci's notebooks.

"I remember that one," she said, studying the picture of a human flying machine on the cover of one of the books. "I told him it would never work."

The air changed so swiftly, a breeze swept Dez's hair across her face and fluttered the pages of the book. The rose vines stirred.

Someone was about. And not a normal someone.

There at the gate to her front yard stood a marvelous creature. Yes, she could go there. It wasn't as if Ivan Drake presented the smallest threat to her. And she'd have to be blind not to feel an attraction.

Why not indulge? It was all a part of her master plan.

"Fight fire with fire," she said, and stepped out onto the porch.

Ivan waved. "It's day!"

"I see that." She crossed her arms over her chest and heeled the edge of the step with a bare foot. "So I suppose you've come for sex?"

"You know it."

"My, but you are the romantic one."

He offered a smirking shrug. Sweet lug of a puppy dog waiting to be taken in and played with. *Toss me a bone. I'll pretend I'm not out to attack you and take away your very livelihood.*

If she thought about this rationally, Dez knew by entertaining Himself's fixer she was playing right into the Old Lad's hands. It was not a position she wished to place herself in. But if she didn't stand down the fire now, it would come again. And again, and again, until finally Himself sent a fixer so powerful even she couldn't fight it. And that opponent likely wouldn't use seduction as a weapon.

All told, she had best meet this one at the vanguard if she had any hope for the future.

"Come on then," she said to the hopeful puppy. "Meet me around back."

Tossing the box of books aside as she wandered through the house toward the back porch, Dez tugged at the clingy dress she wore. It was an ancient thing, made of white lace, and buttoning all up the front. She'd removed the poufy, ruffled sleeves years ago. This witch changed with the times, but that didn't mean she had to abandon a nice dress because it had been in style before most mortals were born.

Humming a bit of the music that played in the speakers she'd installed all over the house, she smiled at the soundtrack tune. Panpipes and violins invited lovers to a Celtic dance.

Pausing before the screen door, Dez rushed her memory over the prominent lovers she'd had through the years. She took a lover when she chose. And when she did not feel the desire for a lover, she did not have one.

Simple rule she'd followed for centuries.

Leonardo da Vinci being such a lover. Yes, she could claim a few famous names for her bedpost. Da Vinci had been a fling, but she'd encouraged him to seek his passion. He'd not easily been drawn from his studies nor his interest in men.

Denis Diderot had taught her to read by allowing her a first look at his fabulous Encyclopedia plates. And Houdini had marveled at her seemingly effortless magical skills. None had ever known she was a witch, though a few may have teasingly accused her.

Hands on hips, she scanned the horizon. Was the man strolling outside along the cliff lover material? Did she *really* think to go through with the invitation of sex? A counterseduction intent on playing him before he could play her? What did she hope to gain by seducing him? It wasn't as though he didn't want sex. He'd be getting something he desired.

As would she.

"A man can be brought to his knees through passion. No one messes with this witch. And he's going to learn the hard way."

On a shelf near the door sat a few vials of essential oils. The open mortar of vanilla beans she'd crushed earlier wafted an intoxicating scent. Dipping her finger, she drew out the slick remnants of oil and dashed it at the base of her neck and across the insides of her elbows.

A crisp breeze gushed up from the beach and whipped Dez's skirts between her legs as she approached Ivan. He turned and offered his cupped hands toward her. He held something caged within his fingers.

"Is it going to leap at me?" Dez wondered.

"Just take a look." His smile could slay the hearts of women the world over. Little-boy enthusiasm captured on the face of a man. "Do you dare, you who keeps frog hearts in jars?"

"Fairy hearts."

"I don't even want to know how you got that thing."

"No, you probably don't."

"You witches and your need for live, beating hearts." He blew out a breath.

"You're half witch, Mister, so don't give me grief about any gruesome acts."

"Deal. So take a look."

Dez curled her palms over his hands and immediately sensed what he held. It touched her innate air magic, and she related to the motion.

"I found it on the grass, soaking up the sunlight."

She slowly peeled back his fingers to reveal the swallowtail resting patiently on his middle finger, above a plain silver ring. It spread open its wings, but didn't immediately take flight. The yellow stripes within the black scales were slightly faded. This butterfly had been around for a while.

Much like her? If this youngling vampire knew exactly how old she was, would he flee in disgust? Hell, her body resembled a thirty-year-old's, but her mind, well, that possessed memory untold, and heartache and triumph and sadness and joy.

Why are you doing this to yourself? Age has no meaning for your kind. If you don't worry about it, he won't.

And what the heck? Why did she care? It wasn't as if she intended to start doing emotions for the guy. This *daylight foray* was strictly business.

Make that war.

Tracing the lobed tip of one black-rimmed wing, Dez delighted in its delicacy. "I bet your master wouldn't approve of your entomological hobby."

"My days are my own, Dez. Let's not talk about my nights, okay?"

"Fair enough. That includes the grimoire, as well? Off-limits during the day?"

"Promise."

She'd accept the promise, but she'd never completely trust it.

Ivan lifted his hand and set the butterfly on a wavering path toward the ocean.

"Now that you've given me such a neat gift, I have one to show you," she said.

"I thought we were going to have sex?" Ivan called.

Men. Masters of the one-track mind.

"Come on, there's a climb down to the beach over here."

Swept from her feet, Dez hadn't time to protest as the vampire leapt into the air with her cradled in his arms. The next second, he landed on the beach and set her down.

"Or we could jump," she said, wobbling to stand. "You like to play the he-man?"

"It's not an act. It's who I am." A tug to her skirts swirled her up against his body. "You fascinate me, Dez."

"You've known me three days."

"You're the first woman I've met who has challenged and seduced me at the same time. I like that. I know every time I look into your eyes I'll see something new there. You're not like any other woman."

"Like you've been around long enough to gain such dating wisdom."

"So we're dating?"

"No."

"Sex is part of dating, isn't it?"

"Sex." She walked to the entry beneath the cliff, and stretched her body along the rough rocky outer wall. "Is sex. It has nothing to do with romance or dating or happily ever after. It's purely a carnal thing."

He rushed up and blocked her entrance into the cave. "Don't say things like that. Sex is precious. It's a way for a man and a woman to share themselves."

"It's a release." And she was losing focus. She didn't want to talk him out of this. What had become of her seduction skills? Hell, was she really so out of practice?

He shook his head and looked to the side. "I don't know about this anymore."

Seduction going downhill, Dez. Step it up!

"All right, I'll give you the sharing part. Sex is a wondrous act shared by two individuals that, for a moment, brings them close."

"But it's just an act to you? Going through the motions without becoming mentally involved? How can you do that?"

She glided a palm over his chest. The heat of him permeated

the thin black T-shirt, and the definition of his pecs felt like stone beneath the fabric.

"I'm not entirely unfeeling." She threaded a hand into his. "Come with me. I'm going to show you something amazing."

Ivan followed Dez back about ten feet inside the walls of a remarkable cave. It was incredibly light, and the walls were lined with huge cloudy white and pale violet crystal formations. He'd never seen anything like it before.

A sense of calm befell him. Was it because of the cave? Or did being with Dez make him relax?

"It's like a giant geode." Stroking one of the crystal formations, he remarked none of the edges were sharp as he'd seen in small, hand-sized geodes.

"That it is," she said. "This was the reason I bought my house. I was drawn here by the energy of this cave. It centers me to stand in here surrounded by all these crystals. It releases the murkiness from my soul and it protects against magic, too."

"Ah, I understand now. You're worried about me stealing your magic if we have sex?"

When a vampire made love to a witch—and drank her blood—he took small increments of her magic into him. It wasn't something that happened often, because most vampires walked a wide path around witches. But it was the very reason for the war between the nations.

Ivan crossed his arms. "Just so you know, I don't need your magic. I'm one of the most powerful vampire-witch hybrids to walk this earth."

"Aren't you full of yourself?"

Dez snaked up to him. The clingy white lace revealed the dark aureoles of her nipples and the dark landing strip between her legs. Ivan looked all he wanted. Because he sensed this encounter would not go as he wished.

He sensed a duplicity about the witch right now. She wanted to seduce him, and yet another part of her raised caution far higher than passion.

The witch swept back the hair from her face and waggled a finger before her narrowed eyes. "I've more power in my little finger than you do in your entire body, baby boy."

"You calling me a baby? I suppose. You have seen more years than most trees."

"Now that was uncalled for." She pressed her hand against his shoulder.

Ivan felt the shock of it as if it were a Taser, but his shoulder merely jerked in reaction. "Did you just try to blast me with your powerful little finger?"

"Drop it, vampire."

"Why is it when you're angry with me I'm a vampire?"

"Because I don't know what to call you, and it's easier for me."

"Maybe it's because you've more prejudice against our kind than you're willing to admit."

"Trust me, Ivan, you can't begin to know what I'm about."

She slunk against a curved wall of crystals, fitting her body to the hard geometric structure. Easy to imagine the divine suppleness of her figure lying beneath him, naked, breathing heavily, begging for more, more—

"Maybe this was wrong, me bringing you in here."

Ivan jerked out of the fantasy. No, it wasn't going to happen. And why had he expected it would? He'd played this one wrong.

Because you don't know what you're doing, do you? You're not here on a fixer task, you're here for selfish personal reasons. You can't do that. You don't know how *to do that.*

"I thought this cave would be a place of peace, of neutral ground," she said. "The perfect place to come together for some unconditional, no-strings-attached sex."

"War sex."

She nudged up a shoulder into a noncommittal nod. "War sex."

"Sounds exciting, yes?"

"It does. And it doesn't. I'm sorry, I know we stand on the same side, hold the same beliefs, but there's that little situation with you trying to steal the *Grande Grimoire* from me. I just can't get beyond that."

"I'm sorry." Ivan kissed her on the cheek. Apricots and vanilla? Like a warm wintertime dessert. Oh, to taste her! "You're right. I know next to nothing about you. As you do me. But I want to get to know you better. We're rushing things with the whole 'let's have sex for the thrill of it' stuff."

"What's wrong with sex for sex's sake?"

"Not a thing, unless you want to have a more involved relationship with the person you plan to have sex-for-sex's-sake sex with."

She lifted a brow. "Say that again, fast."

At least she was joking.

"No coercion," he reassured. "It's day, and I'm here on my own recognizance. And look." And stretched his mouth wide. "No fangs. Promise."

Her sigh thudded against Ivan's heart. She toyed with his shirt at the center of his chest. "This is the craziest situation. I want you. But you work for Himself. And that I've even come this far with you is so wrong."

"How can I get you to see me for the man I am, Desideriel?" He stroked her cheek, softer than any flesh he'd ever touched. The thrill of it cautioned him. No pleasure would go unpunished, he felt sure. "I have a confession. I work for the devil. And I do my job well. But never in a million years did I imagine that one day my job would lead me to something so wondrous as you."

"Let's go back inside." Dez started for the cave opening. "I don't want to hear this."

And I shouldn't want to say it. Ivan pressed his forehead to the cool flat plane of a crystal as Dez walked out.

Ivan stood on the beach long after Dez had climbed up the cliff. The white sand sifted over his boots. He skipped another stone across the water; it jumped once, and then dropped.

What had that been about? He'd refused sex with a gorgeous woman?

It wasn't as though he'd never had no-strings-attached sex. Happened all the time. Well, a few times a year. He couldn't do the free-for-all gigolo lifestyle to save his lacking soul.

Dez had been almost clinical about their having sex. And if that didn't drop a man's libido like a cold shower, then nothing else could.

Was that part of her plan? Could be.

Should he have been more insistent? Eager to accept whatever she had been willing to offer? Probably. It would have granted him entrance to the part of her Himself felt was weakest.

You stopped her from doing something she felt was wrong, even if she didn't realize it herself.

If it didn't feel right, Ivan wanted no part of it. Coercion or not.

And thinking of the coercion: he sensed tonight would be hell.

Chapter 10

He didn't resist this time. It would be a lie.

Ivan fell to one knee and bowed before Himself. They stood at the opening to an alley between a café and a hardware shop. Willow Cove was quiet, it being past midnight.

"Master," Ivan said.

Himself pressed a hoof to Ivan's shoulder and shoved him against the brick building. "You dally, fixer."

The burn of the obsidian hoof shrieked through his musculature. Ivan fought to remain coherent. "Just doing…my job. Seduction…takes…time."

The ever-present aura of brimstone worked like poison on Ivan's lungs. Devil's cancer, he called it. But this disease couldn't kill him, only make him suffer. He struggled to keep his eyes open, his mind clear.

Himself stepped back and leaned against the wall of the opposite building, one arm cocked lazily at his disjointed hip.

He wore a strange costume of red leather over his lean black sinews.

"Don't think I'm not aware of your feelings toward the witch," Himself hissed. "You think to win a reprieve from your duties with silly dalliances?"

"No, master. Seduction is not so simple as making an imp vomit toads or giving a sin eater back all the sins he's eaten. And even when I do finally gain her trust and she is open to me, I'm not sure how to get the book."

"Take it from her."

"It's not like she keeps it on a shelf in the library."

Flayed across the cheek with steel talons, Ivan's body took the slap and he landed on the ground, arms outstretched before him. The scent of his own blood seeping from his face stirred him. It had been days since he'd had the desire to drink blood. He'd not needed it, for his nights were more pleasure than pain.

"Exactly." Himself clomped two paces out onto the sidewalk. "Your kind needs to feed, Drake. You're not taking blood tells me you're not doing the job."

"As best I can, considering the circumstances."

"Not good enough!"

Ivan pushed up to kneel. A shake of his head momentarily cleared out the brimstone, but it seeped back in, dizzying him, softening him to Himself's command. "Would you suggest pain? I don't think she'll take kindly to torture."

"You've yet to try."

"You were the one to suggest seduction!"

"You watch your tone. I own you, boy."

"Yes," Ivan gasped. "I will never forget."

But could he ever win his freedom? Freedom for his parents? *Not likely.*

Always Himself knew Ivan's thoughts. Which was why he focused his intent on doing the job to his best ability, not clouding his thoughts with doubt or insecurities or even disgust for the fixer's trade.

But now he'd stepped into this strange new seduction—no, he would not think it. He would not give Himself the wicked pleasure.

"You've two days, fixer. For your own personal conceit, I suggest you get that book. But if not, you know I will enjoy sucking the souls from your parents. Had your mother's once already. Tasty witch filled with blackness due to her murderous deeds. Mmm…"

Clenching a hand into a fist, Ivan rolled his head down and away from Himself's smacking lips.

Car headlights rolled to a stop at the curb. Ivan pushed himself up by the wall and turned his bleeding cheek away from whoever sat in the car. Even as he sought to hide the wound, he could feel it healing, the skin sewing itself tight, yet pushing out more blood as it did so.

The car door opened and a frail, blue-haired woman got out. "Mr. Drake, is that you?"

"I'm fine, Mrs. Henderson. You shouldn't be out driving so late."

"Coming home from visiting the grandkids in the next town over." She stepped around the hood of the car. Himself stood at the curb, one leg out jauntily and hands on his hips. "Oh. I don't believe we've met."

Ivan shook his head. Those not attached to Himself saw him as their greatest temptation. Fortunately, the old lady would never see the real creature who stood before her. He felt sure the resulting nightmares of such a sight would drive her insane.

"Did anyone ever tell you that you look like Sean Connery?"

"Why, I do believe they have." Himself stepped forward and offered a talon—hand—for Elise to shake. Which she clasped.

That look of utter adoration killed Ivan. The old woman had no idea she held hands with the devil Himself. In fact, she sighed and touched her chest, a gesture of infatuation.

"Are you a friend of Ivan's?" Elise asked. "The town picnic is this Saturday, and you're welcome—"

"He's just passing through." Ivan leaned against the building. He still couldn't fill his lungs with air, and he didn't want to risk stumbling before Elise. A swipe of forearm across his cheek brushed away most of the blood.

"Just so," Himself said. He stroked the back of his sinewy black hand across Elise's cheek, wrinkled with age. The skin tightened, not so much that the wrinkles disappeared, but Ivan saw the change occur. "That grandson of yours, he's one you'll have to watch out for."

"Why do you say that? The boy is a babe."

"We boys grow to be men, Elise," Himself purred. "But if you don't intend to watch over him, I assure you I will. Ta."

Himself turned and strode away. Ivan was sure he'd teleport right out of sight, but the dark demon didn't. Instead he turned the corner, and then likely disappeared.

Elise gave Ivan a confused glance. "What was I just doing?"

"You stopped to offer me a ride, but my hotel is down the street," he said, imparting subtle persuasion in his tone. "You should head home, Mrs. Henderson. It was good to see you."

She smoothed a hand over her cheek. Did she sense the youth Himself's touch had granted her? But the real question was, after she returned home to look in the mirror, would she accept the offer and hand over her soul for more of the same?

Ivan hated how his master manipulated mortals.

When he saw Elise paralyzed by her own wonder, Ivan walked over and helped her back to the car. "Are you sure you can drive?"

She nodded. "Do I look all right to you?"

"Lovely," he said, and regretted it instantly.

"Ivan, what's up? I just saw you. And I'll be seeing you again. We're calling an emergency council meeting on Friday."

"Mom." Ivan lay across the hotel bed and kicked off his boots. A boat motor growled outside. It was late. Someone must be docking for the night. "I've got a problem."

"A bigger problem than being the devil's fixer?"

"It's that same problem."

"I'm so sorry, Son—"

"Don't start, Mom. We've been through this."

"And we'll go through it again and again. I wish there was a way to atone for what your father and I did to you."

Yes, there were days he felt the same. And then he got over that bit of sorry-assed self-pity. He was no man to pout.

"You can help me with this problem. That'll go a long way."

"You need a denizen of the dark slain? A sin eater punished? Something you can't handle? I'm your woman."

Ivan chuckled. He loved his mother. She was all leather and toughness, and sweet kisses to his brow. The woman used to stand down entire tribes of vampires when her quest had once been to annihilate the species. That was until she had met his father.

Good thing for that crazy love affair. Even if it had resulted in them promising their firstborn to Himself.

"Himself wants me to obtain the *Grande Grimoire*."

"Yeah, so what's new?"

"He's given me two days to do it. I've already insinuated

myself into the witch's life. The one who guards the book. You ever hear of her? Desideriel Merovech?"

"Merovech?" She paused so long, Ivan almost wished he had the ability to read minds. Finally, Ravin said carefully, "I've heard of her. I may have even met her once. She must be very powerful. You know where the Merovech name comes from?"

"Not a clue."

"The Merovingians. Very powerful kings who ruled the areas of what is now France. They were allied with wizards and practiced an ancient form of witchcraft."

Ivan knew the Merovingians had reigned from the 500s to the 700s. Well. Was Dez that old? Not that age meant anything in the grander scheme, but to have lived so many centuries?

"Not any witch is chosen to guard the *Grande Grimoire*," Ravin added.

"I guess so." Memory of being washed out of Dez's house by a tsunami didn't improve Ivan's confidence at beating her with magic. "She knows her magic. Thing is, she knows what I'm after and has been able to block my every attempt, and I have no idea how to convince her to bring it out from wherever it is she keeps it. It's bespelled, I'm sure."

"Did you mention the council's idea about reversing the Protection spell to her?"

"No, but I actually feel she'd agree to that. She's not against vampires. She's like me, really."

"Does she know you're a vamp?"

"Yeah, the wild roses surrounding her house gave that away the first time we met."

"Ouch. Oh, Ivan, I worry about you. Your job is so dangerous."

"Mom." He rolled his eyes and felt like the kid at school whose mother follows him to the classroom door and gives his face a dash with a wet fingertip before sending him off to face the sneering bullies. It had happened once. The bullies had only laughed once, too. "I can handle myself."

"You need a woman."

"I need…" He sighed.

Always a conversation with his mother became a plea for his domestic satisfactions. Shouldn't she encourage him to live his life a few centuries before looking to settle down? She had lived four centuries before marrying.

"I need help, Mom. I cannot fail this task. I wondered if maybe—"

"I could talk to her? Ivan, I don't know. Wait! Why don't you bring her along to the council meeting? If she could understand the need for us to take action, perhaps she might draw out the grimoire so we can reverse the spell?"

"It's a possibility. Dez is compassionate. I think she'd listen to reason."

"You say her name as if she were someone special."

"It's just a name, Mother."

"I'm guessing otherwise."

He rolled his eyes and beat his forehead against the pillow. Mothers were the same, no matter if they were mortal or otherwise. And it gave him a tickle to know she possessed a domestic bone.

"So what's happened since I was last there? I haven't been following the media."

"A lot, and none of it good. Some paranormal sleuthing show actually has video footage of a supposed vampire drinking blood from a victim. I've seen it, Ivan. It's the real thing. While the public still thinks it's a hoax, it isn't going to be long before the video can be authenticated. I've put out a call to Lucy Morgan, a professional debunker and vampire. You know, Truvin Stone's wife. She's very good at proving real stuff a hoax. But she said this is going to be a tough one. We've got to do something. Now."

"I'll be there. And I'll see if Dez would like to come along. Not sure if it'll help, but I'll try anything right now. Seduction is going over like a lead balloon."

"Seduction, eh?"

He could hear the smile in his mother's voice, and Ivan took that as his cue to say good-bye.

Her heart wasn't in the right place.

Or maybe it was, and she wasn't reading it right.

The idea to seduce the fixer in the cave had gone over not at all. Dez had spoken the truth about sex being simply sex. And yet part of her denied that vehemently. The deep, gushing, pulsing, pining inner part of her that recognized heart and soul and want.

"He's confused me. I'm trying to think logically, to do what is right for me. But I'm going at this the wrong way."

She knew that now.

Dez collected the glass jar from the shelf and carried it to the center of the still room where she'd cast a circle in Dead Sea salt upon the slate tile floor. White candles flickered at the four compass points. Rosemary and lavender stirred the candle fumes.

Removing the jar cover, Dez reached inside and drew out the slippery morsel. The fairy heart, about the size of an acorn, pulsed more rapidly at the sensation of her touch. It wanted. It desired.

Just as she did.

It would grant her clarity of heart.

To her right, on the edge of the marble butcher block, lay the long silver pin she'd acquired in the nineteenth century from a magician who'd once used it to pierce dove hearts on stage.

Dez wielded the silver pin before her, drawing it over the

pulsing lump of muscle and ichor in her palm. Stepping forward, she positioned herself in the center of the salt circle.

Closing her eyes, Dez began to hum, and then intonated an ancient form of rhythmic spell. Quickly she was swept into the energy of spirit and air and earth and light.

Holding the heart between two fingers, and bending backward to expose her breast, Dez then spoke, "Bestow upon me clarity of heart."

The silver pin slid through the heart. Ichor-laden fairy blood dribbled down Dez's wrist and dropped, falling through the air, to land on her chest. There, right over her heart. The ichor, glittering and sizzling, burrowed through her skin.

From now on, she would follow her heart, be it to her best interest or the grimoire's. She had lived a rational life far too long.

Chapter 11

The air smelled sweetly of burning peat. Smoke half a mile down the road stirred gray tendrils into the teal and rose sky.

Ivan waited at the end of the walk before Dez's house.

"Like a sleeping beauty waiting behind impenetrable thorns," he muttered. "If she'd hack away those vicious vines it would make my life a hell of a lot easier."

But no one ever said Himself's fixer had an easy life. And Ivan liked that it wasn't. It made it easier to recognize the goodness when that did come into his life. It was rare, but, like the angels he instinctively sensed, he knew it when he saw it, touched it and heard it.

Dez Merovech was goodness.

And he would have to betray her to protect his parent's souls.

He could impart the fact she was very possibly a Merovingian and use that to make her less good. The Merovingian line of kings had been ruthless, albeit that was a mortal's point of view. The

French kings had come into their own through wizardry and witchcraft in a time ill-equipped to accept the practice.

Didn't matter who her ancestors were. A man became who he wanted to be, not who his dead relatives thought he should become.

Really? So why do you consider yourself evil because you were born to it? Shouldn't you be able to rise above it?

Ivan winced at his conscience.

A flash inside the house caught his attention. He called out and waved.

If the witch had something so basic as a phone that would help, but she did not even have a cell phone. Her house was bare of most things normal people put inside their homes. Like furniture. And mementoes. And anything that gave a clue someone lived there.

"Interesting. She doesn't get attached to anything. Like men? Maybe that's why she was so willing to have sex."

Had they made love yesterday, it could have only been sex for sex's sake. Should have gone through with it. Shown her who was stronger, in control.

He would be smarter now. Though he couldn't deny he still wanted her—and maybe he didn't need a commitment to enjoy her.

The screen door screeched open and he waved to Dez. She pointed to the roof and slipped back inside.

"Well, it wasn't a no," he said, and took a running leap. He cleared the vines and landed on the roof before the attic window. Standing and looking out over the treetops, Ivan picked out three church steeples nestled in the village of Willow Cove. "If someone saw me doing this—I'd have to pay them a midnight visit."

He did have a way to persuade the truth into a new reality

for any innocents who witnessed his devilish dealings. It involved biting them and drawing out their blood while he worked the persuasion, but that was a bonus. Blood was his sustenance; he wouldn't deny himself of it ever.

"Too bad the persuasion doesn't work on a witch," he said, as he climbed through the open window.

Or did it?

He actually wasn't sure about that. Could he persuade Dez to give him the book?

"Huh. I'm just thinking of this now?" He turned and closed the window, but not completely. She must leave it open for a reason.

There was the trust issue. She still didn't trust him. She was playing with him. Letting him believe she considered him safe, perhaps even a friend, when really she was fully capable of kicking his ass to China should he even think about using force against her.

But drinking her blood?

When a vampire drank from a victim, that victim then experienced the swoon, an intense orgasm from the blood release. The vampire could persuade the victim into a reverie, and they would ultimately wake thinking they'd merely been bitten by a bug; the wounds might even have healed by then, and they'd believe they just passed out.

Ivan had never bitten a witch. Not because their blood was poison to a vampire—he had no fear of that. But if the persuasion did work with a witch, Ivan might be able to suggest Dez bespell the *Grande Grimoire* out for him to study.

Yes, to study. A simple front to mask more evil intentions. Because now that he knew what the book was about, he did want a few moments with it before handing it on to his master.

First things first. A private jet waited for him at the airport. It would leave in an hour.

Trailing his fingers down the bare walls to the bottom of the staircase, Ivan was greeted with a friendly smile. Dez gestured him into the living room while she plucked a teapot off the stove burner.

He glanced into the still room as he passed by. A scatter of something littered the floor. Salt? Had she been conjuring?

"I expected you," she called.

"And yet, still no brandy."

"I was done with alcohol decades ago."

"Really?" He remembered her coy avoidance of his question to her age. Wasn't important. He was curious, though, now he knew of her ancestors.

"So I've a theory about you," Ivan said, as she shoved a steaming teacup across the counter his way, and then came around to join him in the living room.

"I'm sure it's wrong." Dez sat on one of two wicker chairs in the room. The white wicker reeds creaked when she settled into it. A thick blue chenille blanket hung over the back. "But go ahead. I could use a laugh."

Ivan left the tea on the counter. He didn't need food, liquid or solid, so drinking was merely for show. And tea wasn't his thing; he'd learned that the other day.

He walked over to squat before Dez, bracketing her legs between his splayed knees. Today, crisp bergamot and clove and the creamy tendril of caramel wafted from her. But behind the perfumes he thought he sensed something more visceral. Couldn't be blood. But maybe? Didn't smell like apricots. Though, if she had been conjuring…

"You were saying?" she prompted.

"Yes, I was, uh…you smell so good." He kissed her knee through the thin silk fabric that flowed possessively over her curves. Definitely blood, but not human. Curious.

"Maybe it's not so much a theory as a question. I look around and see not a single personal memento in your home. That tells me you want to forget about your past—"

"Or that I'm not much of a decorator."

"I'll give you that. But. Your shop is beautiful. You know how to decorate. And what about the shop? You don't have customers."

"They're all online."

"So why not close up and simply do online orders?"

"I happen to fancy that shop. It's cute and I like the view. And I get a few customers every day it's open."

"But not from the Rose Club."

"What are you getting at, Ivan?"

Not the answer to what kind of blood he smelled on her. Did witches still use small creatures in their spells? That was positively archaic. However, so was eye of newt, which she seemed to have in good supply.

"You seem pretty eager to have those old biddies accept you into their group. Why? I get you want friends and companionship. As immortals we are forced to live a singular life, and of course we always want what we cannot have. But you don't need the Rose Club. They're old, and they're backstabbers. They're not interested in you for you. They didn't even look at you until I showed up."

"Self-centered much?"

"You know it's true, Dez."

Attention focused on the tea shimmering in her cup, Dez gave a noncommittal shrug. "Maybe. But I happen to know Elise wants to get her hands on my gardening secrets. The rose vines fascinate her."

"If she only knew."

Dez·chuckled. "So you see, it's not just you. Let me make

my own mistakes, Ivan. I've made enough of them over the centuries. This one won't kill me or see me tied to a bundle of fagots, so I'm not too concerned."

He reached to trace the fine line that creased out from the corner of her eye. "So that's how you earned these."

"Age has a tendency to do that."

"They're beautiful." He leaned in and kissed the delicate skin at her eye. "You would be a lesser woman without them."

Bowing her head, she wouldn't meet his gaze.

"You're a dichotomy, Dez. You've closed yourself off from the world. You take nothing from it, and keep it at an arm's length. And yet, you're ready to leap through hoops for a few kind words from Elise Henderson. You must have friends?"

She set her teacup on the arm of the chair and clasped her arms tight across her chest. "Are you suddenly my analyst instead of my betrayer?"

"I'm not going to betray you."

"Truth?"

She wasn't about to let him sweet-talk her. Good. He liked that she didn't accept anything less than a person at full value.

"All right. I will," he corrected, "but only because I have to. But that's truth, not betrayal. And you're avoiding this conversation."

"What one is that? About my desire for companionship? I've had friends," she said sharply. "They die."

A bitter truth; sooner or later any immortal would lose someone close to them from old age. He'd yet to experience that sort of heartache, and, frankly, he had gone to lengths to ensure it wouldn't happen. Another thing to thank his parents for.

But was it something to be proud of?

"Ivan, you're what? Less than thirty years old." She touched his chin with a finger and drew it along his jaw. The touch was softer than a fairy's flight, but more intense than molten lava.

Fairies? Could it be…he'd never smelled fairy blood. And he knew blood did not run through the veins of the fey, but ichor. But for some reason, it seemed the right answer. She did have that beating heart in a glass.

"After you've lived a few centuries you begin to care less and less for close relationships," Dez continued. "The reality is such connections will result in hurt, grief and agony. And yet, it is all you crave. You gain a friend, she dies. You take a lover, he eventually dies."

"Immortality is a bitch, but shouldn't the love and friendship you gain be enough? Knowing you've had opportunity to experience it, if for a little while?"

"You're making guesses, aren't you?" A rhetorical question.

She leaned back and slid her bare foot along her opposite ankle. Glancing aside, her profile showed a different woman than he was accustomed to seeing. This one was harder. The softness of her flesh resembled pure white marble now. Determined, yet weary.

Yes, those fine wrinkles had been earned. The hard way. What Ivan wouldn't give to be able to punish all those who had wrongly accused, tortured and beaten Dez over the centuries, for he was very sure it had occurred.

"It's hard to explain to one so young. You've a long lifetime of learning ahead of you. I do crave companionship, and I have a few good immortal friends, but I've learned to protect myself from emotional damage."

He kissed the side of her knee. If only he could get around behind her knee and lick the sweet flesh there. "I wish I was in a position to offer you trust. Damn, I hate this job." Standing, Ivan paced away from her and beat his fist against a cedar wallboard. "If I could get away from him, I would."

"But at what price? What does Himself use to keep you in check?"

"My parents."

"I'm sorry, Ivan."

He hadn't noticed her movement. Dez's warm hand glided down his arm, and her thin, delicate fingers clasped about his rough, clenched fist.

"I have never known hope," he said. It just came out. The truth of him.

"It's not all it's cracked up to be. Trust me on that one."

He smiled. So much knowing in that comment.

While his nights were filled with unthinkable acts, Ivan had found it difficult to adjust during the day. To bring himself down. And he'd not needed to come all the way down to reality. He could not. Goodness was not his.

Yet, Dez made it much easier to put off the barbed tendrils of the night, and to enter daylight. To become…simpler. More relaxed. More open, even.

"I wish things were different," she whispered against the back of his shoulder. "You're the first vampire I've ever been attracted to."

"Seriously?"

"Quite. And I've met a lot in my days. I've always scoffed at the opposites-attract thing, but there may be something to it."

"We're not so different." He turned and stroked her hair. The glints of gold attracted him to trace from crown to cheek. "We both view the world the same. No man is better than any other. The witches and vampires should all live peaceably alongside one another. Which reminds me."

"Hmm?"

"There's a council meeting this afternoon. Would you like to come along with me? It'll give us some time together. To just…be."

An invitation to attend the Gray Council had initially turned Dez off. But she'd given it a few minutes' thought, and finally the idea of attending one did appeal. As Ivan had said, she'd been secluding herself from the world.

It wasn't fair he could read her so well.

Yet, what better way to step back into the world than to familiarize herself with the war and work to find a way to stop it?

And it gave her time to spend with Ivan. She would now be given a glimpse into the side of him directly opposite to the fixer who did the devil's deeds.

Clarity of heart, indeed. She had followed her heart today. Pray it would not lead her astray.

A private jet whisked them to Minneapolis in less than two hours. Dez didn't like flying much, and she went to the bathroom to freshen up while Ivan chatted with the pilot.

A limo waited to whisk them downtown, and they drove toward the city. The bustle of the big city put her off yet at the same time intrigued her. Life moved about her. It smelled like gasoline and industry and pine trees and restaurant fumes. Nothing like her sleepy little oceanside village.

She'd once lived in Paris for fifty years in a little apartment in the Second Arrondissement. That had been during the end of the eighteenth century, following the revolution. Another time of war, but she'd been an observer, secluding herself away from its politics.

Before that, well, she knew the workings of small European villages all too well.

Life had certainly sped up since then. It didn't scare her; it made her want to watch and not look away. To draw it in, yet without actually participating.

And what was so wrong with that? Hadn't she served her time out at the vanguard of life that now a little seclusion was deserved? She was…tired. Not so exhausted with life that she didn't wish to face it, but certainly, these recent decades had become a time of rest for her. To breathe in and take stock.

But she contradicted herself by wishing to be accepted by those old biddies, as Ivan had pointed out.

Why *did* she want to join the Rose Club? It wasn't as if she desired to attend meetings and discuss soil pH or plant germination techniques with blue-haired, wrinkled old women—who were a hell of a lot younger than she.

Had Elise looked younger this morning at the grocery store? There had been something about her Dez couldn't quite pin…

And maybe that was it. Did she feel the way to insinuate herself back into the real world was by starting with the geriatric set that, by all means, she should be a part of?

Who did she think she was, trying to coax a young stud like Ivan Drake to have sex with her? He was a virtual child.

Yet, when he'd touched the fine lines at the side of her eye with such reverence, Dez had softly exhaled. He understood her life had been a struggle. And she had felt utterly beautiful in that moment when he'd kissed her softly.

Further seduction tactics? Or the real Ivan Drake?

"We're here."

Ivan stood outside the car, the door open. Dez hadn't even noticed him get out. Was it because she had become hard of hearing in her old age? Senile?

What am I doing? She gasped at her crazed thoughts. *Why am I thinking like this? The spell…is it wearing off so quickly?*

Perhaps this was how her heart worked. Ready, willing, yet unsure. A little frightened, actually.

"You nervous?" he wondered.

Yes. But only about the unknown future of her heart.

Business she could handle. Nervous about attending the council?

"Why should I be?" she said, and accepted his hand and rose out of the car.

Wanting to look presentable, and maybe a little imposing, she had donned a simple black skirt with heels and white silk shirt. A pearl choker hugged her neck. Yeah, she could do imposing. And she had every right.

Keeping a secret smile to herself, Dez contained her anticipation as they road the elevator to the twenty-fifth floor. A doorman greeted them. Ivan shook the mortal's hand and asked about his wife.

Interesting how the devil's right hand functioned so seamlessly in mortal society.

"In here," Ivan said, and then pulled her close before he opened the door. "I really like you, Dez."

She clasped one of his hands and gave the knuckles a rub. "Why do I feel like my high school boyfriend is spilling his guts to me?"

"I'm going to guess you never went to high school."

"Touché. But why the confession now? Are *you* nervous?"

"A little." His serious expression was exchanged with a smirk. It made his eyes more deeply inviting. And now she teetered even closer to undone. A nice feeling of being unfurled that she wouldn't press back.

Rather, her heart would no longer deny emotion.

"My mom and dad are inside. I should warn you, Mom is always on a mission to get me married and settled down. She wants grandchildren."

"Ah." That confession proved a buzz killer. Dez straightened and adjusted a loose strand of hair behind her ear. "Did you tell her about me?"

"A little. She's the one who suggested I bring you along."

"Oh, that can't be good. Will she be sizing me up as potential wife material?"

"Probably. But don't worry, her bark is much worse than her bite. She's mellowed since she met Dad. I wanted you to know the deal."

"*You* haven't been sizing me up as wife material, have you?"

"I just met you, Dez. First sex and now marriage?" he said with a teasing lilt. "Woman, you are easy."

"Yet you've gotten neither from me. Two points for the witch following her heart."

"Speaking of hearts." Ivan pressed her against the wall. Focusing, she could pick up his heartbeat, faster than hers, almost like a hummingbird's wings. "You still have that fairy heart in a jar?"

"Why do you ask?"

"Just wondering. I…smelled blood on you earlier. Not your own. And it looked like you'd been working in your still room."

Damn, he was good. "I'll never tell."

"Right. But only because I've guessed correctly. I wonder what a witch can do with a fairy heart and a circle of salt?"

"Gotta be interesting," she replied.

Ivan pushed the double wood doors open and stepped inside. A long, plain room, tiled in white marble and sided to the west with floor-to-ceiling windows, was peopled with a dozen men and women.

He brought Dez around to his side, hands held, and introduced her to the council.

All the witches in attendance got up from their chairs, went down on one knee and bowed before her.

Chapter 12

Every witch in the room had bowed to Dez—including Ivan's mother.

Ivan blew out a breath and looked to his father, who shrugged. Nikolaus Drake hadn't a clue what had just occurred. The other vampires in the room were equally as clueless.

"We are honored to be in your presence," Abigail Rowan offered to Dez.

Abigail was the appointed leader on the witch half of the Gray Council. She had fought the early war at the turn of the century against Truvin Stone but had turned peaceable much the same time Stone had. But for her petite frame and tiny voice, she was a powerhouse.

She offered Dez her seat, which was at the head of the table.

And Dez took it, offering a brief smile to Ivan. Stunned, he assumed his usual position by the window.

Abigail then made a more formal introduction. "Gentlemen

and ladies, this is Desideriel Merovech, the keeper of the *Grande Grimoire*. For those vampires out of the loop, she basically sustains the witch nation with her sacrifice to protect the book of all spells."

"Ivan invited me to listen in," Dez explained. "I admit I've been a bit out of touch recently. I don't do television or media. But I feel the strife, as I cannot avoid the connection to the witch nation. The war has increased measurably?"

"It's at a dangerous level," Nikolaus explained. "News media have video of vampires feeding. We've sent out cleaners to take care of that situation, but it can only elevate. We need to stop the war now."

"There's been a suggestion," Abigail said, speaking softly and respectfully to Dez, "that perhaps the Protection spell should be reversed?"

"I thought you weren't behind that," Anastasia, the younger witch, said to Abigail.

"I was informing Ms. Merovech where we stand. What else is there to do?" Abigail paced the length of one side of the table. Her white silk suit whispered softly as she moved. "We don't have a large enough force of vampires and witches who stand at neutral to stop those who insist on taking down the other side. We are overwhelmed."

"I agree," Ravin offered. "We can't allow the mortal world to even begin to suspect we might be real, that vampires may be stalking them at night, or witches might be waiting around the corner to curse them."

"That's nonsense," Francois said.

"But it is what they will believe," Ivan interjected. "We know the mortal mind. It hasn't stopping chasing chimeras since the beginning of time, and yet, it doesn't want to believe there could be others unlike them. If beings of the night and magic did exist? Monsters, all of us."

"It is far truer than I wish to imagine," his father agreed.

The council continued to offer news of the media focusing on vampiric- and witchcraft-related happenings around the world.

Ivan observed the conversation, but he didn't remove his gaze from Dez. She must be someone great to the witches for them to have reacted in such a manner. Was it merely because they knew she was the keeper of the *Grande Grimoire?* He knew it was one hell of a book, but now he was really curious.

To sustain the witch nation? That suggested quite a lot.

And his mom had said she'd met Dez once. Yet now she acted as though he'd taken her utterly without warning.

Absolute serenity held Dez's features expressionless and soft as she listened to the various council members debate whether to send out destructive forces or to consider the spell reversal.

Gorgeous, he found himself thinking. And for once he wasn't coerced to do a thing about it, except stand to the side and bask in her beauty. And what was wrong with that? Didn't he deserve beauty? To admire and enjoy the presence of an intelligent, sexy woman?

And he had no intention of stopping until the sun had set. And then? It was on to seduction, yet another untaxing task.

This fixer had taken a strange turn down an intriguing path. Away from destruction. And that felt damn good.

"Ivan?"

Oh, right. Paying attention. "Huh?"

"Have you verified the reports on the west coast? About the witch burners?"

"Honestly, Dad, I haven't had time. I sent Marcus out to Los Angeles to report back. I'll check in with him immediately after the meeting."

Vampires had hired actual witch hunters to stalk their enemy. Which wasn't going so far as the witches recruiting werewolves to increase their forces.

"Let's reverse the spell," Ivan found himself blurting out. "We know it's the only thing that'll put an end to this massacre on both sides."

Dez's serene expression grew harder. Had he ever noticed the jewel intensity of her eyes before? Or was she using witchcraft right now to influence him in a way that softened his stance? Because he felt like reneging that comment, and it took tightening his jaw and turning away to pace along the window to avoid it.

A fairy heart, eh? Some kind of spell for the heart, he suspected. Had she worked it against him or on herself?

"Ivan is right," Dez announced. "Perhaps there is some benefit to be had in reversing the spell."

The room stirred and Ivan felt the energies of magic and ancient immortality increase. His muscles relaxed, and he turned back to Dez. She had not worked the spell on him. His attitude toward her hadn't changed at all. He desired her, as he had from that first kiss he'd stolen on the porch.

"But at great loss to the witch nation," Abigail argued. "If we no longer have poison blood in our arsenal, we have nothing against vampires."

"You're supposed to be neutral," Dez said, not judgmentally, but the tone of her voice made Abigail bow her head.

"Referring to your blood as a weapon to stock an arsenal?" Nikolaus Drake tossed at Abigail—now *that* question was filled with judgment.

"The vampires will not continue to retaliate," Ivan argued. "Perhaps initially they will, but once they realize the witches present no danger, they will stand down. I know it."

"*You* know it." Dez bowed her head. Her long fingers curled into soft fists. "But I don't think *they* know it."

"I'll make it happen," Ivan countered. "If I must die trying, I will do it."

And he and Dez held a challenge in their fixed stares. Would she fix him as only another witch could? Bind him in her stare and steal some of his magic?

Ivan blinked. He wasn't about to surrender now, much as the notion appealed on a sensual level.

"We'd need to develop an educational program," Ravin suggested. "Do we have enough to form small factions to send to the major cities to get this started?"

"I'll look into it." Nikolaus stood and paced over to Ivan. "Only one problem. We have no means to reverse the spell."

The witches exchanged glances across the table, which all fell back to Dez.

And Ivan looked to Dez, beseeching her. "Why not?" he asked.

"Because," she stood and quietly announced, "there's but one witch who can reverse the Protection spell. The original crafter of the spell must do it."

"And we don't know who that witch is?" Ivan asked.

"Nope." Nikolaus hooked his hands over his son's shoulders. "Happened eight centuries ago."

"I'll find out," Ivan promised again, determined to make this happen.

"You're too busy," Ravin offered. "We can put someone else on it."

"No. I can do it. Just…give me a few days. I've a lot on my plate. But it will be done."

He clasped Dez's hand, and thanked the council members for allowing her admittance, then led her out the door.

When they stood in the elevator and the doors closed, he

nudged her against the wall and dipped his nose into her hair, which smelled of so many different scents it would take him a long, slow night to figure them all out.

"One question," he said. "Who the hell are you?"

It gave Dez a subtle thrill to see the uncertainty on Ivan's face. Himself's dark and dangerous fixer at a loss? Bet that had never happened in his short three decades on this earth.

But she wasn't one to gloat, or even feel superior. She had always considered herself equal to all others, no matter their abilities, upbringing or financial record. And yet, to the witch nation, she was revered. The guardian of the *Grande Grimoire* could be nothing but.

The elevator dinged. They'd reached the bottom floor. Ivan held her as the doors slid open, wanting to keep her back.

"We'll talk in the limo," she said. "I presume we're rushing right back to Maine?"

"We'll make a detour to my place, if you don't mind. I want to check with Marcus and make a few other necessary calls. Should I bow as you get into the car?"

"Don't be a child, Ivan." She walked out and strode down the marble hallway, not caring if he strayed behind after a comment like that.

That was another reason why she kept her lifelong occupation a secret—men could never deal with authority or power in a woman.

Once through the revolving door, the city bustled. An open-air market, thick with flowers and fresh vegetables, lured with bright colors and tantalizing aromas. As Dez stood before the limo waiting for Ivan to open the door, she toyed with walking over to check out the farmers' stands.

The air hummed. And when she focused, closing her eyes

and reaching out for tendrils of magic, she found very little. Immense steel buildings and industrial pollution dampened the elemental forces witches summoned to aid in their magic. The magic was out there, but it was weak.

So there was an advantage to living in a small, lazy town. And the ocean increased her energies and made her water magic all the stronger. She wanted to test it right now.

So she did.

As Ivan opened the back limo door, Dez spread her arms out and tilted back her head. She had only to tap into the electric violet force that lived within her core to summon the rain.

"A downpour! Get inside, quick," Ivan said.

She took her time, gliding across the leather seat, and even rolled down her window to thrust out her hand to catch a few cold droplets. He slid in behind her and directed the driver to his home.

"You did that, didn't you?" Marvel sparkled in his eyes.

This was not an evil man, but one who sought direction and did what he must to survive and to protect his own.

"I wanted to test my magic in the city." Dez tapped the moon roof where raindrops pounded relentlessly. "I don't see how a witch can survive here with all the pollutants and electricity and industry to zap her strength."

"Their numbers dwindle daily," he offered quietly.

And they both knew it was not because of the city.

The limo drove in silence, save the patter of the rain. Dez could feel the consternation vibrate from Ivan's being. Emotions battled within him. His need to ask, but also his need to respect, made it difficult for him to relax next to her.

So she eased his frustration.

"They revere the keeper of the *Grande Grimoire*," Dez offered. She wiped away a streak of rain that wet the back of her hand. "That is all."

"But how did they *know* you? Do you know all of them?"

"They know me in the sense that I belong to the book and it belongs to me. I've never met any of them, save your mother."

And that was one relationship she prayed would remain stale.

"It is a sensation or feeling that comes to them, I'm sure. It's hard to explain. But whenever I meet a witch, they know me. Most may not understand why they put the two together—me and the grimoire—but they are respectful. It's much like the shimmer the vampire feels when he touches another of his kind. An innate knowing."

"When did you know my mother?"

"End of the nineteenth century. She's a force."

"That she is."

"Your father…he is remarkable as well. All those tattoos."

"Got them before he was transformed."

"Of course. You look a lot like him. Tall, dark, proud. Imposing, the two of you."

He lifted her hand and kissed the back of it. "I couldn't take my eyes off you during the meeting."

"I know. I could feel your gaze on my face, and in my heart. Felt good."

"Did you feel it here?" He stroked the underside of her chin, leaning over to kiss the side of her neck.

Goose bumps shivered awake on Dez's flesh, and she sucked in a breath. This boy was dangerous. "Yes, I did."

He lingered over her vein. She knew the thick carotid, if he pierced it with his fangs, would bleed out. Did the vampire not instead go for the jugular?

A brief moment of fear intensified her reactions. Her nipples hardened. Hairs rose on her arms. Dez crossed her arms over her chest, and sat up straight.

"What's wrong?" Dark eyes lingered but inches from her

face. "That little whimper wasn't because you were turned on. You…you're frightened of me?"

"It surprised me when you kissed me here." She stroked the side of her neck. It was so hot. The vein pulsed roughly. "I've never been bitten by a vampire. When a vampire takes a person's blood into them, you take a part of their soul. I'm not willing to give a part of myself away, not to anyone."

"I won't bite," he whispered. "Promise."

"I've seen your fangs drop when you've been holding me. I want to fight it, but…can you?"

"Yes, I can. I don't need your blood, Dez. And I didn't mean to scare you."

And why had she reacted so? Hadn't she faced worse foes in her lifetime? This man wasn't even a foe, really. Not during the day. They both wanted the same thing. And come nightfall, well, she could understand his relentless pursuit of the book—the poor man had no choice.

What's happening, Dez? Losing it around this powerfully sensual man? You know he wants you; you want him. So why not let it happen?

She'd tried that once already. The vampire had morals, was what had happened.

Yet she had been acting rationally at the time, not by her heart.

Still she tried to resist the spell. But the truth of her fluttered in and out of her thoughts like the fairy whose heart had served the spell.

Just let it happen. You wanted to follow your heart. Succumb.

"Can I kiss you?" he asked. So innocently. Not about to simply take a kiss now without her permission.

"I feel I've offended you, if you have to ask such a thing."

"Not at all, Dez. We're learning each other. We're bound to take some curves and detours on the way."

He tilted her chin to look at him. As his fingers glided through her hair, the apprehension shivered away and true desire did rise. "Your mouth is perfect. Small and thick and so curvy. I know it's cliché, but it is like a rosebud."

"Isn't any rose belonging to a witch bad news to you?"

He smirked. "Will you stab me with your thorns if I take a kiss?"

Goddess. He would undo her with sweet words like that.

"Try it, and see what happens."

He touched her mouth first. Testing, perhaps? No thorns. She hadn't any she wished to release on Ivan. At least, not during daylight.

His breath heated her lips before they crushed mouth to mouth. And like that very first moment when the day begins and the world is quiet and coming to life, Dez felt an awakening within her.

Overhead, rain stormed upon the moonroof glass, beating an erratic tempo to the steady pound of her heartbeat. Summoned at her command, it would plunder the world until she gave it permission to cease.

Pressing a hand to Ivan's chest, she found his heart worked much faster than hers, perhaps racing the rain. He would never win that race. But it wasn't necessary; all that mattered to Dez is that he tried.

Lingering on the press of their mouths, Ivan didn't go farther. Not a demanding "take charge and show you who is boss" kind of kiss, this. No, this one seemed perfectly willing to exist in the moment. To learn her.

The connection felt right. No gaggle of geriatric rose growers could ever give Dez this kind of satisfaction. Was that it? She didn't so much desire friendship as good, solid contact.

A closeness that defied reality and instead moved deep inside her to fill the pleading emptiness.

Dez clutched Ivan's shirt. It was a button-up, and the blue silk had been without a wrinkle at the council meeting. Now, she clenched the fabric and drew him in closer. He moved an arm around behind her waist, and fit her body up against his. To keep their embrace, she wrapped her leg around his back.

She was the first to open her mouth and dare him to venture deeper inside her. Like a lover fitting himself into her in a slow, sure way, his tongue invaded her mouth. A button on his shirt zinged her hard nipple. Dez arched her back, pressing her breasts up high against his chest.

And he did not break the kiss. Marvelous. More precious than any memento absent from her house. And one she would remember for all her days, as many and endless as they would be.

"The scent of your blood is strong, Dez," he murmured against her mouth.

"You said you wouldn't—"

"It's sweet and yet, spicy. Like you. Have you ever inhaled one of your perfumes and felt dizzy?"

"All the time."

"That's what you do to me. I don't feel entirely in control of my senses. Like if I tried to stand and walk away right now, I'd wobble and have to catch myself from falling."

"All that from the scent of my blood?"

"Yes." And the prick of a sharp tooth snagged her lip.

Dez stiffened. Not prepared for this, and certainly unwilling to be forced into anything she was sure she did not want.

"Sorry." Ivan pulled away, wiping the back of his hand across his lips. "It's reactionary sometimes."

She understood vampires and that drinking blood was a very sexual thing. A vampire got aroused; he wanted to have sex and bite. Or, if he bit someone, that too caused arousal and it could lead to sex.

"I meant what I said about no biting. Am I safe with you, Ivan?"

"What?" He shook his head. Clearing away the desire to bite? "Oh yes. Dez, you can trust me. It's day, and—"

She pressed a finger to his mouth and slid up to kneel before him. The leather seat felt like butter beneath her knees. "And I want you, Ivan."

"Sex for sex's sake?"

"Can you deal with that?"

He nodded. Dark eyes flickered back and forth between hers. He nodded again, more eager this time. "Promise I won't bite. But I can't promise the fangs will stay in hiding."

She tapped his bottom lip, and dipped her finger inside his mouth. The canines on the top row had receded again, but they were sharp to the touch.

"I don't want the submission that comes with your bite."

"I can't imagine you submitting to anything, Dez. I'll follow your lead."

"We're here, sir."

Ivan smiled against her mouth. Oh, she wanted to eat that smile! Gobble it down and strip off her clothes right here. Sex in the back of a limo?

"The elevator takes less than thirty seconds to get to the forty-second floor, where I live. Can you wait that long?" he said.

"Let's race."

Chapter 13

It had been a while since he'd been home, but Ivan employed a maid who stopped in every Sunday. He didn't bother with the lights as he and Dez entered the apartment, wrapped around one another. Kissing. Groping. Undressing. He was halfway between control and surrender.

"The bedroom is down the hall. I haven't been here for months, but—"

Dez pushed him.

Ivan landed on the thick, overstuffed sofa in the dim shadows of the living room. "You think so?"

"I know so, big guy." She shed her shirt, which he'd succeeded in unbuttoning—okay, so maybe ripping it open and sending the buttons flying wasn't exactly *unbuttoning*. "You're going to pay for this. That was one of my favorites."

He stretched an arm across the back of the sofa and said, "I quiver in fear."

A fine brow arched above her left eye. "You did not just say that."

He spread his arms wide. "Have at me, witch."

"You know I can pin you with a little air magic."

"Sounds kinky."

She strode to the end of the sofa. Braless, her breasts sat high and firm, her nipples deeply colored. Like wine, yes; the gorgeous rosettes would taste wickedly delicious. His body hummed with anticipation.

The air electrified. Magic brewed. Ivan's hackles suddenly went up, seeking defense—but as quickly, he relaxed. She wanted to use magic on him? Bring it on.

A thrust of Dez's hand sent a force at him he didn't try to defend. His shoulders pinned against the cushions, his hips sank and locked against the sofa as if she were physically pressing him down.

Ivan stretched out his legs. "Is that all you've got?"

Another wave of her hand tore the shirt from his muscles, rending stitches free and ripping fabric.

Dez bent over him, her eyes glittering. The tip of her tongue snuck out to wet the crease at the corner of her mouth. "How about this?"

A tiny movement of her forefinger caused the zipper on his jeans to unfasten and begin to slide down.

"Careful," he cautioned. "Don't let it get stuck on anything—"

"Big?"

Oh, did he love a good tease. Good thing it was daytime, and he had control.

As for his morals about having sex merely for sex's sake? Hell, he was a man bred for demonic slavery. He'd argue his angel side later.

An attempt to lift his hand found it remained pinned at his side. Some sort of grounding earth magic, surely.

"You don't want me to touch you?" he challenged.

Propping herself over him, one hand to the back of the sofa, and the other tracing long fingertips down his chest, Dez merely shook her head. "I think I want to play with you awhile first. Any objections?"

The light touch of her, gliding from his pecs down to his belly button, did not preach patience. But all good things… "Do as you wish. I am yours."

"I like the sound of that."

Another splay of her hand swept away her skirt to reveal she wore nothing beneath but a landing strip and legs that went on forever.

Straddling him, Dez hovered over his body, not touching, and so teasing. One foot, clad in a fuck-me black leather spike heel, dug into the white cushion.

Dig that into me, Ivan thought. It was pain he would willingly suffer.

The tip of her tongue dashed out, and she leaned forward to lick a trail from one nipple to the other. The sweet, tightening ache of her touch made him even harder. His cock bobbed at the opening of his pants, but it couldn't wriggle free to do some tormenting of its own.

"How many witches have you had sex with, Ivan?"

That came out of the blue.

"None," he managed, in a desperate attempt to not moan. "Why?"

"You've never slept with a witch? So how do you know it's not dangerous, you being half vampire?"

"My parents."

"Right."

She snuck lower, slickering her tongue down the ridges of his abs. Each ridge she rode hot and slow. The want for her drove him to a pinnacle of panting desperation to do some touching of his own. As if manacled, his wrists fought against her invisible power.

Normally a vampire took his life in hand to have sex with a witch. The fact her blood was poisonous to the vampire kept them from carnal relations. Though to the brave vamp who succeeded, the spoils were worthy. A vampire took some of the witch's magic into himself each time they had sex, and he in turn drank her blood.

And the thought of her apricot elixir sent his fangs downward, ready, wanting.

"Mercy." If he were free, he'd have Dez on her back and be inside her right now.

But this slow pace? Yeah, he could give it a try. Not as if he had a choice.

"You're torturing me," he hissed.

Drawing up the length of him, she pressed her body upon his. Fitting her chin into his clavicle, she licked the underside of his jaw. A wicked succubus intent on stealing his desire.

"I'm not that cruel," she protested sweetly. "I want to learn this part of you, Ivan. The unclothed, unprepared side."

"Unclothed? I'm still wearing my pants."

And then he was not. Seams ripped and the thick fabric tore away from his body. And his cock nestled against her mons. Yes, there, where it belonged. At the entrance. Ready.

"Put me inside you," he gasped, still unable to move. "Please, Dez."

"Soon. Can you feel my heat? I'm so wet for you, Ivan. The heat of you seeps into me. You're strong. A powerful combination of witch and vampire. And the smell of you, dark and spicy, yet unlike anything I've ever captured in a bottle. Mmm…"

"Oh, bloody Mary, Joseph and that other guy. Maybe I'm not so keen on your brand of torture. I need you, Dez."

"Your fangs are showing, vampire."

"Can't help it. Won't bite. Promise. Ah!"

She giggled and nipped at his neck. "What if I tried to bite you, lover?"

"You want my blood? You can have anything you wish from me. It is yours."

"So soon you're willing to give yourself to me? I think it's because your hard-on is straining for some action."

What was she doing to him? Wasn't this the part where she rode him to orgasm and then they had sex all over the house until they landed, exhausted, in the bedroom?

"What do you want from me, Dez? Is this the spell you performed with the fairy heart? To gain control over my heart? You have it. You needn't a spell for that."

She sat up, grinding her wetness against his cock. Ivan moaned. He couldn't move his hips to press himself up tight against her hot pussy.

"I want nothing," she said. "And I want you to want the same. Nothing. I can't give you anything, Ivan. Not a commitment. I—I don't know how."

"I won't ask anything of you. Not emotionally."

"I don't believe you."

"I don't know how to do that, anyway," he said. Was it a lie? It worked right now. "I just want sex, Dez. To be inside you."

She lay down on him and nuzzled her lips against his ear. "I want you inside me, too. Your cock, not your teeth."

"Agreed. And no commitments. No promises. As simple as that."

"And we can keep it simple?"

"Wh-what's wrong with me? Am I so unappealing that once is all you can manage?"

"Truth? You're everything I've not had after centuries of pining for a perfect man. The right one." She leaned down to lick below his belly button. His ab muscles tightened. "The only one." Her tongue teased the head of his cock. "That is why you're dangerous to me."

Seriously? She felt that way about him? Cool.

She moved up again, her breath whispering along the edge of his ear. "The spell was for clarity of heart. My heart. Every move I now make is as my heart wishes, Ivan. My heart desires you."

And he felt his shoulders release and his hips rise up with the force he'd been exerting into them. Free, Ivan sprang up to kneel and coved Dez against the back of the sofa, one hand to either side of her arms.

"Do as you wish," her rosebud lips whispered. The smile she delivered curled deliciously.

Sitting back, and tugging her around to straddle his legs, he growled, "Ride me." And he fit her onto his length.

Like an exotic dancer from the Orient, she shifted and glided and snaked her body upon his. The friction was incredible. This dance he could do endlessly.

"Oh, Dez."

He felt her reach down and clasp her hand about the base of his cock, holding back his climax.

Stroking her breasts, he thumbed the nipples. Her moans were sweeter than the scent of her blood. Unrestrained, and wicked, her voice hummed a sensual music.

And one perfect move. Release of his cock. A slide of her hips. A squeeze of her inner muscles.

Ivan climaxed. And so did Dez. And he had never in his life

reached such a tremendous pinnacle. It must be magic. It had to be magic. But he knew a more regrettable truth.

They were made for one another.

Two hours later, they had successfully christened the kitchen by making love up against the cool glass refrigerator door. Then they'd aimed for the bedroom, but had gotten sidetracked in the hallway beside an original John Byam Liston Shaw lithograph. Dez knelt before Ivan and licked along his length. Intent in his pleasure, she expertly worked him to another climax. Probably his fourth for the day.

But four was nothing. They found number five under a cool, massaging pulse in the shower. And outside on the terrace that overlooked Washington Avenue, a blanket wrapped about their naked bodies, number six quietly arrived with the two of them bent over the railing and their exhaustion slowing the rhythm to a sweet, lingering orgasm.

Now, they'd finally made it to the bedroom. Dez was impressed by the décor, touches of art deco and imported Indian fabrics in brilliant emerald and turquoise. She figured he'd hired a designer. No man, not even a vampire rich enough to buy the Eiffel Tower could put together such a room. Unless he was gay. And Ivan Drake was not gay.

She lay snuggled into the goosedown pillows on the bed. Ivan sat before her, the back of his head nestled between her breasts. They sort of snoozed, and then one would wake the other with a tickle here or a lick there.

Right now, Dez threaded her fingers through his hair, still wet from a shower and smelling like apple shampoo. This felt right. Natural. Like something she could live with for a while.

And that was the dangerous part.

There were so many things working against the two of them.

To even begin any sort of relationship—well, she wasn't about to fool herself it could happen.

You followed your heart. Accept that.

Besides, as a lover, the man could not be dismissed.

Truly, in all her centuries, she had not come upon a man so intent upon her pleasures, and so focused in taking his own. It was as if he'd come to her knowing her body already. And no man ever did. Though some could claim an expertise in making love, the fact remained that every woman was different. And each time a man took a new lover he had to learn anew.

Ivan's learning curve had shot right to the top. He knew her.

And that was a weird thing.

"Do you ever use magic?" she wondered. Stroking his hair, she closed her eyes. The wet strands slicked through her fingers like ribbons of grass. Yes, this was what it felt like—to be undone.

"Only when I need it. I've mastered earth and water and am working on air."

"You may have taken some of my magic with the sex."

"Not intentionally."

"I wouldn't mind if you did gain some of my magic," she offered. "I'm not greedy. I've enough to share."

"Thanks." He turned his head and his cheek nuzzled her breast. A blink of his lashes tickled her nipple. "But I think I need to drink your blood as well to really take away some of your magic. And I meant it when I promised I'd never bite you. I don't need your blood, though I must admit…"

"What?"

"I don't think I can ever truly fall in love unless I have my lover's blood, too. You know? That small sacrifice, a piece of my lover's soul. It just…feels right."

"Then we'd better not fall in love."

The suggestion quieted them both. The scents in the room, wet bodies and sex and steam and shampoo, lingered like a luscious cloud.

No, love wasn't an option if blood was a requirement. Dez could expect nothing less from Ivan. And though she'd known her intentions were to merely enjoy sex with him, the twinge to her heart spoke of deeply hidden desires that ached for love.

That damned clarity spell.

"So what do you call this?" he asked. "Sex for sex's sake?"

"It was a hell of a lot better than that, Ivan. But yes, I suppose."

"Doesn't have to be."

"Yes, it does." Blowing out a wistful sigh, she stroked the dark hair from his eyes.

"What time is it, anyway? It's not night, is it? Doesn't feel like it."

"Because then you'd feel the coercion?"

"Yes, and I should not be naked, or anywhere near you when that happens. Just, you know…I don't want to lose the trust you've given me. It means so much to me."

He turned and kissed her belly, then laid his cheek on it. "So about the book," he started slowly. "If it holds all the spells, then…"

"What is it, Ivan? Want to erase some of your spells that didn't go off as planned?"

"I could do that?"

She smirked. "Technically, yes. But you'd have to actually have the book in hand to reverse it."

"And that's not going to happen. No, I would never seek to change anything in my past. It is what is was, and the future is what I make it. But…"

"You can't reverse anyone else's spells, either, if that's what you're thinking."

"To be expected. But what sort of information is listed for each spell? The maker?"

"Yes. And the complete spell, including ingredients and chant, of course."

"What about if someone ordered the spell? Would it show that?"

"Like some mortal goes to a witch to ask for a love spell hoping to make the gorgeous man across the street fall in love with her?"

"Yeah, sort of. Hell, I'll just say it." He sat up and stretched out his arms, which tightened the muscles across his broad back. Then nestled beside her against the pillows. "I've always wondered about the so-called accident my parents made when selling my soul to Himself. Like, maybe it wasn't as accidental as they believe."

"You think Himself may have orchestrated it?"

"Over the years, I've pondered it often. My parents, they are so good. I know they would have never purposefully done this to me. Not in a million years. And it was a misplaced love spell that brought them together in the first place. My mother told me she was making it for Himself, but she had no idea who the bastard intended it for. Would the grimoire reveal that? Who Himself had originally intended the love spell for?"

"Maybe."

He kissed her. Right there. At the rise of her derriere, the dimples of Venus he'd so fondly devoured but a few nights earlier. And Dez felt her body go jellylike and had no desire to resist his insistent attention to those twin divots.

"Oh, fairy hearts are strong and proud," she murmured. "What a wicked spell I've woven."

"A true spell, though? You are following your heart, not being coerced?"

"Not at all. This is my truth, Ivan. I want to be here, right now, in your arms."

He murmured against her flesh, "Perhaps if my parents had not raised me to be good, I would not care now, but I do. It is an ache, something missing from me. My very soul, I know that. I've always believed without question I am evil."

"Why the assumption?" She nestled her chin in hand and closed her eyes to his tongue dance.

"Because it is true."

Now she flipped over and tucked herself against his chest. So close to him, and staring into his dark eyes. "Why must you become what you believe you were born to be? Why not become what you aspire to be?"

"I...never thought of it that way."

"Will knowing make it easier? You said you didn't blame your parents."

"Yes, but if *they* could know the truth... I'm sorry, Dez, it was a stupid thing to ask."

And it was at that moment Dez could not deny what she'd been desperate to hold back. This man was special to her. And she did trust him.

In her heart, she had already made a decision about Ivan Drake.

"I want to show you something."

"I think I've seen all of you," he said with a chuckle. "What's left?"

"This."

And a huge weight dropped onto the end of the bed, startling Ivan to sit and slide up next to Dez.

There, nestled upon the sex-scented sheets, lay the *Grande Grimoire*.

Chapter 14

"Is that what I think it is?" Ivan leaned over the book, but didn't touch.

"It is."

It was huge, but not as large as he expected a book containing every spell ever cast by all the witches in the world should be. About two feet wide by three feet long, and thick as his fist. It was covered in a rich, red, watered satin and had no symbols on the front save the elaborate gold arabesque work stitched along the edges.

He placed a hand over it, and then retracted it.

"I won't touch it." Ivan sat back, hugging his side against Dez. The warmth of her sent a shiver up his spine. "I don't want to take it from you, and if I touch it, then I won't be able to stop."

He glanced out the window. Close to twilight, the sun was low in the sky. "Why'd you do this? Why now?"

"You wanted to read your mother's love spell."

"Really?"

"Yes. And the council meeting got me to thinking."

Just as he and his mother had hoped.

But things had changed in the course of an afternoon. Ivan didn't want Dez to do anything she was uncomfortable with.

She didn't want their sexual hijinks to become a relationship? He'd have to work with that. She wasn't willing to share her blood with him? A roadblock to them becoming as close as he wished, but he would also have to deal.

She hadn't wanted to show him the book. Well, what was up?

"Perhaps the Protection spell should be considered," she said.

She leaned forward and without even touching the book, cast aside the cover. The pages began to flutter at the direction of her dancing fingers. They were so thin, like pages in a telephone directory, but perhaps even thinner. And colorful and filled with images and text and…and—

"Depth," Ivan said, marveling at the page opened before him.

He leaned in, tucking his hands to his stomach, and examined the page. It looked like parchment, thick and crinkled and, if he touched it, he suspected it would feel rough. Perhaps he even detected a fine hair that hadn't been scraped from the ancient hide during the tanning process. The odor of wet wood curled beneath his nostrils.

An elegant hand had written a spell he didn't want to begin to read, because the feeling that if he read it then it would become whole cautioned him.

But this spell was safe from his comprehension. "Latin?"

"You don't read Latin?"

"Never had the patience to learn. Though my mother taught me a few important words. Is the whole book in Latin?"

"No, there are many different languages throughout. Depends on whoever crafted the spell. This one was used to drought a farmer's crops. See here the wheat seeds and the dirt." She touched a few grains of dark earth and they moved, as if sitting loose upon the page.

"How can that be? The thing is—the pages are so thin. And yet, it looks like I could reach in and snap that wheat shaft in two. It's magic."

"Of course it is." Clutching a wrinkled white bedsheet to her breast, Dez leaned in and blew gently. More pages fluttered before them. "Here's a death spell crafted in the seventeenth century."

"Who is that image of?" Ivan tilted his head. It was a holographic three-dimensional picture, and the image of a woman's face appeared at the lower right corner of the page.

"The spell crafter. All spells are identified with an image."

"Show me the love spell Himself ordered my mother to cast."

Humming absently, Dez danced her fingers over the book and the pages swished by rapidly. Ivan felt so many pages must surely bring them to the end, but it never seemed to go much farther than a few pages.

"You have an intimate command of the book, don't you? You speak to it."

"In a manner. We've been together a long time."

Yes, as far back as when the Merovingian kings had ruled France. Stunning. This woman he was losing his heart to was a dozen centuries older than he. The knowledge she must have. And wisdom!

And he, a mere baby boy, as she'd once called him. At once Ivan revered Dez, marveled at her and, as well, desired any small attention she might gift him. He could learn so much from her.

Then you mustn't destroy her.

Pushing aside the dark thought, Ivan wanted only to be in the moment, not struggle with a coercion he knew would be upon him soon enough.

Pages fluttered, and scents of herbs and earth and some rather foul things whispered into the air. Ivan detected cranberry in one instant, and in the next he could taste the blood of a beating frog's heart pulse at the back of his throat.

"I believe this is the one," Dez said. She kissed the corner of Ivan's mouth and gestured he should move closer.

He inspected the spell, in English, and he read the first few lines before forcing himself to stop. The holographic image of his mother appeared in the corner, below a drop of blood that looked ready to spill off the page. And there, black flesh and obsidian horns.

"That's the one," he said in a whisper. "It was intended that my mother craft the love potion and hand it over to Himself, but my father surprised my mother—he was intent on killing her that evening—and instead he fell in love."

"A good thing," Dez said, and nestled to his side, her breast falling heavily against his bare arm. "Else I would have never met you."

Ivan kissed her. He glided a thumb over her hard nipple.

But he could not dismiss the spell so quickly. Looking over the page, he wanted to reach in and touch the narrow glass vial that contained a gold liquid, but tucked his hands under his legs to keep from doing so. A familiar fragrance drifted upward, and he recognized it as his mother's perfume.

"I don't see any names. An intended target."

"Let's see…" Dez drew a finger down the page, discerning the handwriting Ivan recognized as his mother's. Brimstone now combined with Ravin's perfume. "Normally, if the recipient was mortal, there would be a picture and a name and sometimes even a genetic family tree. But all I'm sensing is Ravin Crosse's presence and another. A very powerful vampire."

"My father."

"The intention is firm. There doesn't seem to be deception or even a sense of accident. The spell was spilled over Ravin Crosse, I know that."

"And then my father bit her. But he had intended to kill her."

"Really? Nice guy."

"Only because my mother first tried to kill him with a blood bullet. They didn't know each other then. It was vamps against the witches, as usual."

"I see. Yes, I can feel the anger, the driving need for vengeance. He drank a lot from your mother. So much it should have killed her. But he also drank in the love spell."

Dez sat upright and withdrew her hands to her lap. She closed her eyes and said, "As intended."

"What?"

The spell read plainly upon the page. Dez had felt Himself's influence as she'd drawn her fingers over the paper. It had been no accident that brought together Nikolaus Drake and Ravin Crosse.

"Himself planned this all along?" Ivan pleaded. "He planned...me?"

"I believe so," she answered. And a sigh was all she could offer.

It pained her to witness the frantic race of emotions crossing Ivan's face. If Himself had intended the two natural enemies to come together, that could only mean he had known the result would be Ivan—his future fixer.

"You can reassure your parents they are not to blame," she tried, and stroked a palm down Ivan's arm.

He flinched, but didn't pull away. "Yes, I suppose."

"I know what you must be thinking."

"Do you? I bet you can't begin to imagine how I feel."

"Betrayed. Tricked. Used."

"Manufactured for evil intent. This is incredible." He caught his forehead in his palms with a smack.

"Do you want me to leave you alone for a while? Maybe I should go find that half-empty bottle of wine we left somewhere in the hallway?"

Dez began to slide from the bed, but Ivan clasped her arm and pulled her to his body. Together they fell to their sides and spooned upon the wrinkled sheets. He drew her tight to his chest.

"Just be with me," he whispered. "I need you."

And they lay there for an hour or more while the room grew gray with shadows. Dez sensed when the coercion prickled into her lover's psyche, for he briefly stiffened, sucked in a gasp, almost pushed her away, but yet, then drew her even closer and kept an iron embrace about her arms.

She knew there was great danger with the book lying exposed on the bed while she lay in the arms of the fixer.

But at this moment, Ivan Drake needed her more than she needed to defeat Himself.

That's your heart speaking. You may like to think beyond the spell now, witch.

No, she didn't want to. Dez would much rather be where her heart intended than anywhere else in the world.

"You can't reverse another witch's spell, can you?" Ivan asked. "You being the keeper of the grimoire? I know no witch can reverse spells that don't belong to them."

"That's not entirely true. But we like others to believe so. Anyone can reverse a spell; they have to be determined and have the right connections."

"Himself?"

She nodded. "You wouldn't want to reverse your parents' love spell."

"No, never. I would cease to exist. And despite my trials, I wouldn't sacrifice a day with you for freedom from a thousand years of suffering."

And she felt the same. Was this love? It didn't happen so quickly. Did it?

No. Not in twelve hundred years had it ever happened like this.

"I was wondering about the Protection spell." Ivan blew softly across the back of her shoulder. "Do you think another witch could reverse it?"

Dez tensed in his arms. Her muscles stretched along his relaxed torso and her nipples tightened even harder, slipping from his loose touch.

"If it's too risky," he said, "we don't have to talk about this anymore. It must be nearing sunset. Christ, it's already dark."

He sat up abruptly. Dez turned to embrace him, but the black design looming but inches from her face stopped her.

"You don't feel the coercion?" She traced a finger down the back of his neck. Did the black tattoo move? Quiver at her touch?

"Not at all."

Was he lying? She had known the moment darkness had fallen specifically from his reaction to it.

Follow your heart.

She felt so close to him, more than the blissful comfort sex had granted. She could relate to his betrayal in a way he could never imagine.

"I need to show you something," she said in the smallest voice. "To share with you. It's been so long since I've ever felt so close to a man."

Her eyes traced his, seeking, wanting.

Ivan nodded, feeling a trifle unsure what she needed at this moment, but willing to follow her direction.

The pages in the grimoire opened to a double-paged spell.

A musty odor rose, yet the second note sprang up, fresh thyme rubbed raw.

Ivan looked over the spell. The diagrams depicted what he guessed were witches bowing before fanged men. Vampires. Blood spattered the entirety of the page. It jeweled on the paper, as if to lift the thin sheet would tilt the crimson liquid creeping to the margins. Witches' blood. Poison to vampires.

"I can't read the words. Are they even words? Doesn't look like any alphabet I've ever seen."

Dez pressed a hand over the bottom corner of the page nearest her. "They're not words in the sense you need to under-stand and define them. They're more intonations and a cadence. This spell is old. Witches once cast using thoughts and rhythm and sound. It's an experience, like becoming one with the spell."

"I become one with my spells. I hum…I work with incan-tations and tones. It's how my mother taught me. But I've never seen it written out like this before."

He spread a hand over the diagrams. One of the drawn female faces cringed at his movement, as if he would slap her. Ivan drew back his hand. "No reversing this spell, though, that's for sure. Unless we can find a witch who understands this. It is an amazing thing, whoever cast this spell, to free a nation of enslaved witches. Is there a picture of the original caster?"

"I don't believe so." Dez bent over the book, dropping a billow of the sheet over the corner of the page, and spreading her hands over the pages as if to discern the very tones of the long-ago recited spell. "There's something I need to tell you, Ivan."

"Is this going to be a good tell or a bad tell?"

"Would it matter?"

"No." He drew her close and kissed the top of her head. "Whatever you want to say to me is good. It's just you and me now. And you know things about me. My darkness. My craving for goodness. And that makes everything right."

"That's hope, yes?"

"Maybe. It's trust, that's for sure. You can tell me anything, Dez."

"Very well." She let out a breath, and then reached for the grimoire, carefully closing it, and grasped it to her chest. The book was huge, and she looked a child clutching it. "Ready?"

"I am," came the brimstone-laced growl.

The room grew dark. And Ivan knew they'd made a terrible mistake. Before Dez could send the book away, Ivan's scream of pain halted her.

Himself held her lover before his fearsome, demonic form. The darkness secreted most of the devil's hideous appearance, but Dez had seen it before. It was an image she would never forget.

How had he gotten to her? She had always taken measures, planted devil traps and warded her surroundings—*not home,* but at Ivan's place.

She had let down her guard, left herself completely unprotected. She had chosen heart over logic. Yet she had not been fully prepared to face the consequences.

Himself must have been waiting for this perfect opportunity. Using Ivan as his pawn, the bastard had finally found a way to put his talons to the *Grande Grimoire*.

Fingernails digging into the white silk sheets, Dez demanded Ivan's release.

"You hand over the grimoire," Himself said. He gouged his talons deep into Ivan's bare chest. Blood oozed out in crimson rills. "And you can have this pitiful excuse for a fixer. I don't know what I saw in you, boy. Fucking the witch was a splendid plan. But falling in love with her was not allowed."

"I—" Ivan couldn't speak. Pain stretched his face. His arms clawed out, as an insect's legs kick when pinned.

Dez knew Himself could not simply take the book. If he could, it would have been done centuries ago. He must have her permission to even touch the grimoire. And he had never approached her personally to demand it, not until now.

Now that she was unguarded.

"You're killing him!" she shouted.

Indeed, the black talons had begun to rip open Ivan's chest. Rib bones snapped and organs were exposed in luscious gore.

Sick with the sight of her lover's suffering, Dez dropped the book and crawled to the edge of the bed. What spell could she use? She tried wind and whipped it up to a tornado, but Himself stood firm even as the torrent whipped Ivan's legs from the floor and splattered his blood against the walls.

Dez stopped the spell, for it further tortured her lover. Rain would merely make the monster chuckle. And swarming insects he would gobble in delight.

A simple bell was all she needed.

"Hand it over, witch."

"No!" Ivan managed to shout.

Some inner part of the vampire oozed from his body. No vampire could heal from such a wound, especially not if Himself touched his heart.

"Very well!" Dez shouted. "The book is yours!"

And the atmosphere lifted. The darkness receded. Ivan dropped to the floor in a sprawl.

And the *Grande Grimoire* no longer lay on the bed.

Chapter 15

Smoke infused the bedroom. Billowing black clouds receded into the corners. A distorted figure lay on the floor against the wall. Blood painted his chest and arms—and that looked like an organ protruding from his gut.

Dez choked out a gasp. She scrambled off the bed and rushed to Ivan's side. But she stopped two feet from his sprawled body where her toes slipped in the vampire's blood. The crimson liquid was everywhere. Thick and dark, Ivan's life invaded her senses. Exotically enticing even as the disgust pushed up her bile.

He was conscious, trying to mumble something. The pain must be beyond measure.

Don't touch. Do not comfort him.

"What have I done?"

The *Grande Grimoire* no longer lay on the bed. A book Dez had guarded for over a thousand years without fail.

"Gone."

And the slightest twinge of liberation allowed her, for the moment, to stand there and take it in. An exhalation washed fickle relief through her being. Gone was the responsibility. Gone was the constant worry and fear. Gone…

Her lover might die. Had she sacrificed the book to spare Ivan's life, only to see him die?

Bending, she stretched out her hands, her fingers curling, wanting to touch, to comfort, but she couldn't do it.

Ivan's hand scrabbled through a pool of blood. Dez stepped back to avoid contact.

"I may have destroyed the entire witch nation."

To speak her sin brought reality crashing upon her.

Dez stumbled backward, looking about. The room blurred and seemed to move. She was naked still. Had to find clothes. Had to…*run*.

Snapping her fingers and muttering a spell, she called up some clothes. A soft white blouse cloaked her shoulders and breasts, and snug gray corduroy slacks fell to her ankles. Black heels clasped her feet.

Staggering, Dez shoved her fingers up through her hair. "I have to make this right. Why did I do it?"

For one man? One man she had known did not have her interests to heart. A man who had plainly told her he would betray her.

Yet they'd made love the entire afternoon. She had fallen deep into a murmur of bliss. It was something she had never in her life had—the connection with another of her kind, the understanding. And it had been wonderful.

And he'd been desperate to discover his truth. To know his parents could have never been so cruel to him.

"Yes. I…did it for you." She glanced to Ivan.

He looked at her now. Dark eyes, spattered with his own

blood, blinked. The tips of his fingers curled. He cringed, and Dez heard rib bones snap. His body was beginning to heal.

"I...love you?" No louder than a sigh, certainly quieter than a whisper.

It felt right to say it, even if she wasn't sure of it. Love?

Their being together had made this happen. Himself had never been able to approach her before, to demand the grimoire. Thanks to decades spent studying diabology early in the twentieth century and creating foolproof methods to keep back the devil, Dez had done so effortlessly. But with his fixer present, and without a single ward or spell to guard her against the devil, Ivan had acted as a sort of conduit for Himself's entrance.

Dez thought she had seen the last of Himself a century earlier.

"This is all too much."

She had to get out of here. Clear her head of the heart spell. And if she remained, tended to Ivan—*touched him*—she'd never be able to think straight.

He'd be fine. Slowly, he'd heal, and then his master would reward him for finally bringing the *Grande Grimoire* to him.

And yet, the war between the nations would be stirred to a head now that Himself held the spells of all witches in his talons.

"Oh." Catching herself against the door frame, Dez forced herself to stagger out from Ivan's bedroom and through the apartment.

She ran out into the hall and onto the elevator, her heels clicking erratically. As did her heart.

She didn't know this city. Didn't matter. She needed air. Sanctity.

She needed to run from this mistake.

Ivan twisted in on himself as the debilitating pain of his healing muscle and flesh and bone rendered him utterly inca-

pable. He could not move to stand or push himself out of the
pool of his blood.

He'd tried to call out as Dez fled the room. His voice resided
in his pain right now.

She'd left him. Alone. Suffering.

What she must have thought; to have handed over the
grimoire to Himself to save him. He understood Dez must not
be in her right mind.

And that scared him worse. She was frantic. And she was
alone in the city. She wouldn't be safe.

He pressed a palm to the floor and tried to move onto one
knee. His gut felt as if his insides had been wrenched outside
his body. And they had.

Bitch that it wasn't so easy to kill him. Because the pain was
still there. And it blinded. And pain meant life. He was quite
literally indestructible.

Falling forward onto his chest, he moaned as the parted rib
cage crushed against the floor.

Evening must have arrived hours before. Dez couldn't place
herself in time as she stepped outside Ivan's building and took
the sidewalk with no care for direction. The air held an unwel-
coming chill. Surrounded by tall buildings, she couldn't spy
the moon or a single star, some navigational mark to give her
direction.

She missed her home. There it was safe.

Was that what she had done over the years? Shelter away in
a safe environment, literally closing herself off from the world?
As Ivan had pointed out, she craved connection.

So much so, she'd given up the grimoire in a desperate
attempt to keep a connection. A connection that probably
wasn't as strong as she wished. Well, it couldn't have been.

They hardly knew one another. And yet they did. Good sex did not make for a strong relationship. But trust did.

"Relationship," she breathed. "This is so not you. You were the one to demand he agree it was just sex. What have you done? Did he bewitch me? Was that it?"

She knew better. There had been no magic in the room beyond which their bodies had created when they'd joined together. Ivan had not used persuasion or influenced her magically in any way. She had wanted to show him the book. It was the most secret part of her she'd wanted him to know.

Truly, she had gone over the edge. Her mind was cracked and she was not acting to character.

Yesterday, she might have welcomed such a change. To try new things, to open her heart to a relationship. To awaken from her slumber.

"That damned heart spell!"

Seeking her truths had resulted in finding them. And Desid-eriel Merovech possessed some dark truths.

Would Himself start unraveling spells immediately? What of any new spells made? Would they be recorded in the book now?

She didn't know. She didn't have answers to anything. She wanted… She didn't know what she wanted. The world to stop and cycle in reverse, erasing her mistake.

"Impossible." Though she'd take it.

Because along with the unraveled spells, her life would also come undone. She guarded the book, and in turn it guarded her. Her life belonged to the book. She had taken a vow centuries ago. Her agreement to protect the book had been forged into its pages. It had been written in her blood. Her heart beat because her blood flowed upon the page. Unlike other witches, she did not require a source once a century; the book held the key to her life.

Now that the book was no longer under her guardianship, the spell could be broken. Her blood would seep from the page were it not cared for properly.

And when the last drop dissipated, so would she.

A city bus rumbled by on the street, spitting up water from the previous rain onto her ankles. Dez stopped on a corner to wait for a green light.

The sky was forgoing twilight for true night, yet the city lights gave everything a gaudy glow. Looking about for the first time, she couldn't spy a landmark—not that she'd recognize one in this city if she stood immediately before it. Neon flashed everywhere and the thump of a distant boom box suggested she shake her booty.

She should catch a cab. And then where? Maybe there was a hotel close by. She didn't have cash. She had nothing. When Ivan had whisked her onto his private jet this morning, she'd been going along for the adventure. And the sex.

Had a little sex reduced her to such a fool?

"I have to face the Gray Council. I must expose my wrongs."

If only to get help. She wasn't sure what the council could do. They'd wanted the Protection spell reversed. Impossible now with the grimoire gone. No longer would they revere her, for what did she have to protect?

Could Ivan's mother offer advice? Dez had recognized Ravin immediately, though she wasn't sure the witch remembered her. It had been the Belle Epoque, in Paris, when she'd known the boisterous slayer of vampires. They'd had a common friend, Dominique San Juste. Dez was sure Ravin had been more than friends with the absinthe-addicted fairy.

"What am I thinking? She's a youngling. A loose cannon. And now she's married to a vampire and her son is the devil's fixer. What the hell happened with that chick?"

Dodging to the right to avoid a man who walked too close on the sidewalk, Dez stumbled and caught herself against the abrasive corner of a brick building.

How soon before her life began to leak away? Surely Himself would go immediately to her life spell and suck her blood from the page? Her death would be easy for the Old Lad.

Of course, she knew he never did things the easy way. Himself enjoyed the play, the macabre manipulation of earthbound souls.

A hand grabbed her by the upper arm, and wrenched her backward. Stumbling in her high heels, she was dragged into the darkest depths of a narrow alley.

A thought to scream emerged, but then confidence rose. A couple of mortals set on hassling her? No problem. She wasn't so freaked by her own indiscretions she could not defend her very life.

She was slammed against the brick wall, and her breath chuffed from her lungs. She momentarily lost her vision and the white light spell that had been on the tip of her tongue.

Three of them stared her down. Not mortal. Their auras were crimson, with specks of ash. Vampires.

Fangs glinted menacingly. Dez's heart ricocheted against her ribs. Did they know she was a witch? There was no way they could know. Or did they usually gang up on innocent mortals in such a manner? Hell, she'd thought vampires were merely after her kind, but if this is how they acted toward everyone…

"Want a bite?" one of the churlish vamps asked. "You look like you could use a nibble. Don't worry, it'll only hurt for a second. Me first."

The biggest and strongest of the threesome lunged for her.

Dez bit her lip. It hurt, and she could have let the vampire bite her, but no vampire was going to stab his fang into her neck.

Spitting, her blood landed on the vamp's cheek as he closed on her.

The contact worked fast. Smoke spiraled from his cheek. He slapped a palm to it. "What the hell?"

"She's a bloody witch!" one of the others cried.

The big one faltered and stepped away. Dez expected the other two to flee in horror, but they did not.

"We know how to take care of witches," one of them hissed.

A gloved hand slapped over her mouth, hard. She could not move her jaw to bite or spit. Another of the vampires shackled her hands behind her back. Her shoulder scraped against the rough brick, and Dez purposefully pressed in deeper, hoping it would cut her flesh and draw out blood.

Meanwhile, the biggest vampire exploded. Her blood had traveled his bloodstream, and the poison—thank the Goddess the Protection spell still worked—had literally eaten him from the inside out.

"Watch the chunks," one of her captors said. "It's got her blood in it. Stop squirming. We're going to burn a witch tonight—"

And then another of them was gone. Flying through the air. Landing on the wall with a dull clunk.

And Ivan stood in his place.

Chapter 16

Ivan did not stand strong and tall and fierce, but bent over and clutching his bleeding gut. There was yet an open crease from his chest to belly.

Dez struggled against the one who held her hands. "Let me go!" She tried to spit over her shoulder, but the move was impossible.

"You helping a bloody witch?" the one vampire called to Ivan. "Looks like she's already torn you to pieces. Ha! This one's mine, buddy. Stand off."

The vampire Ivan had tossed as if a football, reappeared and attached himself to Ivan's back. He brandished a knife and drew it across Ivan's throat.

Using but the command of his magic, Ivan stretched back his arm and sent the vampire flying. This time, he landed thirty feet up on the wall, and the fall to the ground knocked him out cold.

Clutching his bleeding throat, Ivan stumbled for hold against the wall.

Dez, desperate to end this insane nightmare, kicked out, which landed her feet against Ivan's shoulder. She shoved hard, pushing her attacker into the wall. A few spoken words brought a downpour of rain. And hail. The tiny but bulleting ice bits proved enough of a surprise that her attacker let her go.

Scrambling away, Dez pressed her hand against the brick wall, and dragged it across the rough brick. A vampire grabbed her by the shoulder. She spun about and smacked him across the cheek with her bloody palm.

The rain washed away her blood.

The vampire, not sure if he'd been blooded by a witch, stood there for a moment, waiting.

Which gave Ivan enough time to barrel into his chest and land the two of them on the ground.

Dez stepped back and began to recite an ash spell—difficult to render, but the results would prove spectacular. If the vampire were beyond his mortal lifetime, he would be reduced to ash. If not, nothing would happen. Which was why she'd didn't bother to focus the spell. It would hit all three vampires, Ivan included.

Slapping her palms together over her head focusing her energies, Dez dove into herself and swept into the soft violet energy that came easily with the frenzy of the moment. It electrified her extremities and gushed toward her fingers. Spreading out her palms, she released the spell.

The vampire pummeling Ivan in the open chest dispersed to ash. But the vampire lying on the ground remained.

"Let's get out of here." She knelt over Ivan. He was badly beaten, bloodied to a mash. His throat yet bled, but the cut was smaller than the original ear-to-ear slash. "Hurry, before the other comes to."

"An ash spell?" he wondered, as she helped him to stand. The two scampered out onto the main street where hail plummeted the tarmac. "You could have killed me."

"You're too young. I knew you'd be fine. Ouch, the hail is getting bigger."

And though he was grievously hurt, Ivan coved her into his embrace and bowed his head over hers to protect her from the pummeling hail.

And Dez began to cry because, yes, she really did love this vampire who was also a witch, and who seemed to care for her beyond the wicked coercion that forced him to seduce.

And that was why she had to leave him again. She wasn't good for him. And if Himself had his way, she might be dead before sunrise.

Pushing away, Dez began to run. Bulleted in the face and shoulders by pebbles of hail, she endured, for to return to Ivan's gentle embrace was too much. She didn't deserve him.

No longer must she follow her heart.

Ivan dragged himself inside his apartment. Soaking wet, he collapsed on the marble landing. Exhausted and literally wrung through a diabolic wringer, his body fell backward, splaying out in the foyer. The shadow at the back of his neck didn't pulse, or if it did, he was beyond noticing pain.

"Dez." Her name on his tongue sweetened the ache. Momentarily.

She'd run from him. Again.

Was she angry because she'd given up the grimoire to save him? She shouldn't have done it. He would have gladly sacrificed his life to keep the book out of Himself's hands.

And to keep Dez safe.

Years of battling witches had given vampires expertise in

avoiding spat blood or long fingernails drawn across flesh. Dez would have been no match to the threesome had he not shown.

And that thought raised new worries. She was still out there *alone*. Nothing would prevent her from encountering more vamps. They were hungry for witch blood.

What if the Protection spell had been reversed when Dez had been attacked? She would have had no means to hold them off until he got to her side.

Ivan wanted to believe that eventually the vampires would back off when they realized the witches were no longer a threat. But there would be initial casualties.

Dez could have been one of those casualties.

Shoving his fingers through his hair, he then dropped his arms, and they fell slack. His body healed rapidly. He needed to remain still to allow it to happen.

"Maybe it is a stupid idea. The Protection spell should remain intact. It's the only fighting chance the witches have."

And a guarantee the war would never end.

No matter what decision was made regarding the spell, he had to get back the *Grande Grimoire*. If Himself found a way to reverse any of the spells, then calamity would ensue.

And what if he reversed his parents' love spell?

"No, he wouldn't give up his precious fixer."

Or so he hoped.

Dragging himself up to stand, Ivan clutched his aching chest. It had completely healed, but he still felt as if his organs had been rearranged and stuffed back without care. As they had been. His throat had healed from the knife slash. That had hurt like a bitch.

Flexing a fist, he pumped the muscles until his veins bulged. He could crush a few skulls if need be. But the only skull he wanted in hand was the hideous distorted cranium stretched over with black flesh. Himself.

"You rang?"

Ivan smirked. He knew if he thought about his master, he'd come. And how to stay away after all that had happened?

"You're looking rather peachy," Himself tossed out. "That inner-organ colonic I performed on you seems to have left you renewed and ready to face the day once more."

Ivan turned and went down on one knee. Coercion was not required this time. He wanted to show his fealty, to put himself in the position of the slave. The only way he could gain any ground was to do it from the very pit and claw his way up through the detritus.

"Master."

"And still devoted. Such a dear."

Brimstone invaded Ivan's pores as Himself stalked the floor behind him. The scrape of hooves on marble prickled across his scalp. "I appreciate the opening to snatch the grimoire, but such a plan was not as you'd intended, was it? You weren't going to grab the thing for me."

"I—"

"You've become enamored of the witch!" The heat of Himself's breath burned across Ivan's neck. The shadow dug in deep, prickling about his spinal column with barbed needles.

"Was she worth it? Does sacrificing the entire witch nation to my whim satisfy you less than the fuck you had with her?"

"I wasn't thinking about the task. It wasn't evening at the time," Ivan offered.

"Liar."

Flailed across the chest, Ivan took the lash with a grunt yet not a flinch. The icy cut burned into his skin, but then healed as quickly. Himself did like to strip flesh and watch his victims squirm.

"You love her."

"It's none of your concern," Ivan hissed. "You have the book. The task is complete."

Himself flicked at the air with his talons. The clicking sounded like a death beetle scrambling across porcelain.

"What are you going to do with it?" Ivan dared to ask. He remained kneeling, but now he looked up to meet the malicious glow in Himself's red stare. "The grimoire."

"Nothing." Himself strode across the room. He paused by the wall and leaned a multijointed elbow against it in repose. "Not a damned thing. Ha ha!"

"I don't understand. You can unravel every spell in that book. Create chaos. Calamity. Destruction."

"Ah, you appease me with your suggestions to deliciously macabre mischief. True, I could. And I believe I will take apart a few spells, as it suits me. There is one in particular to entice me to no end. It's that Protection spell you're worried about, yes?"

It wasn't as though his master never knew everything about him. Ivan nodded. "Go ahead. Reverse it."

"You'd like that, wouldn't you?"

He wasn't so sure anymore. There were complications, either way.

"I'll tell you why I wanted the *Grande Grimoire* now, of all times."

Doing a strange soft-shoe dance across the floor, Himself spun dramatically and landed in a crouch upon the sofa.

"It is because I don't wish that spell reversed. You see, I want to sit back and watch the witches and the vampires tear each other to bloody shreds. To bring the mortal world to their knees as they discover what dark denizens walk amongst them. It'll be such splendid chaos!"

Huh. That was a new one. To steal a book so he could then

not do a thing with it. And he was right. Without intervention, the two nations would destroy one another. And the mortal world would unknowingly step in to make it happen.

The chaos the Gray Council feared would come to pass. No one would be safe. Not the vampires, because mortals would begin to hunt them, or the witches the witch hunters would burn as if torches standing in line. And mortals would die, for the vampires and witches would not be taken without fear or fight.

A supernatural apocalypse would ensue.

"What can I do to get it back?" Ivan pleaded. "I will do anything in the realm of my power. Just name it."

That got Himself's attention.

The towering devil stalked over to where Ivan knelt. The sickening stench of brimstone coiled up his nostrils and tightened Ivan's throat, but he remained staunch.

One hoof landed on the marble five inches from Ivan's knee. Pale dust from the crushed stone rose. One touch of that hoof would burn into Ivan's flesh. Not like he couldn't take the heat, though, was it?

Why not become what you aspire to be?

Dez had it wrong. Ivan was evil to the bone. Else he'd not have a literal devil riding his back.

"Why do you insist on being so obstinate, boy? You are mine, and yet you've fought me from day one."

"Wasn't my choice. Don't the people who sell you their souls generally do so of their choosing?"

Now he fixed his gaze to Himself's. Drawing in courage, Ivan spoke, "You manufactured me. And now I serve you because I must. But because of the parents you chose for me, and their morals, I will never completely be yours."

Black talons swung through the air, but stopped millimeters

from Ivan's skull. Himself clutched his appendages into a clacking fist. "Just so."

No, he had not won so easily. Ivan could never win. Himself may allow him that belief, but Ivan would never fool himself about the balance of power in this relationship.

"I want to tell you a story."

Inwardly, Ivan rolled his eyeballs. What the hell?

Himself peered over his shoulder at Ivan. "It's a love story."

Yikes.

"Always in the mood for a good romance," Ivan forced himself to respond.

"Excellent." The beast of dark temptations and master of souls seated himself on Ivan's sofa and crossed his disjointed legs. Hoof swaying as he rocked one leg, Himself stretched an arm across the back of the sofa and sighed. "Where shall I begin?"

Determined to get through this fiasco, Ivan waited patiently for the devil to begin his tale.

"She was snow and fairy tales," Himself recited. "I saw her first during winter. Pure white fox fur surrounded her face and wrapped the muff about her hands. She breathed and the air iced before her. Yet in her eyes lived warmth."

This was a love story starring Himself? "You don't know love," Ivan blurted out. "You cannot!"

"What is love?" Himself spat, twisting forward and sneering hideously. "It is everything and nothing. No man can discount another man's love when it is so vast and varied."

"You are no man," Ivan hissed. But he was finished. It wouldn't do to argue. And he'd best not, if he wished to gain any means to the grimoire. "Continue. I want to hear the devil's version of love."

"It was far more grand than any love you have had, boy.

What love can bring down literal walls and see me—*me*—pleading for absolution from the pain of it all?"

Himself had been reduced to such? Perhaps he *had* loved.

But Himself was a liar and the great tempter. He could spin a tale at will, one to serve his needs, to change outcomes and effect disasters. Why it was necessary to create a love story at this moment baffled Ivan.

"I began to woo her. Visiting her daily. Bringing flowers. Sitting in her parlor and chatting about the world. I knew she was a witch. She saw me, well, you can imagine."

Yes, she must have seen her greatest desire when looking upon Himself. Poor woman. She hadn't a chance, surely.

"She was amused by my familiar, at the time. A sweet blonde urchin abandoned by her parents. She followed me everywhere. Most thought her my child. I let them have their fantasies.

"I eventually won over this woman's heart, I believe. Yes, I know there was a moment when she was completely, irreverently in love. She would have died for me. But no matter how I begged, no matter how she succumbed, she would not give me her soul."

"Did she know what it was she had fallen in love with?"

"In the end, yes. And that is when she spurned me. By that time, she was completely under my thrall, but there was a tiny spiral of hope within her that fought. Much like yourself. Idiot fixer."

Ivan liked the woman already.

"I asked for her hand. She refused. I threatened her friends, her family. She refused. I took away all things in the world she cared for, coveted, desired. She refused!"

Himself stood abruptly and paced his floor-crackling steps before the sofa.

"She refused! And yet, I loved her deeply. My desiderata. I was crushed. My kingdom fell around me, and I did not care. I could not have the one thing I most desired."

"So you let her live? Even after her refusal?"

"Of course. I could not remove from this world the one thing that gives me pleasure yet to this day to consider. She exists yet. And that is what I want from you."

Himself stalked to Ivan and lifted him up by the chin. The talon dug deep, piercing through to the underside of Ivan's tongue. Blood spurt across Himself's arm.

Leaning in, nose to nose with Ivan, he muttered in the sepulchral tone that made Ivan sweat icy chills, "Bring her to me. Willing. Ready to become my bride. And I will hand over the *Grande Grimoire*. And…"

He released Ivan from his taloned hook and stood tall, towering above Ivan's faltering gaze. "…if you are successful, I will give you back your soul."

Chapter 17

"Who is she?" Ivan asked.

His soul returned? He would do anything.

"I'm not telling." Himself strode over to a floor-to-ceiling living room window that overlooked the city. He put a hand through the glass, moving it like liquid, to tap the air outside. The glass fogged. "That is for me to know and you to struggle to discover. Wouldn't be sporting of me if I gave you a clue."

"Not even an address?"

"Not even."

"But…she was a witch?"

"All you're getting. I won't put a time limit on this task. But know, every day you do not bring my bride to me, I will rip out a handful of pages from the *Grande Grimoire* and reverse the spells. Delicious chaos. *Ciao!*"

Himself stepped through the glass and disappeared.

Ivan pressed his hand to the glass and flinched away. It was molten, and it moved when he touched it. Blisters bubbled on his fingertips. He could probably follow in Himself's wake, but he had no earthly desire to journey to wherever it was Himself resided.

"My soul?"

With but one task his soul would be returned to him.

Could he take his soul into his body without it being destroyed by the evils he had committed as the fixer?

Ivan had decided years ago it was a better thing he did not have a soul while serving Himself's needs, for the damage to it would be irreparable. He'd seen sin eaters and soul thieves poisoned by the heinous crimes of the souls they tapped. It wasn't pretty.

"My soul," he whispered in awe.

He clasped a hand over his heart. The heavy thuds pulsing against his palm billowed to elation. And all he had to do was find a bride for Himself.

Without a name. Or a location. Or a description of her appearance.

"Hell."

Indeed.

Himself paced up to the wooden podium where the *Grande Grimoire* had been placed since he ripped it from the witch's protection. She hadn't known what had hit her when he'd dropped into her world.

The fear in her eyes had been delicious.

And regrettable. Regret always proved more splendid than pleasure.

Slashing a hand before the book opened it to the center. Pages rippled and with but a thought, Himself commanded it to the guardian's spell. Rather, it was a blood debt agreed upon when the witch had taken on the task of protecting the book.

Glistening blood purled down the center of the ancient parchment. It coiled along the graceful curving lines of her signature, filigreeing about that name as if it were an intended design.

Himself leaned over the page and drew in the scent of blood. Centuries old, and brewed like a valued whiskey to a smoothness that defied description.

A dash of his tongue touched the glimmer of crimson. Just a taste. The blood skittered across his tongue and scurried over his palate.

Casting back his head, Himself bellowed out in triumph.

His parents' loft in the Mill District looked out over the Mississippi River. Construction on a nearby restaurant filled the air with the sounds of jackhammers and trucks hauling in lumber. Ivan knew as he entered, without knocking, that his father was not around. It was midnight. He was most likely out prowling. Not for blood, but to keep the streets as safe as he possibly could.

Nikolaus Drake had taken it upon himself to form a crew of vigilante vampires. They didn't go after witches. Instead, they sought the vampires who went after innocent witches. When caught, they didn't kill the vamps, but instead gave them good reason to reconsider their ways. Those reasons being forced baptism (if the vampire were not baptized) which would give the vamp a healthy fear of the holy, or a torture session that would leave even the staunchest vamp with a bad taste for witch.

Ivan wished he had more time to join his father on his nightly missions, but his nights were not his own. And so long as he focused on finding the nameless bride for Himself, the coercion did not rear its head.

"Oh, Ivan." Ravin popped out from a bedroom door to his right. "You surprised me."

He lifted the half-made patchwork quilt she held draped over one arm. "I guess I did. Quilting? Mom, don't tell me—?"

"Not my handiwork; belongs to your father. It was with your grandma's things from their lake cabin. I've spent the past few weekends going through her belongings because Nikolaus couldn't bear it."

Nana Irene, Ivan's mortal grandmother on his father's side, had passed away two months earlier. She had not been aware her son had been changed to a vampire in the nineteen seventies and had been forced to abandon his chosen profession of brain surgery because of it. Nor could Grandma and Grandpa Drake have guessed the woman their son had chosen to marry was a witch.

Or that their first and only grandchild had been born with a ransomed soul and was attached to the devil Himself.

"I miss her." Ivan threaded an arm around his mother's shoulders and led her into the living room.

Lights from the bridge that crossed the river twinkled in a swag design. Soft tunes whispered from the computer speakers. Ravin liked heavy metal, so the bluesy tune surprised him.

"I'm glad Grandma never learned the truth about us."

"Irene was a good woman. Strong. Outlived her husband by twenty years. Nikolaus really misses her, but he's strong. It's hard to be immortal."

She tugged him down to sit beside her on the couch. Ivan put up his boots on the glass coffee table and snuggled into the plush cushions.

His mother had been alive since the sixteenth century. He used to love hearing her tell about the real history the books never mentioned. "When did you stop caring?" he asked.

"I've never stopped caring, Ivan. I've learned grief is a natural part of life. But it should never consume you, as I once allowed it to consume me. Remember that on your two hundredth birthday, or when your mortal friends have all passed."

"I have very few mortal friends."

She clasped a hand in his. "Safer that way. So what are you up to? No task this evening?"

"I've a bit of a puzzle, and I'm hoping you'd have some information. But first, I have some good news for you. I hope you'll think it's good news."

"Shoot."

"It's about the love spell that brought you and Dad together." Ivan sensed his mother tense up beside him, so he quickly explained. "I saw the original spell in the *Grande Grimoire*."

"She showed it to you? But that should never—"

"Mom, just listen. I wanted to learn the truth, to know what I've always suspected. That you and Dad were never to blame for what you think has made me the fixer."

"But Ivan, we—"

"Did Himself ever tell you who the spell was originally intended for?"

"No, but—"

"Because it was always intended for the phoenix vampire and the witch slayer. Both of you. Himself orchestrated bringing the two of you together with the intention of creating some sort of super vampire with incredible powers. Me. All the better to serve Himself with."

"The grimoire revealed this? Are you sure, Ivan?"

The hope in her voice gave Ivan the resolution he had craved over the years. "Yes, Mother. It was not your fault."

She exhaled. Taking it in, surely. "You're not just saying that?"

"I don't lie easily, you know that."

"Oh, Ivan, this should make me feel better, but you know I still grieve your pain. When your father agreed to offer his firstborn's soul, he believed fully he would never have a child because he didn't want to spread the vampire taint to an innocent. And I, well, I was no better."

"Let's not speak of it ever again. Please? We should constantly strive to move forward, never looking back, for we cannot change the past."

"How did you get to be such an amazing person?"

"My parents." He leaned over and kissed the crown of his mother's head. "You gave me heart."

"And I curse myself every day for it."

"What? Why?"

"Ivan, were you not so caring perhaps it would be easier to bear your bane. I never thought much about that until I saw how you suffer at Himself's whim. I wish I had raised you differently. More…indifferent."

"Really?"

"Yes. No. Oh, hell. You're a great man, Ivan. It makes me so proud every time I look at you."

"Mom, you're embarrassing me."

"That's my job. Besides, I was never allowed to be a PTA mom or a dance chaperone, so you gotta let me take my props when I can."

"All right. I think I can live with a little embarrassment now and then. But I've something else to ask you. How well do you know Himself?"

She shrugged. "Not well, and let's keep it that way."

"Did you know he was once in love?"

"Ha!" Ravin slapped her knee and gave Ivan a shove. "You're dreaming."

"I should be, but he told me the story of being in love with a woman who was that close to becoming his bride. She loved him back, or so he claims."

"Yeah? Who was she? Medusa?"

"Mom."

"Ivan, I know Himself appears to people as their greatest temptation, but love is pushing it a bit far."

"I wouldn't know. He's only ever appeared to me in his true form."

"What?" Sudden worry in her dark eyes surprised Ivan. Rarely did his mother lose her cool. "You've never told me that. Ivan, that's, it must be…oh my Goddess."

"I'm used to it. In fact, I'm glad it's not any other way. Couldn't imagine doing what I've done for something that resembles a gorgeous woman. That's one ugly son of a bitch."

"Goddess help me and my son."

"Mom, listen. Himself has given me a chance to have my soul."

"He's a liar. Don't trust him, Ivan."

"I know that, but what he wants in exchange is enough to make me believe he may be true to the bargain. Supposedly this woman he loved is still alive. He wants me to bring her to him. And then he'll give me the *Grande Grimoire*."

"It's gone?"

Hell. He shouldn't have revealed that. Ivan made to stand, but his mother tugged him back down and put an insistent hand on his knee.

"Did that idiot witch hand it over to Himself?"

"Mother, watch your blood pressure."

"I don't have a blood pressure problem. But I do have a problem with stupid women kowtowing to Himself."

Ivan lifted a brow, but didn't remark that his mother had experienced a rather idiotic moment with Himself when she was younger. "She did it to save my life. Out of love."

"Oh." Ravin sat back. Then she sat upright. "Really? But you're virtually indestructible."

"Himself was ripping my insides out and allowing them

to spew onto the floor. I still don't think my intestines are back in order."

"Ah." His mother laid her head on his shoulder. "I can't hate a woman who tries to protect my son. Even if she may have sacrificed the entire witch nation in the process."

"Himself doesn't want to unravel all the spells. Maybe a few. Every day I don't find his bride, he's going to undo a handful of them. But not the Protection spell. He wants the two nations to go at it and rip each other to shreds."

"Asshole."

"You always call them as they are, Mom. So that's what I'm asking you. Do you have any idea who this woman could be? My master isn't telling."

"I don't know. I've never heard tales or rumors of such a remarkable thing. But I can ask around."

"Please do. I'll keep my cell phone on. Time is key. I've got to run. There are imps to interrogate and all sorts of dark denizens to pummel for information."

"I hope you find the right one." Ravin followed him to the front door. "For you to win your freedom from Himself would be the world to me."

He leaned in and kissed his mother's forehead. "It'll happen. Tell Dad I said 'Hey.'"

The gray-limbed imp hit the concrete wall with a satisfying splat. Tongue lolling and eyes bulging, the creature began to peel away its shoulder from the hard surface when Ivan punched it in the general region where he expected a gut should be.

"Mercy!"

"No mercy for a miserable imp." Ivan twisted his fist.

"We have the same master. What did me do to piss you off?"

"You breathe."

"Not actually—yeow! All right, already, what you want? Himself in love? Never heard something so ludicrous."

"You've been with Himself for three centuries, Malavarious Stout. You'd better not be lying to me."

Sensing with a bit more pressure on the gut, the imp's eyes would actually pop from their sockets, Ivan adjusted his torque. He didn't want to destroy the thing, just cause it excruciating pain.

"Black David tells me you used to serve Himself in his lair."

"Black David is goblin and goblins suck dirt!"

"You'll be eating dirt if you don't spit out answers right now."

"There was a girl once!"

"And?" Ivan slammed his forearm across the long neck of the thing, choking off its air. "What was her name?"

"Me never have names. She was slut. One time. I think she went insane. Died pulling out hair and eating insects like candy."

"There must have been another you recall. Someone who caused Himself no small amount of frustration? Lovesickness?"

"Nope. No silly love birds for that dude. Though...Paris?"

Now he was getting somewhere.

"What about Paris?"

"Me wasn't there with him then, but he did talk about Paris. That splendid time, Himself say. Strange thing to hear from His Darkness. That's all me got, fixer. Now let go!"

Ivan wrapped his fingers about the imp's neck and flung it down the alleyway. It hit a trio of aluminum garbage cans. The thing scampered away on all fours, cursing Ivan in a language he associated with evil, for it was a wicked tongue.

"Paris, eh?"

Striding down the alley, he pondered a trip across the ocean.

His cell phone jingled. Ivan shuffled in his pocket for the iPhone. Mom. "Find anything?"

"All I've got for you is the nineteenth century," she said.

"And Paris," he said. "Didn't you spend some time in Paris in the nineteenth century?"

"Toward the end. I was a bit of a bohemian. But the only devil I dealt with back then was absinthe. Nasty stuff. Sorry I couldn't have been more help, Ivan, but the witches I asked didn't have anything, either. Although…"

"It's a great help, Mom. I think I'm off to Paris. I hate to leave while things are so volatile."

"They're volatile everywhere. You can get a read on the vampire/witch relations in France while you're there and report back to me. The sooner we can get our hands on the *Grande Grimoire*, the better."

"But the problem remains. We still won't be able to reverse the spell. Not without the original creator."

"I have my suspicions about that. You going straight to the airport, or you stopping by to see your girlfriend first?"

"She's not my girlfriend."

"She saved your life," Ravin intoned hopefully.

"She's a lover, all right? And I don't want to talk about this with my mom."

"Okay, but you should have a talk with her before you leave. Trust me, son. It's an intuition. Bye."

Chapter 18

There wasn't much he needed to pack for Paris. Ivan was accustomed to traveling the world—at Himself's bidding—and so was equipped with a million-dollar-limit credit card and an amazing capability to overcome jet lag. Must be because he needed little sleep. But the long flights did drive him stir-crazy.

His parents owned an apartment in the Seventh Arrondissement in Paris, and he had free rein to use it as he wished.

He tugged on a clean muscle shirt and padded out to the living room. Steam from the shower misted apple scent throughout the apartment. He had thought about stopping by a bookstore on the way to the airport, but he found the tattered copy of Mervyn Peake's *Gormenghast* under the bed. He'd been working on that book for decades.

With iPhone in hand, he could catch his e-mail and have all his contacts literally in his palm. And he'd uploaded a copy of

Le Pacte Des Loups, the French werewolf movie, and *Dangerous Liaisons* to watch in case the book grew tiring.

Ready to leave, Ivan cast about his apartment, ensuring all lights were switched off. He didn't want to step off this continent until he'd talked to Dez. Was she still angry with him? Or rather, at her need to protect him, which had inadvertently resulted in dire consequences?

"Of course she is," he muttered.

He wasn't sure how to approach their situation. Did they have a situation? Even with her warning a relationship could never be, he still liked to think so.

While Dez seemed able to brush off their antics as a casual afternoon, he could not. Learning her body now made him more eager to learn her heart and soul. They were two alike. He just needed to convince her of it.

Switching off the air conditioning and grabbing his wallet and a small carry-on bag, Ivan opened the front door—and walked right into Dez.

A fall of hair swished across one green eye and she flipped it aside with a twist of finger. That small motion stirred Ivan's desire.

"I'm sorry, you're going somewhere?"

"No, come in." He gestured her inside. Her presence lifted his mood measurably. And no, it wasn't night. She smelled wildly extravagant. "Persimmons and something else," he said, sniffing at her hair.

"Cinnamon and a little myrrh thrown in for good measure. Ivan, I had to see you."

Reluctant to look him fully in the eye, she drew her gaze over his body as she fidgeted with the single diamond button at the vee of her stretchy black shirt. The please-bite-me curves of her breasts teased wickedly.

But Ivan couldn't help but notice the bruise on her forehead.

Must be from last night's struggle. It killed him to know she could have been harmed worse.

"Thank the Goddess, you're...*whole* again." She swallowed. Finally her gaze held his. And tears wobbled at the corners of her eyes. "Are you?"

He hugged her, taking his time and sensing she was initially reluctant for the contact. Why did it have to be so difficult for her to surrender?

Because you will never be free from Himself. She doesn't want that.

Wrapping his palm across the back of her head, he pressed his cheek to the top of her hair. God, he didn't ever want to let her go. To protect her until his end days would be a dream.

But he could understand her fear. The last time they'd been together, she had watched him get his insides torn from his body. Not a sight he wished upon anyone.

"I'm completely healed."

"It's because of me you were tortured."

"Eh, it was the same-old-same-old. There's not a brand of torture Himself can inflict upon me he hasn't already tried once or twice before. I'm fine, Dez. Holding you in my arms makes me better than fine. But what about you? All in one piece?"

She nodded. "Just some scrapes."

"I wish you would have stayed with me last night. Why did you run away?"

"Because I didn't want *this* to happen." She put up a palm, which was riddled with red cuts. "This...feeling stuff."

Ivan took her hand and kissed the palm. If only he had the power to heal her simple bruises and cuts, he would give up his own ability to heal. Hell, he'd let the devil pummel him nightly if in return he were granted the talent to heal the woman he adored.

"Feeling stuff," he reiterated. "You mean the part where

your heart beats fast and you can't find the right words because you know nothing will come out right?"

A smirk lifted the right side of her mouth. "I thought the one without the soul was supposed to have the most trouble with that."

"I may be soulless, but that doesn't make me any less caring. I'm so glad you came to me, Dez."

"I couldn't stay away from you. I, uh…" Now a smile tickled her mouth and she shook her head, spilling her hair half across her face. "Well, if I can get beyond the torture, and your near death, then all I find myself thinking about is us. Yesterday afternoon. Making love. Something happened then, Ivan."

"You felt it, too?" And here he'd thought it had been just sex to her.

He captured a few of her fingers at the crook of his palm. She didn't want to step closer. A woman unsure. It made him warm with the anticipation of her confidence.

"We're right for each other, Dez. We fit together—"

"Sexually," she hastened to say. "But I'm still unsure about a relationship. You know I didn't want that to happen."

"We can move slower."

"We've already jumped a speeding train," she said. "And I think…Ivan, I'm bad for you."

"Again, shouldn't it be the one lacking a soul saying that? You're not bad for me, Dez."

"I could never give myself completely to you, in the blood, as I know you desire."

"I can live with that."

"No, you can't. It's a part of who you are. And…and…I have secrets."

"We all have secrets."

"Yes, but—"

He caught her in his arms. "Will you come to Paris with me?"

"What? Is that where you're headed? I shouldn't have come. If you're in a hurry—"

He had to tug to keep her in his embrace. The cinnamon notes of her perfume enticed him to nip her earlobe. He couldn't divine the origin or the scatter of scents, but for every kiss he pressed to her hair, and there at the corner of her eye, he excavated yet another intriguing layer of aroma.

Go further, and you'll be sniffing apricots. There, it is dangerous.

"I could stand here all day holding you, kissing you. Breathing you," he said. "Don't walk away. Tell me why you've come. Or is it so simple you wanted to be with me?"

"I don't think anything can ever be simple again. Not in my life. I came here because I'm desperate, Ivan. I have to get the *Grande Grimoire* back."

"That's no secret." He kissed her and grinned widely.

"What are you smiling about? This is serious business, I—"

"I know how to get it back," he said.

But she wasn't listening. "—if only I'd reversed the spell when I'd had it in hand."

"What?" Ivan gripped her by the shoulders. Her hair shivered across the back of his hand. "Reversed the—? Dez, are you saying…?"

She nodded. A small, perfect smile awaited his reaction.

If she thought to reverse the Protection spell, then that could only mean— "You were the one who created it?"

"I did," she said. "Eight hundred years ago and some months. Give or take a few days. Told you I had secrets."

Ivan snapped his touch away from her. She suddenly appeared so…much more than he could have ever imagined. The witches at the Gray Council had known greatness in their presence.

And now…he felt it, too.

He dropped to his knees before her. Dez shook her head, but he wouldn't have it. Reverence for this witch flooded him. She was responsible for crafting a spell that had protected the entire witch nation from slavery for eight centuries.

Impossible to fathom, yet easy to accept. He'd always known she was powerful, a match for him any day, even with the devil riding his back.

"Stand up, Ivan. I've given the grimoire to Himself. I deserve no false worship."

He wrapped his arms about her hips and nuzzled his face aside her stomach. "I love you, Dez. That's all. I love you."

"Oh really? An afternoon of sex does little more than stoke lust. Ivan, you don't even know me."

"You're in my blood."

"I am not. And I never will be."

He stood and for some reason it felt disrespectful to tower over her, so he stepped back, down the step in the foyer, which brought them eye level. "You are a savior to my race. At least half of me."

"So now you're calling me some kind of grandmother to the witches? I don't think grandmothers have sex with their progeny. And I'd really hate to rule that out of our relationship."

"So would I. And you just said 'relationship.'"

"So I did. Hell!" Tossing up her arms in surrender, she looked at that moment more naïve and desperate than Ivan had ever seen. A true princess in need of rescue from the dangerous thorns.

"God, Dez, I love you. It feels right to say that. I love you. And I know how to get the book back. Then the world will be right. And we can be right."

"Oh yeah?"

"Himself set me to another task. And get this." He leaned

in to press a lingering kiss to her mouth. "If I succeed, he'll not only give back the *Grande Grimoire*, but he'll release my soul to me."

"Ivan, that would be wonderful for you."

"Beyond wonderful, and that's why I'm headed to Paris. My research has led me there. Nineteenth century, but I figure if I ask around, maybe utilize the ancient vampire networks in the city, I can come up with results."

"What are you looking for?"

"Get this." Planting his feet, Ivan looked Dez squarely in the eye. "Himself was once in love. And, he wants me to find the woman who spurned him and bring her back to be his bride. It's another bloodless task! I just have to find one woman. I don't have to beat anyone, or make them see nightmares or destroy their lives. I simply deliver the blushing bride down the aisle to her demonic husband. How easy is that?" He checked his watch. "The jet is waiting. I should be at the airport right now."

Kissing her, he cupped his hands in the silken depths of her hair, imprinting his senses with the softness, the mixture of scents, her tiny moan as he parted lips with hers.

"I hate leaving like this, but—"

"Go. I understand."

"Sure you don't want to come with me?"

Dez shook her head. "I should catch a flight back to Maine."

"I'll return to you as soon as I'm finished. It would be a nice surprise if those damned rose vines were cleared away from your porch."

"Right. Ivan?"

"Yes, love?"

She turned, arms crossed over her chest. The smile was forced. He understood. His departure was sudden. He didn't want to leave, but if he made it quick, it would be easier for both of them. Because all he really wanted to do was kneel before her again, strip away her clothes, and pay her worship.

"So what you're saying to me," she said, "is that you'd sacrifice one woman to save many?"

"Hell yes! One witch for tens of thousands? Doesn't that seem fair to you? I gotta run. My flight is waiting."

"Sure. Uh, do you mind if I stay here awhile? I want to watch the sunset from your view."

"No problem. The door automatically locks when you leave." He kissed her soundly. "I'll see you soon."

"Right." Dez waited as Ivan's footsteps echoed down the hallway to the elevator.

She shivered, but not from the cold. "Maybe you're not the man I thought you to be, Ivan Drake."

Chapter 19

Dez's flight arrived in Maine at seven in the morning. The news on the cab's radio was dismal. And she knew, instinctually, it was undone spells.

A man who had struggled with cancer for decades and was miraculously healed two years ago dropped dead earlier that morning, his body filled throughout with cancer.

A world-famous musician took the stage last night, only to stumble off, dumbfounded, and apparently unable to play the guitar as he had become known for. His fans revolted. He was now hospitalized in critical condition.

A Bahamian village saved from last year's vicious hurricane had been swept into the sea early that morning. No survivors.

Vaccines just administered to infants in ten states across the nation resulted in instant death to dozens.

A lottery winner renowned for great charitable acts had

killed himself an hour ago. A letter detailing his so-called deal with the devil was found near the body.

That last one didn't sound like a spell, but one never knew. Witches were as susceptible to devilish deals as common mortals.

It had begun. And she wasn't sure how to deal with it. Exhaustion tightened Dez's neck muscles. Though immortal, she still needed her eight hours of sleep, unlike vampires, who survived on but a few a day.

She figured Ivan must be setting foot in France by now. To begin a search for a woman he would condemn to Himself's whim.

The idea of it made Dez physically ill. Sweat beaded on her forehead, and she wished the taxi would drive faster. Maybe she was coming down with something. She could cast a spell to ward off infection, but she wasn't sure what would come of all spells now that Himself held the *Grande Grimoire*.

Would any spell cast be recorded as usual? Would the spell even work? Or would it be repelled back toward the caster resulting in—well, who could know?

It had been more than twenty-four hours since Himself had taken it. She hadn't heard of any calamities within the witch community. Nothing worse than the war already at hand.

Which was odd in itself. Was Himself biding his time? For what?

She rubbed her elbow. The vampires who had attacked her in the alley had slammed her hard against the wall. A rough scab darkened the skin, and her palm was still raw. As soon as she got home, she planned to mix up a lavender healing unguent that should take care of the swelling.

If Ivan hadn't arrived when he had she felt sure that might have been her last few moments on this earth.

It had been foolish to walk alone in a city she did not know.

But even more foolish had her blood not had the power to repel vampires.

While Ivan's goal to secure the *Grande Grimoire* was magnanimous, she knew he would then ask her to reverse the spell.

Could she do it? Condemn witches to the mercy of vampires worldwide? While the Gray Council's discussion had provided some good defense—there would be a few casualties initially, but the vampires would quickly back off—Dez wasn't so sure.

I must think on this.

"We're here, ma'am."

She hadn't realized the cab had stopped. Dez paid for the ride and stepped out into the fresh sea-misted air. Breathing in deeply, she infused her wanting soul with the cool dampness of the world. And instantly she began to feel better. Home always felt right.

The rose vines stirred as she approached the front door. A warning. They would not otherwise have movement.

Unless there was reason.

As she gripped the doorknob, Dez's heart began to thud. Was there someone inside? Had her house been robbed? By vampires?

Maybe it would be wise to call the police.

"I can handle a few vampires," she muttered. And then, rubbing her bruised elbow, she realized she probably could not.

The door was still locked. No windows were broken. If it had been a vampire, he would have had to leap to the roof to find the attic window, which she remembered now she hadn't thought to close and lock before leaving with Ivan.

"Shoot."

Calling up a white light, she pulled it over her body and spread it out in a perimeter of ten feet. If there was an intruder inside, she needed the wall of protection to keep it back. It would give her time to summon a spell to counterattack whoever may be inside.

Pushing open the door, Dez stepped out of her high heels so her steps wouldn't click on the wood floor. Quiet hummed loudly.

What did she own that a burglar would want? Not a thing, save her oils and simple necessities. All spellcrafting articles—silver athames, minor spell books and a few priceless gemstone amulets—she kept securely in another realm, waiting for her to call them out for use.

Perhaps whoever had been inside was now gone?

No, the roses would have been still then. Ivan's suggestion to cut him a path had been answered with a smirk. He knew better.

A floorboard creaked beneath her heel. Dez cringed. Forgot about that one. But as she peeked around the corner into the living room, she abruptly cut off a rising scream.

"Ivan?"

He sat on the wicker chair, smiling, arms held out for her.

Fear shedding quickly, Dez rushed to him. The white light stopped her ten feet from her lover's arms. "Sorry, I didn't know who was inside."

She dismissed the light with a slashing gesture before her body and crawled onto his lap. A kiss released her apprehensions, and she snuggled in for a hug. Until now, she hadn't realized how much she missed him. And it had been less than eight hours.

"I thought you were in Paris?"

"I couldn't go. Sorry if I surprised you. The white light was entirely warranted. I flew directly here after I changed my mind and decided I'd sit and wait even if it took you days to arrive home. Smells like you here. Like every scent in the world."

"The roses didn't give you trouble?"

"They did. But I heal."

That he'd suffered the torment of those thorns to wait for her further deepened her guilt.

"What made you change your mind about going to Paris? You can't refuse Himself's task to bring his bride to him."

"I can."

"At great suffering and the sacrifice of all chance of ever getting back your soul. Ivan, this is the hope that you've never known."

Could she allow him to make that sacrifice? She wanted to. It was a selfish desire.

"Listen," he said, as he kissed the crown of her head. "I couldn't stop thinking about this nameless woman as I was waiting for the jet to taxi onto the runway. Who is she? What horrors had she experienced when Himself pursued her? What right do I have to make her again suffer? And who says one soul is a worthy trade for thousands? Isn't one soul as valuable as many? Whoever she may be, she is not insignificant. I won't do it. I won't condemn her to a dreadful fate."

An immense relief waved through Dez's body. Melting into Ivan's strength seemed the easiest thing. He was a good man after all.

Now, how to convince him of that?

"I'll have to find another way to get back the grimoire. I'll…have to stand and fight alongside my father. Perhaps together we can hold back the vampires. If only we can bring about a pause, a moment for both sides to stand back and catch a breath. To think."

"This war is worldwide, Ivan. It is an immense task." But she wouldn't call it impossible.

She had no right to dissuade him from such a valiant goal. Dez had sent many a knight off to battle with her favor as promise. The champion needed that support—that hope. "I will join you in the fight. I…"

She hadn't opportunity to think further on the decision to reverse the spell.

"Do you remember the spell?"

"No." She clung to her lover, curling up her legs and snuggling even closer. "Sorry. I need the grimoire. There are no words, but I need the intonations to get it right."

"But you'll do it if we get it back? Reverse the spell?"

"For the first time in my long life, I'm not sure what to think, what decision is right. Or rather, which decision is better, because neither can ever truly be right. You won't sacrifice one soul for thousands. So why should I reverse a spell that could result in the deaths of many to save many more tens of thousands?"

Ivan's sigh echoed her indecision.

"I will abide by whatever the council rules," she decided. "Perhaps this dilemma shouldn't be left to one person."

"I'll be there for you, Dez. I swear it. No more rushing off or leaving you to fend for yourself against vampires."

"It was stupid of me to leave you, especially in your condition."

"I've healed. I always do."

"Do you?" She pressed her ear to his chest. His heart pounded soft, steadily. That night in Ivan's bedroom she had seen things she had never seen before. Hideous torture. Her lover suffering. It hurt to remember it. "What of your heart? Does that ever heal? Ivan, I may have many centuries of living to claim over your few decades, but you…you've survived tremendous opposition. How do you do it? What keeps you standing?"

"My parents instilled extreme stubbornness in me. I guess I have them to thank. Not that it's been easy. And now, I have a reason to want to go on. You. Is that…okay?"

"You and I?" The warmth of him seeped into her flesh. Dez tilted up her head and kissed him under the chin. In his eyes she saw the strife, the utter desolation he must suffer daily. "Yes. I love you for saving one soul before thousands. And I love you for wanting to save the thousands as well."

* * *

Sex with a vampire? Never in eight centuries had Dez given the notion credence. Her idea of the vampire presented as unruly, easily aggravated and untamed. And while every girl entertains dreams of a bad boy, at some point in her life, Dez had had her share.

So why was she crawling over the incredibly toned body of a half-breed vampire, dragging her tongue up his abs and aiming for his nipple?

Because she wanted to. Because she'd couldn't *not* touch him.

"Would it spoil the mood to ask how many lovers you've had?" Ivan groaned, as Dez flicked her tongue over the hard jewel of his nipple. "Just curious. You've been on this earth for so long."

"Too many to count," she said, and nipped his flesh in punishment for the question. "You like it rough, eh?"

"I get enough rough stuff with my night job."

Yes, his night job. Sun beamed across the pale white floorboards. The high noon bells rang in Willow Cove. She was safe.

"You know, history tells us the missionary position was most oft used in medieval times," she said. "Only now are humans becoming more exploratory in sexual positions. But I know for a fact quite a few different positions were very popular in my younger years."

"Is that so? You going to demonstrate?"

"Slide those pillows up under my stomach and let me show you."

The man took orders well. Dez, rolling to her stomach and adjusting the pillows before her knees, slid her arms along the sheets and curled her fingers over the end of the bed.

"I love you this way," Ivan murmured, as he moved behind her and gripped her hips.

"I like it when a man takes control."

"I could never control you, Dez. But I will master you." He slid inside her completely.

Mastered by her vampire lover? Oh yes.

They woke to spy the moon, full and white, at the corner of the bedroom window. Sex all afternoon had lured them both to a drowsy, blissful slumber.

Ivan sat at the end of the bed. His short black hair spiked every which way. The powerful muscles strapping his back flexed as he leaned forward. Creases from the sheets had carved lines into the back of one of his arms.

Dez crawled across the bed and pressed her breasts against his cool back, and wrapped her legs around his hips. "Master," she whispered.

"Only in bed, all right?"

"Of course. We both know I rule when it comes to magic. I could have you on your knees with a mere flick of my fingers."

He pressed his head back aside her cheek. "I'd like that."

Tracing the dark design that stretched from the bottom of his skull down to midback, Dez drew away when he flinched.

"Sorry. This tattoo, it's sensitive?"

"It's not a tattoo," he said, his tone strangely weary. "You know vamps can't keep the ink in their flesh because we heal so fast."

"That's what I've always believed, until I saw this. Then what is it?"

"I call it my shadow. It's Himself's mark. It digs deep, Dez, way into my gut. I can feel Himself before he even arrives in the nerve-scraping tingle that vibrates from that damned mark."

"Like a witch mark, then. Except this one is for real."

"What do you mean?"

"In medieval times, suspected witches were tormented and

very often murdered if it could be proven they bore a witch mark. It was a sure sign she was in league with the devil. Most often the woman was not a witch, yet she believed so strongly that she convinced herself she had powers. And the marks were moles or birthmarks that colored the skin like port wine. Such a pity to watch the senseless murders."

"Well, I *am* in league with the devil. Should the inquisition come sniffing at my heels, let them have at me. I'll give them a fight they won't see coming."

He drew her hands up and kissed her thumbs. One, then the other. "I have to leave."

"The coercion?"

"Yes. It prickles along the shadow. I think I've another task waiting for me. But whoever is waiting to deliver it can't enter your warded home. I'm sorry."

"You shouldn't piss off your master. Go. But not without one more kiss."

Ivan turned in Dez's arms and they spilled across the bed. The pale pink sheets billowed in the wake of their motions. Ivan kissed her and pressed his tongue over her lips and into her mouth. And he moved his cock inside her. Easy, slow, finding a lazy rhythm that pleased them both.

"Would it be silly to say you fit like you were made for me?" Dez whispered.

"No more silly than me confessing I never want to make love to another woman again. I want you forever, Dez. Is that asking too much?"

"You've a lot of centuries ahead of you."

"I live in the moment. Yesterday is gone. Who knows what tomorrow will bring?"

"Tomorrow will bring another tomorrow, and yet another." She hadn't forgotten her own whispered confession that she loved this man—made just moments after Himself had ripped Ivan's insides out.

Had she meant it? What of her staunch insistence they not begin a relationship?

"I love you so much."

This is what you've craved, Dez. Connection. Not the group of chatty hens who only want you in their club for what you can give them. You want this. *And you should do as he insists: love for the moment, not the future.*

"I love you, too, Ivan."

And he came inside her, his body tremoring and his arms shaking as he supported himself above her. Tension tightened his face, and then he gasped and surrendered to it all. His entire face smiled. Those whiskey eyes danced.

This expression Dez could look at every morning, night, and every moment in between. It felt right. She loved this vampire, who was also a witch. Who was also chained to Himself.

A kiss to the top of her breast and he delivered a teasing nip in its wake. "Duty calls."

"Off to pummel the evil and demented?"

Ivan rose from the bed and searched for his pants. "You know it." He flashed a fang her way. "Besides, the scent of you is so strong."

The glint of that sharp fang intrigued her, but Dez knew well to remain where she sat and not invite his hunger any more than her mere existence already did.

"Could you do me a favor while I'm gone?" he asked.

"Anything."

He zipped his jeans and tugged a shirt over his head. A sheen of perspiration made the thin blue sweater cling in all the right places. No amount of fabric could disguise those steel-hard abs.

"Call my mother and ask her to address the council regarding reversing the spell. I want to have their permission so we're ready when I get the grimoire back. I'll leave my phone here." He set a cell phone on the nightstand. "It's pretty simple to figure how to use."

"You think I don't know how to use a cell phone?"

"I'm guessing not."

Dez curled up her legs and toyed with the edge of a sheet. She hadn't told him everything. He didn't need to know it all. Already she felt less, weaker, drained. Himself had to be tampering with her binding agreement in the grimoire.

If Ivan got the book back then she needn't fear for her life. But she didn't want to give him an excuse to go up against his master—no one could win against Himself.

"I don't know how you intend to get the *Grande Grimoire*, but if you do, and the council agrees, I'm your witch."

"It'll happen." He leaned in and kissed her shoulder. A tweak to her nipple, and he bid her good-night and headed upstairs to the attic to make his exit.

"Oh, Ivan Drake." Dez snuggled back into the pillows. "Had you been alive in medieval times, I do believe you would have been a dragon slayer."

Or perhaps a true prince riding rescue to the princess sleeping behind the thorns.

And because she loved Ivan, Dez was torn inside. She needed to be truthful with him, to surrender to her one regret. To step forward and take responsibility.

In doing so, Ivan could get back his soul.

Instead of heading directly to the shower, she eyed the cell phone that Ivan had left on her bedside table. Call his mother?

Dez knew Ravin Crosse. And Ravin knew things about her. Maybe. Dez had never been sure how much the slayer had known about her dalliances late in the nineteenth century.

Surely, if she did know, she would have warned Ivan against her previously.

"I can't fool the world any longer."

Decided, Dez grabbed the phone. She hated technology, but the device was pretty enough to entice her to play around with it a bit. It prolonged the inevitable, her nervous touching of the screen, and sliding around the pictures and viewing various screens.

She had merely to touch the icons to operate the thing. "Hardware for idiots. My need to never get a computer must have been waiting for one of these things to be invented. Not bad."

The call list popped up. The first two entries were Nikolaus Drake and Ravin Crosse.

"She had only meant to help." Ravin had been insistent Dez was making a mistake all those decades ago. "And now I'm dating her son. What a strange world this is. Ravin Crosse was the last witch I ever expected would settle down and have a family."

Diving into this relationship with Ivan would make Dez a part of Ravin's family.

To be part of family.

"That's what I've wanted. The connection. I've just been approaching it the wrong way. Family."

It could happen.

If she avoided her truths.

"No. I've got to come clean. Ivan has only given me truths. It's time I gave him mine."

She tapped the entry for Ravin Crosse.

Ravin recognized Dez's voice immediately, but her tone was guarded. Fine with Dez. She didn't want to have a girlfriend chat, because they'd never been girlfriends. And until Ivan told his mom about his new lover, then she wasn't going to spring that salacious bit on her out of the blue.

She relayed Ivan's request that the council approve the spell reversal, which Ravin was eager to do. Yet, Dez wasn't prepared for Ravin's insistent question.

"Have you told him your secret?"

Ravin knew. As all witches did.

"About the grimoire, yes," Dez answered.

"No, the other. He needs to know."

Yes, that other secret. The one Ravin had tried to stop from happening. But no, she could not have known the details. The truth of Dez's regrets.

"He's my son, Desideriel. I won't suffer the witch who deceives him."

And Dez remembered the first time she had come across Ravin, bent over in an alleyway, long skirts tattered, and legs spread as she leaned over something. Dez had smelled the blood on the air, and she'd heard the cry of the vampire as blood droplets had splattered his face. It had been startling to Dez, at the time, how quickly a vampire could be reduced to ash.

A potent force, Ravin Crosse.

"You're right. I won't lie to your son," Dez said. "Not any longer."

She set down the phone. A shiver traced her arms and neck. Coiling in on herself, she rocked forward and pressed her palms and forehead to the bed. Fingers curling, she dug into the sheets.

No more unspoken truths. You have to help him get his soul back.

And there was only one way to do that.

"Remove my protection. And stop hiding my past."

Dez raced downstairs and out to the porch. She kept a garden spade out there. The plastic-handled shovel leaned against the wall. She grabbed it, and hurried down and around the corner of the house.

* * *

"'Bout time," the clacking bone figure said as Ivan landed on the beach about five miles north of Dez's house. "I've been waiting since nightfall."

"Busy." Ivan walked past the skeletal creature he knew common mortals could not see, for it was a death-wraith, a collector of souls. "What's the task?"

"I'm supposed to remind you of the hunt for Himself's bride."

"It's on my list," Ivan said. He toed a pearlescent shell half stuck in the sand. "That all?"

Ivan's body suddenly flew through the air and landed on a rocky outcrop. Arms flung back with the force, Ivan felt his shoulder bones dislocate. Did none of the devil's minions ever do things half-assed? Just a little slack on the pain, once in a while, was all he asked.

"Chill." He snapped his shoulder forward, fitting it into the socket, and wincing at the searing pain. Yeah, it hurt like hell, but what didn't in his pitiful life? "I said I'm on the case."

"This is a bit more urgent than you understand. Himself told me I should give you a clue, since it appears you're far more stupid than a common corpse imp."

To be compared to the zombielike corpse imp twanged at his pride.

Ivan spat into the face of the wraith. Didn't have any effect; his spittle went right through the hole in the skull and exited out the back.

"If Himself wants results, he's going to have to cough up her name."

"I have no name. But I have a location."

"That'll work. So where am I off to?"

The wraith pointed a bony finger up the embankment, toward the village that glimmered like a constellation fallen to ground.

"What? In Willow Cove somewhere?"

The wraith slammed Ivan against the stone. "The witch, idiot! The witch is Himself's bride!"

"No, she's…" *Not* got stuck in his throat.

Himself and…Dez?

She was one thing only I desired. My desiderata.

Desired things.

Everyone desired. Every…thing. Every demon.

Falling to his knees, Ivan shouted as a means to release the sudden throbbing pain that didn't twist his limbs so much as annihilate his heart.

Chapter 20

Huffing breaths, accompanied by rhythmic soughing beats directed Ivan's attention from the roof to around the side of Dez's house. He walked wide, to avoid the writhing rose thorns.

A glimpse of pale fabric caught the moonlight. She wore see-through pink silk, yet it clung to her body with dirt at her legs and hips. Her face was smeared with more dirt. She didn't see him come up behind her.

"Dez!"

He made to grab her away from whatever it was she seemed so intent on digging, but a whip-fast rose vine snaked up and snapped at him.

"Ouch! Dez! What are you doing?"

"What I should have done the moment I discovered Himself's wicked game."

Deep in the hole, the tip of the shovel clanked against something. Dez dropped the shovel and fell to her knees. She began digging in the thick dirt desperately. Wildness cloaked her eyes. She grunted as she pried and heaved at whatever was stuck in the ground.

Much as he'd been raging, Ivan pushed back the hurt and deception. Something was terribly wrong with Dez. He'd left her in bed, soft and smiling and with promises of love. And though the world had been dumped on its skull since then, he couldn't care about his own troubles right now.

"Talk to me." This time he grit his teeth and bore the pain of the thorns that coiled about his ankle. He bracketed Dez about the arms and lifted her up from the hole.

She kicked and struggled.

The thorns dug in deeply, tightening about his ankles.

"I can save your soul," she shouted. "Let me go!"

A shock of electricity zapped Ivan in the chest. It flexed out his arms, making him drop Dez, and sent him soaring through the air. The vines ripped from their roots as he landed roughly on the ground. She'd zapped him with some kind of earth magic.

Ivan's fangs descended and he snarled. "Not in the mood for silly magic tonight, witch."

With little effort, he sent a blast of wind forceful enough to topple Dez from her feet, but not strong enough to hurt her.

She wanted to save his soul? Digging in the dirt wasn't going to make that happen. Hell wasn't underground, or deep within the depths, as some people believed. Hell was manifested right here on earth. Himself was everywhere, always.

The shovel soared through the air, missing Ivan's head by a fraction of an inch. Did she mean to harm him? What was wrong with the woman?

Scrambling across the grass, Ivan gripped the shovel. A jab at the ground severed a vicious vine wrapped about his ankle.

Dez brought up something from the hole. A dark, round object crusted with dirt.

Ivan plunged the shovel down on another twisting vine. But he didn't see the vine stab out from the rooftop. He took a thorn to the cheek. It burned through flesh and scraped his gums.

Dez hurled the object toward the cliff. It landed with a thud and broke apart.

"One down, nine more to go," she said, and wrenched the shovel from Ivan's grasp.

He gripped her hair and tugged her to him. Using the force of their connection, he stumbled backward, struggling with the vine that now coiled about his neck while holding Dez less than gently, but securely.

To rip away the vine tore the thorns through his neck. Ivan growled and spat his own blood. He landed on the ground, a wriggling woman fighting him. An army of vines snaked and literally hissed but inches from his heels.

He dragged Dez toward the cliff, putting a safe distance between him and the maniacal plants. Pinning her to the ground, palms to her shoulders and knees to her thighs, he swallowed down his own blood and breathed through his nose.

The healing was slow, and Dez's face was spattered with his blood, but Ivan used the long seconds to steady his anger, bring down his urgency to attack with fangs—for wouldn't the blood make everything better?

"Dez, this isn't right. You've gone insane. Stop struggling. I don't want to hurt you. Please…I don't know how to make it better."

Her struggles had begun to lessen. Tears spilled across her cheeks, plowing pale trails through her dirt-smeared skin.

"I can do it," she murmured.

"Do what, Dez? What was that thing you dug up?"

"A ward against Himself. Oh, Ivan. I'm so sorry."

What he'd just learned. Were they both thinking the same things?

Why hadn't she said anything before?

The pink fabric slid away from one breast. He wanted to embrace her, pick her up and carry her to bed and slide inside her, closing his eyes to her betrayal.

His whole life had been a betrayal. He should expect nothing less. But he wanted so much more from Dez.

"I was given a task." The slither of silk and dirt on skin filled his senses. "Or rather a reminder. Himself is quite eager to have his bride returned to his clutches. It is…all that he desires."

How it cleaved his heart to say those words. *She is mine!*

And yet, Dez had never truly been his. He hadn't mastered her. They had only been lost in the freedom away from reality for a few hours in bed.

A very small voice said, "I know."

"Do you?"

Rolling to her side, she closed her eyes. Did she ponder her secret? Or summon an escape?

The urge to use his magic, to make her look at him, to force up the truth from her heart grew strong.

Do not. She is fragile.

"Dez, I need you to look at me. To hear you speak the truth."

With a wave of his hand, he drew the silk up over her breast. "You said you loved me."

"I do." The slightest warble at the end of her statement. She knew he knew. "You want to find the bride? Will that prove my love to you if I give you her name?"

"You know it?"

She pushed up to sit, yet did not turn to face him, her eyes desperate to avoid his gaze. Shards of what Ivan now recognized to be pottery, thick with dirt, littered the cliff edge. A devil pot. He remembered Dez had mentioned she had surrounded her house with them. Bespelled with ancient magic, they could keep back Himself.

Ivan began to direct her chin up with a touch of magic, but he paused. No, this must only be truth. Nothing about this conversation—*that he didn't want to have*—must be forced or conjured with magic.

"You know her name," she said, so softly he felt the surrender in her voice. It tasted like an ache at the back of his throat, like nothing he would ever purposefully seek. "I should have guessed you'd find out."

"Why, Dez? Why didn't you tell me?"

She put up a palm, a barricade between the two of them. Still not looking at him. Long lashes fluttered as her vision flickered from the cliff, to the pot, then out across the ocean. Afraid, or perhaps unwilling to face her truths?

"Please know I never kept the truth from you to deceive. It is a secret I had hoped to take to my grave. It is something…I cannot speak."

So it was true. So very true.

Ivan's heart pulsed. Once. Twice. Could she hear it break? Did she notice his falter? That he winced as the heartbreak tore wide his insides? Could she be aware that this might be the greatest pain he had ever experienced? Yes, even worse than having his insides ripped from his body.

Not five feet away, the rose vines stirred, stretching toward him, but fell short of reaching him with their deadly thorns.

Logically he knew Dez must have been lured into Himself's clutches. It was how the Old Lad operated. With deception and temptation no mortal or immortal could refuse. He could hardly remain angry with her.

But to have fallen *in love* with the very devil Himself?

He *could* get his head around that. The bastard must have appeared to Dez as her greatest temptation. Seduction was easy for one so skilled in manipulation of desire and want.

But surely, sooner or later, Dez had to have learned the truth of her suitor?

"Shall I tell you my horrid tale?" came her pale voice, a haunting moth fluttering so close to the cliff. "Then you can decide whether or not I am still worthy of your love."

Ivan spun to face her. She was worthy.

Do you really believe that?

And who was he, the devil's fixer, to pass judgment?

"You didn't want a soul to know," he said. "You should keep it private, as you've wanted it to be. I…have to learn to accept this. And figure how to get around it now. I can't bring you to Himself. I will not."

"Why not? How can you love me now you know I once loved Himself?"

She admitted her love for the prince of darkness. His master. Ivan swallowed.

"Doesn't the truth turn your stomach? Your task should be easy to shuck off now. Deliver me to your master and be done with me. It is just. If you do it, Ivan, your soul can be yours. And the *Grande Grimoire*—"

"Would mean nothing without you to reverse the spell. He's got that one figured out, I'll give him that. No, I'll think on this."

"The longer you think, the more spells Himself unravels. Did you hear the news this afternoon? It's happening."

"I won't sacrifice you, Dez. I…" He couldn't say it. Not now. *I love you.*

Did he? *Could* he?

"If you don't bring me to Himself, I'll call him here and step up on my own," she said. "As soon as all the pots are dug up, it will be possible." She reached for the shovel.

"No!"

Ivan threw a containment spell at her. It wrapped her arms close to her body and closed her mouth so she could not speak. The pink silk tightened about her flesh, transforming her to a glamorous, sodden mummy. She was not in pain, but he needed time. Time to think. To figure things out.

She could not do magic when bound—or so he hoped.

"I'm sorry. It's necessary to keep you from doing something irrational. I won't have you bringing Himself here until I've thought things through. You're not going to sacrifice yourself, that's all there's to it."

Suppressed mumbles pleaded with him.

"I'm taking you inside. You need a shower, and I need to think."

Within minutes, he'd cleared the roof, and laid Dez across her bed. Caressing her face with both hands, he leaned before her. Oh, the sweetness of her! Apricots. He could taste them on his tongue.

Ivan paced away from the temptation. "There's a way around this, I'm sure of it."

She shook her head negatively.

"Are you angry at me for this spell?"

Another negative nod.

"Will you promise you won't call Himself if I release you from it?"

She nodded yes.

Ivan kissed her, and swept away the spell. The sudden release of her muscles spilled Dez across the bed. She coiled to a fetal position and rested her head along one outstretched arm. Dirty hair fell over her face.

"I'm sorry," she whispered.

"You've nothing to be sorry for."

"I just wanted to help. If I could have destroyed all the protective wards about my home, I could have opened it to Himself."

Ivan sat on the bed behind her. To spoon up next to her would increase the coercion. He fought it at this moment. At the same time he battled his own innate need to lean over her and pierce a vein. Drink her in. Finally *know* her.

He must not. This was a battle he must win.

How easy would it be to call up Himself and say "Here she is"?

"Let's get you in the shower."

"I don't need your help."

"I know that, but you're not getting rid of me that easily."

"I don't want to get rid of you, Ivan."

"Then promise no more digging?"

She sighed, and wiped at a streak of dirt on her forearm. "I'll grant you a reprieve from the easy return of your soul for a while. But just a while."

She sat up and suddenly gripped him by the head. "I was alone. Had been for centuries," Dez said softly. "He…seduced me. I had no idea."

"It's your secret, Dez, keep it."

"I can't speak it, but— You've no soul to harm. Please, let me fix you in my gaze, and show you what I dare not speak."

With an accepting nod, Ivan allowed Dez to bracket his face with her palms. Briefly he closed his eyes. It would be painful for her, he knew. But despite his reluctance, his concern for her…he wanted to know.

Opening his eyes, he stared, unblinking, into Dez's wide, tearing eyes. The fix began instantaneously, so skillfully she worked the stare. Within two heartbeats, his pulse synchronized with hers. His flesh warmed and he began to perspire.

And he saw what she wished him to see in his mind…

* * *

The iron structure was not complete, but he recognized it. The Eiffel Tower, beginning its thrust into the gray winter Paris sky.

Laughter bubbled in Ivan's thoughts. Hers. Dez danced with a partner in top hat and tails. Her face beamed. Suggestive glances were exchanged with the man who twirled her beneath his arm.

Lucien Black. The name formed in Ivan's mind. Now he bowed before Dez, dressed impeccably in narrow black trousers and a tailed greatcoat. The starched shirt beneath spoke of attention to detail and fastidiousness, and his gloves were white silk.

The cane he carried flashed as he swept his arm toward a waiting carriage. It was capped with a silver skull. Two inlaid diamonds glinted in the eye sockets. Dez's eyes sparkled with secretive greed.

Dez showed Monsieur Black to the door of her Victorian home. He bent to smell the red roses he'd brought as a gift.

"I prefer white," Ivan heard Dez say.

And the color dripped from the red petals as if blood, purling down the stems and sliding over Dez's hands. She didn't startle. She knew the man was a witch, very likely a more powerful witch than she.

"Ghastly." A wicked giggle escaped. She did adore his dark humor.

The kiss made Ivan wince, though he did not blink out of the witch's stare. This kiss claimed Dez. It was a perfect kiss. One to render a woman undone.

He was an enigma. Bewitching her with his sensory

magic, though he did not use magic. But the sweet perfume of him, the utter heat of his presence, and the splendid sensations from his touch mastered her as if a spell.

A woman with black hair who carried silver stakes at the crosses of her corsets pleaded with Dez.

Ivan gasped.

His mother. Ravin Crosse sat at the absinthe café where she met her lover, Dominique. Ravin cautioned Dez against a man she knew little about.

"My heart knows him," Dez replied. And she began to distance herself from Ravin's knowing diatribes.

A coachman presented Dez with a box, tied with black grosgrain ribbon and bejeweled with paste garnets. Inside, a dress of deepest midnight glittered with movement as if black metal kissed by silver.

The dress slid over Dez's head with a whisper. The moment she reached behind to fumble for the tiny diamond buttons, they secured themselves.

A long train ruffled with the silver metallic shimmer should have hampered her steps, but she walked back and forth and twisted quickly. The dress moved as if it anticipated her actions.

"Tonight, he can have me if he wishes."

For Lucien Black spoke all the words she wished to hear. His kisses claimed her soul. And her soul had been wanting for a very long time.

"I have lived too long. I have had happiness, but more so, sadness. I deserve this," she stated. "And I will have love."

* * *

The walls of Lucien's castle were fashioned of chipped obsidian. Flecks of mica glittered within the glossy black stone. A full moon cast gorgeous cold light across the façade. Dez reached to run her palm over the stone. It was strangely warm and smooth as polished rubies.

The inside was as empty and dark as the outside. More of the glittering stone covered the walls of the vast foyer. Elaborate frescoes were carved at the top of the walls, depicting bacchanalian scenes of excess and debauchery. Grotesques glittered in the black stone and cast waggish tongues at her as they sipped nectar from goblets and from between the legs of nubile women.

Dez loved the decadent atmosphere. It soaked into her pores and heightened her emotions. She tugged at the low neckline of the dress, imparting coolness to her heated breasts.

Will you be mine?

The words were not spoken aloud, rather, Dez heard them in her mind. And yes, she answered, she would be his.

Chapter 21

"No, please do not look away."

His lover's voice reached in to pull him up from the drowning. Ivan had slipped under. He could withstand a witch's fix. But could he withstand knowing?

"Please?" she whispered. "I was not entirely beguiled."

He nodded and swallowed, and looked away. And when he returned his stare to her, she did not relent…

As she walked through the dark halls of Monsieur Black's castle, certain truths made themselves evident.

This man, who was a witch, was something more. He could conjure flame and blood and water without thought. Perhaps he possessed a bit of wizard in his arsenal.

There was something so large, monumental even, about Lucien. Perhaps demonic? She would not doubt if he dallied in demonolatry, as some dark witches were wont to do. Did he have ties to the devil Himself?

Dez believed in a dark being who tempted souls and breathed chaos. So many witches had been murdered, burned and hung because mortal idiots and inquisitions believed they were in league with the devil. But it was the devil inside mortal man in which Dez believed most strongly, not a dark horned beast.

He sat upon a throne of shiny steel. Her dark enchanter. The man of her dreams. Shadows crept about him, concealing his face, and the hands resting at the ends of each arm on the throne. A glint of white flashed where eyes should be.

The sight gripped Dez as if barbed arms had burrowed deep into her being and pricked at her nerves all along her spine.

"Lucien?" Dez's heartbeat literally stopped. She pressed a palm over her chest. No, still there, beating desperately, yet muffled, as if frightened to a meek cower.

Fear flooded Ivan's thoughts. It was as though he stood there in Dez's place, looking upon the prince of darkness.

"You have come of your free will, Desideriel Rosaline Merovech?"

Shadows cleaved to every part where she should have seen his flesh.

An odor, acrid and strange, clung to the back of Dez's throat. Brimstone.

Had she made the right choice? To come to this man's home, alone, and with intentions to debauchery? Did she really know him, as Ravin had tried to convince her? What were his intentions? He could be anyone, anything. A lecher. A madman. A murderer.

I want him to be my lover.

She had denied her heart too long. Had she not a right to happiness?

"Such doubts trouble you," Lucien said. He slid forward and took Dez's trembling hands. "But I must be true before I accept your submission."

"My submission?" She tugged her hands from his. "Wh-who are you?"

"I am your greatest desire, Desideriel. And you, you are my desiderata."

The Latin word sounded extravagant and lush—yet its meaning chilled Dez's blood. "I am not a thing to be owned. Perhaps I've made a mistake."

And she turned to walk away—only to stumble into Lucien's arms. He'd moved so quick. His kiss conquered as swiftly.

And in the depths of the luscious claiming, Dez whispered, "Yes, I desire you."

"Will you abandon your life for me? Move from your home into mine?"

"Yes." She found her answer without delay. "You have me, Lucien."

"You will have no other lovers before me?"

"Never."

"No friends, no family, no accomplices of the heart?"

No friends?

"Yes. No."

She couldn't stop saying yes, yet she was too intelligent to be foolish like this. Her heart struggled against logic. Rational thought fought to vanquish desire. And since her heart had been exercised so little over the centuries, the other side of her managed a brief success.

"But love does not require such sacrifice as you suggest, Lucien."

"I must have it that way. Become my bride."

Dez stood in the entrance to her home, the Seine behind her. A shackle had been sprung free from her wrist. And she breathed in.

Away from Lucien's home she mastered her fickle heart with ease.

"I cannot sacrifice my freedom for a husband. No matter how desperately I desire his attentions. I cannot marry Lucien."

And later that evening, Dez watched as the shop where she purchased her magical supplies burned to the ground, along with the keeper and his family.

Each day that followed without her returning to Lucien's castle brought another devastating end to someone she cared for. She knew it was his doing. Himself? The very devil?

She knew in her soul what her heart did not dare to believe.

Dez stood in the open doorway of her home, looking upon the coal black carriage that belonged to Lucien Black.

"You are the devil," she said to the elegant man who stood at the bottom of her stoop. "You have taken everything away from me that I have ever cared for."

"You still have me, my desired one."

She wanted to lunge at him and kick and yell and scream. Instead, Dez's legs bent and she fell into Lucien's arms. She had succumbed to Himself's charms. And she only wanted to feel the safety his arms offered.

* * *

Dez stood before an altar of bone, clutching a silver athame as she awaited the arrival of her diabolic fiancé. So much she wanted love, to be cared for, to be desired.

She would do this. Because she had nothing left.

Tonight she would cut open a vein and offer herself to the dark lord for eternity.

Tonight she would…

Try to fight it.

"I cannot do this."

Her heart had been annihilated by Lucien Black's truths. And yet, Dez felt as though she could never gain the devotion, admiration and desire from another man, ever. And she needed it, she craved it. Her body longed to be worshipped and adored.

It was as though she were halved inside. And the greater half sought love, while the lesser half still clung by its bloody, loosened fingernails to the hope for salvation. To do the right thing. To escape.

His entrance filled her veins and pores and the very air with the sweet stench of brimstone. He approached from behind, and she cautioned herself from turning to look at him. He would not be as she had seen him previously, as the man she had fallen in love with.

Can you love a creature? The very devil Himself?

No, she could not.

"You already do," a deep voice curdled up Dez's spine. "My bride, I am giddy with the expectation of your sacrifice. You will be mine in blood, soul and body. I shall drink out your soul as my vow to you, Desideriel."

Faltering, Dez stepped forward. She dropped the athame. It clinked upon the obsidian floor. Falling to her knees, she then shuffled backward, trying to get away, to distance herself from the sight of evil, of chaos. Of temptation gone bad.

Horns and black muscled flesh and distorted joints and red eyes. That was what she took in, processed, as the scream clawed up from her mouth. And for the first time, her eyes were opened. Logic defeated heart.

"I will not!" Dez cried. "I refuse!"

"Bitch!" And he slapped her.

Her body soared across the room and landed against a wall. Bones broke and the blood scent crept out from cuts.

Every day following, Himself returned to the altar room. And every day, Dez, weakened without food or drink, shouted an effusive "No" at him. The passive torture continued for a fortnight. Dez could no longer shout, she could barely breathe, but she would never change her answer.

"No."

And the world fell away from her. The walls of the castle began to crumble. The darkness shattered and the gray desolate night showered her with cold reality.

It was all gone. Lucien Black. The altar. The castle. Her hopes and desires.

Dez lay in the middle of a snowy field, bleeding and near death.

But she was happy.

Ivan dropped his head to his chest and sucked in a breath.

Dez had released the fix. His eyes watered as if walking through smoke. His body trembled—with knowledge.

"So now you know." Dez settled onto the bed, putting up her legs and leaning into the pillow. Still dirty from digging in the mud, she swiped at a smear on her cheek. "I went willingly to Himself, and I went against my will. Even after your mother's warning. But it was love. For a moment. Until my eyes were opened. I'm so ashamed.

"I was taken in by a farmer and nursed back to health. Later, I returned to my home, which still stood, to my surprise, and I began to study diabology and taught myself to craft the most powerful spells against Himself. My devotion was to keeping that bastard out of my life. Forever.

"All I had wanted, he offered. Companionship. Connection. Love. He was right when he told you it was my only weakness. What a pitiful woman I am to be so easily devastated by emotion. I...I followed my heart."

They exchanged flickering glances. Both knew that Dez had followed her heart once again. Yet did she feel the same devastation this time around?

"We must never regret what we don't understand." Ivan slid up close and kissed her. "You were not of the right mind. He bewitched you. He is the master of bewitchments and temptations and seductions. You could not have won—and yet you did. You survived, Dez. I'm so proud of you."

"Don't say that. I was a ridiculous fool led about by promises of sex."

"You were strong. So strong."

With one sweet kiss Dez felt the last century of angst slip away. So easily Ivan accepted her and all her faults.

"I'm not one to throw stones," he said. "You're talking to a man who every night goes out and does the devil's deeds. If anyone should be fleeing this relationship, it should be you."

"Despite my initial reluctance, I love that you consider it a relationship. I wish it could remain so."

"Why can't it?"

He kissed the indents at her clavicle. Such intention in so simple an act. Dez shivered at the magnitude of his touch. No man had ever claimed her and yet released her in the same act.

"You're not going near Himself. If I have to bespell you to keep you here, I will."

Maybe he wasn't quite ready to release her. "My magic is stronger than yours."

"Dez."

She sighed, not wanting to cause Ivan alarm. "I won't do it. And I don't wish to bring the fixer's wrath upon me. The very last thing I want in this world is to be within smelling distance of Ole Brimstone-Breath again. But I don't see a way around it."

"Forget about my soul. I wouldn't want to contaminate it with my work anyway."

"What about the *Grande Grimoire?* We need it back so I can reverse the spell."

"Are you sure you can't remember it?"

"Ivan, it was so long ago. And it wasn't in words, remember? It was intonation and presence."

"Should be a lot easier to remember than a bunch of Latin mumbo-jumbo. Will you at least give it some thought? See if anything comes to you? What if you do a memory spell? Open your mind to the past?"

"I'd have to go backward through time. Relive so much."

"I wouldn't ask you to relive anything that makes you uncomfortable. Yet, what you've told me—can anything be worse?"

"No. I would put being tortured, put to the question, and almost drowned far below falling in love with Himself. Yes, that was the worst." She clutched his shirt. "I'll do it. For all of us."

Another kiss rendered her blissful. And it was the finest undoing she could wish for. Not even the devil Himself could impart so masterful a kiss and still make her understand they were equals. No man would master Dez's heart. But Ivan could have her trust.

"I need to leave. Promise you won't do anything foolish?"

"I promise, but why do you need to leave?"

"The coercion."

"Then go. I'm going to do the memory spell. I may be out for a while. I'll have to throw up all the wards I can conjure to keep my house safe while I do, so don't be threatened if you're not able to enter."

"How long do you think it will take?"

"A day, maybe two."

"I'm heading off to the council. Preventive magic must be done to stop the mortal world from finding out our secrets. I'll be busy, too."

"Are you sure it's all okay between us?" she wondered. "It doesn't have to be, you know."

"It is." He kissed her forehead. "So long as we're always honest with one another, nothing can keep me from your arms."

"I love you. I'll call you if I learn anything."

He did not offer the admission to love, but Dez did not expect it. Yet her heart ached for it.

Chapter 22

The Gray Council had not been surprised to learn the Protection spell was in danger. And they didn't blame Dez for handing over the *Grande Grimoire* to Himself after Ivan honestly laid everything on the table. That he had fallen in love.

Love, the great forgiver. Everyone on the council had nodded, smiled a little and then got down to discussing tactics. They didn't fear Himself. The Great Tempter merely had plans to sit back and watch the two nations tear each other apart. All focus had to go to the war.

Nikolaus's team would summon recruits to push back the vampire forces against the witches, while the witches had to be cautioned of the imminent possibility of losing all power over vampires. Neither side would like it. But it seemed the only way to begin.

And so the council parted, each with directives and missions and headed to all corners of the world.

Ivan had his own mission. And this one would hurt.

* * *

There was no task for Ivan this evening. Obviously Himself expected him to haul in Dez and present her to him as if a roast upon a platter.

Not going to happen.

Not after everything he had seen in Dez's fix. She had not been innocent, but by the time she'd realized who had been seducing her, her heart had already surrendered.

That bastard would answer for his malicious pursuit of Dez.

But Himself wasn't answering Ivan's call. No matter how much he thought of the Old Lad appearing before him, or imagined himself prostrating before the hideous black devil, no prince of darkness appeared.

"Ignoring me, the old bastard. Lucien Black? He never has been overly creative."

Briefly he wondered at how easily he'd accepted Dez's confession. His lover had once been Himself's—no, he was beyond that. He *would* be beyond that. When finally he faced his master.

Ivan formed a plan to summon his deaf master. He clacked a few skulls together in the shipyard outside of Portland. The imps knew nothing about Himself's whereabouts.

Ivan could be sure Himself was aware of his summons, so he didn't waste too much time rousing further dark minions, because even if they had a clue, diabolic coercion could take that clue from their thoughts like mist creeping out from a graveyard.

He landed in New York City and took a cab to Brooklyn. Ivan knew the name of the bar, and the clientele were strictly nonmortal. She would be there. And she would lure Himself to Ivan.

Paying the cabbie, Ivan stepped toward the rusted iron door guarded by a hulking wraith with glowing eyes. The bouncer didn't ask for Ivan's credentials, and merely moved aside, holding open the door as Ivan walked through.

One good thing about working for Himself, he carried a sort of carte blanche pheromone that alerted others they'd better not mess with him.

One would expect dark and black and dismal for an immortal bar populated with vampires, werewolves, vixens, imps and other assorted creeps. But Crimson was entirely red, even the lighting. Red drinks were served by waitresses with plump red lips who wore barely-there strips of red leather and a dull sheen to their red-pupiled eyes.

Ivan had found a few of his jobs hiding out here. He didn't like the atmosphere. It smelled dank and of stale sex and evil.

Striding through the main room that glittered with fairy dust—yeah, the real stuff—Ivan spied a cheesily costumed maven toward the back of the room. Red vinyl devil horns capped a flow of ridiculously curly black hair. A red devil tail lured the eye up to the sweet ass barely concealed by more red vinyl.

She bent over a pool table—red felt, and yes, the balls were all red—and aced a combination bank shot. Tattoos crawling up her leg grew more defined as Ivan approached. A mermaid with scaled tail snaked across her thigh. The aquamarine mermaid's eyes followed Ivan's approach. And when he got close enough to touch, the tattooed mermaid screamed.

He gripped a hank of the woman's black curls and jerked her back. Scent of blood painted her lips. An inordinately long right fang slid over her lower lip, advertising she was a vampire.

"Bloody Mary," Ivan hissed at her ear.

She didn't struggle, and instead tossed the pool cue onto the table in surrender.

"Good girl. Let's talk over there, shall we?"

She gave a sexy "meow" as he pushed her away from the

table. The hungry eyes of the weres and vampires who had been gathered around the sex-kitten vamp followed them away.

"What do you want, fixer?" she pouted, as they found a dark corner. "I'm in the mood for some sweet pain."

Ivan pushed her shoulder to the wall and leaned in. He didn't like smelling blood on other vampires. It was putrid to him. But he knew it turned on most other vampires. However, there was certainly nothing wrong with the body squeezed into the red vinyl and the full breasts pushed up high and crushed against his chest.

Ivan shook his head to focus. He wasn't here for a trick. And any treats this gal had to offer would hurt.

"I may be the fixer," he said, "but you're his favorite. Thought you might come in handy, Bloody Mary."

He leaned in and licked up from her jaw to the pulsing miniature heart tattooed at her temple. She squirmed, but snaked her hands about his waist. The mermaid on her thigh purred, and Ivan thought he heard the sound of a tail swishing through water.

It didn't take long. And when Ivan's back hit the concrete wall and he felt his shadow crackle to life, he could but smile as he dripped down the wall. Rankled, but happy for it.

"What are you doing, boy?"

All around, the bar rustled with scrambling bodies, eager to flee the brimstone stench of Himself. Greatest temptation? Nah, Himself hadn't taken time to cloak himself this evening. Everyone saw exactly what Ivan saw.

And it was never pretty.

Bloody Mary curled up to Himself and kissed one of the black muscled pectorals that looked like burned flesh stretched over a corpse. "Master."

Himself sent her flying with a sweep of his hand. "Insolent.

"And you." The creature of darkness stomped over to Ivan,

who now slid up the wall to stand firmly. "She's mine. You know that."

Affecting calmness, Ivan shrugged. "You've been ignoring me. I had to get your attention somehow."

He was aware he'd not knelt to give Himself the respect due. His shadow pulsed with stinging needles, attempting to coerce him to his knees. But Ivan maintained his stance, even while his shoulder blades cringed and every nerve in his jaw screamed.

"You have it." Himself glanced aside. Bloody Mary crawled along a wall. Her leg looked broken. She'd heal. "Speak your piece, fixer."

"Why don't *you* get your bride? You know her name. You know where she lives. This little game you're playing with me doesn't make sense. If it's the book you wanted, I don't understand how she plays into your ultimate goal."

Himself chuckled, low and from his gut. "Desideriel Rosaline Merovech, illegitimate daughter of the Merovingian king Dagobert III, is the one thing in this infernal realm of mortality I cannot touch. She has mastered spells of diabology against me. Repelling me is an art she has taken to extremes. I couldn't have snatched her out from her bedroom if I wanted."

"You. Powerless against a mere witch?"

A talon strafed Ivan's cheek. He felt it strike his teeth, so clean the cut.

Bloody Mary purred at the scent of blood and began to crawl along the base of the pool table toward them. The mermaid now splashed on her opposite thigh in a pool of red water.

"Better," Himself began, "to have the one man who loves her do it for me, wouldn't you say?"

Of course he would know Ivan's feelings toward Dez.

"Besides, it is the price you must pay for your soul."

"I don't need a soul," Ivan snapped. "It is not something you can dangle before me like diamonds or blood. I refuse to bring Dez to you."

Ivan's body slammed face-first against the wall. A slice of talon stripped open his suit and shirt to reveal his bare back. Icy prickles moved along the shadow. Himself breathed upon his flesh.

Bracing himself for insurmountable pain, Ivan waited. But the numbing red poison of Himself's shadow did not pierce deep. It did not pierce at all. Instead, something strange happened.

Held there by an invisible force, Ivan could but close his eyes and experience as an outline of warmth traced the design of his shadow. It prickled sweetly. It glowed. Spreading. Swelling. It was unlike anything he had ever known before.

Sunshine upon a womb, glistening in a newborn's eyes. Innocence unmarred by doubt, fear or devastation.

Exquisite bliss. A wondrous kiss of light and goodness.

Ivan let out a gasp. Hot tears rolled down his cheeks. He felt it. It was…it had to be—

His soul.

And then blackness ripped away the light. Ivan collapsed against the wall, landing on his ass and clutching his hands across his shoulders.

"Bring it back," he moaned. "I want to feel it again!"

"That was just a taste," Himself growled. "Now. Go. Bring her to me, and you shall have back your soul."

Chapter 23

The clatter above in the attic didn't surprise Dez. She capped a bottle of peppermint oil she'd opened to reignite her exhausted senses, and tugged up her silk robe to avert a shiver of expectation.

Twenty-four hours had passed. She only completed the memory spell two hours earlier. To no avail. She needed to see the written Protection spell. Her mind simply would not put forth a vivid recollection.

That cautioned her, for perhaps there was a reason for such difficulty. She now struggled with whether it would really serve to end the war. But she pushed worries aside now that *he* was in her home.

It was as if he had entered her. Each step Ivan took down the creaky wood stairs heightened her desire. Dez pressed both hands to the marble butcher block over which she concocted her perfumes. Peppermint stabbed at her senses, prickling up into her skull. A medley of wormwood and cardamom and anise swirled a heady mixture in the air.

A danceable tune played softly on the radio. Another means for Dez to rise up from the intense concentration of the spell and to insinuate herself back in the real world.

Ivan's arms fitted about her waist. Wide, firm hands crossed her belly and pressed her back against his body. Her derriere snugged his cock, hard and vital. Hot breath whispered at her nape. He trailed a tongue-dashing kiss down the column of her neck.

His hand slid inside her robe and the heat of his palm seared an indelible burn up her torso. He cupped her breast, squeezed the nipple. His moan pleased her.

"Cloves?" he murmured at her ear. A nip followed. And a zip. He released his pants and shoved aside her robe.

"Cardamom," she corrected. "Sharply sweet."

Sliding forward across the marble table on her arms, Dez spread her legs for her lover. First he slipped an exploring finger inside her. He knew exactly where to go, there, at her clit, which was swollen and wanting.

"Peppermint," he moaned. One of his hands slapped onto the marble to steady himself. "It clears my head."

Dez reached around and captured his cock. "Sex and the scents surrounding us. What a heady blend."

He followed her direction, and slid up inside her, pressing her body forward. Her breasts crushed against the cold marble. They captured the rhythm of the music. He seized her hips and began to plunge deeply. Endlessly. Effortlessly.

"Must have you," he cried. "All of you. Ever after."

A vial of capped neroli oil toppled and rolled off the table. The thin glass cracked open. The dark, intense sweetness spilled into the room and Dez inhaled deeply as she climaxed. Neroli sex. She would never forget that scent.

The force of Ivan's climax pushed her hard against the marble. Her sweat-shimmered breasts warmed the hard stone. Ivan grasped her by the shoulder and drew her up and around into an urgent kiss. He lifted her to sit upon the table. She wrapped her legs about his hips. The slick remnants of his climax buttered her stomach and his.

"I've fallen so hard for you," he murmured into her mouth as he kissed her, "that I don't know how to surface. Don't want to."

Tucking her head against the heat-torqued muscle along his neck, Dez placed a palm over his heart. It beat furiously, racing the music. The scent of him, of the room, made her giddy.

"There's a dance in the town's park tonight," he said. "The big end-of-summer to-do. I want to dance with you beneath the stars, Dez."

"Something a little different than the dance we just did?"

"A little." He kissed her on the nose. Though his eyes were dark, flat, Dez fancied if he had a soul they would glitter madly. "So what do you say?"

"A dance with my dark lover beneath the harvest moon? Sounds lovely. Give me a bit to shower and change?"

He caught her fingers as she slid away, and tugged her to his chest. "Don't shower," he said. "I love the smell of our sex."

"All right. Then give me five minutes."

Dez wore some kind of black lace dress that hugged her body and slipped down her shoulders in a wide neckline that revealed the tops of her breasts. The skirt, long and slender, trailed across the ground behind her as they danced. She looked like a lace doll, something Ivan should be careful not to break.

But nothing was unbreakable. Including his heart.

Because right now, as he held Dez close and could feel her

heart beating against his, Ivan felt the pieces of his heart clatter against one another. Which was how it must remain. Broken.

He tucked his head down into her hair and closed his eyes so he couldn't see the world or know if anyone else dancing around them could see his pain.

He had felt his soul. And he wanted it back.

"Another?" Dez asked. A smile exposed a sweet, regretful wisdom of ages. "Or should we sit the next one out?"

He pulled her hand to his mouth and kissed the knuckles. "Let's walk. Get away from the world for a while."

"I want to look at the ocean with the moonlight on it," Ivan said.

Hand in hand, they strolled the wooden plank sidewalk that fronted the stores along the bay. They had to cross the street two blocks up to pass her shop and take the gangwalk down to the beach. In no hurry.

But Dez sensed the darkest, most devastating conclusion waited when they reached the beach.

He's taking me to Himself.

She knew. Instinct had never screamed more loudly. She walked hand in hand with the fixer. It was night. He was likely deep in coercion.

Ivan's sigh rippled across her shoulders like a bitter winter chill.

"I've never met another woman so strong as you," he said.

Dez looked to the side. Tears threatened, momentarily. She could do this. She *would* do this. Ivan had not even three decades to her twelve centuries. He deserved to know the world with a soul. And if she could give that to him, then so be it.

"So you've not been around a lot of women, then?" she tried on a light tone. "If I am the only strong one you've met? And I've not even a muscle when compared to your mother."

"My mother is a softy at heart." He swept her into his arms. Yes, it was like gliding into a Fred and Ginger move. And it ended with a long, warm kiss.

He overwhelmed her in stature and could break her with a twist, but the gentleness of his touch made Dez want to cry. And for the second time she found herself fighting tears.

What was with her tonight? She was strong, as Ivan had said. She was simply doing what she had to do.

But in doing so, she would never again see her lover.

Sniffing back a tear, Dez thought Ivan was going to say something, when he released her and stepped away into the street. Old-fashioned black iron streetlights glowed dimly as the city argued against using too much electricity. The trees, strung with Christmas lights, were lit, though only until after the dance. Here it was quiet, save a distant strum of violin and the occasional thump of timpani.

They had the street to themselves. And Ivan gave no caution for standing in the middle of it. Standing at the edge of the curb, one foot dangling over the curved edge while she observed, Dez nestled her hands to hips and tilted her head.

Ivan walked with closed eyes, hands lifting as if to hold a load, but his muscles were loose, his posture so…open. Fascinated, she didn't say a word.

"Do you feel them?" he whispered, and though he stood some thirty feet away, his voice carried through the clear evening darkness.

"Them?"

He turned to her and spread out his arms as if to encompass the world and tilted back his head.

Whatever he felt, it looked blissful. But then Dez wondered if it were Himself's minions come to aid the fixer in his evil task.

A shiver curled across her shoulders—yet in the next instant a sweltering warmth moved over her flesh. Calming, reassuring.

This is right. She did not smell brimstone or sense imminent danger.

"What do you feel, Ivan?" she asked, as he stepped down the curb.

Right there, ten feet from her and at the edge of a white line painted to mark the road, Ivan fell to his knees. Surrendering. Holding up his arms to embrace…

"The angels," he said. "I can feel them. Always, when I walk into their presence they make themselves known."

He looked to Dez. Tears glittered in his eyes. She checked her breathing and caught a gasp.

"But I've never seen them. I've no right." He clutched his arms across his chest and swayed forward. Something struggled within, for he gritted his jaw and shook his head violently. "I cannot do this! I won't do this!"

Dez rushed to him. Kneeling, she glanced back to assure none of the townspeople paid them mind. Ivan clutched her hands and held her curled fingers to his mouth.

"What won't you do?" she asked. "Take me to Himself?"

He shook his head furiously.

"You have to, Ivan. It's the only way you'll ever have your soul. You want to see the angels? That is your hope, Ivan. So get up and finish this. I knew when you came to my house tonight what you intended."

"I'm so sorry. This isn't right." He stood and strode away from her, but stopped and again put out his arms. Were they pushing him away? Warning him against dire actions? "They torment me with their presence, the angels. I want to know goodness, and it is so close."

"You can have it by bringing Himself's bride to the docks."

"Never." His refusal ground out harshly. The planes of his face tightened. "I would never sacrifice you, Dez."

"Then I'll do it myself."

Scooping up her skirts and kicking off her heels, Dez took off in a run. She quickly crossed the rough tarmac and landed on the creaking plank sidewalk, only to be swung up and into the air. Ivan swept her into his arms.

"No!" She pushed against his chest and arms. He remained implacable. "I'm doing this, Ivan, and you can't stop me."

Summoning an exhale she blew, and with it, infused the power of the winds.

Ivan released her and was pushed up against the facade of her perfume shop. "All the magic in the world is not going to stop me from protecting you, witch."

Thrusting out an arm, he put out some kind of magic Dez couldn't feel or sense. So she continued on her course, and ran smack into the invisible wall ten feet beyond where Ivan stood. Her palms flattened in the air before her, and no matter how hard she pushed she could not repulse his magic.

So she tapped into her violet energy and called down the rains. And the invisible wall washed away before her. But it also turned into a storm because she wasn't guarding her emotions, and her magic always took cue from them.

Instantly soaked, she stumbled on the train of her dress and fell into Ivan's arms.

"Don't fight me on this," he said.

No, she didn't want to. Standing in Ivan's arms she had never felt so right. But she would not steal his choice away.

Tossing back his head moved the soaked hair from his eyes. "If you offer yourself to Himself then I'll have my soul. Great. And terrible."

"Terrible?" Steadying herself against his rain-slick arms, she clung to him. *Just take me away from it all,* she wanted to beg, but she hadn't survived twelve centuries of strife and challenge to walk away now.

"I love you, Dez. If you're not in my life, then it won't be worth living, soul or no soul."

"Don't say stupid things like that. You're in lust. There are plenty of women in this world. You'll get over me."

"I don't want to get over you. And I know you love me. Don't you see?" He kissed her and the rain slickened their contact. Cool droplets slid down Dez's throat and she crushed her mouth hard to Ivan's.

One last kiss. One to remember him by.

And her next thought was to punch him or lay him out somehow. Stride over his fallen frame, and march down the dock to the beach where surely Himself waited to claim her as he had not been able to that cold Parisian winter.

But her body wouldn't move.

"Are you using persuasion on me, vampire?"

"Yes."

She slapped his face, but he took it as if a nuisance.

"You're not leaving my arms, Dez. I don't care if I have to persuade you for the rest of my life. You're mine. I won't hand you over to another."

"Don't do this," she said, and the tears burst free. "You have a chance at freedom."

"Holding you in my arms is all the freedom I need. You see, even now, when the coercion is clawing at my neck and spiking at my nerves, I don't feel it. Because your body next to mine counteracts that wicked evil."

"Impossible. He'll rip you apart if you don't do as commanded. Then who will be alone? Me without you? I don't want to consider that, either. What are we going to do, Ivan?"

"Oh, bother."

The twosome turned to spy a figure walking toward them. A tall, dark man who parted the rain as he neared. But this was no Moses.

"Ivan?"

Had she not been standing in her lover's arms, Dez would have rushed to the man walking toward them. And kissed him.

He appears to you as your greatest temptation.

It was Himself—and he looked like Ivan.

"Oh, hell," she said.

"Does he look like me?" Ivan whispered.

Of course, he saw Himself in his natural form.

Dez nodded.

"Damn." Ivan moved to stand before Dez, protective, and yet, she tilted to the side to see around him. "We were to meet down on the beach. I'm sorry, Dez, I've betrayed you."

"No," she whispered. "You've never had a choice in serving Himself."

"You're late. And I do tire of the theatrics." Himself waved a hand and the column of air that blocked the rain from him widened about two feet out to either side of him.

Ivan and Dez still stood in the downpour.

"I won't do it." Ivan stretched back his shoulders and took a firm stance. "It's been seven years since I took the devil's shadow. I've survived rather well. I don't need a soul."

Himself as Ivan tilted a moue at Dez. She almost sighed. He was exactly as her lover, except, for reasons she knew were dangerous, he seemed to attract twice as much as the real Ivan. Those eyes were liquid with more emotion than she'd ever seen. And his mouth, firm, yet willing, ready to slay her with a kiss.

"Will you come with me, Dez?" Himself asked. He extended a hand. Ivan's hand.

"She's not going anywhere."

No, she could not do this. She'd never wanted to consign herself to so hideous a fate at the turn of the century. She would not do it now.

But could she, ultimately, be so selfish?

"I—I refuse," she said, and tensed her fists for her stuttering reluctance.

"Well, someone owes me something. Either the fixer shucks his insistent need to resist complete surrender, or you, witch, must become my bride. Which will it be?"

Both looked to one another. Rain droplets spat off Ivan's nose and pinged in the air between them.

"Drake here could save your witchy hide and sacrifice himself completely. Become the fixer he was born to be. Such a gesture."

"No man is born to anything," Dez protested. "He had no choice!"

"So brave you are, little witch. It would see his parents off the hook for eternity. You want your mother's soul safe from me, don't you, Drake?"

"Isn't there a rule about you taking a soul twice?" Ivan hissed.

His mother's soul had once already been in Himself's clutches? Briefly, Dez wondered what kind of family the Drakes were. But then she shook off the disparaging thought. When involved with Himself, no one could master their own will. It wasn't possible.

"Or," Himself stroked his fingers along his jaw, Ivan's dark stubble carving it ruggedly, "Miss Desideriel Rosaline Merovech could step forward and take my hand, thus setting Ivan Drake and his family free of my bonds forever."

"And with his soul?" Dez prompted.

"We accept neither bargain!" Ivan broke in. He turned to Dez, enforcing his determination on her with a fierce glare.

Yes, she agreed. Mostly.

"Then we are at a standstill. A high noon duel of pistols, so to speak." Himself turned and paced, hands behind his back.

"Let her choose!" Ivan suddenly said.

"No, Ivan, I can't." She didn't want to be responsible should she choose incorrectly.

Himself turned and cast Ivan's dark glittering gaze upon the two of them.

"Between the two of us," Ivan explained. "If she chooses you, then she is yours, and I remain your slave for eternity."

Dez's heart dropped to her gut.

"Two birds with one stone?" The false Ivan preened a finger along his square jaw. "I like those odds."

"But if she chooses me, we walk away from your coercion, your influence, your hideous devil's cancer, and I get back my soul."

Himself perused the bargain with a finger tapping Ivan's lips. "Very well. I like the odds, and I know she'll not be able to resist my temptation."

And Dez smiled, because she now knew she must turn away from whoever attracted her the most.

Chapter 24

The rain ceased, and the two figures of Ivan standing before Dez began to quake. Water droplets flew from the Ivan she knew was her lover. The two men shivered frantically and began to bobble closer to one another, as if magnetically attracted.

Dez didn't want to take her eyes off the right one. But when the frenzy of vibration became a blur of flesh and hair and clothing she knew it would be impossible. The two merged as one whirr of motion. An agonizing groan barked out.

And then it was over.

Both men stood still before her. Identical. One looked to the other, and the other followed, only a fraction of a second behind the first.

The one on the right turned to Dez, and the other mimicked in eerie silence. Neither spoke. If Ivan spoke she would know his voice, feel it in her heart.

Maybe.

Why didn't he make some sort of "this is me" movement? Perhaps the coercion would not allow it. Would she be allowed to ask them to remove their shirts so she could check their backs for the shadow? If they were identical, probably Himself bore the same mark.

Searching frantically over the two for some difference, a drop of rain remaining on the brow of her lover, the slyest smirk curling the lip of Himself, Dez took her time. She did not want to give away that she was afraid.

Afraid she would make the wrong choice and condemn them both to a wretched future. For if she chose incorrectly, she would become Himself's bride and Ivan would remain the soulless fixer.

And never again would the two of them kiss, or make love, or have opportunity to begin the forever Ivan had offered her.

Cautioning her heartbeats, or they would leap outside her body and dance a tribal beat, she pressed a palm over her chest. The lace dress was saturated, including her hair and skin.

Both Ivans were completely dry.

The Ivan on the left shoved a hand in his front pants pocket. The Ivan on the right did the same, a nanosecond behind the other.

"Don't move, either of you," she said. "I cannot choose with distractions."

"Very well," both men intoned at the same time. One of them wrinkled a brow and gave the other a discerning look, which was returned.

It was apparent that if Ivan were able to give a clue to Dez about which one he was, Himself immediately matched it. And how to know it wasn't a distracting clue offered by Himself to confuse her?

She was going to have to use something other than her sense of sight for this one.

Dez closed her eyes and settled her inner noise. Sounds of the distant party music faded. The hush of the ocean slapping the beach offered up a rhythm she grabbed and followed until she centered herself.

Ivan's scent carried over the brisk sea salt aroma. Dark, masculine—nervous. She popped open an eye, looking the direction from where the scent seemed strongest. She looked right down the middle between the two men.

She could put a fix on one or the other. Witches were able to look into another witch's eyes and see into their soul, draw up their truths. Or show them their own, as she had with Ivan earlier. No, that wouldn't work. Neither had souls. Or would Himself be so filled with damaged and stolen souls she would see that?

What of her heart? Surely, she could pick out her lover by following her heart? The fairy heart spell had dissipated, but she no longer needed a spell. She knew what it felt like to follow her heart to Ivan. And once already she had denied her heart to Himself.

You've done this before, Dez. You can do it again.

Pray it worked.

"I need to ask a question," she said. "I know Ivan will answer truthfully, and Himself will likely not, but it won't matter."

"Then why ask?"

She eyed the Ivan who had queried. Himself would be concerned about something so trivial. Or not. Oh, for a clue!

Crossing her arms loosely before her, palms curling about her forearms, she nodded and decided to go ahead with what may be futile.

"Tell me, Ivan—" both men looked to her with the same eager attention "—what is it in the world you desire most?"

She looked to the Ivan on the right. "You first. And you," she looked to the other, "may not echo his answer. Is that possible?"

Neither nodded. She wasn't going to have the answer so easily.

"Go ahead," she said to the Ivan to her right.

"You, my love," he answered with the slightest tone of affection, but more neutral, as if he were attempting to keep emotion out of it.

The other Ivan did not mimic his twin.

And Dez did not spend too much time contemplating the answer. It had been quick, easy and felt honest. Her lover had admitted to her he desired only her. Of course, Himself would guess at that as well. And did not Himself genuinely desire her?

"Now you." She nodded to the Ivan on the left.

He swept a hand across his jaw, which was mimicked by the other, and answered as easily as the other, "My soul."

Dez's heart sped up. *Of course.*

Yes, that was it, wasn't it? Above all else Ivan desired his soul. Yet, what a selfish choice. Would her Ivan be selfish?

No, it's not selfish, it is an innate desire. If he is being honest, then he must choose that which means most to him.

She looked from one to the other. Neither offered anything more than a smile. Noncommittal. Emotionless.

Did Himself hold Ivan in sway so he could not break through the bonds of this hideous twin spell? But then, why did not Himself give the upper hand? Unless he had it, and his success was so subtle even Dez did not pick it up, save for subliminally. And then if he did give some signal that would suggest Dez choose him, then she must be suspicious.

You're thinking about this too much. You have their answers. Go with your heart.

"Well?" both men asked. "Which do you choose, Dez(ideriel)?"

Wait. One of them had said Dez, the other Desideriel. But she hadn't been watching their mouths to see which it was. And to concentrate, to try to determine which had spoken longer or had said that last part of her name…

That had been her chance. The answer to her dilemma, and she had lost it.

"Decide," they both said.

Dez pricked her ears, should they again say her name.

"End it," they said.

Could she request they speak her name? But if the real Ivan spoke first, Himself would know he'd made a mistake.

No, she had to do this. And now.

"I…" Stepping forward, Dez reached out. Her fingers trembled in the chill air. And now the ocean breeze swept about the train of her skirt, disturbing her concentration.

Choose wisely. Choose your freedom. Choose Ivan's freedom. No more thinking. *Who does your heart choose?*

Dez stepped to the Ivan on the right, the one who had answered he desired her, and kissed him. She pressed her mouth to his and did not make it quick. Her condemnation would not be so simple. Nor would her success.

The heat of his mouth did not whisper of brimstone. Nor did it tease of comfort. This man was the one she chose. So be it.

A thunder of rain burst upon them. The ground shook. For beside Dez and Ivan, Himself had transformed into his natural form and stomped the tarmac with a smoking hoof.

And the man in her arms shook his head and surfaced from his prison of mimic. Ivan pulled her to him and kissed her hard.

"No!" Himself growled. "Impossible! It is his soul he wants so desperately."

"I would sacrifice my soul for Dez any day," Ivan said.

"I have chosen correctly," Dez said. "Now you must return the book and cease to pursue me."

"You think so?"

Clenching Ivan's hand so tightly her nails dug into his flesh, Dez braced herself for betrayal. Why did she think to trust Himself?

"Your refusal to keep the bargain," Ivan said, calmly, but with certain warning, "will be deemed by your minions as weak. You think there is chaos between the vampire and witch nations? Watch what happens when hell breaks loose."

"Hell is a constant on this mortal realm. Never forget that, boy. And I never go back on a bargain," Himself growled. "You, Ivan Everhart Drake, may have the witch and your soul. But first…"

Ripped from her lover's embrace, Dez found herself clutched to Himself's side, an obsidian talon pressed against her throat as if a blade.

"Take her if you can," Himself dared Ivan.

It was never going to be so simple as Dez choosing one or the other.

Ivan knew that.

And now as Himself held Dez against his hideous, black muscled body, her feet dangling above ground and her head wrenched back to expose her throat to one of the bastard's razor talons, Ivan felt all the years of suppressed anger and hatred for his stolen soul rise. Quickly, he became something else.

He became a man who would never offer his marks the blessing "Curse your shadows."

He became the vampire who would tear out a devil's spine to rescue the girl.

Lunging, he aimed for Himself's throat, his fingers arching into stiff claws, but something swift and agile dove in front of him. Impact pushed Ivan through the air. He landed on the tarmac with a growl.

A bloody death-wraith cracked a skeletal smile and leapt for

Ivan. Timing the moment, Ivan shifted, rolling to his side, and the wraith's skull hit the hard road, shattering.

Behind the wraith followed a league of others. The sky blackened with their tattered wings and bones.

Ivan jumped to his feet. Punches and high kicks and a few jolts of repulsive magic thrown into the mix fended off the wraiths. They were vicious but easily defeated by shattering their bones.

Vaguely aware Himself stood off to the side, with Dez in hand, Ivan prayed to a God who denied him the angels that the devil would not steal her away while he fought off these nuisance wraiths.

A few lucky slashes put boney talons to his cheek and shoulder and back. Ivan merely cringed and shook off the minute pain. His body healed as quickly as he spun to crush two skulls together. Ash formed in his grip and he shook off the cremains.

The dark cloud of cackling wraiths began to dissipate, and when Ivan felt he'd but three or four attackers left to fend off, the growl of a murk demon set up his hackles.

"Oh, hell no," he managed.

Murks were nasty, skinless creatures that were dumb as stone but stronger than a bull. Ivan knew his physical skills would be put to the ultimate challenge. But why bother?

Kicking away the last wraith, Ivan then formed a white light about his body. He had only time to spread it out six inches. The impact of a murk on the invisible shield wavered about him, but he did not take the hit. The murk bounced, landing its four red-muscled paws with a snarl of drooling frustration. It shook its head and charged.

Again it was repulsed. Which gave Ivan enough time to draw up an earth spell.

The tarmac cracked open between Ivan's feet. He spread his legs, but did not jump away from the mini-earthquake. Instead, he reached down to summon up the earth. Dirt particles swirled up and around the feet of the murk. The beast kicked at the growing coil of earth, and successfully jumped out of it. It romped around behind Ivan.

Sensing the murk building up to charge, Ivan lifted his hand high, commanding the earth in a sinuous arc over his head. The squeal of the murk satisfied him as a tornado of earth enveloped the creature in an inescapable straitjacket that tightened until bits of murk exploded through the sky.

Himself hissed. With a command, he brought up a raucous wave of white shadows from the crack in the earth. Ghosts. And not happy ones. These were *pneumata vulnerata*, spirits of the wrongfully murdered.

Ivan repulsed them easily enough, but even as he did so, he knew what Himself had in mind by sending lesser wraiths and ghosts at him. He was weakening Ivan, and that meant the biggest and baddest were yet to come.

Already he noticed a marked decrease in strength. He could not stand straight for the slash across his gut. He spat blood to the side.

The sight of Dez was all he needed to fortify his efforts. She would not be taken by Himself, forced to become the devil's bride. Never.

Growling out in determination, Ivan swept the *pneumata vulnerata* from before him and sent them in a tangled twist of ectoplasm toward the ocean. Chalkboard-scratching cries rose from the shush of soft waves. Enough to give any grown man a fright.

Ivan thrust back his shoulders and planted his feet in the grass at the edge of the sidewalk. Wobbling, but standing, he sucked in a breath to clear his lungs. Narrowing his gaze on Himself, he silently conveyed he was ready.

"You think so?" Himself said. Wicked laughter shrilled up and down Ivan's spine. The shadow at his neck pierced deeply, bringing Ivan to his knees. "That's better, boy. Now, what is the proper address to your betters?"

Ivan clamped his jaw tight. He would not kowtow to Himself, after Dez had rightfully won her freedom and his soul. "Never," he growled.

"Then let's give this a try, shall we?"

Blood ghouls leapt out from the atmosphere, emerging through a part in the sky. They were shaped like hellhounds, hunchbacked and with long rangy legs, but they were twenty times more powerful, and thirsty for blood and meat.

Sharp, yellow teeth bit into Ivan's leg and pulled him flat, palms gripping at the rough tarmac. The pain in his ankle surpassed that of his shadow. Bones broke.

This was going to be a long night.

Chapter 25

When Ivan's mother and father gave birth to their son twenty-eight years ago, they knew he bore a horrible burden. They had done their best to raise him, instilling morals and a sense of all that is right.

They trained him so he could use his incredible vampire strength to protect not only himself but others who were less fortunate. As well, Nikolaus Drake had schooled him on the growing dissension between the witches and vampires. Some day, he warned Ivan, he might be called to stand between the two factions.

Ravin had worked with Ivan until his mastery of witchcraft surpassed all that she knew. When their son was sixteen the blood hunger emerged and he came into his vampirism. The infusion of blood to his wanting vampire soul strengthened him beyond measure.

Ivan Drake had become an incredible force upon this mortal earth.

But never before had he been forced to fight the legions of Hell.

Clothing shredded, and bleeding from every pore, Ivan staggered before Himself. Dez was still crushed against the devil's disgusting form, but her screams and struggles had worn her out. She'd watched helplessly as Ivan had been met with imps, demons, murks and dark denizens of every sort. And he'd mastered them all.

Until his body would not allow it.

Collapsing before his wicked master, Ivan struggled to keep his eyes open. Every part of his body felt open and raw. And yet, he did not feel anything. The bringer of pain had gone beyond pain. Numb, cold and…so hungry.

A single night as the fixer, shaking down marks and enforcing Himself's word always found him ravenous for blood. Now, after battling legions, he felt as though he needed to breathe in blood to survive. It was that essential. The taste of his own blood, copious and salty, merely teased.

"Extraordinary," Himself offered. Sepulchral and cold, the devil's voice crept over the open wounds on Ivan's body and pierced with that familiar prick to raw nerve ending. "You impress me, boy. I am really going to miss you."

Did that mean he had won?

Not so easily as this. It simply could not happen.

Give Dez to me. Release her.

The words formed in Ivan's brain, but he could not mouth them.

"Yes, she must be yours," Himself cooed. The prince of darkness spoke so softly now, the sound actually comforted Ivan. "Completely yours. You are famished, vampire. So hard you have battled and with great success. You have mastered my legions. And now you must restore your strength. I've blood for you."

"Yes," Ivan whimpered. "P-please."

"She will feed your ache. Take from her, Ivan Drake."

And he saw the crisp piece of paper Himself held in clenched talons, and recognized it as torn from the *Grande Grimoire*. Like parchment, the paper, and riddled with tiny script Ivan couldn't read from his ground-hugging sprawl. Crimson beaded across the page like a strand of rubies glinting in the moonlight.

Himself crushed the page in his claws, twisting it. Blood rilled along the edge of the page.

What spell could it possibly be?

And Ivan intuitively knew. *Her spell.* The blood bond that tied Dez to the *Grande Grimoire*.

"No," Ivan managed.

She would not want this. She had been adamant about his not drinking her blood. No matter this was not from her body, but a mere page. He would not. He could not—

Scent of flowers purled in the atmosphere. No, it was sweeter than any summertime blossom, juicy with fragrance. Ivan recognized it. Once before he'd accidentally cut her and the aroma had overwhelmed, seeping into him and becoming an insistent ache he would forevermore chase. Apricots.

"No," he moaned. He wanted to roll to the side, to look away from the bejeweled edge of the paper, but the fight had depleted him.

Such delicious crimson jewels shimmering above him.

"Yes," Himself whispered. "It is Desideriel Rosaline Merovech's blood pact written upon this page. Taste her. Consume her. Take her completely and she is yours. I walk away. You have back your soul. I renege my bride to you."

She was never your bride, Ivan wanted to shout.

So weak. He could but think of moving. But thought did not manifest movement.

So...delicious...The bouquet of her life embraced Ivan.

Must have blood. Dripping across his tongue, forging through his tattered body. Renew. Become. *Make her yours.*

Ivan summoned a lost store of energy and pushed up. Growling fiercely, he spread his mouth wide. A droplet of crimson parted from the paper. It fell as if through a fog, slowly, anticipation silencing Ivan's heartbeats and the sound of Himself's rigorous breathing.

The drop infused gorgeous fragrance into the night. It entered Ivan's senses even as it still plummeted downward. No devil's cancer could overwhelm the sweetness of her blood. Exploding within him, the scent, the taste, the dream of Dez's life.

I belong to no one. If you drink my blood, you would take a part of me I am not willing to grant.

"No!"

Slapping away the blood droplet as it neared his face, Ivan crawled forward and landed on the dew- and ash-laden grass, where legions of demons had just been exterminated. He would die of hunger before he would consume a drop of Dez's blood.

"Stubborn, resistant fool! You have been this way since the first day I seized your miserable soul."

The thud of Dez's body landing on the ground near Ivan made him want to weep. Dead or alive?

"I chose incorrectly," Himself hissed. "What a waste of time. That is the last time I try to manipulate a fixer from the womb. Bah!"

The midnight bells began to ring in the Catholic church down the street. A call to Willow Cove to settle in for the night. A reminder of the greater powers that comforted and guided all souls.

A wicked deterrent to the devil Himself.

Himself stormed about and clomped off. His strides took up

speed and he quickly changed into a ball of fire that rocketed down the road and out of the town.

"Oh goodness!"

Ivan managed to lift himself on his elbows. Elise Henderson stood before him, lavender skirts shimmying about her narrow ankles. Strappy sandals exposed red-polished toenails. She dropped a matching lavender purse near her lavender shoe.

The crumpled, bloodied page from the grimoire sat but a pace away on the grass.

Hell, the last thing Ivan needed was a civilian discovering what had gone on here. Though Dez needed immediate attention, he would not be responsible for the one act that resulted in the mortals finally having proof of vampires.

Beyond the alcohol-laden scent of old lady cologne, he fixed to the aroma of the woman's blood. Not sweet, but mellow and aged. Appetizing, for his hunger did not relent. And he didn't take a moment to struggle with morals.

"Help," he muttered, and reached up for Elise.

She knelt and began to fuss over him. "What's happened to the two of you? Were you robbed? Oh dear, you're bleeding, Mr. Drake. And your clothes; it's as if you've been mauled. Oh… I feel so…warm suddenly. You're—what are you doing, Mr. Drake? The way you're looking at me. It's been so long since a man…has…looked…"

Ivan latched on to Elise's neck. It was quick. Clean. He persuaded her into a dream of a long-lost lover come home from the war. One she had often, but it usually ended in tragedy. This night he gave her the happy ending she desired.

And, too, he whispered of her beauty. That never must she tamper with her appearance. Wrinkles or no, she would always shine.

And when he'd drunk enough to rise to his feet and stand—

but not nearly enough to sufficiently heal—Ivan lifted Elise's lax body and carried her to a park bench. She'd wake in a while with no memory of the bite he'd licked to warrant a fast healing. And perhaps she'd smile at the memory of her dream.

"May all your shadows be cursed," he said.

Staggering, he then turned to Dez, who sat with legs sprawled. Hair tousled about her weary face. Her lace dress was torn from hip to ankle. Blood shimmered at her neck, coagulated pearls of crimson. Must have been cut with a talon. Such a devastating sight.

Apricots. Sweet, sweet…

Ivan bit hard on his lip. The lingering taste of Elise's blood would not serve to repulse his hunger.

"No." He squeezed a fist and looked to the sky.

He'd taken blood. It would serve him for a while.

Dez lunged for the crumpled paper and spread it open. "My blood bond to the grimoire. It's been removed."

"What does that mean?"

"The page is still intact, so I'm not sure. Had the blood been drained, or a mere drop drunk…" She looked up to him. "Why didn't you take it?"

"It would have brought your death," he guessed.

She nodded. "I'm not sure what will happen now. I don't think I'm bound to the book. Where, where is the grimoire? That black demon lied!"

Halfway to standing, Dez's body was thrust back against the wall of her shop. A force chuffed out her breath and her arms curled about something heavy and big.

"The grimoire," Ivan said. He swept back his wet hair and offered to take it from her, which Dez relinquished gratefully. "Let's get this back to your house and safely tucked away."

"The Protection spell." She splayed open the book in Ivan's

arms. Pages fluttered beneath his chin. "I'll do it right now. If it's still here. It's what the Gray Council wants, yes?"

"Yes, we are prepared for its reversal. Dez, are you all right? You've been through so much. This can wait."

She shoved the book into his grip. "Hold this. It must be done now before that bastard comes back for round three."

And she drew her finger across the page, nodding as she murmured the tones, remembering, pulling into her spirit the instant so long ago when first she'd crafted this spell.

A sweet tone vibrated in her throat. Dez tossed back her head and thrust out her arms as she called upon the world, the elements, and the very web of the witch nation.

It didn't last long. Ivan felt a pulling sensation within him, as if his blood were being sucked toward his pores, and it quieted as Dez hummed the final tones.

The world became very still.

Dez stood, head bowed, her hands out and shaking. "Forgive me if this destroys my fellow witches," she said. "I feel it is right, as I felt so many centuries ago that creating the spell was right. We are strong. We can overcome and renew. If presented with a challenge we will find a new way to accept and embrace it. All things have a cycle. This cycle is complete."

"It is complete," Ivan agreed.

Wide green eyes held his. No smile in the irises, but a sense of accomplishment brightened them fiercely. Dez nodded at Ivan. It truly was complete.

"Now to put this away for safekeeping, until I can find a replacement to take guardianship."

Chanting the seclusion spell, she swept the book out from this world and into that other realm which she kept close and where she stored all her pertinent supplies.

"You did it." Ivan swept her into his arms.

"I love you."

"I had hoped you did. For every demon, imp or wraith I destroyed, I hoped it would bring me one step closer to that love."

"You made it. I'm all yours."

"And hope has finally been mine."

Exhausted and yet elated, the twosome joined hands and began to walk toward the edge of town.

"How did you know who was the right me?" Ivan felt compelled to ask. "I couldn't do any more than follow my body's will to move. Every time Himself gestured, I did. And when I tried to make a significant motion, it became something benign. I was completely under his control."

"But you answered truthfully about desiring me over your soul?"

"I did. So how did you know?"

Dez tucked her head against his shoulder. "I didn't. I had a fifty-fifty chance of picking the right Ivan. So, I crossed my fingers and hoped for the best."

"So you basically guessed?"

"What else was I to do? I couldn't read your eyes, or your expression. I lucked out."

"Who would have thought my life would be saved on a whim."

"Saved? I thought you would be killed, Ivan. I couldn't bear to watch after the murk came after you. It wasn't fair. That wasn't part of the bargain."

"Wouldn't have expected anything less from the Old Lad."

"It's over. You're weak. Your clothes are falling off you." She tapped his bare arm, and Ivan gave his wrist a shake, which dropped a shredded sleeve to the ground. Dez pulled away strips of fabric from his shoulders and chest. "You need more blood. Why…why didn't you take mine?"

"I would sooner die than know I betrayed one simple request

that meant so much to you. Mrs. Henderson's blood will sustain me for a while."

"What of your soul, Ivan? Do you feel as if it's within you?"

He placed her hand over his chest. "No. I feel no different. I imagine Himself will overlook that part of the deal."

"But we had a bargain!"

"I'll be thankful if he no longer considers me the fixer. Guess I won't know until tomorrow night. If the coercion digs into me."

"What of the shadow on your neck?"

"It's still there. I can feel it."

They paused at the edge of town. Sunlight glinted on the horizon. Time had twisted when they'd been playing the game with the devil Himself.

"I want to take you home and make love to you all day," he said. "And if the night brings another task, at least I'll know you're free."

"Oh, Ivan."

It wasn't fair. That she had won the *Grande Grimoire* and freedom from Himself?

"Can you get home yourself? I…need to hunt before we can be together."

She nodded. And as he leaned in to kiss her, the scent of her blood seeped into his mind. His desiderata. The only desired thing he could never have.

A homeless man living in a shanty at the edge of Willow Cove served Ivan to renew his strength. He didn't balk at taking advantage of the sleeping man. With the persuasion, Ivan was able to lift the deeply buried dream to handcraft boats to the man's forebrain. He had the skills, and now he would gain renewed determination.

Leaving him with the curse against his shadows, Ivan walked

briskly down the gravel road. Dawn lighted his path and topped the peaks of the white picket fence.

He shrugged a hand through his hair and marveled with a huge smile that Dez had been winging it when she'd chosen him.

But he wouldn't dwell on what could have been. Dez was free, with the *Grande Grimoire*, and that was all that mattered.

The sun dashed pink and gold swashes across the gentle rolling waves below. The air hummed with cicadas and the urgent energy of the ocean. The cool air shifted over Ivan's bare flesh. But shards of his pants revealed everything below the knees. He'd thought to bespell some new clothes when—something was not right.

He scanned the back of the house, eyeing the windows to sight Dez. A shadow moved behind the upper-floor bedroom window. Waiting for him.

Yet he felt the world shift. Vision blurred, and then everything grew sharp and defined. Vision, smell, even the salt in the air pricked at the small unhealed wounds and cuts scattered across Ivan's body.

Would Himself retaliate by taking Dez away from him?

Not that he had her. She was not his. She could never be his. Not while he worked for Himself. It wouldn't be fair to Dez.

Hit with such a force he felt his insides become molten and shift, his limbs splayed out and he could not keep balance.

Falling backward, Ivan hit the ground. The force moved over and through him like worms seeking the inner parts of flesh, muscle and organs. As well, it was warm and encompassing. So bright.

He closed his eyes. His body filled with brilliance. And he did not want to struggle, for he knew this was the moment he'd dreamed of.

When it ceased, he felt different. Full. And empty. Invigorated. And yet, he simply lay there, arms outstretched above his head and legs spread like a vampire Vitruvian Man.

"My soul," he said, and knew it was so.

And then something even more spectacular occurred. Out the corner of his eye, Ivan saw a flash. Not the sun on the ocean. Not a bird's wing taking flight. A blinding wheel spun in the sky, gorgeous with color and radiating love.

"An angel," he whispered. A tear rolled down his cheek. "Thank you."

"Ivan!"

Dez appeared above him. A sweep of red silk spilled across his face as she knelt, and swiped the skirt of her robe away. "What happened? Are you hurt? Is Himself trying to punish you again?"

He slid a hand behind her head and pulled her down for a kiss.

Never before had a woman tasted so exquisite. So…made for him. And the sensation of touch had not until now seemed so fine and detailed. Her lips molded to his as if they were meant to only touch his mouth. The taste of her carried more than a hush of surprise and the soft minty tingle of toothpaste. He could taste her life. Not blood. Life. Full and bountiful and honed over the centuries. Wise with years of experience. Innocent with wonder.

And the angel approved.

Hot tears spilled across his cheek. Dez traced the wet trail with a fingertip, but she did not break the kiss. She wanted to know what was wrong with him. Not a single thing. He was perfect.

Life had just begun.

Epilogue

Ivan paused at the white picket gate before Dez's house and looked over the pile of rose vines heaped to one side, smoldering with smoke and flame. Dez waved hedge clippers at him in welcome, her hands gloved and hair tied off from her face.

"This is too much," Ivan said as he approached, still a bit leery of the vines on the ground. But they had been severed, and when he got close, the thick, cordlike vines did not snake toward him. "What of protection from other vampires?"

"I'll blast them with a category five mini-hurricane. Besides, shouldn't they be relenting on the witch attacks now?"

"They are. The Gray Council reports a remarkable retreat on both sides." Swiping at the smudge of dirt on her cheek, Ivan then leaned in to kiss it. "I love you."

"It's evening," she replied.

He knew what she was asking, and was happy to report, "No coercion. I'm no longer bound to Himself. Look."

He turned and tugged his shirt off over his head. Slapping a hand over his shoulder, he displayed a bare neck, devoid of shadow.

"Bet that feels like a million bucks."

"You can't even imagine."

"What will you do with yourself now you've a new life?"

"I promised my father I'd devote the next year to overseeing the transition. There are a few tribes we've marked that could be resistant and continue to go after the witches. I won't be satisfied until we've achieved complete peace."

"That might never be possible."

"I won't stop until it is so."

"Will you check in with me every month or so?"

"Month? I was thinking my weekends would belong to you. Don't know that I could stay away any longer than that."

"You just want me for sex, vampire."

"You are talented when it comes to sex. But how do I know you're not keeping me around as your love slave?"

"I like the sound of that. Can a person have a love slave and be in love with him at the same time?"

"Definitely."

"Want to help me finish burning the vines?"

"Yes, I'll take over. You shouldn't be messing around with fire, witch."

"So quickly he starts to tell me what to do."

"Now that I've got you, I don't want to lose you."

"You won't. I'll stick around for as long as you'll have me."

"Forever and a day, my love. Forever and a day."

* * * * *

VAMPIRE VENDETTA

Alexis
MORGAN

Dear Reader,

I've always had a thing for vampire stories. Vampires have been the standard-bearers for the paranormal genre. And I love how each author takes the mythology and makes it her own.

For *Vampire Vendetta*, I envisioned a world in which the vampires and humans live side by side. That led me to creating a hybrid species, the Chancellors. As half-bloods, they have the strengths of both humans and vampires—and few of their weaknesses. The hero is a vampire out to restore his family's honour. The heroine is a Chancellor who has experienced prejudice due to her mixed blood.

I hope you enjoy reading Seamus and Megan's story of love and redemption as much as I did writing it.

Alexis Morgan

To Mom—I really miss you.

Chapter 1

Had these humans never seen a vampire before?

Seamus had gone too long since his last feeding and their rapid pulses were straining his control. As he side-stepped his way down the narrow aisle toward the nearest exit, he flashed his fangs at those closest to him, sneering when they shrank back in fear. The only exceptions were a couple of chancellors in the last row. At least they kept their own fangs safely out of sight. Their mixed blood might give them the strength of their vampire ancestors, but they weren't stupid enough to unnecessarily challenge a purebred like Seamus. What a shame. Their blood would've given him a much needed energy boost.

The door whooshed closed as soon as he set foot on the rustic platform outside, and the turbo jerked forward to speed on its way, his existence quickly forgotten. He watched as the train departed, taking his old life with it. From this point forward, he was no longer the person he'd been.

Now wasn't the time to think about that, not when he had to reach his destination before daybreak. He set off at a brisk pace but had to slow down when the path narrowed to little better than a game trail. The uneven terrain made for rough going as sweat dripped down his face and the strap from his garment bag dug painfully into his shoulder. He'd only packed the bare necessities, the kinds of things that a vampire lacking strong ties to one of the more influential clans could afford: well-worn jeans, a handful of shirts, two lab coats and his shaving kit.

In his other hand, Seamus carefully clutched a custom-made case containing the tools of his trade, the ones that he hoped would prove to be his way into the O'Day estate. His newly purchased paperwork listed him as a licensed medic, a far cry from his real qualifications. However, a medical school graduate only a few weeks short of being certified as a surgeon would draw far too much attention, something Seamus couldn't afford right now.

He approached the perimeter fence of the estate cautiously. High-level energy crackled through the wires, pretty much confirming the rumor that Rafferty had forked out big money for first-rate security around his property. Turning east, Seamus followed the fence line, finally spotting a cluster of low-lying buildings in the distance.

"That must be the gate."

Maybe he should be embarrassed about talking to himself, but all he could feel was relief that he was on the right track. Besides, lately, if he didn't talk to himself, he had no one to talk to at all. Once word of his half sister's scandal had filtered through his peers and professors, he'd become totally isolated. It had been weeks since anyone had spoken to him at all except when absolutely necessary.

Among his kind, status was everything. Once that was gone, there was nothing left except for the driving need for revenge. With the death of his half sister, he was the last of his clan, its lost honor his to defend.

The sky to the east already had a faint pink cast. The first rays of the sun wouldn't harm him. However, if he didn't get inside the compound soon, he'd have to rig some kind of shelter to avoid being fried by the rising sun.

He looked at the dry, dusty ground in disgust. His early ancestors had reportedly dug holes and covered themselves with dirt in order to survive. If his life had reached that point, he'd be better off to burn and be done with it. But he still had a goal to accomplish, one that gave him a powerful reason to keep breathing. With that in mind, he picked up speed. He adjusted the strap of his bag one last time and hurried down the slope, eager to get on with his mission.

Outside the gate, Seamus rang the button to announce his arrival, wincing at the effect the shrill bell had on his sensitive hearing. When there was no immediate response, he pushed it several times in a row. A soon as he let up, he heard a stream of cursing coming from the rustic single-story building that sat about twenty meters inside the electrified fence. He huddled close to the scant cover of the gatepost and waited.

A few seconds later the front door slammed open.

An irate male stepped out into the shade of the wrap-around porch with an automatic in his hand and looking pissed off enough to use it. He glared across at Seamus before boldly stepping out into the morning light to open up a control panel on the far side of the gate. After he hit a few keys, the gate rolled open with a loud creak.

At the moment, Seamus was less concerned about his dignity than the effects of the increasingly bright sun. He squeezed through the opening and hustled toward the shelter of the porch. The roof offered some respite, but soon even that wouldn't be enough protection.

In contrast, his silent companion showed no discomfort at all as he waited for the gate to close before joining Seamus in the shade. That combined with a brief flash of fangs identified him as a chancellor rather than either purely vampire or human. Most of Seamus's kind tended to look down on the other two species, but right now the hybrid chancellor was all that stood between Seamus and sure death.

"Come on inside."

The chancellor stepped back to let Seamus lead the way into the office, probably not eager to turn his back to an unknown vampire. Smart of him. Inside, Seamus sighed with relief to be out of the sun. When his eyes adjusted to the dim light, he noted the office had no windows. No doubt a fair number of the estate's residents, including the owner, were severely allergic to the sun.

The man took a seat behind a cluttered desk and waved Seamus toward one of the other chairs. "Dump your stuff on the counter. I'll have to search it before you can go beyond this point. But first, fill out these forms."

He pushed the papers across the scarred desktop and tossed a pen down beside them.

"By the way, I'm Conlan Shea, head of security around here." He gave Seamus a pointed look when he didn't immediately respond.

Seamus picked up the pen and clicked it a couple of times before answering. He met Conlan's gaze head-on. "I'm Seamus. Seamus Fitzhugh."

He immediately looked back down at the paper in front of him and started writing furiously to avoid answering any more questions for the moment. Now that he'd successfully crossed the first hurdle, he needed time to gather his thoughts.

"So, Seamus, when's the last time you fed?"

Conlan was talking about blood, not food, and it was beyond rude to ask a vampire that question. Obviously, the chancellor had no time and no patience to pussyfoot around anyone's delicate sensibilities. They both knew older vampires could go long periods of time with only regular food and no blood. Younger ones, not so much. The last thing a chancellor would want to deal with was a vampire lost in bloodlust.

"Not since the day before yesterday, right before I got on the turbo to come here." Seamus's hand trembled, as much from temper as hunger, despite his best efforts to conceal it.

Conlan rolled his chair back to open the small fridge built into the cabinet. "Looks like I have a couple of A pos and one O neg. Name your poison."

"The A would be fine."

Conlan tossed him both of the As before turning his attention back to the computer. Keeping his eyes focused on the screen afforded Seamus some much appreciated privacy. Watching a vampire drink blood, either from a pack or directly from the source, probably didn't bother a chancellor like Conlan, but most vampires were pretty sensitive about it.

A few minutes later, Seamus tossed the second pack into the trash can. "Thank you. That helped."

"I live to serve," Conlan said with a sardonic smile. "So tell me, Seamus Fitzhugh, what brings you to our little piece of paradise?"

Seamus signed his name with a flourish, striving to act far more calm than he was. Knowing it wouldn't be easy getting inside Rafferty's estate, he should've expected to be greeted by a hard-eyed chancellor as the security officer. Because of their physical strength combined with a fierce sense of right and wrong, the word *chancellor* had become synonymous with justice and loyalty within the Coalition.

Seamus had spent the long hours on the turbo practicing his story, but right now he was choking on the words he'd rehearsed. Finally, he set the pen down and pushed the stack of papers back across the desk and settled for the bitter truth.

"I have nowhere else to go."

If the chancellor was shocked at the blunt statement, it didn't show. Conlan quickly scanned the papers, his eyebrows shooting up when he reached the part where Seamus had listed his marketable skills.

"You're really a medic?"

Seamus let his bitterness show. "I would've eventually become a doctor, but I lost my scholarship because of a scandal. I was asked to leave medical school midyear. Luckily, I had accumulated enough credits to force them to license me as a medic."

"What kind of scandal?"

Once again, Seamus answered truthfully. "It involved a woman. The situation got out of control and destroyed both of us."

Conlan blinked in surprise at Seamus's stark honesty. Maybe he expected Seamus to act embarrassed or even ashamed, but it wasn't in him to cower. Instead, he let the chancellor look his fill. Finally, Conlan nodded, as if reaching a decision.

"Well, okay then. Here's how this will work—we'll check out your story, top to bottom, inside and out. You don't want to be caught in a lie. Rafferty O'Day doesn't offer second chances."

The chancellor met Seamus's gaze again and held it for a few seconds before releasing it. "So you have a choice. If you want to leave, you can wait here until nightfall. If you decide to stay, you'll live here in our guest quarters until I know more about you than your own mother does. Pass muster and you'll meet Rafferty and his wife, Joss, next. It's up to them whether you've found a new home. Clear?"

Seamus nodded. "Yes. I want to stay."

"Let me see your gear, and then we can get you settled in."

The chancellor rooted through Seamus's worldly goods with ruthless efficiency. It was hard not to take offense, but the man was just doing his job. At least he treated Seamus's med kit with respect.

After snapping the lock closed, he handed the case to Seamus. "I can't promise anything, but I know

Rafferty has been hoping to find a licensed medic for the estate. If your credentials pan out, he'll be anxious to talk to you."

Then Conlan hefted Seamus's heavy duffel off the counter and headed for a different door than the one they'd entered through. "If you'll follow me, I'll get you set up. Right now, you're my only guest, so you can have your pick of rooms. There's a common bath at the end of the hallway we keep stocked with towels and the like. Help yourself."

There were about ten doors lining the hallway. A quick peek told Seamus they were all more or less the same, so he settled on the convenience of being near the bathroom. Conlan dumped Seamus's bag inside the door, but then stepped back out in the hall.

"It's been a long night, so get some sleep. I'm going to turn in myself." He paused outside the door. "By the way, the electric fence also separates this facility from the estate itself. One way or the other, you're stuck here until I let you out. If you get hungry during the day, that O neg is still in the fridge. You're welcome to join me for meals while you're here, too. Any questions?"

"Not that I can think of." Especially none he could ask of one of Rafferty's trusted employees, anyway.

"Okay. We'll talk some more tonight."

Seamus listened as Conlan's footsteps disappeared down the hallway to his own quarters. When he was sure the grim-faced chancellor was really gone, he sank down on the edge of the bed. He was fed, safe from the sun and ready for some sleep. The first part of his journey toward vengeance was over and without mishap.

Amazing.

Suddenly, a shower sounded awfully good. Just like the bedroom, the bathing facility was strictly utilitarian in design, but fresh and clean. He stripped off his sweat-stained travel clothes and tossed them in the refurbisher. After programming the water temperature to parboil, he ducked under the stinging spray to wash away the grime and grit from the train and subsequent hike to the gate. Fifteen minutes later, he crawled under the covers and closed his eyes.

Megan's stomach cramped; that was nothing new. She'd been feeling that way for days now, but it was getting progressively worse. In between the waves of crippling pain, she tried to convince herself that the twinge was nothing to be concerned about, but it was a losing argument. When the sharp pangs began to fade, she staggered forward again.

Only a few minutes had passed before the next wave of agony started. The pain built to a sharp crescendo, the intensity worsening with each new attack. It took every scrap of willpower to keep moving when all she wanted to do was lie down in the dirt. If it were only her own welfare she had to worry about, she'd have given in, given up and surrendered to her body's demands for rest.

But she wasn't alone in this, so she trudged on, step by step as the sun slowly rose overhead. At least that made traveling a little easier along the rough path. Her knee ached from an earlier mishap, and she could ill afford to risk an injury that would leave her stranded out in the middle of nowhere.

She was concentrating so hard on walking that it startled her to realize that she'd finally reached the gate.

Tears of relief burned down her cheeks as she rang the bell, asking—no, begging—for admittance. As she waited for someone to answer her summons, she did her best to scrub the dust off her face and straighten her hair. She had no baggage, having abandoned it some distance back when it became too much for her waning strength. Only the small pack she carried on her back mattered.

No one came. She rang the bell again, this time really leaning on it. There was no way to know who manned the gate for her cousin Joss's husband. But if Rafferty had hired a vampire, she might have to wait for nightfall to get in. The sour taste of fear burned the back of her throat as she prayed that someone would hear her.

She was about to give up and sink to the ground when she heard a voice. The yet unseen male sounded more than a little put out about the disturbance, but she didn't care. He could yell at her all he wanted if he'd just let her lie down first.

He finally appeared on the porch, shading his eyes with his hand. She could see his fangs from where she stood, but he had to be a fellow chancellor since he didn't hesitate to step out into the sunshine.

He held a gun in his hand, but kept it aimed at the ground while he punched some buttons. As soon as the gate opened wide enough, she stumbled inside, barely catching herself from falling headfirst through the narrow gap.

"What the hell?"

The chancellor immediately holstered his weapon and loped across to where she leaned against the gate trying to ride out another wave of pain. He did his best to support her as they shuffled toward the porch.

"Sorry, I don't mean to be a bother," Megan managed to gasp as she clung to his strong arm. The pain was back, already sharper than ever.

When she bent almost double, he muttered a curse and swept her up in his arms. She wasn't particularly petite, but the chancellor handled her weight with ease. He carried her carefully, but the motion was making her sicker. If he didn't put her down soon, she was sorely afraid she was going to humiliate herself even further.

Finally, he set her down on a bed. "I'll be right back. Stay there."

Like she needed to be told that. Did he think she was an imbecile? Well, if so, maybe he had a point. Now that she was horizontal, the pain eased up. She only hoped that her reluctant rescuer returned soon.

The door to Seamus's room slammed open with enough force to wake the dead. Most vampires his age slept throughout the day, but the irregular hours in medical school had forced him to adjust. He went from sound asleep to wide-awake by the time the door bounced off the wall and a rough hand grabbed him by the shoulder.

Seamus recognized Conlan by scent even as he knocked his hand away. "What's wrong?"

"You say you're a medic. Well, now's your chance to prove it." The chancellor was already heading back out into the hallway. "Get dressed and then meet me in the first room on the right. Bring that fancy gear of yours because I guarantee you're damn well going to need it."

The familiar surge of adrenaline roared through Seamus's veins as he yanked on a clean shirt and jeans. Picking up the med kit, he trotted after the chancellor.

Obviously someone else had arrived, someone who was in need of medical care. Conlan didn't strike Seamus as the kind to panic. If he said to hurry, he meant it.

Out in the hallway, Seamus's fangs ran out at the sour scent of fresh blood mixed with something else, something foul. The smell grew stronger the closer he got to where Conlan stood waiting for him. The other man stepped aside to let Seamus pass. It didn't take long to assess the situation. He'd been expecting an injury, but instead found a desperately ill female chancellor.

He pegged Conlan with a hard glance. "Stay with her while I wash up—then, would you clean my instruments?"

He weighed Conlan's response, trying to judge just how much help the other man would be. Enough, he decided, even though Conlan clearly was not happy about his guest quarters suddenly being turned into a makeshift hospital.

Seamus set his case down and ran for the bathroom to scrub himself clean. When he got back, he picked out the instruments he'd be most likely to need and handed them to Conlan. "Scrub up and use alcohol to wipe these down. Then wrap them all in a clean towel. I don't need to tell you to hurry."

Conlan glanced past him to the woman hanging off the edge of the bed and retching up blood into a wastebasket. "No, you don't."

When he was gone, Seamus approached his patient. She lay curled up on her side, her arms wrapped around her stomach. He took her pulse and listened to her heart. As soon as he touched her, she stirred and opened her eyes. He answered her unspoken questions.

"My name is Seamus Fitzhugh, and I'm a…a medic,"

he told her, stumbling a bit over the last word. "We're going to get you through this, you understand?"

She nodded and immediately tensed. He helped her lean out over the wastebasket again and supported her forehead as dry heaves racked her body.

When the spasm finally passed, he asked, "Can you tell me your name?"

She answered through gritted teeth. "Megan Perez."

"How long have you been sick?" he asked as he mentally cataloged her symptoms. No fever, but clammy. Racing pulse. Vomiting. Severely dehydrated.

Conlan appeared in the doorway with a stack of clean towels and sheets. "Thought you might need these."

"Thanks. Set them there and bring me a pan of cool water and some smaller rags. After that, find me any emergency medical supplies you have."

As soon as he disappeared again, Seamus picked up one of the sheets and a couple of the towels. "Okay, Megan, I'm going to have to do a quick exam. Are you all right with that?" She had no choice, but he needed her to trust him.

She grabbed his arm, a wild look in her eyes. "Not me. Where's my baby? Is she all right?"

Conlan hadn't mentioned a baby. Seamus looked around the room and spotted a pack lying on the dresser across the room. It was the right shape and size, but way too quiet. Knowing his patient wouldn't relax until he checked her baby, he crossed the room with a sick knot twisting in his gut. Positioning himself to block the worried mother's view, he reluctantly peeled back the tightly wrapped blanket from around the pack, dreading what he was about to uncover.

A pair of eyes, more lavender than blue, blinked up at him as the baby contentedly sucked on her fist. The relief at seeing the child alive was overwhelming.

"Hey, there, little one. I'm surprised you're not screaming your lungs out."

Conlan chose that moment to return. "Why would I be screaming?"

"Not you—the baby."

The chancellor set down the pan and rags near Megan's bed and then looked over Seamus's shoulder. "Holy hell, she didn't tell me it was a baby. No wonder the woman pitched a fit when I took the pack away from her."

Seamus lifted the infant out of the carrier and cuddled her up on his shoulder. He held her out to show his patient. "The baby's fine."

The woman struggled to lift her head, but was unable to hold it up for more than a second. Her eyes, so like her daughter's, caught Seamus's as she tried to talk.

He crossed the room and knelt down beside the bed as she whispered, "Tell Joss, if I don't make it…my daughter…hers now. Promise."

Seamus told her what she wanted to hear. "I promise, but you can tell her yourself when you're stronger."

When the tension abruptly drained out of Megan and her eyes rolled back, Seamus shoved the infant at Conlan. "Here, take her."

Any other time Seamus would've found the panic in the tough-looking chancellor's expression amusing, but not now. He grabbed Megan's wrist and felt for her pulse. It was thready and weak, but definitely still there.

Conlan glanced toward the mother. "Is she…"

"No, but she will be if I don't get some fluids in her. I still need those medical supplies."

"Where can I put this?" he asked, awkwardly holding the baby straight out from his chest.

"It's a youngling, not a *this*." Seamus shot Conlan a disgusted look. "Make a bed for her out of a basket or a box of some kind. Hell, as small as she is even an empty drawer will do. Just pad it with towels or a blanket first."

The chancellor disappeared, allowing Seamus to turn his attention back to his primary patient. He resumed his assessment of her condition. She was practically skin and bones, far too thin for her height and build, as if she'd been too long without even basic nutrition. Nursing the child would have robbed her body's resources, but not enough to account for her condition. Right now, she'd definitely be vulnerable to any variety of illnesses.

Back at the medical center, an array of machinery and a battery of tests would've told him everything necessary to make an accurate diagnosis in a matter of minutes. But here, in the middle of nowhere, he was going to have to go with his gut instincts, and he wasn't liking what they were telling him.

He considered his options. A medic would treat her with IVs and maybe some antinausea medication. If he were smart, that's exactly what he'd do rather than risk blowing his cover story. But maybe he wasn't all that bright or maybe his vow to heal took precedence over his mission of revenge. Either way, it didn't matter. He opened his med kit and triggered the release for the shallow hidden compartment at the bottom.

His hand hovered over the vial he needed to save this

woman's life. Controlled substances weren't as readily available to medics as they would be for physicians. If he used it, he might not be able to replace it, but then he'd already made his decision. Reaching for a syringe, he drew up the full dose and injected it in Megan's hip before he could second-guess himself. Then he sat back and waited to see if he'd gotten to her in time or if his efforts had been wasted.

After all, Megan Perez wasn't sick. She'd been poisoned.

Chapter 2

As the sun went down, Seamus collapsed on the chair Conlan had brought in sometime during the long daylight hours. The antidote he'd given Megan had done its job, although it had been touch and go there for a while. He'd hesitated before administering a full dose of the anti-iron medication. Meant for vampires, it was a dicey move to give it to a chancellor. Despite the genetic characteristics they shared in common with vampires, they were just as much human.

All of which meant that the injection had stood about an equal chance of killing her as it did counteracting the poison, especially in her weakened condition. As soon as the drug hit her bloodstream, it had triggered a series of violent seizures. But once those had passed, her color had gradually improved and the stomach spasms stopped, finally allowing her to rest.

Seamus shifted, trying to get comfortable on the hard chair. Right then, he wasn't sure which hurt more—his feet, his legs or his head. Not that it mattered; he was too busy being exhausted to care. Leaning his head back against the wall, he closed his eyes. The relief lasted all of fifteen seconds before Conlan walked into the room.

"How are they?" At least he kept his voice to a soft whisper.

Seamus straightened up and stretched. "Better. Sleeping for now."

"You okay?"

Why did the man care? It wasn't like they'd spent the day bonding. They'd been too busy emptying basins and changing Megan's bed linens over and over again for them to get chummy. Still, he couldn't deny that the chancellor had followed every order Seamus had barked at him right up until Megan had finally settled into peaceful sleep. Seamus studied the woman's exhausted face.

"She'll need to eat soon, preferably something bland and light." He would, too, but the patient came first.

Conlan nodded and tossed Seamus a warm blood pack. "Why don't you snack on that while I heat up some soup for both of you? I'll also go through some more of the emergency supplies and see if Rafferty thought to stock some diapers. We've already used up the few she'd stashed in the baby's carrier."

Seamus smiled at the worried note in the chancellor's voice. He was willing to bet the man could face down vampires on a rampage without blinking, but evidently a baby without diapers was more than he could handle.

"Soft toweling will do in a pinch." He leaned back again, preferring to feed after Conlan left.

"Odd that she didn't have any luggage," the chancellor said.

Seamus stored that bit of information with the few facts he'd been able to put together. None of it was adding up to anything good. "When you let her in the gate, did she say how she got here? She wasn't on the turbo. I was the only one who got off at this stop."

Conlan leaned against the door frame. "Walked, I guess. I would've heard a vehicle or an air drop."

"Think she might've jettisoned the luggage on her way? Frankly, as sick as she was, I'm amazed she made it this far."

"The thought crossed my mind, too. When the soup's ready, I'll take a run down the trail and look. If it's out there, I'll find it."

"I'm sure she'd appreciate having her own things."

"Back in a few." He eyed the blood pack in Seamus's hand. "Drain that. You look like hell."

When he was gone, Seamus opened his eyes to study his patient. The thought of her out there on that rough trail alone and in pain made him furious. What would've possessed her to risk such a crazy trip instead of seeking medical help? Judging by how thin she was, he knew damn well she hadn't gotten into such bad shape overnight. There was only one logical answer to that—she'd do anything to protect her baby, even if it meant her own death.

So the real question wasn't *what* had driven her to such a desperate move, but *who?* He'd already noted the lack of a wedding ring. By itself, that didn't mean much, although most human pairings went through some kind of marriage ceremony, as did betrothed vampire couples.

He ignored the twinge of bitterness over the outcome of his sister's fractured betrothal. Now wasn't the time.

But Megan was a chancellor with a purebred vampire baby. If she'd mated with another of her own kind, there was only a twenty-five percent chance of that happening. No, it was more likely that the child's father was a vampire.

And maybe that's why Megan had run.

It was guesswork on his part, but it felt right. Other than making sure both mother and child were physically all right, none of this was his problem, but he hated the fear in Megan's pretty eyes. Since Conlan was head of security, Seamus considered whether or not to tell him his suspicions. Then the chancellor and his vampire boss could worry about what kind of trouble might be trailing after Megan Perez.

But revealing Megan's secrets meant endangering his own. A mere medic wouldn't have the training to diagnose and treat Megan's condition. O'Day and Conlan might not know that, but he couldn't risk them finding out.

A few minutes later Conlan returned with the soup. "If you don't need me for anything, I'll head out to look for her stuff. I shouldn't be gone more than an hour. Any farther than that, it will be too dark to see anything."

"We'll be fine."

"I've got to say, you did a heck of a job, kid." His voice was gruff, as if giving compliments wasn't his usual habit. Then Conlan hesitated in the doorway. "I hope she knows how lucky she was that you were here."

A soft voice joined the conversation. "Believe me, I know. The two of us owe you both more than we can repay."

The whispered comment brought both men to full attention. Seamus stood up, setting his unopened blood pack aside. He approached the bed. "How are you feeling?"

Her smile looked shaky, but the expression in her eyes was definitely warm. "I've been better, but I'm not complaining."

Seamus did a quick check of her pulse. "I regret that I couldn't risk giving you anything for the pain."

"I'm just grateful I made it here in time."

Her daughter stirred in her makeshift bed, immediately bringing a touch of worry to Megan's expression. "She's all right, isn't she?"

Seamus nodded as he settled the baby in her mother's arms. "You can check for yourself, but I did a thorough exam. Conlan found some formula among his supplies. Your youngling fussed a bit, probably because of the odd taste, but with some coaxing she took a full bottle."

The new mother's smile grew stronger as she gently unwrapped her tiny daughter. Seamus figured it would take a lot harder heart than his to not enjoy watching a mother fuss over her youngling. It was a shame that life itself would wear away that sweet innocence all too soon.

The baby protested, her cry sounding hungry to Seamus. "Try nursing her if you feel up to it. We can always supplement with another bottle if necessary. Right now physical proximity is the important thing for both of you."

Megan immediately tried to sit up, but couldn't quite make it on her own.

"Here, let me help."

Seamus immediately fluffed a couple of pillows to

put behind her. Then he tried to hand the baby to Conlan to hold, so he could help shift the weary woman up into a sitting position. The chancellor immediately backed away, holding his hands up.

"No, that's okay."

"Come on, Conlan. The baby won't bite. She won't even have fangs for at least ten years." The needs of younglings of all three races were virtually interchangeable until puberty hit.

"It's not that. If I don't head out now, I'll lose the light." He looked past Seamus to Megan. "We were pretty sure that you'd left luggage somewhere along the trail here. I was leaving to go look when you woke up."

The twinkle in her eyes said she wasn't buying that story, not completely, anyway. However, she didn't call him on it. "I had a small cart with several bags and boxes on it. It shouldn't be hard to spot if it's still there."

"I'll be back."

Seamus waited until Conlan disappeared to speak in a stage whisper, knowing his comment would easily carry to the chancellor. "To think a big, tough chancellor would be afraid of someone that small."

"Shut up, Seamus!" Conlan shouted from down the hall.

Seamus chuckled and helped both mother and baby into a better position for Megan to feed her child. "I'll give you some privacy, but I won't go far. Yell if you need anything."

"I will. But before you go, I have to ask you something." The good humor was gone, replaced by a deep-rooted fear.

"What?"

"How sick was I? Is Phoebe in any danger?"

"No, she's not." Time for some hard truths. "Because you weren't sick."

She didn't look as shocked as she should have, and her eyes slid away from his. "Of course I was. I haven't been careful about what I've been eating. Maybe it was food poisoning."

"You're half right—it was poisoning, but not the kind you get from bad food."

She looked past him toward the door. "Does he know?"

Where was she going with this? "Not yet."

"Can you not tell him? At least for now?" Her voice cracked.

"Conlan is the head of security around here. He's your best bet for keeping you and your daughter safe." Not to mention focusing on Megan's problems might delay Conlan's investigation of Seamus for a while.

"Please." The word cost her.

"All right—for now." He'd saved her life, but if he needed to out her problems to save his own butt, he would.

"Thank you." She settled back against her pillow, her focus riveted on her daughter.

He picked up his blood pack on the way out the door. The baby wasn't the only one overdue for a feeding. Out in the hallway, he leaned against the wall, glad for the breather. What a relief that mother and daughter were doing well. It had been a close call.

But she'd rallied after he'd gotten the IV started, although the journey had clearly cost her the last of her energy reserves. She'd be needing lots of fluids and protein to build up her strength.

After kneading the blood pack to mix it thoroughly, he popped it with his fangs and sucked it down. At least it was relatively fresh. According to Conlan, another delivery would arrive sometime during the night.

"Seamus?" Megan sounded hesitant. "I'm ready to lie down again."

He tossed the empty blood pack in the trash and prepared to face his patient, not that he'd ever be a real doctor again. "Let me get the baby settled back in her bed while you eat the soup Conlan fixed. Then you can get some sleep."

A short time later, he let himself out of the room after both mother and daughter had dozed off. The sun would be down in a few minutes, and he could finally escape the closed-in feeling of the dorm building. Fresh air would definitely be a welcome change, as would a chance to be alone for a while. It had been ages since he'd had this much intense interaction with anyone. He wasn't sure he liked it.

He had one, and only one, goal: avenge his sister. His role as a medic had been intended as a means to accomplish it. He hadn't expected to become entangled with any other resident of Rafferty's estate, especially a woman with lavender eyes and dark secrets of her own.

Conlan returned shortly after dark, dragging Megan's cart behind him. Seamus helped him lug the various bags and boxes inside to stack in the hall outside of her room. Neither man wanted to wake up the two females sleeping inside.

After they'd carried the last of the boxes in, Conlan

led the way back to his office. When they were seated at his desk, the inquisition began.

"I've got to know—how contagious is Megan? Do we need to quarantine the compound until we find out if either of us or the baby come down with whatever knocked her flat? The supply shipment is due soon, and I don't want to put the rest of the estate at risk."

Seamus considered how much to tell him and settled for the truth. "You understand that without a fully equipped medical lab at my disposal, I can only make an educated guess about what the problem was?"

Conlan had been leaning back in his chair with his feet propped up on the desk. He immediately dropped them back down on the ground and leaned forward, a lawman scenting potential trouble. "After watching you all day, I'm willing to trust your gut. Spit it out, Seamus."

"I would guess that if we're not sick within twenty-four hours, we should be fine." A safe enough assessment given poison wasn't contagious. "I think whatever it was hit her hard because of her recent pregnancy. If she hadn't gotten here when she did, she'd have died out there on the trail. As it was, I barely managed to pull her back from the edge."

Seamus's fangs ran out to full length, a fact he couldn't hide from Conlan. "I can't believe no one helped her before it got that bad."

By now, the furious chancellor was sporting an impressive set of fangs of his own. Seamus wasn't the only one who hated knowing Megan had gone through hell. Chancellors came hardwired with a strong sense of right and wrong.

Conlan pulled a pad of paper from his top drawer.

"What kind of symptoms should we be watching for? I need to give the boss a heads-up."

"Vomiting, clammy skin, weight loss and possibly gastric bleeding."

Conlan looked up from his notes. "Sounds like fun."

Seamus smiled at his black humor. "Chances are a healthy individual wouldn't get the extreme version Ms. Perez did. She was already weakened from her young-ling's recent delivery."

Definitely time to change subjects. "Which reminds me, why would Megan say that Joss O'Day should end up with her daughter?"

Conlan relaxed, but only slightly. "They're cousins. Joss said they haven't had much contact over the past few years, but were pretty close when they were kids."

"That puts things in a different light. At least it would explain why Megan would risk so much to reach the compound, especially if she thought she was dying."

The chancellor leaned back again, his boots landing on the desktop with a loud thump. "You've got to wonder why she didn't turn to her parents for help or at least go to the local hospital."

"It's hard to think straight when you're that sick. Most likely she didn't know who to turn to, especially if she didn't know who could be trusted."

Seamus knew all about that—feeling so damned alone because he no longer knew friend from foe. After all, that's why he'd ended here up on the outskirts of Rafferty O'Day's estate. The bastard had managed to rob Seamus of everything that had held meaning in his life: family, status, honor. And for that, the vampire would pay dearly.

Something of what he was thinking must have shown on his face because when he looked up Conlan was giving him the evil eye. Before Seamus could decide what would distract his all-too-discerning host, Conlan jerked as if someone had just yanked on his strings. If Seamus hadn't been so lost in his own thoughts, he would've heard the transport sooner.

"Sounds like we've got company."

Conlan grabbed packets of gloves and masks off his desk and headed out the door before Seamus even managed to stand up. By the time he joined him out on the porch, the gate from the estate side had rolled open. The chancellor shaded his eyes, trying to see past the glare of the headlights. Once he recognized the vehicle, he slammed the office door closed and stalked down the steps.

"This is all I need," he muttered as he waited for the vehicle to clear the gate before closing it again.

Seamus hung back to see who had the chancellor looking as if he'd swallowed something nasty. A tall woman climbed out of the passenger's side of the transport as an even taller male slid out of the driver's side. Seamus's chest tightened as his mind jumped to the obvious conclusion. However, the last thing he wanted to do was raise suspicions. If he was right about the couple's identity, he was about to finally meet Rafferty O'Day and his new chancellor bride, Josalyn Sloan O'Day.

He'd hoped to put that pleasure off for a few more days at least, but he had no choice but to act curious and wait for an introduction. He drew comfort from the fact that Conlan also didn't seem particularly happy to see his employer. What was his relationship to the vampire and his wife? Could the man be a possible ally?

There was no use in thinking that way. Without bothering to try to disguise his interest, he listened in on the conversation out in the courtyard.

"Since when do you two run a delivery service?" Conlan tossed them each a mask. "Here, put these on before you come any closer. We don't know whether or not Megan is contagious."

Without bothering to wait for a reply, Conlan picked up a box from the back of Rafferty's vehicle and started toward his office. Rather than be left alone with Rafferty and his wife, Seamus decided to lend a hand without waiting to be asked.

He nodded at the couple, careful to keep his expression neutral, but friendly. They picked up the remaining two cartons and carried them inside. He noticed one was a blood cooler. Good. At least he wouldn't go hungry.

Conlan's small office was even more crowded with the clutter of supplies and two additional people. Rather than hang around, Seamus set his box down with the others and started for his room.

"Get back here, kid." Conlan sounded more like he had when Seamus had first arrived, but Seamus had the impression that his bad mood wasn't directed at him.

"Seamus, this is Rafferty O'Day and his wife Josalyn, Joss for short. They own the roof over our heads and the floor under our feet."

There was no mistaking the bitterness in Conlan's voice. Before Seamus could decide what to think about that, the security officer continued on. "Rafferty, Joss, this is Seamus Fitzhugh. He's the one I told you about."

Rafferty ignored his employee's poor manners and

stepped forward, his gloved hand held out. "We have you to thank for saving Megan's life. We both owe you for that."

Seamus forced himself to accept the handshake. "Ms. Perez is a fighter."

Joss smiled and followed Rafferty's example. Her grip was every bit as strong as her husband's. "Even so, it was a miracle that we had a medic appear at just the right moment. A person with your credentials would've been welcome, anyway, but your timing couldn't have been more perfect."

"Glad to be of service. Now, if you'll excuse me, I'll get out of your way."

He sensed their surprise at his abrupt departure, but he had to put some space between himself and the O'Days. Even though their gratitude seemed genuine, he wanted nothing to do with it—or them. Of course, it was easy to be gracious when they were the ones in a position of power. Not that he'd let his resentment show.

What had Petra ever seen in that man, anyway? No amount of money was worth shackling herself to a bastard like O'Day, especially considering the price she'd paid for doing so. The vampire obviously thought he ruled the world. Well, once Seamus established himself on the estate, they'd see who really was calling the shots.

Conlan stared after Seamus, wondering if he'd only imagined that sudden predatory gleam in the vampire's eyes. It was gone before he could be sure. He didn't want to raise any unnecessary suspicions about Seamus at the moment. After all, the kid was running on empty, same as he was. Under the circumstances, they were both entitled to be a bit testy.

But neither would Conlan ignore the possibility that Seamus wasn't exactly what he seemed. Tomorrow would be time enough to start digging into his past. If there was a problem, he'd find it. A question from Joss jerked him back to the conversation at hand.

"When can I see Megan?"

"Last I looked she was sleeping, but you can peek in on her and the baby, if you'd like."

After Joss left, he turned to Rafferty. "Why don't you ask your questions? I'm hungry and short on sleep. The longer this takes, the less likely I am to have many answers."

The vampire didn't blink at Conlan's blunt offer, but he didn't act all warm and fuzzy, either. Rafferty had hired Conlan because Joss had asked him to. Conlan had accepted the offer because he'd had no other options. It didn't make for the friendliest working relationship.

Rafferty pulled up a chair. "What do you know about the medic?"

"So far, just what he told me. He lost his scholarship because of a scandal involving a woman. He had enough credits to get licensed as a medic. He says he had nowhere else to go."

Steepling his fingers, Conlan stared at them briefly before continuing. "He's hiding something, but I don't know what. All hell broke loose right after he arrived, so I haven't even done a preliminary check. Judging by how he handled himself today, though, his credentials are legit. I was damn glad to have him here when Megan Perez collapsed coming through the gate."

Rafferty sat up straighter. "How bad was it?"

"Bad enough. I can't believe she walked all the way here."

"What was she thinking? If she'd sent a message to Joss, we would have picked her up." The anger in Rafferty's voice was clearly due to frustration.

"My guess would be that she didn't want to stay in any one spot long enough to wait for an answer or a pickup. Our young medic isn't the only one with secrets."

"You didn't say what the baby is."

Joss rejoined them. "She's female and a full-blooded vampire. Megan didn't mention the father, and I didn't press."

Rafferty frowned. "Well, that narrows it down to either a chancellor or a vampire, not that it matters. If Megan wants a home here, she's got one."

Then he shot Conlan a look. "So does Seamus Fitzhugh. Tell him we'll come back for him and Megan as soon as she's fit to travel."

Conlan held his coffee in a white-knuckled grip. If Rafferty wasn't going to follow his own rules, then why bother having them at all? "I'm not worried about your cousin, Joss, but I haven't had time to check into Seamus's story at all."

"I know, but I think this exception is necessary. We need a medic, especially until we know if Megan will make a full recovery. Do your normal search. If he proves to be a problem, I'll handle it." Rafferty rose to his feet and walked out.

Joss hung back for a few seconds. "Thanks again, Conlan, for contacting us immediately. I appreciate it."

"Just doing my job."

Despite his curt response, Joss smiled at him. "I know, but I sleep better knowing that you're here. Rafferty does, too, even though he won't admit it."

"Don't worry about me and Rafferty. We understand each other just fine."

She laughed. "Oh, I know you do. It's like watching two peas in a pod that don't really like each other."

He followed her to the door. "Liking each other has nothing to do with us trusting each other, especially when both of us have a tendency to bite first and ask questions later. However, because of you, we try to be civil."

"If you call what passes between the two of you civil conversation, I'd hate to see you when you're rude." Joss softened the comment with a quick kiss on his cheek.

He opened the gate and watched them drive off. Time for some sleep and then he'd start digging into Seamus Fitzhugh's past. He'd feel a heck of a lot better if he had a nice fat background report in hand before letting the young medic out of his sight.

After all, Joss might be Rafferty's wife, but she was the last real friend Conlan had.

Chapter 3

Megan eyed the huge breakfast Seamus had set in front of her. When was the last time she'd really felt like eating at all? It didn't help that she felt a bit self-conscious wearing nothing but a nightgown in front of someone she barely knew. How silly was that? During the worst of her illness, Seamus Fitzhugh had seen far more of her than what the rather demure gown revealed.

But he was a vampire, reason enough to be on her guard around him even if he had saved her life.

At the moment he was too busy walking her daughter back and forth in the small room to pay much attention to Megan herself. She didn't want to get caught staring, but she couldn't seem to pull her eyes away. There was no mistaking the strength in Seamus Fitzhugh.

Sure, part of that was standard equipment for vampires, but there was something about him that reminded her of tempered steel. As if he'd been sorely tested, but survived the experience all the stronger for it. It was there in the set of his shoulders and the faint lines that bracketed his mouth.

Whatever had happened had left shadows in his intensely blue eyes, which also reflected a powerful intelligence that at times saw far too much. He hadn't asked her many questions, but she could feel them coming.

"Little one, your momma needs to eat every bite on her plate," he crooned, the order intended for Megan although he was looking at the baby. "Or we'll have to spoon-feed her."

"I'm eating, I'm eating," Megan groused. Did the man think she was an idiot? As a nursing mother, she was still eating for two. She took another bite of the eggs.

He still stopped to check out the contents of her plate. Her steady progress evidently pleased him because he resumed his pacing.

"Hey, pretty girl, I still don't know your name."

Megan could take a hint. "Her name is Phoebe Perez."

"A beautiful name for a beautiful girl." Then he wrinkled his nose and grimaced. "And you're still beautiful, little Phoebe, even if I do have to change your diaper. Again."

"I can do that." Megan started to set the tray aside.

The medic headed right for the makeshift changing table. "Concentrate on eating your breakfast. You have years of diaper changing ahead of you. I'll take care of this one."

While he very efficiently handled that little chore, she considered the best way to broach a touchy subject. Finally, she just spit it out.

"Have you updated our medical records?"

He gave her a hard look. "No, I haven't had access to a computer yet. Why do you ask?"

"Because I haven't registered Phoebe's birth and want to keep it that way for the time being."

If Seamus was surprised, he didn't show it. Instead, he finished bundling Phoebe back up in her blanket before answering. He turned back to face Megan, speaking softly.

"Conlan still thinks you were sick with an infection."

Her heart jumped in her chest. "And is that what you think now?" she asked, although it was a sure bet he didn't from the expression on his face.

"Rather than your being poisoned?" he asked, tossing the problem back in her lap. "No, and it wasn't an accident, either. You really need to tell Conlan and Rafferty."

She could no longer look him straight in the eye. "No, and no matter what you think, it was some kind of infection."

"Believe that if you want to. But antidotes for iron poisoning don't work on infections, and that's what I gave you."

Fear threatened to choke off her breath. "So why aren't you telling him the truth yourself?"

His eyes were glacier cold. "Let's just say you're not the only one with secrets and let it go at that."

He turned his attention back to the daughter, his voice softening again. "So, let's see, little girl. Coalition law states attending physicians must keep careful records, especially for infants and children, complete with the mother's name, the father's name and the species of the child in question."

He stopped in front of Megan. "Unfortunately, there was no attending physician anywhere in sight when you and little Phoebe arrived at the compound, so none of that could be done. However, if I were to suddenly stumble across a doctor, legally I might have to report the services I've rendered, as well as an accurate diagnosis."

With an enigmatic look on his face, he lifted Phoebe high against his chest and swayed gently, cupping the back of her head with his hand. "Personally, I don't see that happening anytime soon, especially since Conlan mentioned that Rafferty had been searching for a medic to service the estate. I would take that to mean there are no physicians living there now."

Relief washed over her. "Thank you, Seamus."

He merely nodded, clearly uncomfortable with her gratitude. "Now, finish eating."

Eventually her pursuers would find her trail, but she was too tired to think about that. For the moment, she and Phoebe were safe; that's all that mattered. After being on the run for weeks, the knowledge that she could relax enough to really sleep was a blessing. Once she recuperated enough of her normal energy, she'd be better able to make plans.

If Seamus really did have his own secrets, that explained why he didn't seem all that curious about her reasons for wanting to keep her daughter's birth a secret. Odd that Conlan O'Shea, the chancellor in charge of security, had yet to ask her a single question about how she came to be at the gate. Maybe it was because she was Joss's cousin. Once he'd verified that much, he'd left it up to Joss and Rafferty to decide what to do about her.

Joss had promised another visit soon. Megan appreciated all the vampire medic and the security chief had done for her, but seeing her cousin had meant a lot, too. She just hoped her presence on the estate didn't bring a heap of trouble down on everyone's head.

Seamus murmured something about a sleepy girl and gently settled Phoebe in her bed.

"Thank you," she whispered. "For everything."

"It's not like I have anything else to do." He straightened up but didn't look in Megan's direction. "Get some rest."

Megan stared at the closed door. She hoped she hadn't offended him, especially since he knew the truth about her illness, if not the reasons behind it. She didn't really know how far she could trust Seamus. Rather than worry about it, she took his advice and let herself drift off to sleep.

His departure had been abrupt, bordering on rude. Maybe he should feel bad about it, but Seamus couldn't muster up enough energy to care. Yes, the baby girl was a heartbreaker, and Megan herself was an attractive woman, or would be when she was back to full strength. But he needed to put some distance between them and soon, because he was fighting a powerful urge to protect her and the baby from whoever had sent Megan running. The strength of that impulse was a shocker. It had been a long time since he'd cared about anything but his own troubles. Now wasn't the best time to start.

He couldn't risk getting any further involved in Megan's predicament. That didn't keep him from wanting to beat the asshole senseless who'd left that fear in her eyes and poison flowing in her bloodstream. Worse yet, he'd gone along with Megan's request to protect Phoebe's unregistered birth. If that came to light, he could lose his medic license.

Granted, he didn't much expect to live any longer than it took to bring down Rafferty O'Day, but he still needed to maintain his cover story. Would it look suspicious to the chancellor to find out that Seamus was willing to risk his future for a woman who was little better than a stranger?

It was too late to worry about it. The damage was already done. If necessary, he'd deal with the fallout.

He wandered toward Conlan's office in need of something to eat—blood or food, it didn't matter. Either would help him stabilize his volatile mood. The door to the security chief's office was closed. Despite the thickness of the wood, Seamus's vampire senses made it possible to hear Conlan talking to someone. From the tone, the conversation was definitely not a happy one. He hesitated, unsure of his welcome.

Conlan solved the problem for him, calling out, "Seamus, if you're going to eavesdrop, you might as well come in and sit down. At least you'll be comfortable."

As soon as Seamus sat down, Conlan rolled his chair back toward the fridge and pulled out a pair of blood bags and tossed them across the desk. Even as he was playing host, he didn't miss a beat in railing at the voice on the other end of the line.

Finally, the chancellor disconnected the call and slammed the phone down on the desk.

"God, save me from idiots!"

While Seamus fed, Conlan shuffled through a stack of papers. From appearances, all he accomplished was moving the pile from the right side of his desk to the left and back again. When he cursed and started back through it a third time, Seamus had to stifle a laugh.

Conlan heard it anyway. "You think this is funny? I hope not, because I can tell you right now that I'm in no mood to be laughed at."

Seamus managed to maintain a straight face. "Sorry. I think perhaps I choked a bit on this excellent blood, and you may have mistaken that for a laugh."

"Yeah, right. I must have."

Conlan gave up on the paperwork altogether and leaned back in his chair, as usual propping his feet on the desktop. "So, how are your patients?"

"Fine. When I left the room, they were both falling asleep, which is normal for a baby and the best thing for the mother."

Not to mention him. And at least while they were sleeping, they weren't looking at him with those huge lavender eyes that drew him like a moth to a flame.

Conlan nodded. "Makes sense. How soon can they be moved?"

"It depends on how they'd be traveling and how far."

"About half an hour's ride. Joss and Rafferty are anxious to get Megan and her daughter settled into a house on the estate right away."

"I'd say late tomorrow should be all right. If either Megan or her daughter are going to develop any complications, we should know by then."

"Sounds good. Be packed up and ready at dusk tomorrow. Someone will be here to drive all of you into the estate." He rolled his shoulders to loosen up tight muscles. "I wouldn't be surprised if Rafferty comes for you himself."

Seamus's surprise verged on the edge of shock. "I thought there was a waiting period before I'd find out if I was accepted."

Resentment glittered in the chancellor's eyes. "Yeah, well, the rules are supposed to apply to everyone who walks through that gate. However, since Rafferty elected himself God around here, when he says break a rule, we stomp it into little pieces. He wants you close by for Megan and her baby, so you get a free pass on the waiting period."

"And you're not happy about that?"

"Don't take it personally. I don't trust anybody. Besides, that free pass only extends to the waiting period. I'll still have my shovel in hand digging into your background even as you drive out of the gate."

"Shouldn't take you long. Medical school doesn't leave much room for a social life."

Then he injected what he hoped was just the right note of mild concern in his voice. "But there's one thing I should probably tell you. Coalition law requires all newborns be registered. Megan Perez never registered Phoebe, and I agreed to keep it that way."

The chancellor's sole reaction was a slight narrowing of his eyes. Seamus bet he'd been an intimidating interrogator at some point in his life. That steely-eyed stare and blank expression would've broken a harder man than Seamus.

"So, why risk your license for a woman you've only barely met?"

Good question, one that Seamus had no real answer for, none that made any sense under his own precarious circumstances. If Conlan O'Shea was a stickler for the law, as most chancellors were by nature, Seamus might have just screwed up his only chance to get inside the estate. He gave the only explanation that made any sense at all—the truth.

"Someone had her running sick and scared. I wasn't going to be the one to lead the bastard straight to her."

Conlan nodded. "Good decision. I'll let Rafferty know in case it blows up in our face at some point. We try to maintain a low profile, but we also protect our own people."

Seamus was unsure if he was now included in that group, but he wasn't going to press for that information. It was enough that Rafferty was willing to let him onto the estate proper.

One step closer to bringing the vampire down.

"Well, I'm going to go for a walk. If you need me for anything, give a holler."

Conlan turned back to his computer. "Will do."

As soon as Seamus was out of sight, Conlan opened the file he'd started on the young vampire. The information was pretty thin, although the lack of it wasn't a concern in and of itself. It was early in his investigation, and as the kid had said, medical school was a tough discipline that left students little time for getting into trouble.

Yet, according to Seamus's own confession, he'd managed to get entangled in a situation that had resulted in him losing his scholarship and being forced to leave school, all over a woman. At first Conlan had a hard time believing that, but this latest confession gave some credence to his story. If Seamus was willing to risk his professional career for Megan Perez so soon after meeting her, what would he have been willing to do for someone he knew far better? Especially if that someone and Seamus had a more intimate relationship.

Conlan updated his notes with both his impressions and the facts about the registration irregularity. As a former investigator for the North American Coalition, he knew how to build a case, block by block until the whole took shape and stood on its own. Seamus might be exactly what he seemed—a well-intentioned, competent medic who'd screwed up big-time.

But Conlan's gut twitched when he read over the scant details. Something was missing. And although Conlan realized he liked the vampire, he wouldn't rest until all of the blanks were filled in.

By the next evening Megan was getting tired of the same four walls and of lying in bed. It was a relief when Conlan stopped in to tell her to get packed up because Joss was coming to take Phoebe and her to their new home. It hadn't taken long to get their meager belongings organized. The only downside of moving out was they were taking Seamus Fitzhugh with them.

The jerk! Despite his compassionate attention when she'd been so sick and afterward with Phoebe, he'd quickly grown cold and distant. Had she offended him somehow by asking him not to register Phoebe? He could've insisted on following the law, and she would have understood. At best it was only a delay tactic. Eventually Banan and his family would figure out where she'd gone to ground.

She stuffed the last of her things in the box and sealed it. Before she could look around for something else to keep her hands busy, there was a soft knock at the door.

"Yes?" she called in a soft voice.

"It's Seamus, Ms. Perez. May I come in?"

Ms. Perez? What happened to calling her Megan?

"Yes, of course." She opened the door and stood back to let him in. She was surprised to see him wearing a lab coat and his stethoscope around his neck. His hand held his med kit in a white-knuckled grip.

His eyes instantly went to where Phoebe lay sucking on her fist in her sleep. For a brief second, his expression softened. But when he turned in Megan's direction, the chilly distance was back in full force.

"Is there something you needed? I'm trying to finish packing before Joss gets here."

He looked decidedly uncomfortable, which meant she wasn't going to like what he had to say. Rather than ask, she waited him out.

Suddenly, his eyes focused somewhere over her shoulder, as if he couldn't stand to look her straight in the eye. "Medical protocol dictates that I do one last examination before we risk your traveling any distance, Ms. Perez. You know, to ensure there aren't any complications that would put you at risk."

Despite his naturally pale vampire complexion there was a definite hint of pink in his cheeks. For that matter, she suspected she blushed, too.

"Are you sure this is absolutely necessary?"

His eyes flashed dark with anger. "I assure you, Ms. Perez, I'm not in the habit of putting patients through unnecessary examinations. It is standard procedure before anyone is released from a medical facility. I'd be considered derelict in my duty if I failed to offer my services."

Her stomach churned, and she felt cornered. But he

was right. If she'd been in a hospital, she wouldn't have questioned the need for the exam.

"I apologize, Mr. Fitzhugh. I didn't mean to insult you."

He nodded. "Shall we get started, then?"

The awkwardness didn't go away as he listened to her heart and lungs. The rest of the exam was quick and thorough, the touch of his gloved hands gentle.

"Any more nausea or cramping?"

"No. The infection is gone."

He gave her a hard look. "So we're back to that again. I repeat—there was no infection, Ms. Perez. You were poisoned. Ignoring the truth is not only foolish, but dangerous."

Why did he insist on confirming her worst nightmare? "I knew I'd been losing weight, but that was because I hadn't been eating right. I picked up an infection. That's all it was."

"Fine, lie to yourself if you want to, but someone had been feeding you an iron supplement meant for vampires. In large enough doses, it's toxic for both humans and chancellors."

She doubled up in pain, but this time the cause was emotional, not physical. "He said I needed it for her."

"Well, whoever *he* is, he lied. Phoebe's needs are the same as any other youngling until she hits puberty. I'm sure Conlan or Rafferty O'Day will help you bring charges against him for attempted murder."

She didn't have to think twice. "*No!* That's the last thing I want to do."

Seamus was looking at her as if she'd grown a second head. "The bastard tries to kill you, and you still want to protect him?"

"No, I want to protect my daughter."

"Very well, but you know he'll try again. Don't wait until it's too late to seek help."

As he peeled off the gloves, he met her gaze. "You should be fine for the duration of the trip. Continue to rest as much as possible. Light exercise is fine, but nothing more strenuous than walking. Concentrate on eating lots of fresh vegetables and protein."

"I will."

"If you change your mind or if you need me for anything…uh, medical, that is, please don't hesitate to ask."

Then he was gone without another word, leaving her alone to get dressed again. Somehow she thought the thirty-minute drive to Joss's home with Seamus in the same vehicle was going to be the longest half hour of her life.

Because of their mixed blood, Megan and Joss could travel in daylight, but that wasn't true for Seamus or Rafferty. The hours dragged by until finally there was a knock at her door. Joss poked her head in and smiled.

"Hey, are my two favorite cousins ready to hit the road?"

The friendly welcome in Joss's voice was all it took to have Megan's eyes burning. She blinked back the tears as she embraced her cousin. "It's so good to see you."

Joss held her at arm's length for a few seconds. "Megan, I'm so glad you came to us. Rafferty and I won't press for details, but we're here for you. You'll spend tonight at our house, and tomorrow you and I will look at the cottage we thought you'd like. There are other choices if it's not what you have in mind."

Megan managed to smile through her tears. "I'm sure it will be perfect, Joss."

"I'll get Rafferty and Conlan to load the transport. After we grab your medic, we'll head home."

Megan bit back the protest that Seamus wasn't *her* anything. She was in no position to fault someone for wanting to maintain some distance, and she certainly didn't want to make things awkward for him with Joss and Rafferty. Once she and Phoebe were settled in their new home, it was doubtful that she and Seamus would have to see each other except when Phoebe needed a checkup.

The men made quick work of stowing her luggage as well as Seamus's. Finally, the four adults and Phoebe were settled in the transport. Megan rolled her window down to say goodbye to Conlan.

"Thank you for everything. I don't know what Phoebe and I would have done without your help."

The chancellor looked uncomfortable with her gratitude. "Take care of that pretty daughter of yours."

"I will. Once I'm settled in, I'd love to have you over for dinner to show my thanks."

He jerked back as if she'd just insulted him. "That's not necessary."

She watched in confusion as he stalked away. "Did I say something wrong?"

Joss shook her head. "Don't take it personally, Megan. Conlan—"

Rafferty finished the sentence for his wife. "Is a jerk most of the time."

Joss punched her husband on the arm. "Rafferty, cut

the man some slack. Conlan's had his problems, but then who hasn't?" Joss smiled down at Phoebe in her arms. "Except this little lady. She has all of us wrapped around all her adorable little fingers. Isn't that true, Seamus?"

The medic, riding up front with Rafferty, had been silent since getting in the car. If her cousin or her husband thought his withdrawn attitude odd, neither gave any indication of it. That he finally answered surprised her.

"Phoebe is and will always be a heartbreaker."

Then he turned his head to stare out the window into the night. An odd thought crossed Megan's mind as she watched him from the backseat. Despite there being four other people in the enclosed space of the car, she'd never seen anyone look quite so alone.

Chapter 4

Seamus paced the length of the room and back. If the sun didn't set soon, he'd go into a total meltdown. Feeling caged, he started another useless trip across the carpet and counted off the minutes until he could escape the confines of Rafferty O'Day's home.

He'd already consumed three packs of blood, but they'd barely taken the edge off his hunger, much less his anger. Right now, his craving for blood demanded more than sucking it out of plastic. No, far better to plunge his fangs into the soft flesh of someone's neck and take a long, deep pull of life pulsing straight from the source—rich, vibrant and still warm. Somehow he doubted Rafferty would extend his hospitality that far.

It had been decades since the blood hunger of his kind had shaken Seamus's control. But right now his enemy was just down the hall, patiently waiting for

Seamus to make an appearance. To make nice. To petition to be part of Rafferty's new world vision. Instead Seamus wanted to stake the bastard, and that only after he found a way to destroy everything that meant anything to the older vampire.

That was the problem with schemes based on sketchy intelligence—they fell apart at the first sign of an unexpected complication. Clearly his original plan had been shortsighted, not extending much past finding a way into the estate to study Rafferty O'Day from a distance. Instead, thanks to Megan Perez's untimely arrival, Seamus was the hero of the hour, an honored guest in Rafferty's own home.

Wearing out the carpet was getting him nowhere. He stopped in front of the dresser and forced his reflection to appear in the mirror. Good thing he did, because he looked as over the edge as he felt with his hair standing up in ragged spikes and his clothes disheveled. He finger-combed his hair and tucked in his shirt as he concentrated on slowing his pulse. His host might be willing to give Seamus a free pass because of his service to Joss's cousin, but that didn't imply blind trust on his part. If Seamus appeared rattled or was acting guilty, the older vampire was bound to wonder why.

After one last glance at the mirror, Seamus let his image fade and braced himself to face his host. Outside of his room, he paused to listen. A soft murmur of voices drifted down the hallway. He recognized both females and Rafferty himself. Great. He'd have preferred a private audience.

When the voices went silent, he realized the others had heard his approach and were waiting for him to join them. Further delay would only make things more difficult. He carefully schooled his expression, going for reluctance to interrupt his hosts' visit with Megan.

Joss looked up and smiled as soon as he came into sight. "Come on in, Seamus. We were just making plans to give Megan a quick tour of the estate. We'd like you to join us."

Just what he needed—more time shut up in a transport with his enemies. "If you're sure I won't be in the way."

Rafferty answered that one. "Not at all. While we're out, we can stop by the infirmary, so you can take a look around."

All of which would prevent Seamus from having free run of their home while they were out playing host to Megan. That last part went unsaid, but that didn't make it any less true.

"Then I'm sorry to have kept you waiting."

Megan had been awfully quiet, her eyes focused on her lap. Finally she looked up. "We were actually waiting for Phoebe to wake up from her nap."

Right on cue, the youngling in question announced her need for attention with a loud wail. Megan was immediately up and moving, barely giving Seamus time to step out of her way. He fought the urge to follow her, preferring to be with her and Phoebe than being left alone with the O'Days. He was also fighting a strong urge to take care of Phoebe's needs himself and to find out how Megan was feeling.

Joss moved up beside him, her hand coming to rest on his arm. He flinched, causing her to quickly withdraw her touch.

"Sorry." Keeping her voice low, she told him, "I just

wanted to thank you again, Seamus. We would've lost her if you hadn't been there."

The last thing he wanted was gratitude, especially hers. "No thanks are necessary. Besides, I couldn't have done it if you hadn't had the foresight to make sure Conlan had all the right supplies on hand."

Rafferty entered the conversation. "Which brings me back to the infirmary. First thing, go through the inventory and make a list of anything that's missing because we only bought the basics. There's bound to be more we need, especially now that we have a licensed medic on-site."

"I can do that."

The vampire looked as if he had more to say, but Megan was back. Joss held out her hand to take the baby's bag.

As Megan relinquished it, she said, "We'd better get moving. I'd like to get settled in the cottage tonight."

Joss looked both surprised and hurt. "Surely there's no rush, Megan. You just got here."

"I know, but I don't want to be an imposition."

"You won't be. Besides, you need time to recuperate." Joss turned to Seamus for support. "Doesn't she?"

Talk about awkward. The physician in him agreed with his hostess. Those dark circles under Megan's eyes and her bone-thin appearance demanded more rest, more care. But he recognized a kindred spirit as well, one whose entire world had been gutted and bled out by the selfish act of another. Trust would be a long time returning in Megan's life even if she felt guilty for doubting the very people she'd turned to for help.

He compromised, knowing neither woman would be happy, but it really wasn't his problem.

Rather than see the disappointment in Megan's eyes, he focused his attention on Joss. "She needs another twenty-four hours to make sure there aren't any lasting side effects from the medication I gave her. But barring complications, there's no reason she shouldn't set up housekeeping by herself."

Megan stepped in front him, forcing Seamus to acknowledge her presence. "In case you didn't notice, Mr. Fitzhugh, *she* is right here, and *she* can and will speak for herself. I'm not an idiot nor an invalid. If I didn't think I could take care of myself and my daughter, I'd say so."

He had to admire her courage, facing down a vampire who outweighed her by a good eighty pounds. Males of any of the three species didn't take well to someone getting right in their face, but vampires were especially prone to attacking if provoked. He ignored the faint pain of his fangs running out and his body's predictable reaction to an attractive female's challenge.

"Don't put words in my mouth, Megan." He fought for control. "I didn't say you were an idiot or incompetent. I said, *medically* it would be better if you took it easy one more day. That's all."

She stared up at him for several seconds, her own fangs slipping down far enough to show. Finally, she nodded. "Okay. Twenty-four hours."

Then, remembering they had an audience, she pasted a bright smile on her face. "Joss, Rafferty. I don't mean to sound ungrateful, but I've been on the move for a while now. It will be a relief to begin to build a stable home again."

* * *

An hour later, Rafferty pulled up in front of a squat building, obviously designed for function rather than style.

"Here's your new place of business." He tossed Seamus a set of keys. "Check it out, and let me know what you think."

"You're not coming in?" Which would be a relief.

Rafferty shook his head but kept his eyes trained on the building. "I'm going to catch up with Joss and Megan. Despite what she said earlier, I'm thinking both Megan and her daughter will be ready for some rest."

Then he turned to face Seamus, his green eyes hard as jade. "I'm willing to cut you some slack for a couple of reasons. One, you saved the life of someone who is important to my wife. And two, we need a medic on-site.

"Having said that, I will be keeping a close eye on you myself until Conlan gives you a clean bill of health. He's an obnoxious jerk, but he is thorough. If there's something that's likely to bite you on the ass, you'd be better off telling me now, especially when it comes to your ability to take care of my people."

Seamus should tell the bastard to take his job and shove it, but that would be counterproductive. He settled for righteous indignation. "I'm qualified, with primary emphasis on our species, but with enough experience with the other two to do the job."

"That's more than I had hoped for in a medic." Rafferty gave Seamus a short nod. "Go ahead and look the place over, especially the supplies we stocked. Make a detailed list of what you'll need to set up shop. Divide it up by what you *have* to have and what you'd *like* to have. When you're ready, we'll talk budget and set up an inventory system to automatically replace what you use."

"I'll work on it tonight." Seamus reached for the door handle, needing more than ever to get away from his new employer.

But the vampire wasn't done with him. "One more thing. There's an attached apartment for your use. It was stocked with only the basics, too, but I've set up an account for you at the supply depot."

Rafferty looked away again, his eyes focused on the distant horizon. "You're not the first one to show up on my doorstep with little more than the clothes on your back. Don't let pride keep you from taking what you need."

"I don't like charity." Especially Rafferty's.

"Then consider it an advance against your wages." Rafferty's mouth quirked up in a small smile. "And believe me, as the only medic on the place, you'll earn every dime I'm paying you—and then some."

It was all he could do to nod. This time, when he started to open the door, Rafferty let him escape but rolled down the window.

"When you're done, call the house. The number's by the phone in the office. One of us will come for you."

"Sounds like a plan."

Seamus waited for Rafferty to pull away in a cloud of dust before unlocking the door of the clinic. Once inside, he leaned against the wall and closed his eyes. Maintaining control around his enemy was a bitch, but then he hadn't planned on having so much direct contact with the vampire.

Of course, if he convinced Rafferty he could be trusted, it would make it that much sweeter when he finally carried out his plan. But there was one other thing he hadn't counted on—actually liking the older vampire or at least respecting what he was trying to do here on his estate. Their impromptu tour of the grounds had revealed a well-run, burgeoning enterprise.

Most of the humans who made up the majority of the workforce had retired to their homes for the night. Many had waved and smiled as Rafferty's transport had passed by. Odder yet, both Joss and Rafferty had waved back, often calling to people by name. Seamus was pretty sure his late father would've been hard-pressed to name more than a handful of humans by name. It was probably only a ploy to make the cattle work harder for less pay, but it obviously worked.

Speaking of working, he'd better get started himself. He flipped on the lights and got his first clear look at his new temporary place of employment.

Megan looked around the cottage; there had to be something that demanded her attention—a dirty dish that needed washing, a towel that needed folding— anything at all. She and Phoebe had been living in the place for only just over a week, not enough time to make much of a mess. Besides, she'd cleaned the place thoroughly the day before. And the day before that.

Now that her energy levels were improving, she needed something to keep her busy. Anything to keep from thinking too hard about the mess her life had become. Cut off from friends and family, she was now surrounded by nameless strangers.

Well, except for Joss and her husband, but she couldn't claim to really know either of them. It had been years since she'd spent much time with Joss, and she'd only just met Rafferty. Of course, there was Conlan, the gruff chancellor security officer, but he was some distance away at the gate. And finally, Seamus Fitzhugh, new to the estate himself. She wanted to trust someone, anyone, but for Phoebe's sake she had to be careful. Her daughter's life depended on it.

Rather than think about that or the troublesome circumstances surrounding her new job, she double-checked the supplies she'd put together for Phoebe. Right now her daughter was sound asleep in her crib, so peaceful, so pretty, so blissfully unaware of the dangers that inhabited their world. If it were up to Megan, Phoebe would remain innocent and unscarred by life for as long as possible.

To that end, she fully intended to stay within the electrified fences and walls of Rafferty's family estate, no matter who showed up at the gate demanding that she surrender her daughter to their care. Both of the O'Days had been remarkably supportive during the time she'd been there, not to mention patient. She knew she should share the truth of her situation with them, but she'd grown too accustomed to living a secret to make confiding in someone easy.

For Phoebe's sake, eventually she'd confess all to Joss in order to take legal action naming her cousin and Rafferty as Phoebe's guardians, just in case something happened to her—say, like being poisoned. Once again, the medic came to mind. She owed him her life. If only he weren't a vampire— but he was, and she'd never risk involvement with another one.

There was nothing left to do but stare at the clock until the sun went down. Once it did, she'd be on her way to her new job. And her new boss—Seamus Fitzhugh.

The soft purr of a well-tuned engine caught her attention. She turned on the outside lights and slid open the peephole as a transport slowed to a stop in front of the cottage. As soon as she recognized Joss climbing out of the driver's side, she leaned down and gave her daughter a quick kiss.

"Okay, little girl. Here's where the whole trust thing gets started."

Bracing herself for separation anxiety, she opened the door and stepped outside. "Joss, come in. Are you sure you don't mind watching Phoebe for a couple of hours?"

"Not at all. I live to spoil her rotten." Her cousin grinned. "In fact, Rafferty will be along in a minute to help with that."

"You didn't come together?"

"Nope. We wanted to leave one of the transports here for you to use, so we drove separately. There he is now."

Joss held out the keys. "So here, and don't protest. We keep a fleet of vehicles for everyone to use. It's part of the whole package."

Megan wasn't sure she believed that, but she was willing to accept the small lie. "I appreciate all of your help."

"You'd do the same for me. Now trade me my favorite little girl for these keys. You don't want to be late for your first night on the job."

It hurt to hand off her daughter, but she did her best to hide it. "Mr. Fitzhugh said he'd only need me for a couple of hours tonight."

"I know, but anytime you need a break, all you have to do is ask." Joss's expression turned fierce. "And Phoebe will be safe with me and Rafferty."

Tears burned her eyes. "That means a lot, Joss."

"We'll handle whatever comes, Megan, up to and including toxic diapers." Rafferty joined them. He smiled down at Phoebe before meeting Megan's gaze. "You know if there's anything else we can help you with, all you have to do is ask."

She'd been expecting the offer. She forced herself to face the vampire. "I know. I'll think about it."

"Do." He softened the order with a wink. "I promise you and your child will be safe here."

"Thank you, Rafferty." Her eyes burned, but she was done crying. "Now, I'd better get to work. Wouldn't want to anger my new boss on the first day."

"Good luck!"

She drove away while she had the strength to do so. Starting from the minute she'd found out she was pregnant, it had been just her and Phoebe. Now, being separated from her daughter was ripping a hole in her heart. Even if she'd only be gone a short time to go over her new duties with Seamus, it was still hard. Once she knew more what the job entailed, she'd have to make arrangements for Phoebe's care.

She absolutely hated that, but she couldn't live on Joss's charity, either.

The infirmary was only a short distance from her cottage, close enough that she could've walked. She was just as glad to get there and get this first encounter over with. She still wasn't sure how, out of all the people on Rafferty's estate, she came to be working with Seamus Fitzhugh. It wasn't as if she had a medical background, but evidently he needed her computer skills. Time to get moving.

* * *

A transport pulled up out front. Seamus set down the list he'd been staring at for the past fifteen minutes as he waited for his new coworker to arrive. Technically he supposed he was her boss since Rafferty had put him in charge of the clinic. Since he had no desire to be in charge of anything, much less Megan Perez, he'd show her what needed to be done and then concentrate on his own duties. Maybe their paths wouldn't cross all that often.

Megan was going to build the database for the estate's medical records. When he and Rafferty had gone over the inventory, the discussion had turned to the logistics of providing adequate care for the various inhabitants of the estate. It came as no surprise that Megan Perez wasn't the only one who would prefer not to update her official records with the North American Coalition anytime soon.

At Rafferty's suggestion, Seamus was to see the patients as needed and make note of any treatment rendered. At some point in the future, should they ever get a licensed physician, then they'd decide what to do about the regulations that demanded that all doctors report to the Coalition Medical Department.

It was splitting hairs when it came to compliance with the law. At best, the North American Coalition was a loosely organized governing body whose main function was to oversee any interactions where the three races crossed paths. As long as no one complained about their records being incomplete, the Coalition wasn't likely to care one way or the other.

But in any case, Rafferty would be the one to take the heat, provided the vampire lived that long.

With that happy thought, Seamus opened the door for Megan just as she was reaching out to ring the bell, startling her. For the space of a heartbeat, the two of them stood frozen, her hand reaching out, his eyes locked on hers. Finally, she jerked her arm back. He retreated a step. Both of them drew a deep breath.

He finally found his voice. "Sorry, Ms. Perez…Megan. I didn't mean to startle you. Please come in."

She sidled past him in the hallway, only stopping when she'd reached the more spacious waiting room. He took his time locking the door, needing that short break to get himself back under control. He'd thought over the past week that his memory had exaggerated his body's powerful reaction to the skittish chancellor. But no, one look into those pretty, but worried, eyes had his adrenaline pumping hard.

He joined her in the reception area, careful to keep his distance. Her face looked softer, more rounded than he remembered. Good, she was definitely on the mend.

"How are you?"

She managed a small smile. "Are you asking as my medic or making polite conversation?"

He laughed, the tension between them easing. "Both, I guess."

"Better and fine. Phoebe and I have settled into the cottage that Joss picked out for us." She frowned. "Where are you staying?"

"There's an apartment attached to the clinic here. It was intended to be used for whoever is on call. But since I'm it for medical staff right now, I'll be living here."

He hated knowing the food he ate and the roof over his head came straight from his enemy, but there was no way to avoid it here in the middle of O'Day's family estate. Something of what he was thinking must have shown on his face because Megan gave him a sympathetic look.

"Feels like charity, doesn't it?" She pretended an interest in the design of the receptionist's desk. "Joss says I'm being silly, but I'm used to earning my keep."

"Is that why you took the job working here at the clinic? To earn your keep?" What had he expected? That she'd chosen this particular job in order to spend time with him?

She gave him a rueful grin, one that revealed a small dimple in her right cheek. How had he missed seeing that before? He realized, while he'd been staring at her, he'd missed what she was saying.

She didn't seem to notice as she continued, "Of the open positions, this one was the closest fit to my skill set. I've designed record systems before for a variety of businesses. I don't have a medical background, but I figured you could help me with that."

"Out of curiosity, what were your other choices?"

Megan's serious expression was belied by the twinkle in her eyes. "Right now I could be driving a tractor, baling hay or learning to be a transport mechanic. Can you imagine? All those possibilities, and yet I chose to work here."

"Amazing. What were you thinking?" he asked, enjoying the banter far more than he should. "Instead of being out in the bright sunshine, you get to spend your time in a back office here in this lovely concrete building. Or as I've come to call it, the bunker."

The teasing light died in her eyes. "That was a big part of the attraction."

Because she didn't want to risk being seen by the wrong person. "Well then, let me show you around and then I'll introduce you to your new domain."

It didn't take long for Seamus to show her the clinic. When they returned to the reception area, he ushered her into the office she'd be using.

"I downloaded a copy of a Coalition medical records form for you to use as a template but with some minor changes. It's all there in the folder by the computer. I'd also like a color-coded filing system for the hardcopy of the patient charts based on species."

She nodded. "Any preference on colors? Like red for the vampires, white for the humans, and pink for the chancellors since we're somewhere in between."

He raised an eyebrow. "I assume that was a joke."

"Not much of one, since you didn't even smile." Not that she even tried to look apologetic.

"All right. It was cute, but I'd still prefer something like blue, green and yellow."

"Okay, one boring filing system coming up." She walked around the desk and sat down.

Seamus finally smiled. "I'll be directly across the hall if you need me. I thought you might want some time alone to get settled in and maybe make a list of any supplies you require. That's all we needed to talk about tonight. The clinic opens for business the day after tomorrow at four in the afternoon."

Four o'clock? But he was a vampire. The vampires she'd known usually didn't work while the sun was up. "You'll be working during the daylight hours?"

"It's not a problem for me. When I was in training, they

varied our hours all the time to acclimate us to different sleep patterns. We're going to start with being open from late afternoon until midnight, which should be fine for all three groups. Since the humans work the day shift, they can come in at the end of their day. Same for most of the chancellors, although their schedules seem to be more erratic. Any resident vampires can take the later appointments. I'll handle emergencies as they arise."

How odd. In her experience, the vampires she'd known had expected the other two species to change schedules to accommodate their preference for the night hours. Back when she thought she and Banan had a future together, she'd actually traded a job she'd loved for a lesser one because he'd demanded it. What a fool she'd been. She should have known then that he was all take and no give.

Seamus picked up on her mood change. "Is something wrong?"

She forced a smile. "No, sorry, my mind wandered off."

"And not to a happy place, judging by the expression on your face."

Darn, he was far too perceptive. "No, it wasn't. Now, I've already taken up too much of your time. I'll make that list for you."

She walked into her office. *Her* office. It was amazing what a mood lifter that simple expression was. She looked around, surprised at the spacious feel of the room, despite the lack of windows. The furniture was pragmatic rather than fancy, but the computer was top-of-the-line. Rafferty obviously spent his money where it counted.

She jotted down both a supply list as well as some

questions for Seamus about what kind of records he wanted to keep. It occurred to her that neither he nor Rafferty had mentioned anything about billing for the services rendered. She'd have to ask about that. Maybe they planned to hire a bookkeeper, but until the clinic got busy, she should be able to handle that, as well.

Satisfied with the start she'd made, she crossed the hall and knocked on the door frame before entering. "Got a minute?"

"Sure. By the way, no need to knock if the door's open. I'll close it if I need privacy." Seamus looked up from his computer screen. "Have a seat. I'll be with you in a second."

While he finished up, she looked around his office, noting there was barely room to walk between the single bookcase and his desk. Then there were the piles of books on the floor along the wall. Why was he holed up in such a cluttered space while her office was so roomy? Even his name plate on the door was held on with tape. How odd.

When he stopped typing and sat back in his chair, she asked him, "Shouldn't you have the bigger office? All I really need is a place to set a computer while you have all this to deal with." She waved her hand toward the stacks of books piled around the room.

His eyes slid to the side. "I liked this one better."

"Right, everybody wants to run into an obstacle course whenever they walk into their office." What was he trying to hide? "Want to try that again?"

A look of anger flashed across his face. "Okay. I thought you'd need room for a crib and a changing table for Phoebe. This office isn't big enough for all of that."

Had she heard him right? "You want me to bring my daughter to work with me?"

"You mean you don't?" He looked both surprised and a bit defensive. "I thought you'd worry more if she wasn't with you."

Her eyes burned. This vampire was little better than a stranger, and yet he'd known without asking how hard it would be for her to leave Phoebe. What could she say to that? "That's very kind of you."

"I'm not being kind at all. I'll get more work out of you if you figure you owe me." He definitely looked more grumpy.

Obviously he didn't handle gratitude well, so she changed the subject. "Here's the supply list you wanted. I guess I should add a crib and changing table."

"I already ordered them. They'll arrive tomorrow. I'll get them assembled before you're due to arrive."

"Thank you, Seamus."

"It's nothing." His pale skin flushed. "Back to your duties. We're it as far as staff goes. Rafferty is on the lookout for a receptionist and a medical assistant for me."

"And a billing clerk?"

He shook his head. "Rafferty's not charging his people for medical services. He says it's all part of the benefit package, which he hopes will entice more highly trained applicants to move to the estate."

Why did that look as if it left a sour taste in Seamus's mouth? As long as he was being paid by Rafferty, why did he care?

"Would you mind if I take the computer home with me to study the programming?"

"No, that's fine, although I don't expect you to take

your work home with you on a regular basis. I meant what I said about your needing time to rebuild your strength. I respect your need for independence, but if you find the hours are too much, say so. We'll work around it."

"And I said I'm feeling fine." If she sounded defensive, too bad.

He wasn't buying it. "Do I have to remind you that it's only been a week since you almost died? Don't push yourself. You won't do either of us any good if you have a relapse."

She stood up and glared down at him, her hands clenched in fists. "And this isn't the first time I've had to remind you that I'm the best judge of what is and isn't good for me."

He stepped around the desk to loom over her. "And was it your good judgment that got you poisoned in the first place?"

That did it. She'd never slapped anyone in her entire life, but his arrogance shattered her control. His vampire reflexes kicked in, enabling him to catch her wrist before her hand made contact with his face. Her temper flamed hot as she struggled to pull free of his grasp. Instead of letting her go, his other arm snapped around her and yanked her up against his chest.

"Seamus."

She meant to yell his name, to protest his rough treatment of her. But the single word came out as a whisper, almost a prayer as his lips touched hers and their burning anger changed into a whole different type of heat.

Chapter 5

She tasted honey sweet with just a hint of hot spice.

He'd wondered about that; now he knew. Her tongue mated and danced with his, both of them lost in the moment. Touches were tentative, gentle. A brush of fingertips there, a slow caress tracing a curve, a slight squeeze. How long had it been since someone had touched him at all? He couldn't remember. Their bodies shifted and aligned perfectly, her softness against his hard strength.

Warmth, all delicious temptation, slid through his veins, running out his fangs and making him want to savor far more of this woman than a simple kiss. Her blood called to him, arousing his craving to taste life in its purest form. He broke off the kiss and nibbled his way along the elegant curve of her jaw and down her neck. There, he found it—the soft flutter of her pulse running so enticingly close to the surface.

He gently raked the tips of his fangs across her skin, asking permission without words to take this exploration one step further. But instead of offering herself up to him, she gasped as if in pain and shoved him backward. The unexpected move, combined with her chancellor strength, caught him off guard. Once again his vampire reflexes saved him.

The chill in Megan's eyes left no doubt that the moment had passed, leaving only their original anger hovering between them. Despite his disappointment, he had to admire the way she stood her ground, refusing to cower before a fully aroused, fully enraged vampire male. He fought hard to bank his temper, his frustration and the powerful need to take her right there amidst the clutter on his desk.

They remained frozen in place, both breathing hard as if running a race. Finally, he blinked and stepped back, breaking the spell. More distance would be needed if he was going to resist the urge to touch her again.

"Go home, Megan." He forced the words through the tightness in his throat.

"But…"

He held up his hand to stop her. "I know. We can't. We won't." When that didn't seem to satisfy her, he added, "Hell, Megan, if anyone ever asks, I'll even swear we didn't. But you need to leave. Now."

She nodded as she backed toward the door. "I'll tell Rafferty to find someone else."

That would probably be the smart thing to do, but right now he wasn't feeling all that intelligent. "No, you won't."

To his amazement, rather than blow up again over him

trying to boss her around, she laughed. "Wasn't your trying to issue orders what got us into this position?"

This wasn't the position he wanted to try out with her. In fact, he could think of several, but in that direction lay madness. If she could lighten up, so could he, even if it killed him.

Forcing a great deal more good humor into his words than he actually felt, he said, "Okay, Ms. Perez, let me rephrase that. I would most humbly appreciate it if you would not demand Rafferty find you another job."

"Why? It's not like you have a lot invested in my training or anything."

"This might be the only job where you can bring Phoebe with you. I'm the only one who knows there's a very real threat to both of you. That is, unless you want to come clean with Rafferty or Conlan and tell them somebody wants you dead."

His words hit her hard, making her flinch. He didn't regret saying them, though. He'd saved her life once, but that was no guarantee he'd be able to again.

"What if your vampire lover tries again? I might not get to you in time if you're working days or on the other side of the estate. What if he goes after Phoebe the next time?"

"That won't happen because he wants her. It's me he's finished with." He could tell that admission cost her a lot. She shrank in on herself, once more looking like the desperately ill woman she'd been when he first met her. Then her shoulders snapped back, her spine ramrod straight.

"I'll keep the job, Seamus, but only if you promise this won't happen again. It was nice. Actually way beyond nice, but I've learned my lesson. I won't risk getting involved with another—"

She stopped midsentence, unable or at least unwilling to continue, but they both knew what she'd been about to say. She wasn't willing to get involved with him because he was a vampire, just like Phoebe's mysterious father. That was all right. He couldn't afford to get involved with anybody, regardless of species. He had his own agenda to follow.

"We'll write it off to a momentary weakness that won't happen again. We'll make sure of that. Do we have a deal?"

She reluctantly nodded. "All right. I'll be back tomorrow afternoon with Phoebe. If you change your mind before then, call. I'll understand."

"I won't change my mind."

"Unless there's something else, I'll go pack up the computer and leave."

"I'll walk you out." He braced himself for the argument sure to come.

Once again, she surprised him. "All right, but just this once. After all, Rafferty is very careful about who he lets in. We're safe here on the estate."

Seamus knew for a fact Rafferty hadn't been all that careful. After all, he'd let Seamus in, hadn't he? But wisely, he kept that little bit of information to himself.

It didn't take long for Megan to gather up her computer, the file and her keys. Seamus waited for her by the front door of the clinic, not wanting to crowd her. Even more, he didn't want to test his control around her. When she was safely tucked into her transport, he stood in the doorway and watched her drive away, not wanting her to feel like he was hovering.

As soon as she was out of sight, he changed into shorts and a T-shirt. He'd already established a routine of taking a late-night run, using his need for exercise as an excuse to learn the layout of the estate. So far, he'd taken a different route each time, but made sure to pass by Rafferty's home at some point.

Unlike the infirmary, which had no windows in the walls, Rafferty's house was definitely more high-tech. Heavy-duty shutters protected the vampire leader from sunlight during the day, but they opened at night to allow in the evening air. Each pass through the area netted him more information, learning the behavior patterns of the locals, including Rafferty and his wife. As he ran, he noted whose dogs barked, where the vampires lived, whose lights went off early.

Once he started official office hours, his chances to scope out the estate would become more restricted. So tonight, he'd take the long way around, and if his route took him past a certain cottage on his way, so much the better. It wasn't as if he was hoping for another glimpse of Megan Perez. He just wanted to make sure she'd gotten home safely.

Yeah, right.

Damn, Conlan could really learn to hate that bell. It was petty on his part, but he continued to ignore the summons until he finished reading the report from one of his operatives. Once he'd signed off on it, he took his own sweet time stepping outside. The security lights were on, bathing the latest stray in stark relief.

Vampire, judging by his size and the time of his arrival. Conlan drew his weapon and walked toward the gate.

The jerk flashed his fangs with a hiss. "It took you long enough. I'm sure your boss won't appreciate knowing how incompetent his lackey is."

Charming. So not only vampire, but one from a top-level clan. It didn't matter which one, the behavior was always the same: arrogant, demanding and a pain in the ass.

Well, two could play that game, too. "Sorry. You don't have an appointment. Next time, call before you decide to show up unannounced."

He smiled, showing off his own impressive set of fangs. "Now if you'll excuse me, I have things to do. You know, important lackey stuff."

Back inside, he counted down the minutes until either the bell started up again or his phone rang. It didn't take long. As tempting as it was to ignore the phone, he knew better than to ignore Rafferty O'Day.

He kicked back in his chair and put his feet up on the desk. "Hi, Rafferty. What's up?"

"Shea, why am I having to make this call?"

"Because I'm not supposed to allow questionable characters onto the premises. That's my job description."

Silence. Conlan smiled and started a mental countdown until the explosion. He only got as far as eight, a new record.

"The only son and heir of the Delaney clan is not a questionable character."

"Sorry, boss, but he didn't identify himself. Had I known, I would've let him in. Honest."

"Go do it now. Offer him something to drink while he waits in your office until I can get there to pick him up."

"Will do, boss. Immediately, boss. Is there anything else, boss?"

"Conlan—" Rafferty paused, drawing a slow breath as if praying for patience.

"Yes, boss?"

"Be grateful Joss likes you so much."

"Oh, believe me. I am." Sometimes he even felt guilty about it. "See you in a few minutes, sir."

Then he hung up and headed outside to open the gate. Rather than wait for the vampire, Conlan walked back inside without a backward look, saying without words that the fool was beneath notice and no threat. Coming from a chancellor, the Delaney heir would recognize the implied insult. Conlan stopped short of closing the door, although the temptation to make the vampire wait outside on the porch was strong.

He was already back at his computer working when his guest sauntered in, all arrogance and anger. *Bring it on, punk, and you'll find out why chancellors are employed to keep both vampires and humans in line.*

Opening the fridge, he pulled out a blood pack and tossed it on the desk. "Here. Enjoy."

"I suppose warming it first would be too much to ask."

Conlan kept his eyes firmly on the computer screen. "The kitchen's through that door. Knock yourself out."

The blood pack came flying back across the desk as the young vampire sneered. "Do you have any idea who I am?"

Conlan tossed the pack back in the fridge. "According to Rafferty, you're one of the Delaney clan."

"I'm the heir."

Clearly he expected Conlan to be impressed. He

wasn't. "Congratulations or else condolences, depending on how you feel about that."

"Does O'Day have any idea how insufferably rude you are to his guests?"

"You'll have to ask him yourself. Now if you'll excuse me, as I said, I have work to do." He saved the report he'd just downloaded from his operative and then fired back a list of follow-up questions.

The young vampire leaned back in his chair and propped his feet up on the corner of Conlan's desk. "You might want to update your résumé while you're at it. When Rafferty finds out how you've treated me, I'm sure you'll be needing it."

Actually, that might be true, but Conlan wasn't going to worry about it. Right now he was going to do some quick digging to see why someone of Delaney's status would come knocking on Rafferty's gate unannounced. Ever since Rafferty had married Joss Sloan, his relationship with the upper echelons of the vampire community had been chilly at best. They couldn't shun him completely; his money wielded too much power for that to happen.

But for the heir of one of the snootiest families to show up like this warranted checking into. He'd keep his inquiries low-key rather than risk setting off a major feud between the two clans. Rafferty really would fire his ass for that, but watching out for possible threats to the estate was Conlan's job, after all.

It was always possible Delaney had a good reason for being there. But Conlan's instincts, finely honed after years of sifting through the bullshit to find the truth, were screaming that something was off about this visit. Punks like Delaney usually traveled first-class and with an entourage. Conlan was still trying to make sense out of the scant details in Seamus Fitzhugh's portfolio, but that would have to wait. Right now, he had other fish to fry.

"Well, today's the day."

Seamus didn't bother to check his appearance in the mirror. He might need every scrap of energy he could muster to get through the next eight hours. Even so, he straightened the collar of his lab coat and patted his pockets to make sure they were stocked with the usual stuff—pencil, pen, notepad and some silly stickers for any younglings who came in.

The sound of the front door opening echoed through the building. Time to go. Megan had insisted on coming in early for the official opening of the infirmary. She said it was to give Phoebe time to settle into her new surroundings, but he suspected Megan had picked up on how nervous he was about all of this. Even though he'd used his medical training merely as the means to get through the gate, he found himself wanting to do the job right.

In fact, sometimes he actually forgot about his real reason for being there. Then something would make him think of his sister Petra and all the grief and anger came rushing back to remind him that he had a higher purpose than merely dispensing medication and doing physicals. If his clan was destined to disappear, he insisted on taking his enemies with him.

But it wasn't time for that. Not yet, but soon. Definitely soon. The more time he spent in this charade, the easier it would be for him to forget the debt that was owed, the price that must be paid. And spending hours in the company of Megan Perez and her sweet daughter weren't helping any.

Not for the first time, he wondered what kind of coldhearted bastard not only cast Megan aside, but tried to kill her. A man lucky enough to have Megan in his life should've cherished her. And to be doubly blessed to create a child together? That was such a rarity among his kind.

"Seamus? Are you in there?"

"Coming."

Megan waited for him in the short hallway that led to both of their offices as well as to his private quarters. They'd been careful in their dealings with each other since that kiss two nights ago in his office. Even so, the memory, the potential of it, seemed to hover over them whenever they were in the same room. Maybe if they'd actually carried the encounter through to its logical end, they would've been able to write it off to nerves or proximity or even just plain need.

Instead, they maneuvered around each other, careful not to touch, careful not to linger, careful not to get too close. However, all that their careful dancing accomplished was to emphasize the temptation and his secret hope it might happen again. But now definitely wasn't the time for such thoughts.

"Hi, you ready for this?"

Megan smiled. "As ready as I can be. I'll do my best to funnel the patients through to you in the right order."

"First come, first served…"

"Unless there's blood involved." She finished for him, smiling.

He'd explained the basic principles of triage to her,

but that pretty much summed it up. "That is, if we get any customers at all."

He followed Megan into her office where she settled Phoebe into her crib. "Oh, I wouldn't worry too much about that. Have you looked outside lately?"

"No. Should I?"

"Follow me."

She led the way back to the front entrance and slid open the peephole in the door. He leaned in over her shoulder to look outside, doing his best ignore to the twin distractions of the rapid trip of Megan's pulse and the scent of her skin. He closed his eyes briefly to force himself to focus and took a look outside. Then he blinked twice and looked again.

He stepped back to put more distance between him and temptation. "The line goes all the way to the road."

"I know. It's even longer now than when I came in."

A familiar surge of adrenaline simmered in his veins. "Guess we'd better get ready."

"I'd better give Joss a call. She said if it looked like we'd be busy, she'd come by and take care of Phoebe for me until she goes down for the night."

The last thing he wanted was one of the O'Days underfoot right now. Things were bound to get hectic with that many patients on his first night. On the other hand, it was doubtful he could play a triple role of receptionist, nurse and medic by himself. If Joss could free Megan up to work with the patients, things were bound to go more smoothly.

"That's a good idea." He closed the peephole after taking one more look. "I guess they really did need a medic on the estate."

She smiled on her way to the reception desk. "Looks like. Joss and Rafferty will be more glad than ever that you're here."

Not if they suspected his real reasons for being there, but now wasn't the time for such thoughts. He waited until Megan called Joss before unlocking the door to invite the first patient of the night through the door.

Megan's back ached and her feet hurt, but it was a good tired, the kind that came from a job well done. Other than a couple of small glitches, the past nine hours had flown by. Starting from the initial onslaught, they'd never had more than a ten-minute break between patients all night long. They'd planned on closing at midnight, but around ten o'clock a pair of chancellors had carried in a human with a nasty gash on his leg.

As Seamus had said, blood took priority. Taking him ahead of everyone else who'd been waiting barely caused a stir. In fact, several offered to come back the next night, but Seamus had insisted on seeing each and every patient. If they were willing to wait, he was willing to see them.

She could only imagine how tired he must be. She saw the last patient out and then locked the door and turned off the outside lights. She really wanted to take Phoebe home, but not before she knew Seamus was all right. As far as she knew, he hadn't had a chance to feed or eat all night. Rather than ask, she pulled three packs out of the refrigerator and put the blood in to heat.

He wasn't in his office, so she went on a hunt. He was in the lab looking at a slide with a microscope.

"Seamus, can't that wait?"

He made some notes and then set the slide aside. "That's the last one."

"Good. You've done more than enough for one night. Surely anything else can wait until tomorrow. Come on, I've got blood warming for you."

He gave her a dark look but followed anyway. "Your job description doesn't include waiting on me."

"And I don't plan on making a habit of it." She blocked his office door. "No, you don't need to spend the rest of the night at your desk. Go sit in your living room and I'll bring it to you."

"Megan…"

"Seamus…" she echoed, with a smile. "Look, just go sit. The faster you do what I tell you, the faster I can go home."

He clearly wanted to argue the point, but she walked away before he could. When she returned with the packets, she found him sprawled on the sofa, his head tipped back and his eyes closed. It was the first time she'd crossed the threshold into his private quarters and wasn't sure if she should. Both of them had worked hard the past couple of days to establish a strictly profes-sional relationship.

Feeding him in his home was definitely on the other side of the line they'd drawn. But it would have taken a much harder heart than hers to see how tired he was and not want to help.

"Seamus," she called softly.

When he didn't answer, she tried again, this time re-luctantly reaching out to shake his shoulder.

His eyes popped open as soon as she touched him. "I'm awake. I'm awake."

"Sure you are. Here, take this." She handed him one of the packets and put the other two within easy reach before backing away.

When he didn't immediately feed, she resorted to nagging. "Seamus, that's going to get cold."

He inverted the packet a couple of times to mix it. "I was waiting for you to leave."

"I've seen a vampire feed before. It doesn't bother me."

"Maybe it bothers *me*."

Before she could ask why, Phoebe made her own demands known. "Okay, I hear my name being called. I'll leave you to it."

Joss had taken care of Phoebe as Megan worked the reception desk, staying far longer than they'd originally planned. She'd sworn she didn't mind because Rafferty was out giving an unexpected visitor the grand tour. Once Phoebe settled into sleep, she'd gone home.

"Hey, there, little one. I'll bet you're hungry." Normally, Megan would've preferred to take her home first so she could put Phoebe back to bed after she'd been fed. But right now, it would take too long to pack everything up and haul it out to the transport.

After changing Phoebe's diaper, she took her out to the waiting room and sat down in one of the chairs. These quiet moments spent nursing her daughter were always the best ones of the day. She found the time soothing, the physical connection between them almost spiritual. She brushed Phoebe's wispy hair and smiled.

"Hey there, little one. I love you."

Tears stung her eyes. Maybe because she was tired, but the reason didn't matter. Sometimes it hit her hard how much she'd gone through just to get where she was, safe and with her daughter in her arms. No matter what she'd given up, she didn't regret her decision to keep Phoebe.

This might not be the life she'd envisioned for herself, but she had few regrets. A slight noise caught her attention. Seamus was standing in the shadows across the room, watching the two of them with such stark hunger in his expression. Yeah, she had regrets, but meeting Seamus Fitzhugh wasn't one of them.

If only he was a chancellor, but he wasn't. All the more reason to keep some distance between them.

"Don't let us keep you, Seamus. I can let myself out."

"Not going to happen. I'll make sure you get home safely."

"But—"

He leaned against the wall and closed his eyes. "Megan, we're both too tired to argue. If it weren't so late, there'd be enough people still out and about to make it safe for you to be on your own. So either I take you home or I'll follow you. Either way, you're not going to be alone."

She suspected that he'd find another excuse tomorrow night, but she really didn't want to fight about it. Phoebe had already fallen back asleep; they could go now. Tomorrow would be soon enough to get this matter settled once and for all.

"I'll get my things."

Conlan had picked up the phone half a dozen times in the past two hours. Rafferty hadn't spoken to him since Delaney's arrival two nights ago. If there'd been any problems with the vampire heir's surprise visit, surely Conlan would've heard.

Even so, he couldn't quit thinking about the young vampire's unexpected appearance. Maybe it was just the inborn arrogance of a vampire scion that had gotten under Conlan's skin, but he didn't think so. It was more the kid didn't fit the profile of the usual applicants for residency on the O'Day estate, which made him a bit of a mystery.

Conlan hated mysteries.

"Screw it."

He gave in and punched in Rafferty's number. No answer. He slammed the receiver back down and considered his options. His assistant had arrived, so Conlan could go poke around the estate himself and see what he could find out.

As he waited, he thumbed through the stack of files on his desk. The third one down belonged to Seamus Fitzhugh. So far, all the information matched what the young vampire had given them. Oddly enough, that's what bothered Conlan. It was too perfect. Next, he'd send one of his operatives to quietly interview anyone who might have really known Seamus. But as far as Conlan could tell, Seamus had left behind no friends, no family, no nothing. Hell, he hadn't even had a parking ticket.

Oddly enough, despite his misgivings, Conlan realized he very much wanted to approve the file. He'd liked the young vampire, but that wasn't why. Watching Seamus fight for Megan Perez's life had been like watching a highly trained warrior go into battle, armed with little more than his courage and determination that no one would die on his watch. That kind of heroism deserved to be rewarded.

Unlike the egotistical jerk who'd shown up the other

night, Seamus deserved a chance here on the O'Day estate. Maybe he'd drop in on young Fitzhugh at the infirmary. Before he made a final decision on Seamus's future, he wanted to look the young medic in the eye one more time.

History had proven Conlan's judgment wasn't infallible, but right now, it was all he had to go on.

Chapter 6

Seamus set a stack of patient files on Megan's desk. The brightly colored folders represented the impressive amount of work they'd accomplished on their first night in business. Tonight could be just as busy. In the past, Rafferty had made arrangements for emergency care for the residents of the estate, but that was all.

Much of what Seamus had done last night was routine care—immunizations, medication renewals, minor infections. The one injury had been bad enough, but nothing that couldn't have been evacuated to a trauma center if necessary. He'd stitched the leg wound closed easily enough. The guy would have an interesting scar, but no lasting damage.

Seamus found himself looking forward to what the night's patient load might bring. He wasn't sure how he felt about that. It had been a long time since he'd actually had anything at all to look forward to. In medical school, the heavy workload pretty much insured that all he and his fellow students had time to think about was getting through each shift, grabbing a few hours of sleep and then starting all over again.

How long had it been since he actually had some control over how he spent his days—or nights? Too long. And he was only fooling himself that he did now. He had one goal, one last duty to carry out, and to consider anything else was a waste of energy. He needed to hold the people he met at arm's length, but that was so much harder to do than he'd expected.

It didn't help that the air in Megan's office was rife with her scent coupled with Phoebe's sweet baby smell. There was also a taste of Joss O'Day mixed in, but that was beneath his notice. It hadn't taken long for Megan to make the room her own. The woman definitely had some control issues. She'd given him very specific instructions where to put the files as he finished with them. He had no doubt that she'd even double-check to make sure he'd input the information correctly before putting the patient files away on the shelf.

He couldn't wait to see how she did it. If it were up to him, they'd be filed by species first and then alphabetized by last name. He was betting she'd do the same. But however Megan set up her filing system, she'd be able to lay hands on anything he wanted with easy efficiency—one more thing he liked about her.

Which was the last thing he needed.

He allowed himself one more deep breath of Megan-scented air before leaving her office. There was much to be done to get ready for tonight. But as he headed

across the waiting room, intent on restocking the examination rooms, there was a sharp knock at the front
door of the clinic. He veered in that direction, his pulse
already kicking into high gear to deal with whatever
crisis awaited his attention.

When he threw the door open, there was obviously
no emergency. Instead, Joss O'Day gave him a bright
smile and shoved a picnic basket toward him.

"Hi, Seamus. I figured you'd be up and might appreciate a meal you didn't have to cook for yourself. Megan
said you had a heck of a first night on the job."

His hand automatically closed on the basket's handle,
despite the strong temptation to refuse the gift. He had
no desire to accept any more handouts from O'Day and
his wife than was absolutely necessary. On the other
hand, the better he knew his enemy, the better his chance
to strike hard when the time came. The two of them had
played loose with the rules of their society, with no
regard for the fallout their games had caused. They
would soon learn that such carelessness would come
back to haunt them.

"Would you like to come in, Mrs. O'Day?" he asked,
forcing a note of friendly curiosity into his voice. When
she frowned, he added, "I mean, Joss."

He preferred to use her married name, to maintain
that much more distance, but she'd already insisted on
him calling her by her first name. Neither of the O'Days
stood much on formality, a definite anomaly among the
vampire clans. Another was their willingness to take in
strays, although he doubted they would appreciate him
calling their people that. It was true, though. Rafferty
had made it clear that his estate offered a new start for

anyone willing to work hard, with few questions asked other than Conlan's initial screening of all applicants.

Seamus stepped back into the shadows of the doorway as he waited for her to decide. Even so, there was still too much sunshine for comfort.

Joss didn't hesitate. "If you're sure you don't mind."

He led the way into his office, wanting the solid presence of his desk between them. "You timed this perfectly. I was going to restock the exam rooms before grabbing a bite to eat. We used up a lot of supplies last night."

And he was babbling. To keep his hands busy, he opened the basket. The rich scent of tomato and basil filled the air.

"I hope you like spaghetti and meatballs," Joss said with a smile. "It's one of Rafferty's favorites, so I thought you might like it, too."

"I'm sure I will."

"Go ahead and eat while it's hot."

"Will you join me?"

"No, I'm fine. In fact, while I'm here, I think I'll put together some more patient files for Megan. She showed me how last night, and it will give her a head start. Rafferty is still sleeping because he had a late night with an unexpected guest, and I'm restless."

He would rather she didn't stay, but knew he was fighting a losing battle. Instead, he concentrated on eating, figuring he'd need all his strength to get through what could be another stressful night.

The meatballs were just as he liked them—spicy and no garlic. Back in the day, before the present system of government evolved to allow the three species to coexist side by side, humans thought that garlic would protect them from vampires. The truth was, his species just didn't care for the taste. He wondered if the same was true for chancellors.

Before he could take another bite, he heard something. Was that someone else knocking at the door? Before he could get up, Joss poked her head in.

"You eat. I'll see who it is. If you're needed, I'll holler."

Who else would it be for? He was the only medic in the region.

He set his fork down and listened. He could hear Joss's voice as well as a deeper male one. It was too early for any of the vampires on the estate to be out, so that left the humans and chancellors. As the voices drew closer, recognition kicked in. What was Conlan Shea doing here?

Joss led the security officer straight into Seamus's office. "Seamus, you must be special for Conlan to come calling, especially considering he's turned down every invitation I've made since he hired on."

Conlan's face flushed red. "Sorry, Joss. I've been busy."

"Yeah, right. Well, since you're here anyway, you *will* show up at my house this evening at midnight to eat with Rafferty and me." She gave him a narrow-eyed look. "You wouldn't want to hurt my feelings, would you?"

Judging by Conlan's expression, he really wanted to refuse, but knew he was trapped. "All right, Joss, I'll be there. But shouldn't you ask Rafferty first?"

"You let me worry about him." She smiled, clearly unafraid of her vampire spouse. "Good, that's settled. Now I'm going back to work in Megan's office with the music turned up so I can't hear what the two of you have to gossip about. See you tonight, Conlan."

"All right." The chancellor waited until she closed the door before quietly adding, "I'm sure Rafferty will be thrilled."

"I heard that!" Joss called just before the music started playing.

Seamus fought to hide a smile, but then gave up and grinned at Conlan. "I take it you're not Rafferty's favorite employee."

"True, but the fact that he's not my favorite employer sort of evens things out."

Conlan leaned forward and sniffed. "Did Joss make that?"

Seamus recognized hungry when he saw it. "Yeah. If you want some, come with me."

Without waiting for Conlan to answer, Seamus gathered up the food and put it back in the basket. "We'll have more room next door in my quarters."

Conlan followed him, not bothering to hide his curiosity about Seamus's home. "Nice place. You settling in all right?"

Figuring the security officer rarely asked idle questions, Seamus considered his words carefully before answering.

"Yesterday was our first night to open the infirmary. It was a madhouse, but I liked feeling useful."

"Yeah, I get that." He accepted the plate of spaghetti and salad. "It's probably rude of me to invite myself to lunch, but I love Joss's spaghetti. She makes great lasagna, too."

So Conlan knew her well enough to know her cooking skills. Interesting. "How long have you known her?"

"Since our days as arbiters for the Coalition negotiating agreements between the three species. She was one of the best before she resigned."

Seamus wasn't surprised by that. In fact, Conlan would be surprised to know exactly how much Seamus did know about Joss's time as an arbiter for the Coalition. After all, her actions during that time had set in motion the events that had brought destruction raining down on Seamus's sister.

For that, Joss and her vampire husband would pay. But now wasn't the time for such thoughts. Not with a sharp-eyed chancellor sitting across the table from him.

"She definitely has a way about her."

"That she does." Conlan cut himself another slice of bread. "I understand Megan's working here at the infirmary, too. That's convenient."

Seamus glared at Conlan. "What's that supposed to mean?"

The chancellor shrugged. "Nothing. Just that since she's the only person you knew here, it was nice that you ended up working together. I assume her health has improved."

"That it has. Good thing, too. Try telling her to take it easy and you'll get your head handed to you."

Conlan didn't exactly smile, but his eyes warmed up. "Can't say that it surprises me. Toughness must run in their family. As sick as Megan was, I'm still amazed she made it all the way to the gate. Good thing she did, and better yet that you happened to be there at the right time."

He leaned back in his chair and gave Seamus a hard look. "I'm due to make my final recommendation on your application to live here. Is there anything you want to tell me before I send my report to the boss?"

"Not that I can think of, but if you have any specific questions, I'll try to answer them." Seamus made himself meet Conlan's direct gaze head-on. He hoped like hell that the chancellor was on a fishing expedition and not really expecting to catch anything.

"Do you like living here?"

"Yes." At least he could be honest on that point.

"Why?"

How to answer that? The real truth was out of the question. He picked up his dish and set it in the sink and thought about how he would have answered if he were the man he was pretending to be.

"I won't deny that I've made my share of poor choices, but I'm good at what I do. Most of the patients I saw last night were routine cases, but that doesn't mean the care I gave them was unimportant. The residents here on the estate need somebody with my particular skills."

He turned back to face Conlan. "I'd like to stay."

"Glad to hear that, considering I've already sent your file through with my recommendations that we accept you, Seamus. But make no mistake, if I find that my trust was misplaced, I'm a bad enemy to have."

So was Seamus, but Conlan wasn't his target. "Thank you, Conlan. I don't want to disappoint you."

But he would, and he hated knowing that.

"Well, I've got to go. Thanks for sharing your lunch with me. I've other business to take care of before I have to be at Joss's at midnight." Conlan still didn't look pleased about what was essentially a command performance.

Seamus followed him to the front door. "Look on the bright side. Maybe Joss will make lasagna."

"Even that won't make dinner with Rafferty any more

palatable. Especially if his guest is still hanging around. I don't know why that vampire is here in the first place."

Seamus let a little bitterness seep into his voice. "You mean he's not broke and running from his past?"

Conlan clapped Seamus on the shoulder. "Now, listen, Joss prefers that we think of our residents as running toward their future, not from their past. But to answer your question, this guy is the sole heir to his family's fortune, definitely not the kind of vampire we usually have show up at the gate, especially alone."

Seamus's mental alarms went off. "Did he say why he's here?"

"I can answer that."

Neither of them had noticed the music had been turned off. Joss joined them at the door. "Banan Delaney says that he's heard about our more progressive ways of doing things and wanted to see them for himself. He claims he's been butting heads with his family over how to get the most work out of their human and chancellor employees."

Conlan nodded, as if her explanation confirmed something for him. "Sounds like you don't believe him."

"It's hard to take him seriously when he spends most of his time drinking up our blood supplies and looking bored. If he's asked one intelligent question, I haven't heard it. And there's something off about him when we do show him around."

"How so?"

Joss frowned as she considered her answer. "He seems more interested in who we have working for us than how the work is being done. If he's wanting to change things on his own estate, it should be the other way around. It's almost as if he's hunting for somebody."

For the first time Seamus saw the warrior side in the two chancellors. Both radiated strength and determination, their fangs showing, although not fully extended. If he were this vampire heir, he'd be treading carefully around these two. Ever perceptive, Joss picked up on Seamus's own tension.

"Seamus? Do you know something about Delaney I should know about? Have you met him before?"

Joss's question jerked his attention back to her. "No, no I haven't. I'm afraid I wasn't exactly listening. I've got a lot to get ready before we open again tonight."

Joss seemed to accept his explanation. He wasn't so sure about Conlan, but then the chancellor was paid to suspect everyone and everything.

"Thanks again for bringing lunch, Joss."

"You're welcome. We'll get going so you can get something done."

Seamus locked the door after they left, intending to restock the exam rooms. However, he couldn't concentrate as the conversation played over and over in his mind. An irritating visitor was hardly his concern, but something about Joss's description of the vampire's actions prodded at him.

Was the vampire looking for someone specifically? If so, then the question was who? A chill danced down his spine. As Conlan had pointed out, quite a few of the estate residents had their own secrets to protect, but he knew one in particular who had a vampire in her past.

It was huge leap in logic, but they all suspected that Megan had been running from someone, and most likely that person was a vampire. But what Joss and Conlan didn't know was that she'd been systematically poisoned. If Delaney was indeed Phoebe's biological father, he could be here to try to finish the job and reclaim his daughter.

Seamus's own fangs ran out fully at the perceived threat to Megan. If the vampire tried to harm either female, Seamus would kill the bastard. And it wouldn't be an easy death, not if the vampire dared to threaten Megan. Seamus had dragged her back from the edge of death, and that made her his woman now.

His.

And that realization ricocheted around in his head as he tried to make sense of it. What was he thinking? Megan wasn't his. Never would be. But on a gut level, he knew that didn't matter. There was a connection between them that was forged that first day and had only strengthened with each minute he'd spent in her company.

She and her innocent daughter deserved to live in peace, not be haunted by a specter from her past.

There was no way to know if this Delaney fellow was really the villain in this affair, short of asking Megan point-blank who the father of her child was. Even then, she might not answer. While he admired her desire for independence, he wouldn't let it stand in the way of her safety.

He checked the time. She'd arrive for work in just over two hours. He'd put the time to good use and do some snooping of his own. The news media loved to cover the social circles a vampire heir like Delaney ran in.

It was a long shot, but it might just give him enough information to confront Megan with.

Banan checked his messages and cursed under his breath. So far, his mother, his father and two of his four grandparents had seen fit to send him e-mails. Each and every one of them contained the same demand for an update on his progress. He could sum it up in one word: *none.* He considered sending out a blanket message to that effect, along with a request that they leave him the hell alone, but that wouldn't be smart.

Right now, his relationship with the higher-ranking members of his clan was dicey. If he were to push back too hard, it would be just like them to cut him off without a dime. According to his mother's mother, he'd had more than enough time to pick a nice vampire female from an appropriate family to marry. Not only that, the clan needed an heir to solidify the clan's future and right now his bastard daughter by a chancellor was their only option.

More and more the vampire clans were finding it harder to produce a new generation to carry on the family name. Humans and chancellors, on the other hand, had no such problem. They bred herds of young like the cattle they were. The only plus was that their mixed genes meant chancellor women were capable of producing a pureblood vampire.

When he'd culled Megan Perez out of the herd to breed with, he'd known the odds and rolled the dice. First time out, they'd produced a healthy vampire female. Custom demanded that Megan give the child up to her father's family to raise.

Where he'd gone wrong was that he'd also chosen Megan for her intelligence, not just because she was pretty. Who could've guessed that such a stubborn nature existed under that pleasant facade? Under increasing pressure from his family, he'd resorted to extreme measures to get the child away from her. She should've died from the poison he'd given her. Instead, she'd disappeared.

He ripped open another blood pack and poured it into a glass. It was insulting that Rafferty didn't provide humans for Banan to feed from, but that didn't mean that Banan would stoop to sucking his meal from a plastic bag. He took a long drink and waited for the familiar buzz of the rich liquid to hit. Unfortunately, the packaging process diluted the effect, forcing him to drink more blood to get the same energy from it.

At least his host kept a well-stocked supply of even the rarer types, although he suspected Joss O'Day was growing tired of playing hostess. Too bad. Even though Rafferty had all but severed any ties with the vampire hierarchy, he couldn't afford to alienate them completely. So as long as Banan didn't break any of the household rules, such as direct feeding, Rafferty would allow him to stay.

Because of the sprawling size of the O'Day family estate, it was taking longer to search for Megan than Banan had planned on. It would help if he could access the records on Rafferty's computer, but they were password protected. Before coming to the estate, he'd even paid someone to hack into the Coalition medical files but with no luck. If Megan had received any medical treatment, it hadn't been reported anywhere.

Not for the first time, he wondered if he'd actually succeeded in killing her. While that would save him the trouble of having to try again, that didn't answer the question about where his daughter might be. It wasn't as if he knew for certain that Megan had sought out her cousin Joss for sanctuary, but he'd already exhausted all the other logical possibilities.

Certainly her parents hadn't exactly welcomed her back into the fold. Most chancellors preferred to see their young stick to their own species, increasing the likelihood any resulting children would also be chancellors. And if they gave birth to either a full-blooded human or vampire, the expectation was that the child be given up to their own kind to raise, a fact Banan had been counting on.

However, in a surprise move, Megan had defied both him and her parents by insisting that she be the one to raise Phoebe. Personally, he wouldn't have given a rip if Megan lived or died, but unless he found his daughter and soon, his whole life was going to implode. And that was simply unacceptable.

At last the sun was going down outside. He'd indulge himself with one more blood pack and then take off by himself. As long as he returned by midnight for the requisite meal with his host, he was free to wander the estate. Maybe he'd have better luck this time. Once he knew for sure that Megan was living on the estate, he'd leave.

Back in the civilized comfort of his own home, he'd make plans for the best way to repossess his daughter. Megan would never willingly give Phoebe up to him, even though it was the sensible thing to do. Her rash actions had already caused him great inconvenience and threatened his comfortable lifestyle.

The more he thought about it, it was clear Megan would have to die, regardless of how it happened. A better man might feel bad about that, but he certainly didn't. She'd brought this disaster on herself. After all, cattle shouldn't expect to have any rights. If she'd surrendered his daughter like any reasonable chancellor would have, neither of them would be in this fix. And according to his parents, his failure to control this one chancellor female cast doubt on his ability to rule the clan. Time was running out for all of them.

Megan reached the clinic less than an hour before they'd have to open the door to patients. She fumbled for her keys and hurried inside, ignoring Phoebe's fussing over being jostled. After flipping on her office lights, she set Phoebe down in her crib and patted her daughter on the cheek.

"Give me a second to get settled, little one, and then I'll take care of you. What do you say to that?"

When she turned back to her desk, she about jumped out of her skin. "Seamus! You startled me."

He tried to look sorry, but gave up and grinned. "Sorry, but I was on my way by and heard you talking. I wanted to see if Phoebe answered."

Her pulse continued to race, although not because of Seamus's unexpected appearance. No, the disconcerting effect on her libido was strictly due to his high-wattage smile. When it dimmed a bit, she realized that she'd been staring at his mouth for several seconds, very possibly with her own hanging open and drooling a bit.

Time to get her head back on straight. "I wanted to get in early to catch up on the computer stuff before the onslaught starts again."

He held up his hand to stanch the flow of words. "Don't worry. You're fine. Get your daughter settled and do what you need to. If there's a line at the door,

I'll pass out forms to everyone to fill out. That will keep them occupied until we're ready."

Which reminded her. "Files! We're almost out. That's why I meant to come in earlier." She started to reach for the box of empty files, but spotted a stack already assembled and sitting in the middle of her desk.

"Never mind, we seem to have plenty." She eyed him suspiciously. "Did you do this?"

"Nope, not me. Joss stopped by earlier with lunch for me and looking for something to do."

When he reached for the files, his fingers brushed against hers, sending a rush of warmth dancing over her skin. By the way he quickly stepped back, putting more distance between them, she suspected he'd sensed the connection, too, and didn't much like it.

Rather than dwell on it, she cranked her smile up a notch. "I should be ready shortly."

"No rush, and I should warn you that I suspect Joss is going to come by again. I think she enjoyed being here last night." He sounded a bit bewildered by that.

She wrinkled her nose and grimaced. "I'll talk to her. If I can't do my job and take care of Phoebe, it's not right to expect Joss to step in."

"I don't mind her being here. After all, she owns the place, or at least Rafferty does."

"True, but it's your clinic."

He looked decidedly uncomfortable with that idea. "Not really. One of these days, Rafferty will find a physician to take charge."

"That wouldn't be fair, not after you've gotten everything up and running."

"There's a lot about life that isn't fair, Megan." Then

Seamus made a show of checking the time. "I'd better get moving. Come along when you can. No rush."

Then he was gone, leaving her staring at the empty door and wondering if she'd offended or embarrassed him. Okay, so maybe she wasn't exactly neutral on the subject, but it was clear that Seamus had worked hard to make the clinic opening go smoothly. From what she had seen, he treated each patient with calm, professional courtesy. Despite the crowded waiting room, he hadn't acted rushed, taking the time to make everybody feel important.

He did the same thing to her sometimes when he turned that powerful intelligence in her direction, listening to each word she said as if she were about to utter the wisdom of the ages. Or maybe she just liked to think that she mattered in even that small way to him.

Now wasn't the time for such thoughts. She needed to get to work. After a quick check to see that Phoebe had settled in, she started to head for the reception desk. Before she reached the door, though, Seamus was back and looking worried. Really worried, in fact.

"Seamus?"

"Megan, I just got a call from Rafferty. He's had a vampire visiting the estate this week, evidently checking out the innovations Rafferty has made in how he runs things around here. This guy has been making the rounds with the boss, but he's out on his own right now. There's a chance he might stop by here tonight."

"And you're telling me this why?" Although she couldn't keep the fear from her voice. It couldn't be Banan. It just couldn't. In all the time they'd been together, he'd never shown any interest in where his family's money came from. His talent was in spending money, not making it.

"Don't play coy, Megan. Now's not the time."

He was right. "Did Rafferty mention any names?"

Seamus's eyes gleamed with anger and his fangs flashed as he said, "This vampire's name is Banan. Banan Delaney."

Chapter 7

Megan heard Seamus's words, but they held no meaning. From his worried expression she knew he was telling her something, probably something important. But as she struggled to make sense of them, her head filled with a deep swirling darkness, and she could no longer feel her legs beneath her. Suddenly, she was sitting down at her desk with Seamus's hand on the back of her neck and shoving her head forward.

"Damn it, Megan, put your head down and breathe."

Despite her confusion it registered in the back of her mind that although he was angry, he kept his voice pitched low and calm to avoid disturbing Phoebe.

She managed to choke out, "Sorry, I don't mean to be a bother."

"But you are that," he grumbled, but softly as if he didn't really mean for her to hear his words.

She concentrated on regaining control. When the world quit spinning she pushed herself back upright. Her first thought was to take Phoebe and run, but she immediately rejected the idea as futile. She had nowhere else to go, and now wasn't the time to let fear rule her decisions. Her life and that of her daughter could very well depend on what she did in the next few minutes.

When she attempted to stand up, Seamus backed away to give her room to move but stayed close enough to catch her again. Bless the man, he might not like being a hero, but he was one right through to the core. If she hadn't sworn off vampires, she'd be seriously tempted to… No, she wouldn't go there. There was too much at risk.

"Sorry, Seamus. You always seem to be in the right spot when my life goes into meltdown, although you might not think that's a good thing."

She moved past him to stand over the nearby crib where her daughter was sound asleep, sucking on her fist. It was time for some painful truths.

"You're suspicions are right on the money. Banan Delaney is Phoebe's biological father. We were lovers for a few months."

She tucked Phoebe's blanket in around her and then stepped away from the crib. "I guess that much is obvious, though, isn't it? Either way, I was a fool. I thought he loved me, that we had a future together."

Seamus's big hand came down gently on her shoulder. "A vampire of his status would never marry outside of his class, especially when he's the heir to the family fortune."

"I know that now, but at the time I didn't." Was it bitterness or fear leaving such a sour taste in her mouth?

"He didn't explain the facts to me until I was into my second trimester."

"I'm guessing he feared you'd end the pregnancy if he told you sooner." Seamus's voice was as grim as death.

"Then he didn't know me very well. Phoebe is everything to me and has been since the first day the doctor told me I was pregnant." She sat back down at her desk. "I was so happy. I went rushing home and fixed a fancy dinner—candles and everything. I wanted everything to be romantic and perfect."

She looked up at Seamus, hoping to see something in his expression that hadn't been there in Banan's that night. There was something there all right. It might have been pity rather than sympathy, but even so, he nodded as if urging her to continue.

"I thought he'd propose, we'd plan a wedding and build our lives around our new family. Oh, make no mistake, he acted happy enough. But after that night there was a new distance between us. I kept hoping things would change, but they didn't. A few months later he announced that his parents would be adopting the baby to raise."

"What did your family say?"

"They agreed with Banan's parents. I think they would have preferred that I go into seclusion, hiding my pregnancy from their friends."

When tears streaked down her face, Seamus shoved a handful of tissues into her hand and backed away. The gesture made her smile. The man could face blood and guts without hesitation, but a few tears were obviously scary stuff.

She sniffed and wiped her face. "Sorry, Seamus. I don't mean to dump all this on you."

"I have a suspicion you've needed to unload."

She considered that. "Oddly enough, I do feel better. Or I would, if I knew for certain that Banan wouldn't find me. He tried to kill me once. I can't give him another chance."

"He won't get one." Seamus knelt down to her eye level. "I can keep you and Phoebe out of sight in my place tonight. He might have permission to check out the clinic, but he has no business poking around in my personal quarters."

"Won't he be able to detect our scents?"

"Let me worry about that. For now, let's move the crib and changing tables into one of the exam rooms so they look like they're here for my patients to use. Then we'll get you settled in the apartment."

"But how will you handle the patients alone?"

"I'll call Joss and tell her that I sent you home because we thought Phoebe might be developing a cold. She'll be glad to cover."

"Are you sure you want to get sucked into the mess my life's become?"

"No one deserves to have their life ruined, or ended, by the cruel, homicidal actions of another, Megan."

As he spoke, his eyes turned chilly, his expression hard, belying the gentle touch of his hand on her face. In a surprise move, he pressed a quick kiss on her lips before stepping back.

"Now get your things together. Time's short."

Damn it, Seamus knew better than to let himself "get sucked in," as Megan had put it. But he couldn't live with himself if he didn't do everything he could to prevent Banan Delaney from finding Megan and her daughter. And that's how Seamus thought about Phoebe—she was Megan's daughter. That Banan happened to be the sperm donor was but an unfortunate accident of fate.

If the bastard didn't value Megan, he didn't deserve the child they'd created together. But with the minutes ticking down until the clinic needed to open, now wasn't the time to be considering how best to destroy another selfish vampire scion.

At least Joss was on her way. He was convinced Megan had to trust her secret to more than just Seamus. He'd fight to the death to defend her, but he couldn't provide around-the-clock protection for her and still do his duties—or seek his own revenge.

Again, no time for that right now, either. They'd finished rearranging the crib and baby table in one of the exam rooms, and Megan was safely tucked away in his bedroom with her daughter. Satisfied with how things looked, he had one last detail to take care of. He took the lid off a bottle of rubbing alcohol and headed for Megan's office. Then, oops, he dropped it. And clumsy him, he dropped it again in the lobby. It took quite a while for him to get it all cleaned up.

The pungent odor of the alcohol should mask any remaining traces of Megan and Phoebe, unless Delaney's sense of smell far exceeded that of the average vampire. Next he hurried back to the crib and table and wiped them down with an antiseptic with a strong medicinal odor.

Showtime. He washed his hands, grabbed his lab coat and headed for the front door. He let in a handful of patients, handing each one a blank chart to fill out as they filed past him. By the time the last one was seated in the waiting room, a very worried-looking Joss arrived.

He needed to head off the discussion until they were somewhere more private. "Mrs. O'Day, can I have a moment of your time?"

She followed close on his heels as he led the way into Megan's office. Joss noticed the absence of the crib immediately.

"Seamus, what's going on? How sick is Phoebe? Is it what Megan had?"

He placed a finger over his lips and waited until he closed the door and turned on the stereo before answering.

"Megan and Phoebe are both fine. They're in my apartment right now."

Gone was the concerned friend, replaced by the fierce warrior. "Why? What's happened?"

Where to start and how much was his right to tell? "It probably won't surprise you to learn that before coming here, Megan was being pressured to give up her baby by her parents as well as Phoebe's biological father and his family."

There was no mistaking the anger that flashed through Joss's expressive eyes. "The idiots. It's that kind of stupidity that Rafferty and I are hoping to put an end to here on the estate. Just because it's the way things have always been done doesn't make it right. We hope to make things better for our people."

She slammed her fist down on the desk. "How can they think that anyone else would be a better mother to Phoebe than Megan?"

Now wasn't the time for Seamus to tell Joss what he

thought about the changes she and Rafferty had made. It all sounded altruistic of them, but it was still their own self-centered needs that started it all. They might be happy, but others had paid dearly for their selfishness. But right now, this wasn't about him—or his need to avenge his sister.

"Here's what's going on. Your houseguest lied about his reasons for his visit. Banan's here hunting for Megan and Phoebe. Before she came here, I'm convinced he even tried to poison her, but I have no way to prove it. Right now, she needs to stay out of sight."

"I'll throw that sniveling bastard out on his ass." Joss's fangs would do a full-blooded vampire proud. "That is, if Rafferty doesn't stake him first after I tell him and Conlan what's going on."

"You'd both have to get in line behind me, but I'm not sure it's the best idea. If Delaney doesn't find her soon, maybe he'll decide she didn't come here after all and leave. If we attack, he'll bring the weight of all his clan down on us."

Joss's eyes turned frosty cold. "The Delaney clan be damned. They have no jurisdiction here. That's the law. Even the Coalition's authority is limited within the borders of the estate."

"Maybe, but you and I both know that the law doesn't always protect the innocent, especially when there's enough money involved. Then the advantage goes to the highest bidder."

The words slipped out before he could stop them. Damn it, he could only hope that Joss thought he was talking in generalities. His control was slipping badly. They needed to move on to safer topics.

"Look, we can talk later. I have patients to see. Can you cover the desk out front? All you need to do is have any new patients sign in and give them a chart to fill out. I'll take them in order unless an emergency comes in."

Her eyebrows had snapped back down after her reaction to his last comment, but she let it pass. "Okay, and if Banan does show up, what do you want me to do with him?"

"Let him look around, as long as he respects the privacy of my patients. If we try to control his movements, it will only make him more suspicious. I don't plan on making him feel welcome nor will I keep my patients waiting to answer any fool questions."

He softened the remarks with a smile. "There, do I sound arrogant enough to be a real doctor?"

Joss tipped her head to the side and studied him. "Yes, I do believe you do."

"Good. We'd better get moving. We've got patients waiting."

Banan flexed his hands and forced his fangs to retract. One more day. That was all he had left to find the bitch who'd kidnapped—no, stolen—his daughter. His mother had sent him a reminder that the annual meeting of the hierarchy in the Delaney clan would be held in just over a week. One of the agenda items would be a review of his role in the family businesses. His spending habits had already undergone a close scrutiny, resulting in a tightening of his access to clan funds.

He had to show up at the meeting with his daughter, the clan's first member of the next generation. Without her, he could very well be replaced by one of his distant cousins as the presumptive heir.

More than ever, he wished he'd choked the life out of Megan Perez with his bare hands even if poisoning her with an iron supplement had been a safer choice. After all, everybody needed a certain amount of iron in their diet. Who could have guessed that a healthy chancellor would've had such an adverse reaction?

But instead of dying, she'd fled the city. Her parents were more angry than concerned. He'd quietly hired an investigator to dig into Megan's life to see who she knew that might offer to help her. The file had been remarkably fat, which only emphasized how little he'd really known about her. One by one, he'd contacted her friends and coworkers, expressing his heartfelt concern, and almost gagging on the words. Most of them clearly had no idea where she was, but he was convinced at least a couple had been lying to him.

Unfortunately, he couldn't leave a trail of dead or damaged humans and chancellors in his wake as he continued his search. Once he'd eliminated all the possibilities in her more common haunts, his search had expanded to the areas outside the city. In the end, that had led him to Rafferty O'Day's estate. There was no indication that Megan had been in contact with her cousin Joss, but he suspected she'd grown desperate enough to risk the trip.

If she'd taken refuge here, though, he'd yet to find anyone who would admit to having seen her. Granted, Rafferty's lax standards had attracted a lot of new residents, making it easier for a recent arrival to blend into the crowd. His gut instincts were screaming he was on the right track.

So tonight, he'd visit a few more possibilities. Being limited to the night hours was a problem, but he'd do what he could. He stopped in front of a squat, ugly building—the infirmary. Before making his approach, he watched several people walk out of the building.

Even though the new medic was a vampire, he'd set his office hours to accommodate all three species. How noble of him. It made Banan sick to see one of his own kind catering to the needs of the two substandard species. A vampire should have more dignity than to play nursemaid to humans and chancellors.

But Banan couldn't afford to let his disdain show once he stepped through the door. He rolled his shoulders to ease the tightness that came from too many days away from the comforts of home with nothing to show for it. As ready as he'd ever be, he'd walk through the door and flash his practiced smile at the receptionist. With luck he'd be able to charm her into letting him have a peek at their record-keeping system on the pretext of seeing how it was set up.

That idea tanked as soon as he walked in the door. What was Joss Rafferty doing working at the infirmary? Charm wasn't going to work with her.

Without looking up from what she was reading she held out stack of forms. "Here, have a seat and fill these out."

When he didn't immediately take them, she looked up. "Oh, Banan, sorry about that. Thought you were another patient. You're not, are you?"

"No, I'm not." He smiled and glanced around the crowded waiting room. "Seems like a popular place."

She nodded. "This is only the second night the clinic

has been open, so our medic has a lot of catching up to do for even the routine stuff. I'm here to help with the crush. Once we know more what the real demand is, we'll know how to staff the clinic."

"I was hoping to look around." Especially in any areas they were reluctant to let him see.

One of the humans approached the desk to hand Joss his papers. "Here you go, boss lady."

Joss grinned at the man. "Thanks, Will. It shouldn't be much longer."

"Tell the doc to take his time. I don't mind sitting on my backside for a couple of hours."

"Well, it is one of your better talents."

Both Joss and the human laughed. Their easy familiarity was offensive. Something of his thoughts must have leaked into his expression, because Joss was staring up at him with her own dose of disapproval. It was a good thing he planned on leaving at sunset tomorrow. His welcome here was clearly coming to an end. Charm wouldn't work with Joss, so he went for businesslike.

"I know you're busy. Would you mind if I just poke around? If your medic has time, I'd love a chance to talk to him."

"As long as you don't interfere with the flow of patients." She shot a look across the small room to where Will sat, his head tipped back and his eyes closed. "And just so you know, Banan. According to Rafferty, Will over there hasn't missed a single day's work in ten years except when he broke his leg saving the lives of three young vampires."

Her fangs showed over her lower lip. "So, if the fact

that I treat him as an equal and a friend offends you, too damn bad."

A human hero. Big deal. It was only right the fool sacrifice himself for the benefit of his superiors, but now wasn't the time to share his opinion on that subject. "If I've offended you, I apologize. I also promise not to get in the way while I look around."

"Fine. The hall to the right leads to Seamus's office and the one designated to be used for the office manager and as the record room. To the left are the exam rooms, the operating room, lab and X-ray. Seamus can tell you more about that area when he has time."

She smiled, but it wasn't at all friendly. "*If* he has time. By the way, the door past his office leads to his private quarters, which are off-limits. We respect the privacy of our friends."

Which he took to mean humans and chancellors as well as the vampires on the estate. Yeah, he couldn't wait to get back to his home where the stench of humanity knew its proper role in the world.

He checked out the office with Seamus Fitzhugh's name plate taped on the door, and crookedly at that. How could the man breathe amidst such clutter? Every horizontal surface was piled high with papers and books, including the floor. The office across the hall, on the other hand, held nothing more than a desk, a chair and a couple of empty shelving units.

Once again his sense of propriety was sorely offended. Why would a vampire accept such inequity? Especially when he was in charge of the clinic. It wasn't as if the space in the other office was being used. And what was that smell? It went way beyond the usual medicinal smell he associated with a doctor's office.

He wandered into the manager's office and looked around. Normally, his sense of smell told him a lot about who had been in a given area, including their species. But the acrid odor that permeated this room interfered with that. Interesting. The spill may have been accidental, but it could also have been a deliberate attempt to hide something—or someone.

There were also faint scratches along the wall, as if another piece of furniture had been there. Also very interesting.

"Oh, there you are."

Banan whipped around to find a vampire standing just inside the doorway. "You must be the medic. I'm Banan Delaney."

"Seamus Fitzhugh." He immediately backed out into the hallway. "Joss said you'd like a quick look around the infirmary. I've got a few minutes right now, but that could change any second. It's the nature of the business."

Without giving Banan a chance to respond, Seamus walked away. As Banan followed him back toward the waiting room, he heard a noise coming from behind him. Or at least, he thought he had. He stood listening with his eyes closed to focus all of his attention on the locked door at the end of the hall. But all he heard was a heavy silence.

Reluctantly, he followed the medic as he considered just what it was he'd heard. It could have been nothing or it could have been the muted cry of a youngling. For the first time, his predator instincts went on full alert.

* * *

Seamus clenched his teeth and silently cursed Delaney and his whole family. There was no way Banan's vampire hearing would've missed that soft cry coming from Seamus's apartment. The damage was already done. Short of throwing the bastard out on his ass, there wasn't much Seamus could do but pretend it hadn't happened and continue on with the tour.

He led the way into one of the exam rooms with the unwelcome vampire. "We have regular examination rooms, but also a fully equipped surgical suite."

If Banan was truly interested in how Rafferty was managing his estate, it didn't show. Right now, Banan was staring at Seamus rather than looking around.

"Do you have any questions?"

"What brought you to Rafferty's door?"

Not exactly the question he expected Banan to ask, or maybe he should have. "The turbo, same as most of the people who come here."

Banan's laugh sounded forced. "Sorry, it was rude of me to ask. You're entitled to your privacy."

Banan trailed his fingers across the counter, picking up one of the scopes and holding it up to his eye. "What's this for?"

As if he'd never had his ears or eyes looked at by a doctor. "To check for ear or eye infections."

He held out his hand for the instrument. Banan handed it to him and moved on to study the chart on the wall that showed the comparative bone structure of the three species side by side. Studying medicine quickly stripped away any illusions about the nature of the three species. Although Banan probably didn't care, only a very few differences at the DNA level separated them. Granted, those variations in genetic makeup gave vampires their superior strength, their extended lifetimes, but also their dependence on blood.

The chancellors got the strength but also inherited the humans' ability to tolerate a wider variety of climates, not to mention daylight. Most folks thought the humans got short shrift, but Seamus wasn't so sure. They could live anywhere, under even the most extreme conditions, including freezing cold as well as the burning heat of the midday sun.

Banan turned back toward Seamus. "How late do you plan to work tonight?"

Where was he going with that question? "Office hours officially end at midnight, but I stay until the last patient is seen. Why?"

"I was wondering if you'd like to have dinner with me at the O'Days'. I'm sure they'd hold the meal long enough for you to get there."

"I wouldn't like to impose on their hospitality." True enough. He was having an increasingly harder time socializing with his employers.

"I'm sure they won't mind. I'll be leaving soon, and I'd like more time to talk to you about your plans for the clinic."

Banan's smile looked so sincere. If Seamus didn't know the truth about the aristocratic vampire, he might have actually believed that the man really wanted to spend time with him. If they had met in Seamus's prior life, they might have even been friends, but he'd like to think not. What kind of bastard tried to murder the mother of his own child?

Personal honor should count for something, especially among their kind. Their lives were too long, their memories too sharp to allow for lax morals. Even a hundred years from now, Seamus would still want to hold Banan accountable for his actions against Megan. When grudges could carry on for centuries, one had to be extra careful in the decisions that were made.

Seamus was aware that Banan was still waiting for an answer. "If they have room for me, I'd be glad to join you for dinner."

"Perfect. I'll talk to Joss on my way out." Banan immediately walked away, all pretense of interest in the infirmary gone.

More than ever Seamus was convinced the vampire had heard Phoebe's cry, and that could lead to disaster. He'd finish his rounds as expected, but then he'd have to talk to Megan. She might not like it, but she was going to have to stay in his apartment until Banan left the estate.

If somehow he planted someone to watch the infirmary to see if Megan and her daughter came out, Banan could attack before they could stop him. At the very least, if he knew Rafferty was harboring them, his influential family could cause the O'Days a great deal of trouble. Ordinarily Seamus would've been all for that, but not at Megan's expense.

Once again, he found himself siding with his enemy against a common foe. Of course, as long as Rafferty and Joss thought that Seamus was firmly on their side, his ultimate betrayal would be that much sweeter.

Or so he hoped.

* * *

Three hours later Seamus let himself into his apartment. He was not looking forward to breaking the news to Megan that she was under lockdown for at least another twenty-four hours. She was likely to tear into him but good for making a decision on her behalf without consulting her first.

She was waiting in the living room. He'd hoped that she would've dozed off so he wouldn't have to talk to her, but that was cowardly. Besides, she needed to know what was going on.

"Did Banan leave?"

"Yes, but I'm supposed to have dinner with him at Joss's in a few minutes."

"So it's safe for us to go home now?"

"Not exactly."

He headed for his bedroom to grab a clean shirt. Phoebe was curled up in the middle of his bed surrounded by pillows to keep her from rolling off the side. Megan had followed hard on his heels.

"What's that supposed to mean?" Even though she whispered because of Phoebe, her anger came through perfectly clear.

"I'm afraid he heard Phoebe when he was sneaking around in your office. If so, he might very well watch this place to see if you come out."

"So I'm supposed to hide in here until *you* decide that it's safe for me to leave?"

"Joss thought it was a good idea, too, especially after I told her he'd poisoned you." Oh, yeah, that really helped. Now she'd think they were ganging up on her.

"Megan, I don't like this any more than you do. But

we can't risk Banan finding you. If I knew a way to get you home without impacting your safety, I would do it in a heartbeat."

"Sorry to inconvenience you so much." She retreated to the living room.

Damn it, that's not what he meant. "Megan, that came out wrong. I don't want to see you hurt by him. It's only twenty-four hours, give or take. Surely we can handle staying here together for that long. You and Phoebe can have the bedroom. I'll take the couch when I get back."

"Fine. You do that."

He didn't have time to talk her down off the emotional ledge she was on. He was holding up dinner as it was.

"We'll talk more when I get back."

It was hard to tell if she heard him. She was too busy closing the bedroom door in his face.

Chapter 8

The atmosphere around the dinner table had been brittle, as if the wrong word, the wrong look would've shattered the peace. Joss had made a valiant effort to keep the conversation rolling, but the four males had definitely failed to hold up their end of things. Finally taking pity on his hostess, Seamus had launched into a description of how his first two nights at the clinic had gone. He aimed his remarks toward Banan, but he showed remarkably little interest in anything Seamus had to say on the subject.

Considering the clinic was the reason that Seamus had been invited to dinner, the motives behind the Delaney heir's visit to the O'Day estate were even more suspect. Judging by the hard looks Conlan shot in the vampire's direction, the security officer had his own qualms about the vampire.

Seamus made his excuses right after dessert was served. He'd walked to dinner, wanting the chance to see if he was followed on his way back. It was an iffy proposition because of the risk of Banan offering to accompany him, especially given the vampire's habit of roaming the estate at night. There was no way Seamus could refuse, but he'd make sure that Banan understood that Seamus was heading home to his bed.

His bed. Where right now Megan was probably curled up sleeping. Damn, that was not an image he needed in his head at the moment.

Definitely time to get moving. "Dinner was great, Joss, but I need to get back to my quarters. It's been a long couple of days."

Rafferty followed him out onto the porch. "Thanks for coming, Seamus. I was glad to hear Conlan gave you his approval, and I've heard great things from Joss about the job you're doing over at the infirmary."

"I appreciate their vote of confidence."

"Well, I sleep better knowing you're here for our people. We'll still have to evac anything major, but they'll get the right care beforehand when each minute counts. The wrong decision can cost lives."

Yeah, there were lots of ways lives were lost when people made the wrong decisions, just like when Rafferty had broken his word to Seamus's sister. He stepped down off the porch. "I'd better get going while I still have the energy to move."

"I can run you home, if you'd like."

He wanted no extra favors from his employer. "That's all right. I can use the exercise as well as the fresh air."

"It's a nice night for it. Don't be a stranger."

Seamus walked away, forcing himself to take it slow and easy no matter how badly he wanted to put some distance between himself and Rafferty. It was getting too easy to forget that this wasn't his real life, that Rafferty was the villain, and that being a medic where one was desperately needed wasn't where Seamus was supposed to be.

As soon as he was out of sight of Rafferty's house, he cut across country. He'd circle back when he reached the cover of the trees to see if Banan followed him. So far there was no sign of Delaney, but then vampires didn't have to depend on their superior night vision. Their sense of smell worked even better when it came to tracking their prey.

Seamus strolled into the trees and stopped, breathing deeply of the earthy scents. He couldn't remain there long, though. There was always the chance Banan wasn't coming, but Seamus didn't think the vampire could resist the chance to look for Megan. It was imperative that Seamus be there to keep her safe. He tried not to think about why that was.

When he didn't sense any movement in the immediate vicinity, he left the cover of the trees and continued on a straight line directly toward the infirmary. He was glad for the lack of windows in the building. If Megan was up, it would've been hard for her to resist watching for him, not to mention it would've been far easier for Banan to spy on her. At the entrance to the clinic, he stared up at the stars overhead for a minute before unlocking the door to underscore his statement regarding his desire to enjoy the night.

The air stirred behind him, just the merest ripple,

hardly a breath. Someone was out there, lurking out of sight. Was it Banan? The predator in Seamus demanded to go hunting for blood. As with most vampires, especially the males, the veneer of civilization wore damn thin at times. Right now, his fangs burned with the need to rip into his enemy, and Seamus's instincts screamed for him to charge out into the darkness and rip into the living flesh of his prey. It had been a long time since he'd feasted off another vampire and he missed it.

Banan deserved to bleed for attacking Megan and in such a cowardly way. She had no male to defend her, no family who cared enough to see justice was done. Seamus had been unable to save his sister. Maybe this was his chance at redemption.

And if by destroying the heir to a formidable clan, he would also bring disaster raining down on Rafferty at the same time, so much the better. He stepped into the deepest shadows, slowing his pulse, pacing his breathing until he became at one with the darkness. His stalker stood motionless a short distance away, doing little to disguise his presence.

Seamus smiled, his fangs at full extension, his fingers flexing as he prepared to attack. Between one breath and the next, he transitioned from quiet to killer, traversing the distance to his target in a blur of motion. A twig snapping was the only warning his intended victim got as Seamus launched himself forward to drag the other vampire to the ground. They slammed into each other and came up fighting.

Seamus recognized Banan by both scent and sound. Images flashed through his mind: Megan close to death, dragging herself step by step to get her daughter to safety; Phoebe, so pretty and sweet, almost an orphan; Banan's snooping through the infirmary, looking for the two females. Hatred, pure and clean, sent Seamus's aggression level skyrocketing.

He landed a solid punch to Banan's jaw and another to his gut. Fist fighting was the stupidest thing a surgeon could do with his hands, but right now Seamus wasn't thinking as a doctor. No, the potent blood of his ancestors, predators all, overrode both caution and rational thought. The world narrowed down to a blinding rage that demanded the blood of a fool who'd tried to destroy the precious gifts that life had given him, who yet continued to threaten the two females.

"You don't know who you're messing with," Banan hissed, his fangs bared, his hands scrambling for purchase as he tried to ward off Seamus's furious attack. "Let go of me."

"Hell, no! I'd rather make you bleed or, better yet, die."

Banan danced back out of reach. "What did I do to you?"

Seamus circled to the left, trying to trap Banan back against the wall of the clinic. Before his maneuver had a chance to work, he was blindsided by another male and sent sprawling to the ground. Banan didn't hesitate to bolt, immediately disappearing into the darkness. Meanwhile, Seamus ended up flat on his back with Banan's unexpected ally's hands wrapped around his neck and choking off his breath.

"Damn it, Seamus! It's me, Conlan. Knock it off before I hurt you."

"Not going to happen." Seamus pitched and rolled, trying to break free. "Get your hands off me!"

"Stop fighting me, and I will."

Slowly Conlan's words got through to Seamus, but that didn't keep him from struggling to break free from the chancellor's hold. He finally managed to drag Conlan's hands off his throat and shoved against the chancellor's chest, tossing him backward to land hard some distance away.

Seamus immediately surged back to his feet before Conlan quit bouncing. He fought an uphill battle for control while every synapse in his body fired hot and screamed for blood—Banan's, first and foremost, but with Banan out of the picture, Conlan's would do. Hell, better yet, Rafferty's. It didn't matter as long as somebody bled.

At least Conlan had the good sense to lie still. By going totally passive instead of aggressive, he gave Seamus the chance to regain control. Gradually, when some of the adrenaline burst had worn off, he stepped forward and offered Conlan a hand up off the ground.

"Didn't anybody ever tell you not to break up a fight between vampires?" His voice sounded as if he'd been chewing glass. The bruises from Conlan's choke hold would fade by morning, but right now they hurt like a bitch.

Conlan rubbed his shoulder and tested the mobility in his arm. "Normally I know better, but what the hell were you doing fighting with Banan, anyway?"

"At first, I didn't realize it was him sneaking around." Okay, so that was a lie. Better to derail that line of conversation. "Are you all right? Lucky you, the infirmary takes emergency patients."

Conlan laughed. "I'm fine. Besides, I deserve a few bruises for not getting to you sooner."

"So what were you doing lurking outside my clinic?"

"I was walking back to my transport from Joss's house when I spotted someone sneaking around in the woods. Figuring as security was my job description, I followed him, especially considering what Joss told us about him and Megan after the two of you left."

"That was me you saw."

"No, it wasn't because I saw you go by first. It was that bastard Delaney. I waited to see what he was up to, but he caught wind of me and took off running. By the time I caught up with him again, you two were already swinging fists."

Seamus froze, listening to make sure they were alone. If Banan was still lurking in the area, the young vampire was far better than he should be at hiding his presence. It was almost a shame he was gone. Between Seamus and Conlan, they could have done a bang-up job of convincing the vampire that he was unwelcome.

"He's definitely gone."

Conlan waited until Seamus once again focused his attention on him. "I'm pretty sure he'll hightail it back to Joss's house, and Rafferty will make sure he stays there. I don't trust that punk vampire and can't wait to see the last of him. If I had hardcore proof he was the one to poison Megan, I'd execute the bastard myself and damn the consequences. He's leaving tomorrow whether he wants to or not because I made his turbo reservations myself. Sending him back to his family all bruised up may cause a few ripples, but too bad."

"Tell Rafferty I'm sorry."

"But not Delaney himself?"

Seamus flexed his hands, wishing he had them

wrapped around Banan's neck. "Hell, no. I defend what's mine. He had no business sneaking around the infirmary. If he was here to see me, he should've announced himself rather than hiding."

Conlan gave a noncommittal grunt, leaving Seamus unsure how much trouble he was in. On the other hand, his fighting instincts were still running high. Once his energy burn was gone, exhaustion might kick in. Right now he was ready to defend his actions, with his fists if necessary. It was definitely time to get inside. Rafferty might forgive an attack on an unpopular guest; trading punches with his security officer not so much.

"If you're sure you don't need pain medicine or an X-ray, I'm way overdue for some downtime."

Conlan tested his shoulder again. "No, I'm good. I was going to drive back out to my quarters, but I'll hang around until tomorrow night to escort Delaney off the property myself with a warning not to return anytime soon. If you want me for anything, give me a call."

"Thanks, I will. Good night."

"Same to you. And, Seamus—"

"Yeah?"

"Thanks for watching over our two friends. We'll all sleep better knowing they're not alone right now." He rubbed his shoulder one last time. "Especially now that I know what kind of punch you're packing."

Seamus didn't know how to respond. He settled for a mumbled, "It's nothing. Anybody would do the same."

"That's where you're wrong. Most people wouldn't. See you around."

Then the chancellor disappeared back into the darkness, leaving Seamus staring after him. Feeling out of sync by the whole encounter, he pulled out his keys and let himself inside the clinic.

Although there was no reason to think Banan had broken into the infirmary, Seamus wouldn't sleep easy until he checked all the rooms. Normally, he would've also spent time writing up the last few reports on the patients he'd seen, but he was still too revved by the fight to concentrate. He'd never get to sleep if he didn't find a way to burn off this excess energy.

Which brought Megan Perez to mind. Somehow he doubted she'd be interested in helping him out with that particular problem. Even if she thought she owed him for saving her life, he didn't want to bed her only because she felt grateful. With that unsettling thought, he turned the lights off in the clinic before retiring to his own quarters.

He'd hoped Megan was already asleep. Instead, she was curled up on his couch pretending to read when he walked through the door. He couldn't imagine she'd find a treatise on the blood disorders of ancient vampires riveting enough to keep her up this late, which meant she'd been waiting up for him but didn't want him to know.

He dropped his keys on the table and gave the book a pointed glance. "So which treatment would you recommend? Transfusions?"

"Leeches, I think."

Okay, he hadn't expected that. "You actually read it?"

"No, not really." She closed the book and tossed it aside. "Mainly I looked at the pictures. Nothing like close-ups of blood cells to stir the imagination."

He couldn't help it. He laughed. "Sorry, I didn't have anything better around for you to read. I'm still trying to organize the medical books Rafferty bought for the infirmary."

"That's okay. You weren't exactly expecting to have overnight company."

She studied her hands. "So, how did dinner go? Was Banan as charming as ever?"

"Not particularly. He'd invited me specifically to talk about the clinic, but yet didn't ask a single relevant question. Conlan was there, too, but didn't particularly want to be. Rafferty was quiet, too, so poor Joss had to do most of the talking."

Talking about Megan's former lover did little to further calm Seamus's fight-or-flight instincts.

Megan toyed with a loose thread on his couch. "So now that your dinner party is over and the sun will be up soon, can I go home?"

He might not want to have this discussion, but didn't see how to avoid it. "I won't stop you, but I wish you wouldn't because Banan could still be out there somewhere. Right before I came in, I could feel somebody watching me and jumped him. Conlan broke up the fight before I could corner Banan long enough to learn why he was hanging around in the dark."

To lighten the moment, he added, "I thought Conlan was on Banan's side and tangled with him, too. Fangs all look alike at night, you know."

His attempt at humor fell flat. Megan sounded fierce when she asked, "Banan's not going to give up on finding us, is he?"

Seamus shrugged. "I'd say not, but the good news is he's leaving the estate tomorrow night. Conlan made the turbo reservations himself, but right now he's on the loose. Banan has failed to endear himself to anyone around here, but without proof of anything, all they can do is shove him out the gate."

Megan sighed. "I should have told Rafferty and Joss myself, so you didn't have to. Obviously ignoring the problem didn't make it go away."

"So you *will* stay tonight." It wasn't a question, but a statement of fact. He really didn't want to force the issue, but if he had to, he would.

"Okay, but I'll take the couch." Again that stubborn chin came up.

"It'll be crowded with both of us sleeping on it. Last time I looked, Phoebe was hogging the middle of my bed." He flashed Megan a teasing look. "Let me get you something to sleep in and dig out an extra toothbrush for you. I'm sorry, I should've thought to do that before I left."

"That's okay. Do you have a drawer I can borrow for Phoebe to sleep in? That worked great when we were at Conlan's."

"Not a problem."

He dumped out his sock drawer and carried it out into the living room along with one of his undershirts and a pair of running shorts for Megan. He stood back and watched as Megan gently carried in her sleeping daughter and settled her into the padded drawer.

As Megan leaned down to adjust Phoebe's blankets, her hair fell forward over her shoulders and hid her face. Damn, he wanted to kiss the back of Megan's neck, to taste her sweet-smelling skin with his tongue and then with his fangs. And the rounded curves of her backside would be exactly perfect to cushion a lover's thrusts when he took her.

He had to get away from her before he acted on the fantasies playing out in his head. It had to be the leftover aggression from his fight with Conlan driving his libido. He knew better than to get involved with anyone right now, but especially Megan. She'd already suffered enough at the hands of one of his kind who wouldn't share his future with her. Even if Seamus wanted to, he had no future to offer.

When she started to look up, he ducked into the sanctuary of the bathroom to give them both some space. As he started up the shower, it occurred to him that it had been years since he'd shared living quarters with anyone. He would've expected it to make him feel crowded, especially in a small apartment. But instead, it felt...right somehow. As if Megan belonged not only in his home, but in his bed, and maybe even in his heart.

Now that was a scary thought.

Megan stared at the bathroom door wondering why Seamus had suddenly bolted from the room. Just before he'd disappeared, she'd sensed a change in his mood. What was up with him, anyway? She hoped he wasn't hiding an injury from his altercation with Banan. Neither man seemed like the type to do their talking with their fists, but then they were vampires. Their species hadn't developed all that physical strength for nothing. All she knew was that she always felt safe when Seamus was around, perhaps for the first time in months.

While he was out of sight, she quickly changed into the shirt and shorts he'd brought her. Their size swamped her, but they'd be more comfortable than sleeping in her own clothes. While she waited for her chance at the bathroom, the muffled noises Seamus made in there as he got ready for bed sounded homey and surprisingly soothing. Despite her intimate relationship with Banan, he'd never slept at her place nor had he invited her to stay over at his. Maybe that should have told her something, but she'd been blind to anything but his charm.

Seamus might lack some of that high-gloss surface polish that Banan took such pride in, but she found that reassuring. With him, what you saw was what you got. He had his own secrets, she had no doubt. But inside, where it counted, he was honorable. It was there in the way he approached his patients, as if each and every one deserved his full attention and the best care he could offer.

As much as it frightened her to admit it, she would have been dead without his intervention. She owed him far more than she could ever repay.

The bathroom door opened and Seamus stepped out in a cloud of steam from the shower he'd taken. Bare-chested and wearing flannel pajama bottoms, he looked ready for bed—and she didn't mean as in going to sleep. Without his lab coat and stethoscope to hide behind, he looked more approachable, more powerful and masculine. She noticed the shower had left his smooth skin damp. What would he think if he realized how badly she wanted to lap up those small droplets of water, to taste his essence with her tongue?

But, no, she shouldn't be having these thoughts. Not about a vampire. Not again.

But what she should do and what she wanted to do were two very different things. Her eyes traced the well-defined muscles of his chest down and down until she saw exactly what kind of effect her scrutiny was having on her host. As her own powerful mating instincts kicked in, her fangs dropped down. She licked her lips, the tip of her tongue tracing the point of one of her canines.

Seamus's gaze locked on her mouth. "Megan?"

She rose to her feet. "Seamus?"

Despite the distance between them, the sizzling heat in his eyes caressed her body as if he held her in his arms. Instead, he hovered in the doorway across the room as he waited…for what? Then they both took a step forward at the same moment, forever shattering the last bit of control she had.

This might not be about love. It definitely wasn't about happily ever after. It was about trust. She could lose herself in his arms for a few hours, taste his passion, share hers with him and know that he would shelter her from the world outside. It had been so long since she'd last felt safe and cared for. Seamus had given that back to her with his fierce determination to save her life and to protect her daughter.

His arms wrapped around her, holding her secure against the warm wall of his chest. Her head tucked in under his chin, his erection pressing against her belly. She shimmied against its hard length, wanting nothing more than to be skin-to-skin, to brace herself for the power he'd bring to their lovemaking. Tension coiled deep within her, leaving her hovering on the precipice with just his embrace.

His breath teased her skin as he whispered near her ear, "Megan, God knows I want this, I want you, but are you sure?"

Even as he asked, his hands were already roaming,

learning the curves of her body and how sweetly she fit against him. He closed his eyes and awaited her answer, his conscience hoping she'd back away and his soul praying that she wouldn't.

She raised up far enough to bring her lips to cover his. "Yes," she murmured, her eyes half-closed and dreamy.

"I want this," she said between the small kisses she gave him, her hand slipping down between them to make sure he knew exactly what she was talking about.

"I want you." She smoothed her hand up and down the length of his erection. He'd been aroused before, but now she definitely had his full attention.

He caught her jaw with the tips of his fingers, angling her face to deepen their kiss. His tongue swirled in and out of the sweetness of her mouth, testing the sharpness of her fangs, imagining the feel of them against his throat, piercing his skin.

Just the thought was enough to send him to his knees. It was time to take this to his bed, right where he'd been imagining Megan. With no warning, he swept her up in his arms and carried her into his room, kicking the door closed, shutting out the rest of the world. For these precious few hours, this would be about them, two lovers with no past, no future, no regrets.

He knelt on the edge of the mattress and gently laid Megan down, right where she belonged. Her eyes were huge as she stared up at him, watching and waiting for him to make the next move. Where to start?

He needed to go slow, to savor the experience. Stretching out beside her, he propped his head up on his right hand and considered the possibilities. Finally, he laid his palm at the hem of her shirt, moving his hand upward, tugging up the soft fabric along in its wake to uncover inch after luscious inch of her skin. He paused long enough to trace the pattern of her ribs before moving on to feather his fingertips across the sensitive peaks of her breasts.

"Perfect," he whispered as he leaned down to kiss and nibble his way around the full curves and then teasing her nipples.

Megan arched up off the bed as she tangled her fingers in his hair, pressing him closer, asking for more. He broke away long enough to help her peel the shirt off over her head. When he tossed it on the floor, she raised up and pushed him over onto his back.

"My turn."

She straddled his hips, settling the full weight of her body against his erection. He was pretty sure his brain was going to explode from the incredible sensation. He loved having her pretty breasts right there for him to knead and kiss as she rocked back and forth, the friction setting them both aflame. He couldn't remember a more perfect moment in all his life, and it was only going to get better when they finally shed the last layers of clothing between them.

Megan then moved farther down his legs and leaned over to kiss his cock, the warmth of her breath feeling incredible as she nuzzled him from top to bottom. He groaned when she reached through the fly to stroke him. Megan definitely had a talent for doing exactly what would drive him crazy.

"Keep that up and this party will be over way too soon."

Grasping her wrist, he pulled her hand up his mouth to place a warm, wet kiss on her palm. At the same time, he slid his other hand inside the waistband of her shorts to tangle in her damp curls. He kissed her throat, loving the syncopated beat of her pulse just below her skin.

"Oh, yes," she moaned as he eased one, then two fingers deep inside her slick heat. "Seamus, please!"

It was too soon in their relationship for him to feed from her vein unless she offered, but he could taste her in other ways. He withdrew his hand and journeyed down the length of her body to remove first her shorts and then his own flannels. Her eyes widened with appreciation as she reached out to cup him with one hand and explore his length with the other.

The woman definitely knew what she liked and what she wanted. But he was running too close to the edge to take her yet, not if he wanted to please his lady as much as himself.

He moved back out of the reach of her busy hands. "Open up for me, Megan."

She froze, unsure what he meant. To show her, he wrapped his hand around her ankle and tugged it toward him. "I need you to make room for me."

Cautiously, she slowly spread her legs apart, watching him as if she would bolt if he moved wrong or too fast. He knelt between her feet and then stretched out, as she watched his slow approach with her eyes wide and her breath coming in shallow pants as she waited in anticipation.

He drew in her scent, making it part of him, knowing he'd never walk away from this encounter unchanged. Then he kissed her, tasting the sweet flavor that was hers alone. Her head kicked back on the pillow as her legs opened wider in surrender. He lifted her knees up onto his shoulders, feasting deeply and long until she keened out her release. He gave her but a short reprieve before relentlessly driving her up and over the edge again and again.

"Seamus! Enough, take me now!"

She'd never had such an unselfish lover, one so determined to pleasure her before seeking his own release. Now, as good as it was, she wanted more. She wanted to bear his weight, to feel the solid strength of him deep in the very heart of her, to know the power of his body.

This time he heeded her demand and rose up to settle the tip of his cock against her, and then with one powerful thrust, buried himself fully inside her. He paused, holding himself still with obvious effort, to give her body time to accept him. His consideration for her was stunning in its generosity. She scraped her nails gently across his shoulders and then down his arms.

"Seamus, I'm so ready for this." She lifted her hips up to meet his. Then she arched her head up and to the side, "And this."

Her twin offers snapped his control. He began thrusting, his hips working hard to seat himself deeply within her with each stroke. The tension built with each pounding beat, spiraling tighter and tighter until it shattered. As spasms of brilliant-colored pleasure ripped through her, the pulse of Seamus's own release shuddered deep inside her.

Then in a lightning-fast move, his fangs pierced the side of her throat, and a second wave of ecstasy flooded through them both in a warm gush of blood.

Chapter 9

Banan walked into his room and fought against the urge to slam the door. He'd already drawn Joss's unwanted attention when he'd stormed into the house and stalked right by her without saying a word. She'd had a lot to say, though, ending with ordering him to remain in his room. He was so damned enraged right now, he couldn't be sure that he wouldn't attack her.

Worse yet, he wasn't sure he'd actually win against the chancellor. She'd enjoyed a fearsome reputation in her work as an arbiter. More than one vampire had learned the hard way not to cross her.

Safe in his room, he stopped in front of the mirror and forced his image to appear. Still badly rattled, it took him several attempts to bring it into clear focus. Leaning in for a closer look, he stared at the purplish bruise spreading out across his lower jaw and up toward his eye. His hand gingerly pressed against his stomach, testing the extent of the bruising there, as well.

He knew one thing for sure: Seamus Fitzhugh needed to die—painfully and begging for mercy.

How dare that clanless low-life vampire lay a hand, much less a fist, on a Delaney? Anywhere else but here on this backwater estate, Banan would've summoned the chancellors to drag the medic away in chains. Even that wouldn't be enough to assuage Banan's wounded pride.

No, he wanted Seamus staked out where the morning sun would find him. He played the scene out in his head, savoring the imagined screams and the scent of smoke as the scum slowly caught fire, smoldering at first and then burning brightly until his lungs exploded and the dying vampire could scream no more.

Oh, yeah, that would be so sweet, however unlikely. Gone were the days when the vampires could execute their enemies without due process. He doubted the North American Coalition would think that a few well-placed punches would warrant a death penalty. However, money in the right hands could still purchase justice. He added that to the list of things he needed to take care of once he got back to civilization.

To that end, he pulled out his duffel and began packing so that he could start for the gate as soon as the sun set. Once that was done, he popped open a few more bags of Rafferty's blood supply, concentrating on using up the rarer, and therefore more expensive, vintages. The extra pack or two would go a long way to healing his injuries while he slept.

As he turned out the lights and stretched out between the cool sheets, he thought back through the day's events. He was almost certain he'd heard a baby cry at the infirmary. Better yet, the noise had come from the direction of the medic's private quarters, not from one of the examination rooms.

It also occurred to him that Seamus's attack had been over-the-top savage if all Banan had done was startle him. Normally, a vampire didn't succumb to such blind rage unless he was defending something that really mattered to him. As a recent addition to the estate, it didn't make sense that the vampire would be so territorial about that hideous clinic.

Which meant what?

The answer was obvious. If Seamus wasn't defending *something,* he was defending *someone.* It wasn't too much of a leap to guess that that someone had to be Megan and the baby. Why else would Seamus not mention he had a mate and a child? That wasn't exactly something he could have kept secret from Rafferty and Joss, either, so they were in on it. The obnoxious security officer had to be, too, so add him to his enemy list.

It infuriated him to know Megan had gone straight from his bed to that of a no-name lowlife like that medic. Not that he had any interest in bedding the bitch again. Had the two crossed paths before they'd come to Rafferty's estate? Maybe Seamus was the one who'd helped her escape. He'd known all along she wasn't smart enough to elude his efforts to find her this long all on her own.

Interesting, though, that Seamus was the only one who'd dared to openly attack him. Why? Joss was Megan's cousin and a warrior in her own right, not to mention Rafferty being one of the most powerful vampires around. They must suspect that he was hunting for his daughter, but not that he'd actually tried to kill Megan to simplify his life.

Seamus, on the other hand, had somehow figured it out, making him the only immediate danger to Banan's plans. The only question was what to do about him. The ache in Banan's jaw made it difficult to concentrate, especially with the sun rising in the east and with it the pressing need to sleep.

He'd leave as ordered, but he'd be back. And then there would be hell to pay.

She was cold. Why? Where had all the warmth gone? Megan rooted across the bed, unconsciously looking for that living wall of heat, which had sheltered her so sweetly as she slept. Slowly, she awoke feeling confused and alone.

Where was she? And Phoebe! Bolting upright, the sheets pooled around her waist, making her aware that she was naked. She never slept in the nude. Fear and confusion washed through her mind until she heard the muffled murmur of a familiar voice coming through the door.

Seamus Fitzhugh. Her hand immediately went to her throat, testing for soreness there and finding it. The memories of the time the two of them had spent in this bed, starting in the middle of the night and at least twice more after that. A tentative touch, a gentle kiss and then the passion would ignite again.

What had she been thinking? Her conscience forced her to give the honest answer to that question: she'd been thinking how right it had felt to welcome Seamus into her arms and into her body. Making love with him had been…perfect.

And what a terrifying thought that was! Before she could decide how to react, the bedroom door quietly swung open revealing her lover with her daughter cuddled in his arms.

"I was just going to wake you. Phoebe's finally decided I'm not the one she needs right now."

As he approached the bed, Megan tugged the sheet back up to cover herself, although it was a bit late for that, especially considering Seamus's excellent night vision. She gave up and held out her arms for Phoebe. The sweet baby smell immediately soothed her.

"I'll scrounge us some breakfast. Take your time, though."

He started to lean toward her, but then backed away when she flinched. Guilt washed over her. He'd been nothing but considerate, and here she was treating him so badly. Although he was already on the wrong side of the door, she knew he could hear her, anyway.

"Seamus, I'm sorry. I'm not used to…well, any of this. I've never slept through the day with anyone, not even Banan. I'm not sure how to act."

His voice was muffled by the door, but she suspected he was smiling. "Me, either, if that's any comfort."

Amazingly, it was. For the moment, she concentrated on nursing her daughter, losing herself in the familiar routine. She whispered to Phoebe, telling her the sorts of things that mothers had been saying to their young-lings forever. That Phoebe was pretty, that she was loved, that everything was going to be all right.

She could only hope that last part was true.

* * *

Seamus listened to Megan talking to Phoebe. He didn't mean to eavesdrop, but vampire hearing made that difficult. He loved the sweet tone in her voice and knew firsthand how it felt to be held close and warm in Megan's arms. He'd hated leaving his bed when Phoebe woke up and demanded attention. However, because of him, Megan hadn't gotten much rest during the day and he figured she deserved to sleep as long as possible.

He grinned as he set the table. Megan wasn't the only Perez female who was a heartbreaker. Little Phoebe definitely had her mother's expressive eyes and pretty smile. And both females brought out every protective instinct he had. Sure, he'd promised her that she could go back to her cottage as soon as Conlan escorted Banan Delaney to the turbo. That didn't mean he wanted her to go.

He began cracking eggs into a bowl as he pondered what he should do about that idea. The obvious answer was nothing. One vampire had already betrayed her trust and come close to killing her. There was little doubt that Banan was still out there, still trying to find her in order to take Phoebe away.

Seamus would do anything he could to prevent that from happening, but his own motives for being on the estate wouldn't stand up to close scrutiny. He was living a lie, one that was a direct threat to Megan's cousin and her husband. Granted they were the true villains, their actions directly responsible for the disaster that loomed over their heads. That they also stood the best chance of keeping Megan and Phoebe safe here on their estate was beside the point.

Right? His sister's image popped into his head. Petra

had been much older, but she'd been good to him in her own way. She'd been so beautiful; everyone said so. And now, now she was dead and buried, leaving him alone, broke and clanless. It went against his nature to lie to anyone, especially someone he cared about. After all, Rafferty's lies to Petra had resulted in her death.

Unless he wanted to be guilty of the same crimes as both Rafferty and Banan, he had to reestablish emotional distance between himself and Megan. One night of passion had only whetted his appetite for more of the same, but his hypocrisy had limits.

The bedroom door creaked slightly, warning him that he was no longer alone. He whipped the eggs and poured them into the skillet.

"Can I help?"

"You can pour the coffee."

Between the two of them, breakfast was served up and ready in a matter minutes, another reminder of how well they worked together. He so didn't need that right now.

"Think I'll be able to go back to my cottage long enough to change clothes and pick up a few things for Phoebe before time to start work?"

He mulled over that idea. "Let me give Conlan a call first and see when he plans on shoving Banan out the gate. Once we're sure he's gone, it should be fine."

"Good. We've imposed on your hospitality long enough." She carried her dishes over to the sink.

Last night had been anything but an imposition. It had been incredible.

While Megan washed the dishes, he dialed Conlan's number. He smiled at the gruff response from the other end of the line.

"Conlan, it's Seamus. I was wondering where you are."

"Glad you called, Rafferty. I'm already back at my place, but I'll be out of touch for a while. Delaney here needs a ride out to catch the turbo. I figured you'd like me to play nice and give him a lift."

So Conlan didn't want his guest to know who was calling. "I don't suppose you could put him under the turbo rather than on it."

A bark of laughter carried back across the line. "Good one, boss. Remind me never to get on your bad side. Gotta go now or we'll be late."

"Thanks, Conlan. I owe you."

"Don't worry about it. I'll be sure and collect next time I'm there."

The phone went dead. Seamus hung up. No more excuses for keeping Megan sequestered in his apartment or sharing his bed. He wished he could be happier about that.

"Is he gone?"

He schooled his features to hide his disappointment. "Yeah, Conlan pretended he was talking to Rafferty in case Banan was close enough to hear his end of the conversation. They're on the way to the turbo station. Conlan will make sure Banan really does leave."

"Good. I'll go change back into my own clothes, and then Phoebe and I will get out of your way."

He caught her arm. "You're not in my way, Megan."

Damn, he was going to kiss her again. So much for reestablishing any distance between them. She met him halfway, her lips parting in invitation. His tongue savored the velvet texture of hers. She tasted like dark roast coffee and sexy female, a combination that rivaled the richest vintage of wine. He pressed closer, letting her know without words the powerful effect she had on him.

When they came up for air, he rested his forehead against hers. He wished he had the right words to describe how she made him feel, even if these were the last moments he dare share with her like this. When they wouldn't come, he kissed her again, starting with a series of quick licks at the pulse point on her neck where she'd let him feed.

Oh, God, if he kept that up, she was going to come right there. She arched her head to the side, offering him free rein. He worked his way up the curve of her neck to her ear. That talented tongue of his traced the shell of her ear, the sound of his ragged breathing making her ache for far more than they could share standing in his living room fully dressed.

Earlier, at breakfast, she'd thought he'd been a bit cool, distancing himself from her and what they'd shared during the long hours they'd spent in his bed. Right now, though, they were only seconds from either trying out his couch or maybe even the floor. She couldn't wait to find out which it would be.

"Megan, honey, we shouldn't…"

Not what she wanted to hear. "That's not what you said last night when I did this." She really loved the soft slide of flannel over something so deliciously hard.

His voice grew rough. "But Phoebe…"

"Is asleep. We've got time, Seamus, although it might make me a little late to work." She cupped him with a gentle squeeze.

His breath went out in a rush. "Maybe I can have a word with your boss."

Then he scooped her up in his arms and headed for the couch. When Seamus gently laid her down, she scooted toward the back of the couch, making room for him to stretch out beside her. His knee pushed between her thighs at the same time his mouth found hers. She wrapped her arms around him tightly, relishing the sensation of once again being sheltered by his powerful body.

This time it seemed that neither of them wanted a slow exploration, maybe because they both knew the world outside wouldn't leave them alone for much longer. She worked her shorts down off her hips as Seamus continued to kiss her senseless. When he realized what she was trying to do, he helped her.

After shifting her onto her back, he settled in the cradle of her body. He pushed his own pants down only far enough to free his cock. And then with a couple of sharp thrusts, their bodies were joined again. He guided her ankles high up around his hips.

"Hold on tight, honey. This is going to be fast and furious."

She rocked against him and smiled. "Go for it, big guy."

He grinned down at her response, and then put all his considerable strength into his powerful claiming of her body. She'd never been the focus of such an explosive experience. What was there about this particular vampire who brought out such intensity in her?

Seamus dragged the tips of his fangs across the veins that ran along the side of her neck. He didn't break the skin, but it was still enough to send her rocketing toward ecstasy. When he offered her his vein, she bit down hard. With a shout, he poured out his own release.

Before either of them could do more than lie there in boneless bliss, the world came rushing back accompanied by a loud rapping on Seamus's door.

"Megan? Seamus? Sorry to bother you, but it's an emergency. Rafferty's been hurt."

With a muttered curse, Seamus immediately pushed away from Megan, his eyes bleak. "Get in the bedroom. I'll see what's going on."

She was perfectly capable of getting back up off the couch by herself, but a hand up would have been nice. However, it was clear that Seamus had lost all interest in touching her. With her eyes burning, she picked up her shorts and stalked into the bedroom, her pride the only thing holding back her tears.

Maybe she was overreacting. There was no reason she should feel embarrassed if Joss figured out what she and Seamus had been doing. They were both adults, after all. But as she closed the door, she'd risked one more look in Seamus's direction. She'd never seen him look so grim, so unapproachable. Gone was her smiling lover.

In his place stood a cold-eyed vampire with death in his eyes.

What a screwed-up mess! Seamus heard the click of his bedroom door, well aware that he'd managed to hurt Megan without meaning to. They'd both known they were running out of time.

Joss pounded on the door again. "Seamus, they'll be here with Rafferty in a few minutes. He's going to need surgery, but he's bleeding too badly to wait for the med techs to get here. He needs help now."

Or he could just let Rafferty die. But Seamus kept that particular thought to himself as he yanked the door open.

"What happened?"

"Witnesses said his transport veered out of control and plowed into a tree." Joss was pale, her hands shaking.

"Have them take him to the first exam room."

"Thanks, Seamus. I can't tell you how glad I am you're here for him."

Not if she knew the truth. "I'll be right there."

Joss ran back toward the front door of the clinic, leaving him to deal with his other guests. He knocked on the bedroom door.

"Megan, I'll be out in the clinic with Rafferty."

She opened the door as he stepped away. "I'll join you as soon as I change clothes."

He wanted to tell her to stay away, not wanting any complications until he figured out what he was going to do. He wanted his revenge, but he hadn't expected an opportunity like this to drop in his lap.

"All right."

He ducked into the pre-op to grab a set of scrubs to put on. No time to shower, so he washed up at the sink instead. By the time he was done, he could hear voices out in the waiting room. His breakfast churned in his stomach knowing the next hour could very well be the last one of his life. If he let Rafferty die, and Joss figured out it was deliberate, she'd stake him.

He'd thought he was ready to face that possibility, but evidently his will to live was stronger than his need to punish the vampire who'd destroyed his world. And he knew who he could thank for that—Megan Perez. No one could experience what the two of them had shared and think one day like that was enough. But if he was going to die, at least he was going out on a high note.

Joss was hovering over her husband as they carried him in on a makeshift stretcher. She looked like hell and Rafferty looked worse. It didn't take a medical degree to see why. His right leg was bent at an unnatural angle and jagged bone shards jutted up through the fabric of his jeans. Blood pooled and dripped off the board they'd strapped him to. If he'd been bleeding that badly for long, it might already be too late.

Joss knew it, too. It was there in her terror-filled eyes. "We called for an emergency evac, but they said it would be thirty minutes to an hour before they can get here."

False comfort wouldn't help anyone. "He can't wait that long."

Rafferty needed immediate help if he was to survive. Even with medical intervention, success was far from a sure thing. Seamus weighed his options. After studying the possibilities, he chose Megan on several levels.

He sought her out in the crowd. "Megan, go put on scrubs. I'm going to need an extra set of hands."

She backed away. "You need someone who knows what they're doing."

"Do you see anyone who meets that description around here?"

They both looked at the cluster of humans, all farmers judging by their attire and the dirt caked on their boots. Megan obviously came to the same conclusion because she handed Phoebe off to Joss.

Seamus nodded in approval. "Okay, we need to get moving. We don't have all night."

While he waited, he checked Rafferty's pulse. It was

thready and weak, but the vampire's eyes opened and looked around until he spotted Seamus. Dazed and wracked with pain, he struggled to talk.

"Don't waste your energy, Rafferty. You don't have any to spare."

Still the vampire fought to speak. Seamus leaned down to listen, knowing his patient wouldn't give up until he said his peace. Rafferty finally whispered one single word. "Petra."

Suddenly, Rafferty wasn't the only one who was having trouble breathing. Seamus stared down at his patient. Their eyes met and held as they both came to terms with their shared truth.

Finally, Seamus nodded. Evidently satisfied they'd reached an understanding, Rafferty gave in to the pain and passed out, leaving Seamus wishing he could do the same.

Chapter 10

Seamus pegged one of the farmers with a hard look. "Call Conlan and tell him to get his ass back here. He may be out of range for a while, but keep trying until you reach him. Tell him what's happened."

"Sure thing, Doc."

"I'm not a doctor." Although he really was. "Now let's get Rafferty into pre-op. We've got to get that tourniquet off before it causes more damage."

"What do you mean by 'pre-op,' Seamus?" Joss blocked his way. Every inch of her vibrated with the protective nature of a warrior. "You're just a medic. Do what you can to stabilize him. That's all."

Seamus stared at the bloody mess in front of him. Yes, he could continue this farce of pretending to be less than he was, which would even play into his desire for revenge. It was doubtful that Rafferty would live long enough to make it to the trauma hospital. Without lifting a finger, Seamus could simply let his enemy die.

But that wasn't going to happen. Somewhere along the line, these people had come to mean something to him. Not just Megan and Phoebe, but also the O'Days themselves and the people who depended on the vampire for their living, for their homes, for the second chance Rafferty had offered all of them.

His decision might come back to haunt him, but his vow to do no harm outweighed his vow to avenge his sister. Time to get moving.

"They can't get here fast enough, Joss. He's already lost too much blood. If that doesn't kill him, the trip will. Let me take care of him. Now, before it's too late."

The indecision looked out of place on the chancellor's face. "He's all I have."

"I know, Joss. And if you don't get the hell out of my way, you won't have him for long." Brutal, but it was no less than the truth.

For the second time in less than a minute, he reluctantly made hardcore eye contact with someone and made a promise. "I can do this, Joss. Trust me."

She drew a shuddering breath and jerked her head in a sharp nod. "What can I do to help?"

"Take care of Phoebe." Which would give her something to concentrate on besides her husband.

Next, Seamus dragged Megan along in his wake on the way to the pre-op. "Scrub up and put some gloves on. Then start cutting away Rafferty's jeans while I'll get him medicated."

Megan tried one last protest. "Seamus, what if he…"

"There'll be no *if* about it unless we get moving." He

realized he was barking at her and softened his voice. "I'll point at what I need. I just need an extra pair of hands. You'll do fine."

Then he glanced at his patient. "You both will."

With Megan's help, Seamus had Rafferty stripped, prepped and medicated for surgery in a matter of minutes. Even with his untrained helper, he was able to get IVs started and a unit of blood dripping into Rafferty's vein. Their species could survive almost any wound as long they didn't bleed out completely. With transfusions and the right drugs, the older vampire stood a good chance for a full recovery.

Once the bleeding was under control, the next hurdle would be to get the bones realigned quickly enough. Seamus could still try to stabilize Rafferty enough for transport and let someone else take it from there. But left on their own, the bones would solidify as they were, leaving Rafferty permanently crippled. Even if Seamus got them even partly back in place, it would make it easier for a surgical team to try realign them correctly, but as bad as the break was, it was unlikely they'd succeed.

That left one more option. Seamus could come out of hiding and do the complete surgical repair himself. As soon as the thought crossed his mind, his decision was made. Time to get started.

Megan studied their patient's face. "His color looks better."

"That's the blood doing its work. Now we need to get him into surgery."

Together they maneuvered the gurney into the next room and positioned it by the surgical table.

"On a count of three, we'll lift him over. Are you ready?"

When she nodded, he counted, "One, two, three!"

It was a good thing Rafferty wasn't awake for that because jarring his leg that much had to hurt like a bitch.

"What next?" Megan kept her eyes focused on Seamus's face, clearly not wanting to look at the torn flesh and shattered pieces of bone that used to be Rafferty's leg. He draped the site with sterile dressings.

"Now, we pretend this is a particularly challenging jigsaw puzzle and get to work."

He pulled the tray of sterile instruments over within easy reach. "Luckily, I've always been good at puzzles."

God knew how many hours later, they were finally done. Megan's back ached, her head pounded and her eyes stung from sweat. Even so, there was no place she'd rather be than watching Seamus Fitzhugh perform his magic.

She'd known firsthand that he was good at what he did, but watching him put Rafferty's leg back together was like watching an artist in action. Piece by piece, stitch by stitch, what had been a hideous mishmash of blood and bone fragments became whole again. Right now Seamus was slowly sewing the long incision closed, his tiny black stitches tidy and neat.

"You were amazing." In so many ways, although right now she meant his gift for healing. "I didn't know that medics could do something like this."

Seamus glanced up at her. After a second, he said, "They can't."

"But—"

"They also don't have the training to dispense the kind of medicine that saved your life. Not legally, anyway."

He went back to his work, leaving her confused about what he was trying to tell her. If medics didn't do surgery or dispense the medicine he gave her, then that meant…what exactly?

"Come on, Megan, you're smart. You can figure it out." Seamus snipped the last thread and dropped the small curved needle back down on the instrument tray.

The truth hit her hard. "You're not a medic at all, are you? You're a doctor, and a surgeon at that."

"Half right. I finished medical school and should have been licensed to practice medicine. However, I lack a few weeks of training to finish my residency in surgery." He bandaged Rafferty's leg and then checked his patient's vitals.

After making several notes in the chart he'd started, he covered Rafferty with a warmed blanket.

She stepped back from the table. "Why pretend to be somebody you aren't?"

"My reasons are my own." He adjusted the flow of the IV a bit. "Go tell Joss that her husband came through with flying colors. He'll be asleep for a while, but she can come sit with him until he wakes up."

It was clear she wasn't going to get any more information from Seamus. Whatever was going on in that head of his, he wasn't ready to share, not even with her. That hurt, plain and simple. She'd seen every impressive inch of him during the past twenty-four hours, but right now she was having a hard time recognizing him at all.

"I'll go get her."

The waiting room had filled up since the last time she'd

been out there. As soon as Megan appeared in the doorway, both Joss and Conlan were up and moving in her direction. As tired as she was, she let them come to her.

"Is Rafferty—"

When Joss couldn't go on, Conlan finished the question for her. "Is Rafferty ready to go? The evac chopper landed twenty minutes ago, but we held them off waiting for Seamus to get him ready to transport."

When Megan started to shake her head, Joss blanched and staggered back a step. Conlan immediately wrapped his arm around his friend's shoulder while Megan hastened to correct herself.

"No, Joss, Rafferty is doing fine. Seamus did an amazing job of putting the pieces of his leg back together. He sent me out to get you so you can sit with Rafferty until he wakes up. Come on, I'll take you back."

Conlan followed hard on their heels, his face grim. When they filed into the small surgical suite, Seamus was waiting for them.

"Glad you're here, Conlan. We need to move Rafferty out of here so I can get the room cleaned up and restocked. I could use your help lifting him."

"But what about the helicopter? They won't wait forever."

"Let them go. They can't do any more for him than I have and being jostled right now could actually make things worse. If the ride got rough enough, they'd have to operate again. Thanks to his age, Rafferty's tougher than most. That doesn't mean he's invincible."

The security officer crossed his arms over his chest and blocked the door. "Fine, I'll call them, but then we need to talk, *Doctor.*"

That definitely sounded like a threat to Megan, but Seamus only looked resigned.

"No arguments on that count, Chancellor, but not right now. Let's get your boss situated, and then I need to check if any of that crowd out there is waiting to see me. Once I've seen to my patients, I'll surrender peaceably."

"Can we trust you with their care?" Conlan kept his voice low, probably out of consideration for Rafferty, but still managed to sound belligerent.

Seamus's smile didn't reach his eyes. "Right now, I'm all you've got."

Joss studied her husband's pale face and then the bandage on his leg. "Let him, but I want you with him every minute. I'll stay with Rafferty. Once he's awake, we'll decide what to do."

Then she got right up in Seamus's face. "And if he doesn't wake up, you're dead. Painfully, permanently dead."

Megan tried to shove her way between Joss and Seamus. She wasn't sure what all the undercurrents to this conversation meant, but she wouldn't let them raise a hand to hurt Seamus. No matter what else he'd done, he'd saved her life and Rafferty's, too.

She dragged her cousin back a couple of steps. "Joss, back off. I know you're worried and upset. But in case you've forgotten, he just saved Rafferty's leg, not to mention his life!"

Her cousin leaned in close and sniffed Megan's skin. "Just because you spent the night in his bed doesn't mean he's trustworthy, Megan. We both know your taste in lovers is questionable at best."

Seamus shoved Megan out of his way. "Okay, that's enough, Joss. What happened between me and Megan is none of your damn business. You want to rip into me, fine, have at it. But you don't say another word to her or your husband won't be the only one bleeding in here today."

"*Shut up,* all of you!" Conlan roared. "Joss, you might want to remember that Megan just helped save his life, too. Focus on Rafferty and leave Seamus to me."

Then he turned on Seamus. "As for you, take care of your patients, including Rafferty. I'll stay with you because Joss asked me to, not because I don't trust you to do your best by them."

His face gentled when he finally got to Megan. "Strip off that bloody gown because I suspect that's your daughter calling for you."

Conlan was right. Phoebe was her priority, but still she hesitated. "Seamus?"

There was exhaustion in his stance and great sadness in his face. She instinctively reached out to him, despite everything needing to offer him some kind of comfort. When he flinched and stepped back out of reach, her heart hurt.

"Go on, Megan. I'll be…here."

She left. And if anyone noticed the tears streaming down her face, they didn't say so.

"Boy, when you decide to screw up, you don't mess around."

Seamus opened an eye and stared across the exam room at his unwanted companion—or warden. He wasn't sure which Conlan was at the moment and didn't really care. He figured he was only hours away from being dead or thrown out on his ass. He was too tired at the moment to worry about anyone but himself.

Well, except for Megan. Right now he'd give anything to be back in his apartment, pretending that the hours they'd shared there were more than just a momentary lapse in judgment. He'd known better than to involve her in his problems, and yet he'd managed to drag her right down into the muck with him.

Evidently ignoring Conlan wasn't going to work because he sat up straighter and tried again. "Are you ready for that talk?"

"Does it matter whether I am or not?"

"Not really."

He stood up. "That's what I thought. Let's take this party back to my quarters. I'd kill for a cup of coffee."

"Fine. Let me tell Joss where we'll be."

Seamus walked through the clinic and was glad to see the waiting room was empty. Once he'd gotten Rafferty taken care of, he'd had a steady stream of patients requiring his attention. Conlan had kept his promise to Joss and stayed with him every step of the way, stepping out only when the patient was female and required a physical examination.

As Seamus headed for his quarters, he was surprised to see the light on in Megan's office. He quickly learned there was a good reason for that.

"Megan, what are you still doing here?"

She looked up from the file she'd been reading. "I work here, remember? Unless that's changed."

A rush of unexpected warmth gave him a new surge of energy. "I wasn't sure you'd want to."

"Make no mistake, you've got some explaining to do,

mister, and not just to me." She frowned. "I swore never to let another vampire into my life, but it seems I must trust you on some level. If I didn't, I wouldn't have spent all those hours in your bed."

She picked up her pen and began making some notes, leaving him standing there staring at her in bewilderment. She still trusted him?

When he didn't immediately leave, she asked, "Was there something else?"

"Uh, no."

"Okay then." Then, she closed the file and reached for the next one on the pile. "And, Seamus, don't make me regret last night. Life doesn't offer many gifts like that."

What could he say to that? He'd never been anyone's gift before, and now was sure as hell the wrong time and place for it. He let himself into the apartment and started raiding the refrigerator. Since it looked as if he'd survive the day, he might as well eat something.

By the time Conlan strolled in, Seamus had thrown together a couple of sandwiches, but he had to take care of one more thing before he sat down.

"Go ahead and eat. I'm going to check Rafferty's vitals and give him another dose of medicine." He left without waiting for Conlan to respond. If the chancellor still wanted to babysit him, fine.

Joss looked up from her magazine when Seamus walked into the room. "What are you doing now? Where's Conlan? I thought he was told to stick with you."

"He was. He did. Right now I'm going to check on my patient and give him something for the pain."

A hoarse voice entered the conversation. "I'm done being a pin cushion, Fitzhugh."

Joss and Seamus both turned to see Rafferty blinking up at them. Although clearly still feeling the aftereffects of everything that had been thrown at him, the vampire looked coherent.

Joss hurried to his side. "God, Rafferty, you ever scare me like that again, and I'll operate on you myself—and without drugs."

When the vampire laughed, he winced in pain. Seamus offered them his back as he filled a syringe with Rafferty's medicine, to allow the couple a private moment.

A few seconds later, Joss cleared her throat. "Uh, Seamus, you can turn around now."

He walked around to Rafferty's other side and swabbed his arm with alcohol. The older vampire glared at the needle.

"Is that necessary?"

"Yes, it is. But on a happier note, barring unforeseen complications, it should be the last dose through a needle. You can take pills after this if you need them."

"Good. Now when can I go home?"

"With luck, the day after tomorrow you'll be out of that bed and hobbling around on crutches." He quickly injected the meds and covered the spot with a cotton ball. "When you can manage to walk from here to the front door without hurting yourself, you can go home."

"Why not tonight?"

"Because I need to keep an eye on your surgical site, and Joss needs to get some sleep. She'll need all the energy she can muster to wait on you hand and foot once you're back home."

"I like the sound of that." Rafferty gave his wife an evil look. "And how long can I milk that for?"

"As long as you feed regularly, making it fresh blood whenever possible, you'll be completely healed in a couple of weeks. So take advantage of every minute you can." He winked at Joss.

"Hey, he's hard enough to live with as it is, Seamus. Don't encourage him," Joss protested, although she was smiling down at her husband.

He needed to put some distance between himself and them, both physical and emotional. "Conlan wants to talk to me, and then I'm going to get some sleep. After that, I'll sit with Rafferty so you can go home, Joss."

Before Seamus reached the door, Rafferty spoke again. "Seamus?"

"Yes?"

The vampire struggled to lift his head up so he could glare at him. "Thanks for saving my leg and, most likely, my life. That doesn't mean I'm not going to kick your ass for you once I'm off the crutches."

He could feel the cold steel in Rafferty's gaze from across the room. "Fair enough."

It was too much to hope that Conlan would've given up and gone home. But no, he was firmly ensconced on Seamus's couch, his feet propped up on the coffee table. Memories of how that couch had been put to use flooded through Seamus's mind as he picked up his sandwich and dropped down on the opposite end from Conlan.

At least Conlan held off on starting his inquisition until Seamus had devoured everything on his plate as well as two packs of blood. By now, he was well past caring if Conlan or the whole damn world watched him feed. When the second pack was empty, he tossed it aside.

"Okay, the condemned man has had his last meal. Fire away." Not that he was in the mood for answering questions.

Conlan shifted to face Seamus. "So it turns out you're a doctor, and not just a medic after all."

There was no use in denying it. "Yes, I've finished medical school, but I was asked to leave before I completed my surgical residency. I was specializing in orthopedics, but had extensive practice in general surgery before starting my last round of training. The school refused to grant me my credentials, so the part about being licensed as a medic is true. They didn't even want to give me that much."

"Want to tell me the rest of the story? I'll find out one way or the other."

"Do you really think confession is good for the soul, Conlan? Because no matter what I say, I'm guessing you'll toss me back out the gate and probably in broad daylight. However, for Rafferty's sake, you might want to wait until I take the stitches out."

"Don't be a smart-ass." Conlan was clearly not amused. "As much as I'd like to oblige your death wish, I'm not the judge nor the jury around here. Rafferty and Joss will decide what happens to you from this point on. None of us take well to being lied to, no matter what the reason. I might think the boss is a pompous jerk most of the time, but I do respect what he's trying to accomplish here."

His right hand flashed out and caught Seamus by the collar, jerking him halfway across the couch. For the first time, as he got in Seamus's face, the chancellor let his anger show, along with his powerful fangs.

"You bastard, I actually *liked* you. Hell, I gave my approval on your application even though I knew there was something off about your story, that you were hiding something. The only reason you're not bleeding right now is because you've saved the lives of two people I care about."

Seamus instantly responded with all the belligerence of an irate male vampire in his prime. He broke Conlan's grasp on his shirt and shoved the chancellor back to his own end of the couch.

"Yes, I lied, but at least I was actually more qualified than I claimed to be. I've never used my medical skills to do harm."

True enough, although he'd been damn tempted. Frustration and something that felt an awful lot like shame had him wanting to punch something. Or somebody.

Before he gave in to the urge, he lurched to his feet to put the narrow distance of the small living room between them. Both he and Conlan were breathing hard, the inborn aggression native to both species hard to contain.

Finally, Seamus forced himself to speak. "I had my reasons for why I lied, Conlan. Reasons that have nothing to do with you and everything to do with Rafferty. That's all you need to know."

"That's where you're wrong, boy! Everything around here is my business. I won't rest until I know the truth. The sun's already up, so I know you're not going anywhere for a few hours. I've got a couple of my men and the transport mechanic checking over Rafferty's vehicle. If I find out there's more to this than a simple accident, you'd better hope you've got a watertight alibi."

The anger faded into shock. "You suspect it was sabotage?"

"I don't know yet, but I'm not ruling it out." Conlan cracked his knuckles out of frustration. "But Rafferty's transport was practically new. That the brakes would fail in the one vehicle that he drives all the time might be a coincidence, but I'm thinking not."

Who else would've had it in for Rafferty? Banan, but he was out of reach at the moment. "Let me know what you find out."

"Oh, believe me. You'll be the first to know."

Now wasn't the time for this. Until they knew for sure if the wreck had been an attempt on Rafferty's life, there was no reason to try to convince Conlan that Seamus hadn't been involved.

"Look, I told Joss I'd catch a couple hours of rest and then send her home. You're welcome to sack out on the couch or in one of the exam rooms if you want to stay close by. We'll all think better when we're not running on empty."

Which reminded him, Megan was long overdue to be heading back to her cottage.

"Banan Delaney's gone, isn't he?"

"Yeah, he had just boarded the turbo when I got the call about Rafferty. Why?"

"I wanted to make sure it was safe for Megan to go back home."

Conlan's expression turned sour. "Yeah, and that's one more reason I want to kick your ass from one end of the estate to the other. I shouldn't have been the last one to learn about the poison. I'm still sorry I didn't throw the bastard *under* the turbo as you suggested."

He took a step in Seamus's direction, his fists clenched. "Megan's a nice woman and deserves someone who'll treat her right. You understand me?"

Seamus agreed on both points. "No arguments from me."

"Tell her I'll take her home and check the place out for her if she'd like me to."

"I'm sure she'll appreciate the offer."

As Seamus headed out the door to tell her, he realized that for the first time he regretted being a vampire rather than one of the other two species. At least if he were a chancellor, or even a human, he would be the one to escort Megan and her daughter safely back home.

Instead, despite his superior strength, he was stuck inside and unable to keep his lover safe from harm.

The sound of Seamus's door echoed down the hallway. Megan immediately put her hands back on the keyboard to look busy. The last thing she wanted was for Seamus to catch her daydreaming, especially about him. She'd meant what she told him about still trusting him, but that was true only up to a point. He had some serious explaining to do. After that, she'd make up her mind how far her faith in him would extend.

Her traitorous body clearly had no such reservations. As soon as he appeared in the doorway, all she could think was how much she wanted to brush his hair back off his forehead and how good that stern mouth had tasted when he'd kissed her.

"Hi, there."

"Hi, right back to you."

She shut down the computer and stood up as she was

hit with a powerful urge to walk straight into his arms. "Was there something you needed?"

"Conlan has offered to see that you and Phoebe get home safely."

Conlan, but not Seamus. Okay, so much for those daydreams.

As if sensing the direction her thoughts had taken, he added, "The sun's up."

"Oh, then, that makes sense. It will feel good to get out of these same clothes."

Seamus's smile changed from friendly to something far hotter. "I wish I could go along and help with that."

So did she, despite everything that had happened, but she couldn't give in to temptation. Not until she knew more about what was going on. And Seamus knew it, too. His smile disappeared and the blue of his eyes turned icy.

"Seamus, I can't…"

"I see. That's okay." Although it clearly wasn't. He retreated back into the hallway. "I'll get Conlan for you."

And coward that she was, she let him walk away.

Chapter 11

The smart thing would be to let him walk away, to rebuild that wall of caution between them. Maybe it was because she was so tired, but she wasn't feeling all that bright at the moment.

"Seamus! Come back!"

She sensed him still out in the hallway, trapped between his apartment and her office and unsure which way he wanted to go. He wasn't going to make this easy for her.

"Please."

He reappeared in the doorway but made no move to come back into the office.

"What now, Megan?"

He sounded so tired her heart ached. She came around the desk and walked straight toward him. At first he only watched her, but at the last second, he held out his arms. God, it felt so good to be gathered in close to the strength of his chest, to let his warmth engulf her.

"I'm sorry, Seamus." She leaned her head back to look him in the eye. "I know you have good reasons for…whatever you've done."

"Call it what it is, Megan. I've lied to Conlan, to Rafferty and to you. And if circumstances hadn't forced my hand, I would've gone right on lying to all of you."

It all came down trust, something she'd had in short supply these days. So what could she say to him without giving either one of them false hope? She had to try.

"I had my own secrets, Seamus. If you hadn't been there when I arrived, I would've died. But even so, I was in no hurry for everyone to find out that I have poor taste in men."

Oops. She dropped her head back down against his chest with a sigh. "Sorry. That came out wrong. I meant to say I *had* poor taste in men. Before coming here. Before I met you."

To her surprise, Seamus laughed. Then he crooked his finger and used it to tilt her face back up toward his. "How about we just admit we're both too tired to be having any kind of serious discussion right now?"

While he spoke, he focused on her mouth, as if waiting for something. Permission, maybe?

"Okay, I'll go along with that idea, provided you figure out something else we could be doing right now besides talking."

"How about this?"

Then he kissed her. At the first brush of his lips across hers, the stress of the past twenty-four hours disappeared. His kiss was everything she wanted and not nearly everything she needed from him. Now wasn't the time to push for anything more.

Slowly, he broke away, saying without words that he regretted having to do so. "Conlan's waiting. Go home. Get some rest."

"I'll be back tonight."

He shook his head. "The clinic's closed tonight, except for emergencies. You've been through a lot. Take it easy and spend some time with Phoebe."

"But…"

He put his finger across her lips. "But nothing. I'll have my own big baby to take care of, or have you forgotten that I've got Rafferty staying in the clinic? How long do you think he'll like being confined to bed?"

She giggled, mainly because he wanted her to. "Okay, but if you need me, call."

"I will. Now get packed up. I'm going to get some sleep so I can send Joss home to rest."

"You're a nice man, Seamus Fitzhugh." She raised up to kiss his cheek.

"No, I'm not, but I'm glad you think so." Then his expression turned serious. "I hope nothing you learn about me changes your thoughts on that subject."

"We just agreed now wasn't the time to get all serious." She gave him a gentle push. "Now tell Conlan I'm ready to go."

He gave her another quick kiss and disappeared, but this time looking a great deal happier. She quickly bundled up her daughter and waited in the hall for Conlan. Seamus was right. She needed to rest, to give herself time and space to get some perspective on the monumental changes her life had gone through in the past few days.

However, there was something she'd already learned. Hope was a precious thing, and she'd had far too little of it for a long time. But with Banan gone and Seamus in her life, she had hope again. And that was a good thing.

The alarm went off, jarring Seamus out of a sound sleep. He slammed the palm of his hand down on the clock to shut off the obnoxious noise. Now if he could just make the rest of the world disappear as easily, he'd be happy.

He pushed himself upright and sat on the edge of the bed for several seconds. Okay, time to get moving. He'd promised to replace Joss at Rafferty's bedside, a chore he wasn't looking forward to, but a promise was a promise. Thinking of his vampire host, he thought it was a damn shame that not everybody felt that way.

On the other hand, he'd never seen his sister's eyes light up at the mention of Rafferty's name nor could he imagine her sitting at the vampire's side as he recuperated from a near-death injury. Rafferty had been betrothed to Seamus's half sister but he'd called the engagement off shortly after he met Joss. Seamus suspected that if Rafferty had married Petra, the two would've both been locked into a loveless relationship forever.

He poked at that idea, trying to decide how he felt about it. Without question, he would prefer Petra were alive—period. Despite her shortcomings, she was his sister, and he'd loved her. But was her pride worth the cost of making not two, but three people miserable for the duration of their long lives? Rafferty wanted Joss. Joss wanted Rafferty. That much was clear.

He knew exactly what Petra had wanted: the status from being married to a vampire male from a higher-ranking clan. All things considered, she'd have found Rafferty's cash to be cold comfort. Seamus had learned the hard way status was a fragile thing indeed. Any friendships and other relationships based on it even more so. Events totally out of his control had taught him that bitter lesson.

Now, here he was in the middle of nowhere, surrounded by people he'd known but a short time. Yet, for the first time, he knew where he belonged, what his role in life should be. Hell, he even knew the woman he wanted to share that life with—Megan. How bizarre was that? His honor still demanded retribution for the death of his sister, but at what cost? And who would pay that price besides him?

This was getting him nowhere. Time to go babysit his patient. Do no harm, that's what he'd promised. He now knew for certain that those were more than idle words, that they defined him as a person. Strip him of friends, family, money and anything else of value, and he still had those words.

Do no harm—the bedrock of his soul.

Joss crossed her arms and stayed right where she was. "And I'm telling you I'm fine."

Seamus should have known it wouldn't be easy. "Joss, go home. Don't make me get Conlan to help me drag your exhausted backside out of here."

Rafferty opened his eyes, a slight smile playing

around his mouth. "I'd buy tickets to watch that. And just so you know, Seamus, even with the two of you ganging up on her, my money would be on Joss."

His wife leaned over to kiss him. "Thank you for that vote of confidence, big man."

Seamus threw up his hands. "Fine, she's the toughest thing around these parts. That doesn't mean she can go without food and sleep. You put me in charge of the health care for everyone on the estate, and that includes both of you."

He glared at the couple and waited.

Rafferty supported him. "You heard the doc, Joss."

She stared at her husband briefly before turning her hard gaze on Seamus. "Can I trust you with him?"

He knew what she was asking. He'd already told her the answer to that before he'd dragged the bleeding vampire into surgery and resented having to say it again. So he didn't.

"Not a problem. He's not my type."

She didn't find his answer funny, but at least Rafferty did. "I'll be fine, Joss. Go."

"Okay, but I'll be back."

As she walked out, Seamus followed her. She made it almost across the waiting room before stuttering to a stop where she slumped against the wall. He'd been expecting the collapse, figuring the only thing keeping her upright was sheer stubborn determination. Joss resisted when he tried to support her, but then gave in as tears poured down her face.

Finally, when the deluge had run its course, she stepped back, wiping her cheeks dry with the handkerchief he handed her. "Oh, God, I almost lost him."

"But you didn't. He's a strong man, Joss."

"But not invincible."

"None of us are," Seamus replied. "Will you be all right?"

"No, I'll be okay." She stepped out into the bright sunshine.

"I know." He hovered back in the shadows and watched until she reached her transport and pulled away before locking the door. Time to go face the music.

On the way, he snagged four blood packs and warmed them. Okay, so as a delay tactic, it sucked, he thought ruefully. At the most, it would slow down the confrontation by only a few seconds. Besides, after feasting from Megan's vein while being held in her arms, taking his nourishment from a plastic bag just didn't cut it.

Rafferty probably felt the same way, but right now processed blood was all either of them had. He carried the peace offering into the other room.

"So I guessed right. You're Petra's half brother." Even flat on his back, Rafferty had a commanding presence.

Seamus sat down in the chair Joss had been using. "Yes, although the *half* part never mattered. She was my only living relative."

He held out two of the blood packs. "Drink these."

Rafferty tried to hand them back. "I don't need to feed as often as you do."

"And you'd prefer your wife's vein. I get that. But right now, you're running several quarts low, and she's already exhausted. Drink that or I'll pump it in through a dull needle. A big one. If I look hard enough, I might even find a rusty one."

"Okay, hard-ass. I'll drink it."

After they'd both finished, Seamus disposed of the empties and then quickly checked Rafferty's vitals. "I'm going to look at your leg now. Want me to sit you up so you can get a look at your handsome new scar? Eventually it'll fade away, but it's pretty impressive right now, if I do say so."

"Sure."

When Seamus cut away the bandage, he stepped back to let Rafferty get a good look at his handiwork.

"Son of a bitch! I knew it was bad, but…"

All the color leeched out of Rafferty's face. "No wonder Joss kept checking to see if I was really breathing. I came damn close to losing that leg, didn't I?"

The vampire was the kind of man who'd want the truth. "No, you almost lost your life. If they hadn't gotten you to me when they did…"

"You probably don't want my gratitude, but you have it." Rafferty covered his eyes with his forearm as he pressed the button to lower the head of the bed.

A few seconds later, he asked, "So, you do want to talk about what happened with your sister?"

Now that the moment had arrived to confront his enemy, Seamus found he lacked the words or even the will to do so. Instead, he concentrated on applying a new bandage to the surgical site.

"I never cheated on Petra with Joss, Seamus. There was one night, but—"

"What you did destroyed my sister, Rafferty. I don't need excuses or details." He added one last strip of tape, amazed he could keep his touch gentle when what he really wanted to do was to punch something.

"No excuses offered. But you need to know the details." Despite his calm tone, Rafferty's fangs showed enough to reveal the powerful emotions he was fighting. "I need you to know them."

"It won't change anything."

"Nothing will, but the truth is better than lies and misconceptions. If we're going to find a way to get along from this point on, Seamus, we need a do-over."

The import of his words sank in. Seamus looked at Rafferty in shock. "You're not going to throw me out?"

"Let's just say, it wouldn't be my first choice. Now, are you going to listen or not?"

"I'll listen. That doesn't mean I'll believe you."

Rafferty smiled and shook his head. "God, you remind me of me. Joss thinks I'm the only one this stubborn."

Seamus didn't like that one bit, especially considering his low opinion of Rafferty. Although he had to admit, that had changed since his arrival on the man's estate.

"I said I'd listen. I didn't say I'd sit here and be insulted. How did you figure out who I was?"

"Something about how you were acting today reminded me that her brother was studying to be a doctor."

"And you let me operate on you? You had to know I'd be looking for vengeance."

There was real regret in Rafferty's voice. "Had I known what happened…what the fallout had cost you, I'd like to think I would have done something about it."

"Yeah, well, that's easy to say now when it's too late."

"Okay, Doc, do you want the long or the short version?"

"What's to tell? You broke your word to my sister and it destroyed her. I was just collateral damage."

"You're right, of course. I was betrothed to your sister when I first met Joss. But knowing your sister, did you really think our relationship was a love match?"

"No, of course not. I wasn't blind to my sister's faults. She'd already broken one betrothal when she realized that you were a step up for her."

"And I was looking for a female who could handle all the demands our society places on a scion of a highly-ranked vampire clan. It seemed like a fair trade."

"And then you met Joss." He so didn't want to hear this.

"She was the newest arbiter for the Coalition." Rafferty stared up at the ceiling as he lost himself in the past. "I knew from the first minute she was something special."

He rolled his head toward Seamus. "Imagine—a vampire of my age and experience falling that hard and that fast. Not that I had any intention of acting on it. I was a vampire, after all, and she was a lowly chancellor."

He winked at Seamus. "Don't tell her I said that or both of us will be bleeding."

Seamus didn't want to be charmed by Rafferty's embarrassed admission, but he was. And for some inexplicable reason, Megan Perez's pretty face drifted through his thoughts, yet another "lowly" chancellor who possessed both incredible strength and beauty. He hated knowing he and the older vampire had that much in common.

"Oh, boy, you've got it bad, too." There was a great deal of sympathy in Rafferty's voice. "All the more reason for us to get past this."

"Keep talking."

"I fed from Joss one time while I was still betrothed

to Petra. That's all that happened, but we'd crossed the line and we both knew it. Joss resigned as an arbiter as soon as the Coalition session ended. I went back home and broke off the betrothal."

He sounded tired, by now his voice barely above a whisper. As Petra's brother, he needed to hear more. But as Rafferty's doctor, he needed to make his patient rest.

"We can finish this discussion later, Rafferty. Get some sleep."

The vampire shook his head. "Don't think I can do this again. There's not much more to say, anyway."

"All right."

"Petra didn't take it well. If I'd left her for another vampire, one she saw as her social superior, she would have understood. Or if she'd found another male who was easier to manipulate than I was, but my social equal, she wouldn't have hesitated to dump me. Unfortunately, she visited me while the Coalition was in session and met Joss."

Rafferty rubbed his eyes. "I was so damn careful, but Petra had a real talent for reading people. She knew I was leaving her for a chancellor, and *that* she couldn't tolerate."

That rang true to Seamus. "She would have seen that as insult of the worst sort, especially if her friends found out. She would've never lived it down."

"I planned to wait a while before contacting Joss. To give Petra time to move on, so that no one would make the connection between our breakup and any subsequent relationship I was able to establish with Joss. The nobility of that sacrifice was lost upon your sister."

For the first time, he sounded bitter. Too bad. All of

this was still Rafferty's fault. Their society might have overlooked him having a chancellor mistress, but he doubted Petra would have, especially when it was clear that Rafferty felt far more for Joss than he had Petra.

"Then all of a sudden, I was charged with murdering a human, one I was known to have had difficulties with in the past. I was duly convicted, the main evidence being my knife was found wedged in the bastard's chest."

Rafferty sounded so disgusted, Seamus found himself smiling. "Imagine! What were they thinking?"

"Like I would've ever been that stupid. I don't know how familiar you are with the law when a death sentence is involved, but the Coalition grants the prisoner the right to have one of their chancellors review the case. If the evidence holds up, the chancellor executes the prisoner by any means they choose. If the chancellor finds inconsistencies, they have the authority to set aside the judgment. I chose Joss to hear my case."

"And big surprise, Joss set aside your conviction. You managed to walk on a murder conviction, and married your lover. Everybody lives happily ever after. Well, except for Petra."

A fresh wave of bitterness washed over Seamus, leaving him aching. He lurched up out of his chair, kicking it out of his way.

The vampire didn't flinch in the face of Seamus's fury. "No, actually Joss wasn't the one who cleared me. I knew I didn't have a chance in hell of being exonerated, but at least Joss would make my death painless. Not all chancellors are that considerate. But when Joss reviewed the file, she realized your sister had put a lien against my estate, hiding behind a corporation name.

Instead of handling the final dispensation of the case herself, Joss called in Ambrose, her boss."

Seamus stood up straighter. This part he hadn't heard. If Ambrose was involved, it changed everything. The honor of the top chancellor for the Coalition was beyond reproach. No one among the three species was held in higher regard.

"What did Ambrose find?"

"He brought Petra in and confronted her. She admitted to having framed me. By law, she was tried, convicted and given the same sentence I was. I know it's cold comfort, but Ambrose saw to it that it was mercifully quick."

A heavy silence settled between them. After a bit, Rafferty stirred restlessly. "I can't tell you how sorry I was that it came to that, Seamus. I may not have loved Petra, but I never wanted her dead. Hell, I even understood why she did what she did."

There wasn't anything Seamus could say to that. He'd known all along that there was more to the story than he'd been told. As soon as it became known that his sister had been executed as a murderer, his scholarships had dried up, his residency canceled and his world came crashing down.

"I'm going to sleep now."

Rafferty tugged his blanket up higher on his chest and closed his eyes. He didn't immediately fall asleep, but the pretense allowed both males time to deal with the emotions that the painful story had stirred up.

Seamus rubbed his chest, as if that would make the pain in his heart would go away. Damn Petra, anyway! If she'd come to him, told him what was going on, maybe he could've helped her find a way to get past Rafferty's betrayal.

But she'd thrown the dice and lost, leaving Seamus alone and struggling to find his own way. He hated that she'd been that bitter and unhappy, but hadn't he meant anything to her at all? Obviously not enough to make any difference. As furious as he was with Rafferty, he was just as mad at Petra. God, the whole thing left him tired straight through to the bone. Catharsis might be good for the soul, but it burned a lot of energy.

Conlan had said Joss preferred that those who came to the estate were running toward their future rather than from their past. Right now, he wasn't up to running anywhere for any reason, but he could walk. And if Rafferty meant what he said about wanting Seamus to stay, he'd eventually pick up speed toward a future that held something good, like hope or friendship.

Or maybe even love, added a quiet voice in the back of his mind. And with the memory of Megan's sweet kiss, he dozed off.

Traveling by turbo left Banan filthy, exhausted and more determined that ever to wrest control of the family fortune by any means necessary. By fair means or foul, it didn't matter. And speaking of foul, he wondered if Rafferty discovered the little surprise he'd left behind. Or maybe it was Joss who'd learn the hard way that the brakes on their favorite transport were about to fail. That would be all right, too. It was the perfect gift to show his appreciation for their piss-poor hospitality.

Which brought him back to the misery of the turbo

ride. He could've called for an airlift pickup when he left the O'Day's estate, but maintaining a low profile was more important than comfort. Money also played into his decision.

God, he hated having to conserve funds. As heir, he should have had unrestricted access to the family bank accounts, but showing an improved sense of fiscal responsibility was part of the total image package he was presenting to the older generation. If he'd managed to retrieve his daughter, that alone would've been enough to cement his future role of head of the family. But until he got his hands on her, he had to pretend to comply with the family's expectations.

He'd gotten off the turbo at the first town past Rafferty's stop long enough to make a few phone calls. As luck would have it, one of his distant cousins was up for a little adventure. Riley had long ago burned any chance of ingratiating himself with the current senior generation.

Riley might not be overly smart, but he was greedy. With the promise of money and power, Banan reeled him in with almost no effort. Fool! As if Banan would ever trust anyone whose loyalty could be purchased so cheaply.

Banan checked the time. He had hours left to be cooped up in this metal cage as it rattled along on the track. He couldn't wait until he checked into a decent hotel. One with room service, the kind where they kept willing humans on hand who would offer up their vein for the right price—and their bodies as well, for a slightly higher fee.

Of course, he'd have to be careful not to do any permanent damage. He'd always been hard on his toys, and right now he couldn't risk drawing unwanted attention to himself.

When Riley arrived, they'd make plans for his next visit to the O'Day estate thanks to one of his shady friends who could fly them in and out of a remote section of the estate. From there, they'd have fun checking off all the things he had on his special to-do list. A few drained-until-dead humans would be the perfect start to this particular adventure.

With luck, they'd lay all the blame right at Seamus Fitzhugh's doorstep when they found Megan Perez's body dumped in the woods near the infirmary. Seamus would be lucky if Rafferty staked him before he offered him up to the noonday sun.

And this time, when Banan left the O'Day estate behind, he wouldn't be leaving empty-handed. His parents would be so proud of their granddaughter. They'd hire the best of nurses to take care of her until she was capable of civilized behavior. Say, around age twenty or so. It was, after all, a family tradition.

Chapter 12

Stress was running high in the room. Megan couldn't control the slight trembling in her hands, so she kept them out of sight in her lap. Conlan shot her a sympathetic look, no doubt picking up on her tension despite how hard she was working to hide it. He sat with his leg crossed over his knee, his foot keeping time to a rapid beat only he could hear while Joss methodically tore a paper napkin into small pieces.

Seamus, on the other hand, sat rock still, his mouth a straight slash except for the slightest hint of fang showing. He looked like he'd been through hell and barely lived to tell the tale. Joss and Rafferty had called this meeting to discuss his future, although so far only Joss was seated at the table.

Seamus clearly didn't appreciate anyone having that much control over his life, but the truth was the estate was theirs to run as they saw fit. All decisions were final, but at least they'd invited her and Conlan in on the session, perhaps to ask their take on the situation.

It had been less than a week since Rafferty's brush with death. Without Seamus's quick action and superb medical skills, they'd have been gathered to bury the scion of the O'Day clan. Instead, they had other business to attend to.

She still didn't know what had brought Seamus to the O'Day estate, but it had been bad. Surely he wouldn't have lied about who he was and what his intentions were without good cause. But then her judgment when it came to men wasn't always trustworthy.

Obviously his path had crossed Rafferty's at some point in the past. Other than Seamus himself, only Joss and Rafferty knew for sure and they weren't talking. The only consolation was that Conlan looked as frustrated as she felt.

Finally, she heard the clomping steps of Rafferty making his way toward them. He came around the corner, awkwardly trying to manage his crutches and his injured leg while not dropping a file folder. After maneuvering himself into his own chair, he looked around the table. "Sorry to keep you waiting. Things took longer than they should have."

"Did it come?" Joss nodded toward the file folder.

"Yeah, but I had to grease a few palms to get those greedy bastards moving." He shot a hard look across at Seamus. "I thought the vampire clans had cornered the market on power plays and manipulating people. Those bastards you studied under could teach even the oldest of us a few lessons."

Seamus frowned. "Why were you talking to them? I already told you the reason I didn't finish school."

"Yeah, let's say I hate anyone being backed into a corner through no fault of their own." He reached for the cup of coffee Joss had poured for him. "Dusty work, but it's done."

"What work?" Conlan asked as he reached for a couple of cookies.

Megan watched both of the O'Days, trying to guess what was behind the looks they exchanged. Finally, Joss nodded as Rafferty tangled his fingers in hers, presenting a united front.

"Seamus, here, lied to us about his reasons for coming here. After a long and private conversation on the subject, we've come to terms with the circumstances that made that necessary. The details are not mine to share."

Rafferty waited until Seamus nodded in agreement before continuing. "Our official policy has always been to permanently expel anyone who has misrepresented themselves to us, no excuses accepted."

Megan gasped, ready to protest, but Seamus wasn't acting either surprised or upset. Why?

"In this case, however, there are extenuating circumstances. We're prepared to overlook the misrepresentation for a variety of reasons."

Joss interrupted, "Not the least of which is that he saved Rafferty's life."

Conlan shot Seamus a conspiratorial look. "Which may show a lack of good judgment on Seamus's part."

"Bite me." Rafferty flashed his fangs at his security officer before returning his attention to Seamus. "So, Seamus, we're officially offering you the chance to remain here on the estate. We'd like to think you've found the work to your liking and have good reasons to want to stay."

No one looked in Megan's direction, but she blushed anyway. Was she one of his reasons? She had to wonder, especially because he'd been avoiding her once everything had blown up in his face.

Rafferty tapped the file he'd laid on the table. "However, we don't want you to stay here because it's the only choice you have. Your school had no right to do what they did, and I've encouraged them to rectify their mistake."

Conlan's eyes opened wide as he grinned. "And how many were left bloody and bruised by your style of hands-on encouragement?"

Ever the predator, Rafferty's own smile showed a lot of fang. "Enough to make it fun."

He pushed the file across the table toward Seamus. "This is only a copy. The originals will be arriving by courier in the next couple of days."

Seamus pulled the papers from the file and stared at them, looking a bit bewildered. He glanced at Conlan for some answers. "I don't understand."

The security officer leaned over and quickly scanned the papers scattered on the table. "It's all couched in the usual legal gibberish and fancy words. However, the bottom line is you are now a board-certified physician and surgeon, free to practice medicine anywhere in the Coalition."

Then he clapped him on the shoulder. "I guess congratulations are in order!"

"We'll second that," Joss said, smiling. "As Rafferty

said, we wanted to make sure you had a choice, although we'd really like it if you chose to stay here. What do you think?"

Seamus finally looked up from the papers, his eyes a brighter blue than Megan had ever seen them. He looked at each person in turn, starting with Joss and Rafferty, then Conlan and finally her. She felt the heat in his gaze all the way to her toes. Her heart fluttered in anticipation as they all waited for his answer.

Seamus broke off the eye lock he had on Megan and forced himself to look back down at the stack of papers Rafferty had handed him. His medical degree. He'd given up all hope of ever having it, but there it lay—or at least a facsimile of what it would look like when it was delivered.

Months ago choice had been stripped from his life along with everything that had held any meaning for him: medical school, his sister, his status among their kind. Once his life had veered out of control, he'd been driven solely by his need to avenge his family honor.

He was well aware that everyone was watching him, waiting for him to respond to the amazing gift that had just been handed to him. It was at once too much to take in and not nearly enough to make up for what he'd lost. But again, this was about beginnings, not what-could-have-beens.

He settled for the simple truth. "I don't know what to say."

As he glanced around the table, he could pretty much guess what most everybody was thinking. Joss was proud of what her husband had been able to do, and

Rafferty himself was well aware that the stack of paper would give Seamus back his pride, if not the life he'd lost. Conlan was pleased for Seamus and probably relieved that he wasn't going to have to evict Seamus anytime soon.

There were a lot of thoughts going on behind Megan's lovely lavender eyes, but he wouldn't presume to think he knew what she was contemplating. He'd guess she was relieved in much the same way Conlan was. And like Joss, she was happy that Rafferty had straightened things out for Seamus, although she had no idea why Seamus had run into problems.

And maybe, just maybe, she was hoping he'd stay.

Where else did he have to go? Nowhere.

Who else wanted him? No one.

Did he want to stay? God, yes.

He allowed himself the privilege of reaching over to take Megan's hand in his and gave it a gentle squeeze. He kept his eyes firmly on hers when he announced his decision. "I guess you have yourself a doctor, Rafferty."

Then everyone was hooting and hollering, with Rafferty ordering Joss to fetch the champagne he had on ice in the other room "just in case." She was back in seconds with a tray full of glasses and the wine.

She handed him the bottle. "Here, this is your cele-bration, Dr. Fitzhugh. You pop the cork!"

Seamus managed to do the job with only a minimum amount of the bubbly stuff spilling onto the floor before Joss managed to catch the rest in her glass. When everyone had some, Seamus held his glass up to make the first toast.

"Here's to running toward the future."

The chime of crystal against crystal rang out as they all bumped glasses.

"Here, here!" Joss said.

Even Conlan managed a small smile as he lifted his glass. "Here's to trust well placed."

The words seemed to solidify and hang in the air between them, sending a chill through Seamus. Yes, for the time being they would trust him, but he had to wonder how strong that newly forged bond really was. But for now, he would sip the wine and enjoy the company.

Tomorrow would be soon enough to start planning for his future.

The night was pleasantly cool. The perfect temperature for walking home, his arm wrapped around a warm, lovely woman. He could see it now—him, Megan, at her front door as she debates whether or not to invite him in. He weighs in on the argument, not with words but with a kiss designed to sway her opinion.

But there was another pretty female who had to be taken into consideration—Phoebe. So rather than holding Megan in his arms, he held her daughter. Not that he was complaining—exactly.

The youngling was wide-awake and happy. If Seamus had to venture a guess, Phoebe was ready to be the center of attention for quite some time to come. He shifted his cheery burden to his other arm and snagged Megan's hand. He liked that her fingers felt so right tangled with his as they walked along.

"If I didn't say so before, I appreciate your being there for me tonight."

"Yes, well, I love my cousin and her husband, but no

one should have to face the two of them at the same time without backup." She smiled up at him. "However, you would've done fine on your own. They're smart enough to know that they were lucky to get you."

Luck had little to do with it, but he wasn't going there. "I hope it didn't cost Rafferty too much to get them to issue my credentials."

"You'll probably never know, but he wouldn't have done it if he didn't want to. Either way, it was only fair that the school fixed your records for you. You'd spent years working to become a doctor and surgeon."

"Yes, it's all I ever wanted to do." And would've given it up in heartbeat to get his sister back.

Right now, though, he had an entirely different goal in mind as they turned off the road and walked up to Megan's cottage. She unlocked the door and turned on the lights inside.

"Would you like me to take a quick look around?"

"If you wouldn't mind." Megan looked relieved. "I know it's silly because Banan is gone, but I still worry. I can make tea if you'd like some."

"That sounds good." Well, not the tea, but he'd settle for that just to spend more time in her company.

He started to put Phoebe down in her crib, but she immediately started to fuss. "Okay, little one, you can take the grand tour with me."

The cottage wasn't much bigger than his apartment at the infirmary, but Megan had somehow transformed it into a real home. There were feminine touches throughout: houseplants, soft pillows, bright-colored curtains. When he stepped into her bedroom, he wished that it was Megan and not her daughter in his arms.

"All clear."

He followed her scent into the kitchen and sat down at the table with Phoebe in his lap. He picked up a string of beads and dangled them just within reach of the baby's tiny hands. She cooed happily as she caught at them.

Megan set a cup a tea within easy reach and sat down in the chair next to him. "Do you want me to take her?"

"No, she's fine." In fact, she'd snuggled in close and was starting to look drowsy.

"You have a real gift with her. She's never that content with anyone else, including Joss." Megan snickered and added, "Rafferty always looks like he's worried that she's about to do something disgusting on his favorite shirt."

Seamus brushed Phoebe's soft cheek with his finger. "Then there's Uncle Conlan. He'd die to protect her, but is terrified by the thought of changing her diapers."

"He caught me nursing her once. I've never seen a chancellor turn that particular shade of bright red before." Megan sipped her tea. "Look, she's already asleep."

"I'll go put her down in the crib."

He slowly stood up and carried Phoebe into the small bedroom that Megan had made into a nursery. The baby stirred slightly and then settled back to sleep. He covered her with a blanket and gently patted her on the back. Not for the first time he realized how much he wished he could lay claim to her.

Banan Delaney was a fool for throwing all this away.

Megan was waiting out in the hallway. He supposed he should head back to his place. Dawn was a little over an hour away. As much as he'd like to stay longer, he couldn't risk being trapped here by the sun.

"Well, I should go. Thank you again for being there for me tonight."

"I had a good time. How does it feel to be officially Dr. Seamus Fitzhugh? I'm so pleased for you." Megan opened the door and stepped outside with him. "Does it seem real yet?"

"Not as real as this does."

He tugged her into his arms and kissed her. She smiled against his lips, teasing him with little forays with her tongue over the points of his fangs as they dropped down.

The sensation was exquisite, making him wish they had hours and hours instead of mere seconds. "You have no idea how much I've been wanting to do this all evening."

He nuzzled her neck, allowing himself the privilege of nipping at her throat right where her blood pulsed closest to the surface. She bent her neck to the side, offering him easier access and encouraging him to continue with a soft moan.

Finally, he stopped for the simple reason he had to, now, before it was too late. With her scent and the heat of her blood driving him crazy, he had to walk away or he'd end up taking both her body and her blood right there up against the door. Or maybe in the cool grass at their feet. Either way, she deserved better.

He rested his chin on top of her head as he struggled to regain control. From the bruising hold she had on his shoulders, she was skirting the edge of control as much as he was.

"I'm going to walk away now, but not because I want to." It took him several more seconds to remember how to actually let go of her and step back. "Your kisses should require a warning label, woman."

When he let go of her, she leaned back against the doorway. "I'll take that as a compliment."

"It was meant as one."

"Um, Seamus, I was wondering. Would you like to have dinner together tomorrow night after we get off work? I know emergencies might interfere, so I understand any plans we make have to be flexible."

"You're a mind reader, Megan. I'd love to have you for dinner." He rolled his eyes. "Okay, that came out wrong."

She giggled, her light-colored eyes gleaming in the moonlight. "Yes, it did. I was talking about a meal with real food."

"Let me try that again. I'd love to have dinner *with* you. At my place."

"Great. I'll see you tomorrow night." She slipped back inside, but before she closed the door, she whispered, "But if you play your cards right, you can have me afterward."

He all but flew home. The sooner he got to bed, the sooner tomorrow would arrive. The whole way, her whispered promise played over and over in his head. Was it too soon to be counting down the hours until he could coax Megan into his bed? Probably, but that didn't stop him.

"So tell me, how does my leg look?"

Rafferty hobbled over to peer over Seamus's shoulder at the X-rays backlit on the screen. Seamus let his patient look his fill. Finally, he turned off the switch, letting the stark black-and-white film go dark.

"Hop back up on the table. I want to check a few things." He kept his expression suitably somber, not wanting to give away anything too soon.

"Why? What did you see?" Rafferty pushed himself back up on the examining table and set his crutches aside. "It looked good to me."

"If you've had experience reading X-rays, why do you need me?" Seamus supported Rafferty's lower leg and helped him flex his knee and ankle. "Does that hurt?"

When the vampire hesitated, Seamus gave him a stern look. "Don't try lying about it. I'll know."

"Okay, fine." He shifted restlessly, probably trying to gauge how much he could get by with.

"I'm not Joss, Rafferty. No need to act invincible in front of me."

His boss grinned. "It doesn't work with her, either. She sees right through the bullshit."

Rafferty drew a sharp breath and winced when Seamus poked and prodded at the damaged muscles. "I can tell you this much—I'm tired of being treated like an invalid. But it hurts when I stand too long, it aches enough to keep me awake and I get tired easily. If I didn't know better, I think I was getting old."

Seamus rolled his eyes. "All normal symptoms. Considering how bad it was, it's healing way better than expected. If you'll take it easy for another week, you should be moving a lot better and able to terrorize everybody again."

Seamus picked up the crutches and stuck them back in the supply cabinet and replaced them with a cane. "Give that a try."

"Really?"

Rafferty immediately stood up on his good foot and gingerly put more weight on the broken leg. Taking the cane in hand, he hobbled back and forth across the small examination room. Seamus made a couple of suggestions to improve his patient's gait and stood back out of the way while he practiced.

"Okay, I'm going to let you go home with that instead of crutches. Your wife has agreed to snitch on you if you abuse the privilege."

"Thanks a lot, Seamus. As if she wasn't already hovering enough to drive me crazy."

"Behave, and she won't have to. You can't expect to be over an accident that bad this quickly. You need to keep feeding more than usual because your body needs it to heal."

"Anything it takes to get me back to normal."

As they walked out, Seamus asked, "Did Conlan ever find out what happened to cause the accident?"

Rafferty's expression turned stone-cold. "Someone messed with both the brakes and the accelerator."

"Any idea who'd do something that stupid?"

"Someone with a grudge against me—or Joss. We both use that vehicle."

Rafferty kept his eyes focused straight ahead, making Seamus wonder if his boss thought that someone might be him. He felt compelled to defend himself.

"I was with Megan from late afternoon that day until they carried you in."

They'd reached the front door. The waiting room was empty since Rafferty had been Seamus's last patient for the day. He unlocked the door and held it open.

"I wasn't accusing you of anything, Seamus."

"Maybe not, but it needed saying. We both know I definitely had an axe to grind. The thought had to cross your mind."

"Well, I won't lie about that, but I dismissed it out of hand. I'm thinking it was more likely a parting gift from Banan Delaney. Conlan would love to have that jerk alone for ten minutes behind a soundproof door. Then we'd know for sure."

"It sounds like something that bastard would do. But either way, thanks for the vote of confidence."

"Confidence had nothing to do with it. I figured when you made up your mind to come after me, you'd make sure I knew it was you taking me down and why. It's what I would do if the positions were reversed. This attack was more Banan's speed—sneaky and cowardly."

"I'm not sure whether to be flattered or insulted."

"Maybe a little of both." Rafferty laughed. He walked toward where Joss waited to drive him home, showing off his new skill with the cane.

Seamus watched until Rafferty made it all the way to the transport without mishap before closing the door and turning off the outside lights. As long as nothing new happened, the vampire was well on his way to being back to a hundred percent.

Right now, Seamus had something far more urgent to attend to, or actually someone. Megan. She was already waiting for him in his apartment. He sniffed the air in the hallway. Hmm. She wasn't the only hot thing in his kitchen. Whatever she was cooking smelled delicious.

And so did she. Would it be rude to risk letting dinner burn by coaxing her into his bed before they actually ate? Probably. Oh, well, he'd waited this long. He supposed he could hang on for a while yet, but waiting wasn't the only thing that was hard. He'd had that problem all day long every time his thoughts had strayed in her direction, which had been way too often for the good of his sanity.

Did she have any idea how good it felt to know she was waiting for him?

He stepped through the door and closed it behind him, shutting out the rest of the world. Barring blood and broken bones, nothing and no one better interrupt his plans for the evening.

"Hi. I'm in here."

He followed Megan's voice into the kitchen where she was stirring something on the stove.

"How's Rafferty?"

"About as happy as you can expect a big, tough vampire to be when he's hurting. I let him graduate to a cane, though, so that helped improve his mood some."

"Poor Joss! He can't be fun to live with right now."

"Yeah, well, she knew what he was like when she married him. He's among the most powerful of our kind, but almost dying from something as simple as a transport accident was a real shock to his system."

He paused, thinking about what Rafferty had told him. "Actually it wasn't an accident at all. Someone messed with the brakes and the accelerator."

Megan gasped in shock. "Who would do such a thing?"

"Rafferty figures someone with a grudge against him or Joss—like me, for instance."

She went from concerned to furious in a heartbeat. "He can't possibly believe that's true! You would never do such a cowardly thing."

"Actually, Rafferty agrees with you. Besides, the night it happened I was with you."

He eased up behind her and slid his hand around her waist, moving slowly so as not to startle her while she was so close to the burner on the stove. "As I recall, you kept me pretty busy, both before and after the clinic closed."

He lifted her hair to the side so he could kiss her neck, liking the way she shivered in response. Then he traced the shape of her ear with the tip of his tongue. "The after part was my favorite."

"Keep that up and I'll never finish cooking dinner."

He looked over her shoulder to see what was simmering in the pot. "That smells good. You smell better. Delicious, in fact."

She giggled as he resumed what he'd been doing. Finally, it dawned on him that he hadn't seen the baby. He looked out toward the living room.

"Where's Phoebe?"

Megan leaned back against him and looked up at him over her shoulder. "Seems Aunt Joss wanted to babysit for a few hours. I'm supposed to pick Phoebe up on my way home. You know, sometime around dawn."

Her pretty eyes grew heavy-lidded with promise. "We have almost six uninterrupted hours to linger over dinner…and dessert."

All of his blood rushed south—again. "Perfect. How soon can we eat?"

"In big a hurry, are you?"

He let his hands do a little wandering. "Dessert's my favorite part of the meal, and I've been thinking about it ever since I walked you home last night. I want to make sure we have plenty of time to do any of that lingering you mentioned."

"I thought you might feel that way. Hand me those bowls and I'll get dinner on the table."

"I can't wait."

Chapter 13

Megan refused to be hurried. Yes, they were headed toward Seamus's bed—or maybe his couch, because that was fun, too. But moments like this should be savored, not rushed. Even if it was becoming increasingly difficult to not grab Seamus and drag him to the floor.

But tasting his passion would come soon enough. She'd spent hours putting this meal together, pulling out all the stops. Not that she felt the need to impress Seamus with her culinary skills, but this meal, this night and this man mattered.

Finally, she brought out the dessert, a personal favorite, a light confection of whipped cream and fresh berries. Nothing too heavy, but luscious and bursting with flavor. Seamus's eyes widened at the sight.

"I wasn't kidding about loving dessert," he said as he

eyed the bowl she set down between them. "But why only one spoon?"

She scooped up a bite and held it up to his mouth. "I thought we could share."

If his eyes had been caressing her with hot looks before, the temperature simmering between them ramped up geometrically as he accepted the sweet offering. When she leaned in close and licked the small bit of whipped cream off the corner of his mouth, his fangs ran out to full length. That pleased her. He took the spoon and followed her in the dance, gently feeding her a plump berry smothered in cream.

And that pleased her even more.

"How can something so cool make me so hot?" His voice had dropped low, gravelly thick with the promise of what was to come.

And, please God, soon.

Seamus studied her face as he fed her another bite. The berries filled her mouth with a burst of bright flavor.

"This is wonderful, but I'm ready for our real dessert." He set the spoon aside, calmly picked up the rest of their berries and cream and set it in the refrigerator.

How could he think of such mundane details when she was about to melt into a puddle of need right there on the kitchen table? Then he held out his hand for hers, tugging her to feet. She'd thought he was going to kiss her, but instead he led her out of the kitchen, right past the living room and into his bedroom.

"You cannot imagine how much I've been thinking about this moment, Megan."

When he reached out to cup the side of her face, she turned to kiss his palm, tasting the slightly rough surface of his skin with the tip of her tongue. He groaned and brushed his thumb across her lips.

"I want to take this slow, to make it good for you, but I'm afraid my control is a bit shaky right now."

She loved having that much power over him, to know that her kiss and her touch were enough to bring him to his knees. Which she just had. Literally. He knelt in front of her, laying his face against her stomach as his hands swept up the backs of her legs from ankles straight past the hem of her dress and on up to cup her bottom.

Her bones melted. She slowly sank down, straddling his lap as she lowered her mouth to his. As she tongued his fangs, he freed up his hands to start stripping away the layers of clothing that separated them. Her sweater was the first to go, followed by her bra. He paused in his quest long enough to pay homage to her breasts with his lips and tongue and teeth.

Her turn. She unbuttoned his shirt, taking her time, drawing out the process to torment him, only to realize that she was torturing herself at the same time. Finally, he muscled them both back up off the floor in an impressive display of his vampire strength.

"I need your skin against mine. Please."

She'd never deny such a simple request. No other man had ever looked at her with such stark hunger. Stepping back, she quickly finished the job he'd started, letting him look his fill when she stood before him, wearing nothing more than the smile on her face.

"Your turn."

He immediately toed off his shoes, but she pushed his hands out of the way when he reached for the button on his jeans.

"Let me."

She eased the zipper down slowly, too slowly, given the impatient expression on her lover's face. But he didn't complain at all when she removed his boxers at the same time as she stripped the denim down the long length of his legs. In seconds, all was revealed for her viewing pleasure.

All those lean muscles and supple strength drew her like no other lover ever had. She closed the distance between them, taking her time, feeling his heat long before she actually felt the rough slide of his skin against hers. His hands eased her firmly against him, leaving no doubt about how much he wanted her.

"Kiss me, Megan."

He tasted of whipped cream and berries. His tongue enticed hers to join in swirling play as his arms wrapped around her, gentle bands of steel that lifted her up enough that his erection slid between her legs. He rocked against her core; the slight friction had her wanting so much more.

She raised her right leg, wrapping it around his and opening herself up to more of the same. He murmured his approval, but made no effort to take them to the next stage. As much as she loved his foreplay, it also frustrated her. Finally, she pulled away and gave him a hard shove, sending him sprawling back onto the bed.

His smile promised swift retribution. Perfect. It was just what she wanted.

He liked Megan's playful side and that she wasn't at all shy about what she wanted. What she hadn't taken into account was a male vampire's dominant nature. He was willing to let her have her way with him—up to a point. He wanted to make a few demands of his own, and that moment had arrived.

He remained motionless, waiting for his lady to join him on the bed. She crawled up on the bed, prowling closer, her fangs showing as she made her approach. When he pounced, she was too startled to do more than let out a short squeak before he'd flipped her onto her stomach. He stretched out on top of her, careful not to crush her, but letting her know that this was how it was going to be.

She immediately bent her head to the side, offering herself up to him. Oh, yes, this was going to be good. He nipped at the nape of her neck and rocked against the sweet curve of her backside.

He'd never had a woman all but purr before, but Megan thrummed with pleasure as he let her feel the length of both his cock and fangs. Her scent filled the air as she arched up against him.

With one hard thrust he took her, giving her slick heat only seconds to adjust to the sudden invasion before he started moving fast and hard. She chanted his name in counterpoint to the rhythm he established, making him hunger for far more than the spiraling tension between the give-and-take of their bodies.

Finally, when he couldn't wait another heartbeat, he sank his fangs into the rich flavor of her vein. As he drank deeply, she screamed in release, her body convulsing under his. He paused long enough to give her a small window of relief before once again driving her up and up. Suddenly, there was no sense of time or space, just the pounding of two hearts and two bodies, until in a moment of perfect accord, they shattered in a kaleidoscope of colors and sensations.

Seamus wasn't sure he'd actually survived the experience, but at the moment, he was okay with that.

"Wow." Megan reached back to touch his face. "That was amazing. Or maybe incredible. Or both."

He kept his face nestled in her hair, his arm around her waist as they lay spooned in the bed. "I'd say let's try that again, but it might be a while before I can. I'm pretty sure more than just my brain got fried."

When she giggled, he felt the vibration through his entire body. To his surprise, a certain part of his anatomy immediately stirred back to life. He cuddled closer to share the good news with Megan.

She instantly rolled over to face him, a huge smile on her face. "Hey, is that for me?"

"I do believe it is."

"Perfect."

And he did his best to make sure it was.

Seamus opened the driver's door for Megan, reluctant to watch her drive away after the hours they'd spent together.

"Can I ride as far as Rafferty's with you? I'll go on my nightly run from there."

Her eyes lit up. "Sure, but haven't you had enough exercise for one night?"

He climbed in the other side. "Well, I could be trying to impress you with my incredible stamina...or I can admit that I just wanted an excuse to stay with you for a few more minutes."

"Good answers—both of them."

As she steered the transport away from the curb, the headlights hit the trees across the field that backed up on the clinic. For a second there he thought he spotted someone just inside the treeline. "Can you slow down for a second, Megan?"

"Sure. Is something wrong?"

He studied the woods, but whatever he'd seen—or thought he'd seen—was gone now. "No, everything is fine. I thought I spotted someone cutting across country toward the infirmary. I didn't want to take off if someone needed me. We can go now."

As Megan hit the accelerator, he looked back one more time. Still nothing, but he had the strangest sensation that someone had been there, someone who hadn't wanted to be seen. But until he could verify his suspicions, he didn't want to worry Megan.

He'd take a slightly different route on his run and check out that stand of trees. If no one had been there, fine. Maybe his imagination was working overtime. But if someone really had been watching them from the safety of the deep shadows, the real questions were why and, more important, who?

He wasn't worried about himself, but damned if he'd put up with any more threats to Megan and her daughter.

Megan tapped him on the shoulder. "You're looking pretty fierce there."

He'd been so lost in thought that he hadn't noticed they'd already arrived at Rafferty's house. They both climbed out of the transport, and he looked at her over the roof. "Sorry. I was just thinking maybe that run home was going to be harder than I thought."

She walked around to his side. "I can always drop you back at your place on my way home."

He wrapped his arms around her, pulling her in close.

"No, that's okay. I need the exercise. Besides, I've got reasons to keep up my strength."

"Really? And what might those be?"

"Nights like this one." When he kissed her, the flames they'd carefully banked before leaving his apartment threatened to overwhelm them again. Breaking off that kiss and stepping away was one of the most difficult things he'd ever had to do.

"If I don't walk away now, we're going to put on quite a show for Rafferty and his neighbors. Hug Phoebe for me."

Megan's face was flushed, her lips swollen and so kissable. "I will. I'll see you at work tonight."

"And after?" He hadn't planned on pressing her, but he found he couldn't leave without knowing.

"And after. Now go. The sun will be up before too long."

"I'm on my way."

But he jogged backward until she reached Rafferty's front door safely. Then he took off at a full-out run toward the trees. The last time someone was sneaking around back there, it had been Banan. Since he was gone, most likely it was one of Rafferty's employees with a legitimate reason for being there. But all things considered, he'd sleep better knowing that for certain.

Banan wallowed in the human's blood: his fangs, his fingers and his face dripped with the stuff. He licked a few drops off his hands, savoring the rich flavor. It would be a hell of a mess to clean up, but at the moment he didn't give a damn. It was just a shame that he'd had to take his temper out on this human weakling instead of Seamus Fitzhugh or Megan Perez. Even Rafferty O'Day and that bitch wife of his would've provided more entertainment. Humans simply lacked the stamina for this kind of dance.

Eventually his enemies' time would come. Until then, he'd have to make do. At least the human he'd caught had been female, which meant she'd been good for more than her vein. If he hadn't seen Megan Perez walking out of that medic's place, he would have been satisfied with bedding the human and then draining her dry, offering her nothing but pleasure until the instant she realized he wasn't going to stop. That she'd suffered was not his fault. No, that blame belonged to Seamus Fitzhugh for daring to touch what belonged to Banan.

Even from the far side of the field, Megan's body language had been all too easy to read. She had bedded that damn vampire, no doubt about it. The truth was written in the way Seamus stood a little too close to her as well as in the easy touches.

If dawn wasn't so close, he'd wait for Megan to arrive back at her cottage and teach her a painful—and definitely fatal—lesson about betraying him. How sweet it would be to dump her bloody and abused body on Rafferty's front doorstep. Or better yet, the medic's. Let him explain how his lover had ended up dead, her throat ripped out by vampire fangs.

But right now, Banan would dump his substitute date in the creek and then wash up before getting dressed. The water would wash away all trace of his scent. How long would it be before someone found her? He wished he could risk being close enough to watch the security officer's investigation.

The cause of death would be painfully obvious: death by vampire. A chancellor could rip out a throat, but wouldn't have drained the blood. The only real question was which vampire would Conlan suspect first?

It was probably too much to hope that he'd blame Rafferty, although there was no love lost between the two. Conlan seemed to like Seamus a little too much for him to be the leading suspect. Eventually, though, as the attacks continued, Conlan would have to consider them both.

Once they were all spinning in circles and pointing fingers at each other, Banan would find a way to make all the evidence lead straight to one of the two. He was having too much fun envisioning the various possibilities to decide which it would be.

Playing God with lives was a lot of fun and good practice for when he took over the Delaney clan. Things were definitely looking up. He picked up the body and headed for the creek. Then it would be time to get back to the pickup point. He couldn't wait to crawl into his tent and dream of great times to come.

Seamus normally started off his nightly runs at an easy pace, only picking up speed when his muscles were warmed up and stretched out. However, acutely aware that Megan might be watching, he couldn't help but strut his stuff a bit. He might pay for it later, but after all, a vampire had his pride.

He turned off the road to cut across country, preferring the open spaces where he could more easily lose himself in the waning hours of the night. He loved the quiet peace of these last moments of darkness when daybreak hovered just out of sight over the horizon.

However, tonight he had little time to dawdle if he wanted to check out the trees for any proof that someone had been lurking there.

A few humans were already stirring in their homes, lights slowly coming on as they started their days. Because of the human affinity for sunlight, they were the ones who did most of the manual labor on an estate like Rafferty's, especially out in the fields. Seamus gave Rafferty credit for treating his workers a lot better than other high-ranking vampires did. He valued them as individuals, not just for their muscles and their blood.

Sure, there were drawbacks to living on the O'Day estate, its distance from any other center of civilization being chief among them. However, his progressive attitudes and an offer of a new start left O'Day with no shortage of applicants.

Seamus's role as the sole health-care provider had already brought him into contact with a fair number of the estate's residents from all three species. As usual, the humans outnumbered the other two combined. Most of Conlan's security people were chancellors, which only made sense. To police any given population, you needed staff who could be out in daylight and were strong enough to handle any problem vampires.

He circled back the way he'd come before heading into the trees. A steady wind had come up, making it doubtful he'd be able to pick up any scents. He slowed to a walk as he entered the copse, quieting his own breathing in order to hear better. Other than the rustling of the leaves, the woods were quiet.

He was alone as far as he could tell. Moving from tree to tree, he studied the ground although it was hard to pick out many details even with his superior night vision. A broken twig here, a crushed leaf there, but nothing that said definitively that someone had been there recently.

Even so, his own predatory nature insisted that someone had been there. What he didn't know was who or why, and he didn't like that, not one damned bit.

It was too late for him to do any more checking, but he could contact Conlan and ask him to take a look around while the sun was up. Maybe he'd pick up on something Seamus had missed. Having done all he could for the night, he walked across the field to the infirmary.

Thanks to the specialized training he'd had in medical school, normally he could function for extended periods of time when the sun was up. But after the night he'd had, he needed to seek out his bed. Once he had some hours of sleep under his belt, he'd contact Conlan before it was time for Megan to arrive. There was no use in worrying her unnecessarily. At least she'd already agreed to spend the hours after work with him. He'd keep her safe—and occupied—until dawn.

Yep, it was shaping up to be another busy day—and night.

Dreams for vampires were rare, especially ones as peaceful as this one was. Seamus smiled at the pastoral scene before him and started down the hillside toward the woman waiting for him at the bottom. Megan waved at him, a bright smile lighting up her pretty face.

Before he'd gone three steps, a rough hand clamped down on his shoulder from behind, preventing Seamus from being able to reach Megan. With a simple touch, his dream went from fine to furious. He struck out, ready to take no prisoners to keep the woman he loved safe. Wait? What had his dream-self said? The woman he loved? Was that right? At least here in his dreams, it was true. But what about when he was awake?

Then the jolt of landing a solid punch jerked him out of his dreamworld and dropped him right in the middle of a painful reality. He came up fighting.

"Seamus, damn it, quit swinging! It's me, Conlan. I'm getting damned tired of being used as a punching bag by you."

Conlan? What the hell was he doing in Seamus's dream? No, wait, he was awake now. So make that, what the hell was Conlan doing in his bedroom? Seamus forced his eyes open and glared at the chancellor, who'd wisely put the width of the room between them.

The clock on the dresser said it was still daylight outside, so for the second time the security officer was waking him up to deal with a crisis. It wouldn't be the last, but they definitely needed to lay down some ground rules before one of them got hurt. He sat up on the edge of the bed and waited for the cobwebs to clear or the chancellor to explain himself, whichever came first.

He glared at the security officer. "I understand that you need my services, but next time, call me. I usually don't punch a phone."

"Thanks for the heads-up. Maybe I'll just poke you with a long stick, but for now, get your ass out of bed. I need you. I'll wait for you out in the clinic." Conlan started out the door, but stopped briefly. "And, Seamus, don't make me wait long."

Seamus quickly pulled on yesterday's shirt and jeans.

What had the chancellor's tail in a twist? If it were a medical emergency, wouldn't he have said so? Instead, the chancellor had just looked grimmer than usual. Only one way to find out.

More curious than worried, he left his quarters and headed toward the light pouring out of the closest room. To his surprise, Conlan wasn't alone. Rafferty stood with his back to the door, looming over someone stretched out on the exam table. Seamus's nostrils flared wide as he stuttered to a stop just inside the doorway.

The odor of death easily overpowered the heavy medicinal smell that usually permeated the clinic. That explained why Conlan and Rafferty were both there as well as the high level of tension in the room.

He moved to the far side of the table and studied the still form outlined by the opaque plastic sheeting that shrouded the body. Feminine for certain, but that was the only thing to be learned at first glance.

"Who is she and what happened to her?"

Rafferty's furious eyes snapped up to meet his, the length of his fangs and the deep lines bracketing his mouth only underscoring the high emotions that thrummed in the room. "Why don't you tell me, Dr. Fitzhugh?"

Okay, so that's how it was going to be.

Before Seamus could pull back the plastic to reveal the body, Conlan blocked him. "Do you have any forensic experience?"

"Only what little they showed all of us in school. I'm a surgeon, not a forensic pathologist."

He tugged harder on the plastic. "However, I'm the closest to it you've got. I'm guessing since you're asking the question at all, this woman was a victim of a crime, not an accident."

Rafferty moved closer to the head of the table and pulled back the sheet himself. "Her name was Maggie Travis."

Seamus hissed when he saw what was left of her throat. "Who did this?"

Conlan ignored the question to ask one of his own. "Vampire or chancellor?"

"I'll need to take a closer look. I'll be right back."

He went next door to the operating suite and picked up a tray of sterile instruments and his surgical tele-scopic headgear that would allow him to scan the wounds and flash them up on the computer screen. Not that he had any doubts that a vampire had played long and hard with this poor female. Yes, a chancellor's fangs were capable of inflicting that same damage to her throat, but she'd been drained of blood.

However, he'd follow the protocols as he remembered them from school. Preserving the evidence had to take priority, to make sure that a case could be made against the guilty party once Conlan hunted the bastard down.

He slipped on the surgical goggles. After he adjusted the focus, he turned on his voice recorder. Leaning in close, he studied the wounds, starting with her head and working his way down her body. He noted each wound, each bruise, each violation. Then he repeated the journey, this time with a digital camera. He was dimly aware that both Rafferty and Conlan kept their eyes averted from the body, preferring to watch the computer monitor.

He didn't blame them, knowing it would allow them some small emotional distance from the horrific wounds. Whoever had done this had done more than play with his food, resulting in her accidental death. Although Seamus was no expert, it was obvious the vampire in question had deliberately set out to inflict pain, terror and death, but had at some point lost control. This woman had suffered greatly, and she would have embraced death as a blessed release from the horror of her last few hours of life.

Once he'd completed his examination, he quickly summarized his impressions, keeping his voice neutral, professional, his comments succinct. Then he clicked off the recorder, calmly set his surgical goggles aside and left the room. Out in the lobby, he calmly picked up the closest chair high over his head and heaved it against the wall with a resounding crash, putting all of his vampire strength and rage into the effort.

Breathing heavily, he studied the hole in the wall and the heap of broken wood and torn fabric on the ground. It wasn't enough, not nearly enough to vent the fury churning his gut. He started to reach for another chair, but destroying a room full of innocent furniture wouldn't do a damn thing to help that poor woman.

No, what he wanted, needed was to wrap his hands around the guilty party's neck and slowly, slowly choke the life out of the sadistic bastard. And that only after he'd ripped into his arteries to let his blood pulse out onto the ground.

"Remind me not to piss you off anytime soon." Conlan eased up beside him, but Seamus noticed he was careful not to touch him. The chancellor bent down to pick up the broken chair leg. "I didn't see that coming."

"Why? Because I did my job in there?" Seamus

growled, his voice thick with anger. "My impressions and descriptions may make the difference in a conviction. I don't want the son of a bitch that did that to get off because we didn't preserve the evidence correctly."

"Thanks. You might not have forensic training, but you did a hell of a job in there." He studied Seamus's expression. "Are you up for answering some questions now?"

"What kind of questions?"

"The same ones we'll be asking all of the vampires on the estate." Rafferty had joined the party. "He needs to know where you were this morning, right before dawn."

Okay, so they needed to do this. That didn't mean he had to like it. "I was with Megan right up until she dropped me off in front of your place. From there, I took my nightly run."

"Did you come straight back here?"

Not exactly, but how would it sound if he mentioned his suspicion that someone had been out in the woods? However, the truth was still the better route. Lies tended to come back and bite you on the ass.

"When Megan and I were leaving the clinic, I thought I saw someone standing at the edge of the woods across the field out back. I asked Megan to slow down in case it was someone who might be looking for me. But the next time I looked, there was no one there. I decided to swing through the woods on my way back home to check things out. Either way, I was going to call Conlan this morning to have a look around in the daylight."

Conlan was frowning. "Why didn't you call me when it happened?"

"Because it didn't seem like an emergency and I was tired." He still was. "As I was running, I noticed the lights were on in several of the human quarters I passed. I know some of the farm workers head out pretty early, so I figured it was probably a human on his way to work."

Time for a few questions of his own. "Were you able to narrow down the time of death for Ms. Travis?"

"Near as we can figure, it happened somewhere between three and six this morning. She works the late shift at the dining hall. Her boss said she left a little later than usual to help cover for someone who called in sick. Normally she walks home with a group, but obviously that didn't happen. The last time anyone saw her was when she left work a little after three.

There was real grief in Conlan's voice. "Her family knew she was working late and so didn't get suspicious until close to sunrise. That's when they called me, but some workers had already found the body in the creek before I could get here. At least they had the good sense to back off and wait for me to supervise retrieving the body. My men are out there now combing the area for evidence."

"She was found in the creek? Damn it, I should have guessed that she'd been submerged in water from the lack of blood in the wounds and no scent other than her own." Seamus walked back into the examination room with the other two trailing behind.

"What are you going to do now?"

"I'm going to swab all the wounds to see if we can find any trace evidence. If she wasn't in the water all that long, there's a chance the deeper wounds weren't washed completely clean."

Conlan joined him beside the body. "Those tests take time, and we need answers now. They're also expensive."

Seamus put on a fresh set of gloves. "So what's it to be, Rafferty?"

To give the vampire credit, he didn't hesitate. "Do it. I want my people to know that I'm more concerned about justice than I am the expense. Tell me what I can do to help."

"Use the computer in Megan's office to print out labels with the victim's name, the date and the case number, if there is one. Conlan and I will get the supplies together. Once we're done, we'll all three sign off on when and where the specimens were collected."

"Good thinking. The better job we do in collecting evidence, the better the chance we'll get the death penalty when this case goes to trial."

"So you think we'll catch him?" Seamus asked as he laid out swabs and transport media, along with a scalpel to take scrapings from under her nails.

"If Banan was still here, I'd be hauling his ass in for a long talk. However, I followed up to make sure he really did return to New Eire. He's still racking up charges at the hotel. Too bad."

Conlan ran his fingers through his hair in frustration. "This whole mess just feels like something he'd do, but since he's out of the picture, we'll have to look closer to home. We pretty much have a captive population, and I'll know if someone tries to leave. It will be a process of elimination after we finish tracking everyone's movements."

A shadow passed over Seamus's soul. What if the vampire in question had managed to hide his movements? Would that leave Seamus the only one with time unaccounted for? Logically, of course, the point could be made that he'd be unlikely to help collect evidence to convict himself. But if he'd refused, they would have already slapped him in chains or worse.

All he could do was hope the evidence pointed out who the real killer was.

Chapter 14

Megan answered the unexpected knock on the door to find her cousin standing there. Joss was clearly agitated, looking both upset and angry.

"Joss, come on in. What's wrong?"

"There's been a death on the estate." Her cousin headed straight for the kitchen.

"Who was it?"

Joss sat down and dropped her head down on her folded arms on top of the table.

"Catch your breath while I put the kettle on to boil."

Considering Joss's background in investigative work, whatever had happened had to have been bad to leave her so upset. Either that, or it was someone who'd been close to her.

A few minutes later, Megan poured each of them a

steaming mug of her favorite herbal tea. "Do you want sugar or honey?"

Joss finally lifted her head. "A big dose of honey sounds perfect."

Megan sat down next to Joss with Phoebe in her lap. She'd give Joss all the time she needed to gather her thoughts.

Finally, Joss drew a shaky breath and started talking. "Conlan is investigating a murder that happened near here on the estate. Our first."

Joss's expression was bleak. "One of our human workers, a young female, was brutally tortured and killed this morning right before dawn. Whoever did it brutalized her and then dumped the body in the creek on the far side of the woods that backs up on the field behind the infirmary."

Megan had a bad feeling about where this was going. "Do they know who did it?"

"A vampire, although that's as much as Seamus and Conlan could tell. The creek washed away most of the blood and the scent of her attacker." Joss cradled her mug in both hands, no doubt finding the warmth soothing.

"We have to be careful about assigning blame until all the evidence is in. But frankly, there aren't that many pureblooded vampires living on the estate."

"And it couldn't have been a chancellor?" Not that there were all that many of them, either.

Joss shook her head. "Not likely. Rafferty said the physical damage could have been done by a chancellor, but the body was drained of blood. That makes it far more probable that a vampire is responsible."

"That poor girl! Can we do anything to help the family?"

"We'll know more when Rafferty sees them after the sun goes down. He was out with Conlan in the early morning, but I made him go home and get some rest."

She took a long sip of her tea before continuing. "After they talk to her folks, he wants to accompany Conlan as he interviews the rest of the resident vampires about where they were this morning."

After setting the cup back down, Joss held out her hands toward Phoebe, who immediately dove straight for her. "Seamus helped with the initial examination of the body. I know Conlan and Rafferty were impressed by how well he did, especially since forensics isn't his specialty."

"At least Seamus is in the clear."

When Joss didn't immediately concur, Megan frowned. "He is, isn't he? In the clear?"

"No one is yet, even though they don't want to suspect him."

Okay, that wasn't a clear-cut yes or no. "He was with me last night, Joss, right up until I arrived at your place to pick up Phoebe."

"But was he with you *all* night? Every minute?"

This was getting way too personal. But she wouldn't let them accuse Seamus of something he didn't do in order to save herself a little embarrassment.

"We were together from the time clinic closed until we got dressed again so I could pick up Phoebe. Is that blunt enough for you?" She knew she sounded defensive, but it shouldn't be anyone's business how she and Seamus had spent their time together.

Joss stared down at Phoebe, letting the baby play with her fingers. "I'll pass that along to Conlan, but that still doesn't account for the time after he left you at our place. The closest they can pin down the time of her death is shortly before dawn."

"Seamus isn't a killer, Joss. He'd never even consider doing something so awful, much less carry it out."

She hated—*hated*—the sympathetic look Joss gave her, as if her cousin knew something that Megan didn't, something that would change how she thought about Seamus.

"What is it, Joss?" Not that she'd believe it for one instant.

"It's not for me to say. But the next time you see Seamus, ask him why of all the places in the Coalition he could have looked for work, he chose this one." Joss finished her tea.

"Why can't you tell me?"

"It's not my story to tell. Ask him." She kissed Phoebe's chubby cheek. "Look, I've got to go. Rafferty may need my help with any arrangements that have to be made."

Megan let Joss out. As her cousin drove away, she had to wonder what Joss's real purpose in stopping by had been. Maybe she had needed a break or someone to talk to. But if so, why plant the seeds of distrust between Megan and Seamus? What had happened in his past that would lead them to even suspect him in the first place?

Now that she thought about it, though, he'd been pretty closemouthed about his past. All she knew was that he'd had some problem getting his final credentials from medical school, but not really why. Rafferty had intervened to make sure Seamus had a choice of where and how he lived. All of that made sense, but obviously there was far more to the story than she'd been told.

There was only one way to find out. She'd go into work early and see if she could get answers to her questions. If he was too busy, then afterward they'd talk.

Seamus was at his desk when she arrived. Rather than disturb him, she quietly slipped into her own office and settled Phoebe into her crib before booting up the computer. Although she'd rehearsed her opening lines over and over, she still wasn't ready to face Seamus. No matter how she phrased her questions, it came out sounding like an accusation.

But if their relationship was going to last, truth and honesty had to play a major role. After her experience with Banan, she had zero tolerance for lies or secrecy. Finally, she forced herself to confront him.

She froze in his doorway, neither in nor out, waiting for him to notice her. Finally, he looked up, a smile spreading across his face.

"You're early, not that I'm complaining."

He immediately came around the desk to kiss her. Twenty-four hours ago, she would have welcomed the embrace, but she turned her face at the last second so that his kiss landed on her cheek and kept her arms down at her sides. Always perceptive, he frowned.

"Megan? What's wrong?" He studied her expression, his eyebrows drawn down low. "Have I done something to upset you?"

"No, but I heard about what happened this morning, and it's freaked me out a bit. Are you all right?"

He seemed to accept her explanation and stepped

back to give her some space. "It certainly wasn't fun examining the body, but it was necessary. I'm furious that someone would do such a thing and worried because there's a killer loose on the estate."

"Joss said a vampire was responsible."

"Yes, that was our conclusion, although I'm sure Conlan would prefer that I not discuss the case in any detail."

Seamus poured himself a cup of coffee, looking even more grim. "However, since Joss has already told you that much, I don't suppose it will hurt. We just don't want to release many details while Conlan investigates and builds a case."

"And it definitely wasn't a chancellor?"

"Not with the way the body was drained. It's doubtful a chancellor could've been quite so thorough."

"Are there any new vampires on the estate?"

Seamus shook his head. "No, not since Conlan escorted Banan off the property. That's what has Rafferty so upset. The few who do live here are all long-term friends of his."

Except Seamus. Before she could point that out, he did.

"With the exception of me, I guess. Rafferty and I have a past, and not one based on either trust or friendship."

"If that's how you feel about him, why did you pick his estate when you needed a job? Especially if you don't trust each other."

For the first time, there was a definite flash of temper in Seamus's eyes. "We've been working on changing that. But out of curiosity, what kind of tales has Joss been telling you about me, Megan?"

Okay, so now she felt guilty for talking about Seamus

behind his back. But didn't she have a right to know exactly what kind of man she was sleeping with?

"She didn't tell me anything other than suggest I ask you why you ended up here and not some other place, especially considering how you felt about her husband."

The office was closing in on her as she waited for him to respond. She backed out of the room without waiting to see if Seamus would follow or bother to answer. If he had nothing to hide, it shouldn't matter. But since silence rather than an explanation hung in the air between them, it was obviously a big deal.

She had to get away. "Never mind. It's almost time to open the clinic. Forget I even asked."

After retreating into her office, she slammed the door shut, startling her daughter out of a sound sleep. As Megan comforted her baby, she realized Phoebe wasn't the only one in the room with tears running down her face.

A few seconds later, Seamus walked in without even bothering to knock. His expression was etched in harsh lines. She deliberately turned her back on him, showing how little she feared his temper, as she put Phoebe back to bed.

"Is there something you wanted?" There was no way he'd miss the tear streaks on her face, but she didn't care.

"Hell, yeah. I wanted you to trust me." His words were clipped and cold.

She forced herself to move a couple of steps closer to him to show she wasn't intimidated by his cold show of temper. "What makes you think I don't?"

"If you did, you wouldn't have let a few veiled comments by a cousin you don't know any better than you do me put this wall between us."

He moved in her direction, leaving her no choice but to either stand her ground or retreat. Well, that wasn't going to happen. She'd run from Banan. She wasn't going to run again.

"At least I trusted you enough to come ask questions instead of assuming the worst. Right now, you're the one making assumptions about me." She clenched her fists, her hands aching to shake him senseless.

Two more steps in his direction put him within touching distance. "So what do you have to say for yourself?"

"You want the truth? Fine. I came here to destroy everything and everyone that Rafferty O'Day cherishes, including your lovely cousin, Joss. I wasn't going to rest until they were both dead and buried."

The shock of his blunt confession hit her like a bucket of ice water. Before she could string together a coherent response, he used his vampire reflexes to capture her. She slammed up against the stone strength of his chest as his mouth engaged hers in a battle for dominance. She wasn't going to surrender without putting up a good fight.

Oh, God, he tasted so good, all temper and heat. When her fangs nicked his lip, she lapped up the small droplet of blood, its flavor rich and powerful. He groaned when she sucked at the small wound.

He lifted her up and set her down on the edge of her desk. Was he going to take her right there amongst the files and office supplies? She hoped so, because as long as he was driving her out of her mind with his touches and kisses, she didn't have to think about what he'd told her.

"Tell me you want this." He rocked against her, showing her without words exactly what he had in mind.

How could she say no when his slightest touch set her aflame?

"Yes, I want this." Right there. Right then.

"Good because I have every intention of finishing this the minute our last patient walks out the front door. Be ready."

Then he was gone, leaving her aching with need and with more questions than answers. Even when her common sense warned her to proceed with caution, her body betrayed her. She waited for her heart to quit racing and her hands to unclench before standing up. After straightening her clothes, she checked on Phoebe one last time before heading out to the waiting room to greet their first patients.

She hoped it was busy, because otherwise this was going to be a very long evening.

Banan was in a very good mood. Both well fed and well rested, he had a busy night ahead of him. Of course, he couldn't really carry out any of his plans until after midnight when the clinic closed. It wouldn't do to commit murder when the vampire he wanted to cast blame on had lots of witnesses that he was elsewhere at the time.

The only question was how soon after the clinic closed would Megan be heading back to her own home. If she spent the night rolling around in the sheets with that second-class vampire Fitzhugh, it would definitely complicate things. Yet another crime she would pay for when it was her turn to be his playmate for a night.

For now, he'd wait until Riley returned from running up some more charges from Banan's hotel room. If Rafferty's security officer started nosing around, it would appear that Banan was nowhere near the O'Day estate. The ruse wouldn't hold up to close scrutiny, but it should buy him enough time to accomplish his mission.

Once Riley got back, they'd go have themselves a little fun. Both of them had a taste for dark pleasures, but they had to be careful to make it look as if only one vampire was on a rampage. If Conlan detected more than one pair of fangs were involved, he'd have evidence that outsiders were responsible. Then he'd come hunting with sharp stakes and ready to kill.

Even against two vampires the highly trained chancellor would be a formidable enemy, especially since he wouldn't be limited to the daylight hours. If Rafferty joined him, well, it would definitely get ugly.

The only question left to answer about the night's planned entertainment was if the next victim would be male or female, human or chancellor. There were definite drawbacks to each species. The human, although easier to catch and subdue, would be more fragile. A chancellor would put up more of a fight, but once he and Riley had their victim under control, the fun would last longer.

Decisions, decisions. Rather than get his heart set on one or the other, maybe he'd let fate surprise him.

Seamus had spent most of the evening avoiding any contact with Megan while he tried to sort out the confused mess of emotions her simple question had caused. Damn it, one short conversation with Joss had been enough to sow seeds of doubt in her mind about the kind of man she believed him to be. That seriously ticked him off.

Granted, she had trust issues, but he'd thought they'd gotten beyond that.

On the other hand, if he was completely honest with himself, he hadn't told her the full truth about his past for just that reason. He'd told her he had secrets, let her think that he was perhaps embarrassed by them, but not that he'd actually planned to destroy her cousin and Rafferty.

Oh, yeah, this was going to be a pleasant conversation. He walked out into the waiting room, almost hoping that it had filled up again while he was restocking the exam rooms. No such luck. As it stood, the clinic would close precisely on time.

Allowing ten minutes to explain his past to Megan, he could probably be in bed—*alone*—by one, one-thirty at the latest. Even if he could use the sleep, it sure wasn't how he'd been hoping to spend those hours. But despite his assertion that they'd finish what they'd started in her office, he wouldn't push her into something she didn't want. But, damn, that woman burned bright when she was in his arms. Surely that meant something. If only he knew what.

Megan came out of her office carrying a stack of files. "These are the last ones for the night. Once you've signed off on them, I'll update their patient records."

He took the files from her, wishing he dared to do more than brush his fingers against hers in the transfer. "It shouldn't take me long."

"I'll be working on the pharmacy and supply inventories so we can place an order. We're getting low on a few things."

"Thanks, I appreciate it. Rafferty said once we've had enough time to work out an average rate of usage, we can set up standing orders. That should simplify things."

"Yes, it should." She did an about-face to head back to her office. "Holler if you need me for anything."

Now that was tempting, but he suspected she meant the offer to be work-related. The brief snippet of conversation was such a far cry from the easy rapport they'd shared before. Damn Joss, anyway. He fought back the temptation to rip the files to shreds or maybe destroy another chair. Rafferty hadn't complained about having to replace the one from that morning, but he wouldn't appreciate Seamus making a habit of destroying furniture whenever things didn't go his way.

So for now, he'd go finish up his paperwork, lock the door, turn off the lights and try to convince the woman in the next office that he was still one of the good guys.

Megan was waiting for him out in the living room, but not with the same warm welcome she'd had for him last night. What a difference a single day could make. He guzzled a blood pack to replenish the energy he'd burned thanks to the increased stress the past twenty-four hours had brought. He'd need every advantage he could get.

Finally, he could delay no longer. Time to face those doubts and questions in Megan's mind. He wanted to blame Joss for all of this, and she'd certainly played a part. So had Rafferty. But Seamus thought he'd come to terms with their betrayal of his sister, as well as the poor decisions she'd made herself.

Megan looked up when he walked in and sat down. Although he didn't exactly cuddle up close, he refused to put the length of the couch between them. If she didn't like it, she could be the one to move. When she didn't immediately object, some of his tension drained away.

"Okay, I'm going to start at the beginning and tell you how and why I ended up here on Rafferty's estate. When I'm done talking, you can ask me any questions you might have or you can talk to Rafferty and Joss if you'd rather. But hear me out before you interrupt."

"I'm listening."

So he stared down at the floor, as if all the answers he needed were there. Starting at the beginning, he explained that Rafferty's humiliation of Seamus's half sister had resulted in Petra's attempt to destroy Rafferty by setting the vampire up to be convicted of murder. Only Joss's intervention and finding out the truth had prevented him from being executed.

When he drifted to a halt, Megan reached over to entwine her fingers with his, telling him with her touch that she was still there for him. He took a shuddering breath and started talking again, almost choking over the words.

"Petra was tried, convicted and executed. When her assets were confiscated, I lost my only source of income and the medical school canceled my scholarship. Fairness doesn't mean much in vampire politics."

And then he told her the hardest part of all. "I meant what I said earlier. I came here planning on doing a lot more than confronting Rafferty and Joss. I wasn't going to be satisfied with anything less than their total destruction. I was so angry, I wanted them both bleeding and everything they cared about destroyed."

"So what changed?"

He clung to the note of conviction in her voice that made it clear that she knew his intentions toward her cousin and her husband were no longer violent in nature. Slowly, he turned to face her.

"You, mostly. When I came here, I thought I'd lost all chance of ever practicing medicine again. Fighting to save you from the poison reminded me of how it felt to be a doctor, to hold someone's life in my hands. I realized that even as a medic, I could make a real difference.

"And as much as I hated to admit it, I saw that Rafferty was already making changes that are long overdue in our world. It's criminal that anyone would expect you to give up Phoebe just because she's pure-bred vampire and you're not. No matter how mad I was over what happened to Petra, I'd be a pretty selfish bastard to destroy the one place where you and your daughter could be safe."

Megan immediately let go of his hand and shifted to straddle his lap. She framed his face with her palms. "Now that we've settled that, it seems to me you made a promise to finish our earlier conversation."

"I'm up for it if you are." He flexed his hips to demonstrate that he meant that literally.

Her warm breath tickled his ear. "Want to start out here and end up in your bed?"

"Either is fine with me." He punctuated each word with a kiss. "As long as we get started right now."

What the hell was that noise? Seamus blinked sleepily at the clock as he waited to see if he heard it again. There. Someone was knocking on the clinic door. More than three hours had passed since he'd locked up for the night, meaning it was another emergency.

He eased away from Megan, seeing no reason for her to lose sleep, too. His clothes were scattered on the floor out in the living room. So were hers, for that matter, he thought with a pleased smile. They'd finished up their conversation on the couch and then started a whole new one in his bed. The evening had definitely ended on a high note.

But back to the matter at hand. He was still buttoning his shirt when he turned on the outside light and opened the door. A vampire he didn't recognize was waiting for him. The man was breathing hard, as if he'd run a long distance. He was also dripping wet from the rain that had started sometime during the night.

"Can I help you?"

"Are you the medic?" the vampire wheezed.

"I'm Dr. Fitzhugh, yes. Is there an emergency?" He looked past the vampire to see if he was alone.

"You'll need to come with me. I was working out near the fence when I found an injured female. I was afraid to move her by myself, so I ran all the way here to fetch you. Between the two of us, we can get her back here easily enough."

So why hadn't he called ahead? It didn't make sense, but then not everyone reacted logically when confronted with injuries. Maybe he'd better offer some first-aid classes when he had time to prevent this type of thing from happening.

"I'll get my bag. Once you show me where she is, we'll call for help if she's too badly injured to carry."

The two of them ran at full speed for what had to be at least three miles before the electric fence came into sight. The vampire at his side slowed to a stop.

"If you keep going straight to the fence and turn right, you'll find her. She's under a pair of trees. I'll go back for help."

Then he took off, leaving Seamus staring as he disappeared into the darkness back the way they'd come. Something wasn't right. He'd said the two of them could get the woman back to the clinic. If that was the case, then why was he leaving?

With a growing sense of foreboding, Seamus continued on toward the fence before turning right. Spotting the trees a short distance ahead did little to ease the knot of tension in his chest. Thoughts of the murdered human female filled his mind. Was he walking into a trap? His instincts were screaming that he was, but he had no choice but to continue on.

A few minutes later, he found her—a human female. The rain did little to hide the scent of fresh blood, triggering his fangs to drop down. He slowed his approach, his night vision still able to pick out all too many details from a short distance away. Death was close if not already stealing the last beat of her heart, the last breath from her lungs.

But he had to try to save her. He knelt in the wet grass, ignoring whether it was blood or rain that was soaking through to his skin. He began cataloging her injuries at the same time he opened his medical bag. When he tried to put pressure on her neck, blood sprayed right in his face. When her eyes fluttered open and saw him hovering over her, fangs out, she panicked and tried to move away, her efforts weak and unfocused.

"I'm Dr. Fitzhugh. I need to treat your injuries."

That only made her more frantic. If she weren't already so weak, perhaps he could have sedated her. However, in her condition, it might only hasten her death. Damn it, why hadn't he called for help before leaving the clinic? Maybe they could have gotten her evacuated to the trauma hospital in time.

But judging by the rattling deep in her throat, that was wishful thinking. One breath, another, and then a quiet exhale that ended her life for good. He rocked back on his heels and cursed. If he couldn't save her, at least he could do as much as he could to bring her killer to justice.

Thanks to the rain, he couldn't readily identify the vampire either by scent or sight. The male had been wearing a heavy sweatshirt with the hood cinched down close to his face. Seamus had assumed he'd worn it that way because of the weather, but now he knew it was to prevent him from being able to describe him.

One didn't make it through medical school without developing some immunity to the sight of horrific injuries. But the degree to which this poor woman had suffered at the hands of her attacker made him sick. Shallow cuts meant to inflict pain, but not death, were scattered over her torso as well as her legs and upper arms. There was no mistaking the similarities between this victim and the one that Conlan had brought to the clinic.

It was definitely time to call for help. But before he could dial the phone, he was hit with a blaze of light that blinded him for several seconds. He'd been concentrating so hard on the woman that he'd missed hearing the approach of a pair of transports. He shaded his eyes against the glare, trying to make out the shadowy forms who were now walking toward him.

Was that a gun?

Rather than wait around to ask, he jumped to his feet

and prepared to run like hell. Vampires could survive almost anything other than a head shot, but he wasn't going to wait around to test that theory. He'd head straight for Rafferty's house.

He'd gone no more than a handful of steps when he was tackled from behind. The ground rushed up to meet him, knocking the air out of his lungs. Survival instincts kicked in as he fought to break free. He succeeded in throwing the guy off once, but before he could make it back to his feet a second man joined the party. Together they quickly overpowered him.

His arms were yanked behind him and handcuffs were snapped around his wrists with little care other than to make sure they were painfully tight. So far, his attackers hadn't muttered a single word. The brief scuffle had them all breathing hard.

Seamus muscled his face up out of the mud long enough to identify himself. "Let go of me. I'm Dr. Fitzhugh!"

His captor rolled him over. To his shock it was Rafferty. The older vampire got right down in his face. "I know who you are and what you are, you murdering bastard. When I get done with you, you'll be nothing but dead."

"Are you crazy? I was called out here to treat an injured woman. I didn't kill her."

"She's dead, isn't she? And that's her blood your face is covered with." Rafferty lifted him up to his feet with one hand. Under other circumstances, Seamus might have been impressed.

"Yes, but she wasn't when I got here." Realizing how that sounded, he tried to explain. "I found her lying where you found her. She died right after I got here."

"Sounds like a confession to me. Don't you agree, Conlan?"

"Yeah, boss, it does."

"And you two are idiots if you think I could do something like that."

Rafferty's smile was a horror to behold. "Idiots, are we? You know, I don't much like being insulted."

Then his fist connected with the side of Seamus's head, and the lights went out.

Chapter 15

Consciousness returned slowly, with a jackhammer headache pounding in back of his eyes. Seamus moaned and tried to roll over. Even that much movement made him queasy, confirming Rafferty had most likely given him a concussion when he punched him.

That explained the pain, answering only one of the questions flashing through his head. Where was he? What was going on? He briefly considered those two and came up with nothing other than he was obviously on a bed in a room that was absolutely dark. Even with his superior night vision, he needed at least some ambient light to see. All of which left him in the dark—literally.

He pondered one last question, the only one that really mattered to him: would Rafferty let him live long enough to see if Megan would believe in his innocence?

If he was going to die, he didn't want the woman he loved thinking the worst of him.

A wave of bitterness washed over him, knowing that he'd never said the actual words to her. After the night they'd shared, he'd planned on telling her how he felt over breakfast. He wanted her to know that he meant it even in the cold light of day, not just after a bout of hot sex. Depending on her response, he might have even asked if she'd consider moving in with him. The apartment was pretty small for three people, but until Rafferty hired another person to help cover emergencies, Seamus couldn't move.

What a fool for thinking that for once his plans would play out the way he wanted them to! He flexed his fingers, wishing he could have five minutes alone with that rat bastard vampire for playing him like a fool. He'd choke the truth out of him, and then drain him dry, leaving him alive long enough to stand trial for what he'd done to those two poor women.

It was time to do more than lie in the darkness and brood. He reached out with both hands, feeling for the edge of the bed. His right hand hit a wall, but his left found nothing but air beyond the mattress. Okay, now to see if he could sit up without getting sick. The last thing he wanted to do was to throw up in the darkness.

He made it to semivertical, sitting on the side of the bed as he waited for the pain to ebb to a manageable level again. Before he could stand up, though, he heard someone approaching. Cocking his head to the side, he focused all of his attention into listening.

Sure enough, the muffled sound of footsteps slowed to a halt a few feet away on the other side of the wall.

He stayed where he was, waiting to see what happened next. A rattle of keys and a quiet click preceded a door opening directly across from him. He blinked against the light pouring in from the hallway.

"Conlan."

"Right on the first guess. I'm going to turn on the lights, so you might want to shade your eyes."

Even with the warning, the sudden onslaught of high-voltage light sent fresh shards of pain ripping through Seamus's head. He closed his eyes and held his head in his hands while he waited for the moment to pass.

Conlan made a disgusted grunt. "Damn it, I told Rafferty he hit you too hard. When you're able to eat, here's a trio of blood packs and a tray that Megan insisted on bringing by for you."

At the mention of her name, Seamus forced himself to look up at Conlan. "How is she?"

Before answering, Conlan put the tray down on the seat of a straight-backed chair and then dragged it across the room to where Seamus sat. "She's shaken up. It's not every day a woman realizes she's been sleeping with a murderer."

There was nothing Seamus could say to that, at least until he consumed enough blood to kick-start the healing process. Maybe once his head cleared, he could find a way out of this mess. He quickly knocked off the first two packs and then started on the food Megan had prepared for him.

For the first time since Rafferty's fist had connected to his head, things were looking up. If Megan was worried about what he ate, maybe all wasn't lost. Once he'd finished eating, he reached for the last of the blood.

"Thanks."

Conlan stood across the room, leaning against the wall, his eyes on the frigid side of cold. Seamus wasn't fooled by the chancellor's calm demeanor. It wouldn't take much more than Seamus breathing wrong to release Conlan's pent-up rage.

He popped the top of his blood pack. "For the record, I didn't kill either of those women."

"Save the 'I'm innocent' crap for someone who's more gullible than I am, Seamus." Conlan pushed himself off the wall and glared across at him.

"You had opportunity and motive. I may not be part of the Coalition's justice system any longer, but I'd bet those two things are still enough to get you convicted and maybe even executed. That is, if Rafferty had any plans to turn you over to the Coalition in the first place."

Seamus shrugged and consumed the blood. Already his head was feeling better, his thinking clearer. "Did you find any sign of the other vampire? The one who suckered me into taking the fall for this?"

Conlan sneered, his fangs on full display. "There is no other vampire. And before you ask, we checked on all the other resident vampires on the estate. They were all accounted for, including witnesses. The only one out wandering around by himself was you."

Conlan picked up a notebook off a table near the door that he'd obviously left there earlier. "I promised Rafferty I'd take your statement. Personally, I think it's a waste of my time."

It was obvious that both Conlan and Rafferty already had him tried and convicted, but Seamus had to try to make them listen.

"I'm reasonably intelligent, Conlan. Why would I kill two innocent women and set it up so that the most likely suspect is me?" He fought for control. "I was with Megan right up until a vampire I didn't recognize came banging on the clinic door. He told me he'd been working out near the fence and spotted an injured woman. He was afraid of moving her by himself, so he came and got me. We were going to either bring her in together or call for help if I thought she was too badly injured to be carried."

Conlan looked up from his notes. "And where did this mystical vampire disappear to? When we arrived at the site, you were the only one there."

"He turned back to get more help before we actually reached the woman. At the time I thought it was odd that he changed the plans with no warning, but I had no choice but to go on. I was going to call Rafferty as soon as I determined the nature of the victim's injuries."

Seamus frowned. "But how did you know to come at all? To get there as fast as you did, you had to have been on your way before I even found the victim."

"I was meeting with Rafferty when he got a call from someone saying they heard screams out near the fence."

"Did he say who called?"

"No, whoever it was hung up before he got a name." Conlan looked up from his notes. "Rafferty is trying to trace back to find out, but the number wasn't local. That doesn't mean much, because we don't keep track of cell phones and the like."

Maybe the call was a dead end, but at least Rafferty was looking into it. "The woman was still alive when I found her. When I tried to apply pressure to her neck wound, she roused long enough to try to fight me off, which is how I got coated with her blood. Before I could calm her down, she died."

He couldn't sit still any longer, not with that poor woman's eyes, terror-filled and dead, clogging up his thoughts. Conlan must be confident in his ability to stop Seamus from escaping since he made no effort to block the doorway.

"Go on with your story."

"I was just going to call for you and Rafferty when I saw the lights from your transports. I was prepared to run if it turned out to be the killers coming back."

"Killers? Why plural? You only mentioned seeing one vampire."

Seamus paced the length of the room and back several times before he answered. As he walked, he reviewed his mental list of the woman's many injuries. Finally, it hit him.

"She has bruises on her upper shoulders."

"So? Near as I could tell, she had bruises every-where." But there was a definite glint of interest in Conlan's eyes that wasn't there before.

"I'd have to take a closer look to make sure, but I remember seeing a series of small bruises along the top of her shoulders, like someone was holding her down. And before you ask, the angle was all wrong for it to be the same person who was busy…doing other things."

There was no need to itemize how many ways the woman had been brutalized. Conlan had seen all of it for himself.

The chancellor kept writing for several more paragraphs before he finally set the pen aside. Finally, he stood up. "I'm going to give Rafferty a call."

"Should I borrow that pad to write out my will?" Seamus tried to inject a note of levity in his voice, but suspected he failed miserably.

"Not quite yet. Get some rest. This might take a while." Then he walked out and locked the door behind him.

When had her cottage shrunk to this size? When Megan first moved in, her new home had seemed spacious and yet cozy. Now it was stifling and oppressive. Of course, she was pretty sure the way the four walls were crushing in on her had more to do with her state of mind than any real flaw in the design.

Poor Phoebe had clearly picked up on Megan's foul mood, and it was making her fussy. She wouldn't sleep, and she wouldn't eat. Instead, she demanded to be held constantly. But when Megan tried to cuddle her, her little face turned bright red, her body stiffened and then the crying started.

Megan tried rubbing her daughter's back. "Darn Seamus, anyway. I know he'd calm you right down with those smooth moves of his. Instead, here we both sit, crying and frustrated."

Neither Rafferty nor Joss would tell her where they were holding Seamus. She still couldn't believe that they'd think he was capable of killing not just one, but two women for no reason.

Admittedly, she wasn't the most experienced woman when it came to the males of any species. But despite that fact, she wanted to believe that she knew Seamus

Fitzhugh better than either Rafferty or Conlan did. Maybe her ego didn't want to think she had trusted her heart to a man who would make such sweet love to her and then go right out and kill.

It didn't make sense. She didn't believe it. And she was tired of being kept away from the man she loved. Sure, she'd badly misjudged the kind of man Banan really was. However, looking back, she realized that she'd loved the idea of Banan, not the person he really was. She'd somehow ignored the warning signs that he was all wrong for her.

When it came to Seamus, though, despite his secrets, her instincts insisted that he was a good man, one who could be trusted with her heart. At least Phoebe had finally settled down, although judging by her quivering lip, it wouldn't take much to set her off again.

A new determination settled over Megan. "Phoebe, I'm not going to settle for secondhand information. I want to hear what happened directly from him. He owes me that much."

It was almost dark outside, so Rafferty should be up and about. She'd start with him and Joss. If they wouldn't give her what she wanted, she'd track down Conlan. Surely he'd let her talk to his prisoner. If not, she'd fix Seamus another meal and then sit back and watch for Conlan to deliver it. Yeah, that would work.

"Okay, little one, we're going to find him. And heaven help anyone who gets in my way."

As she spoke, Phoebe relaxed in her arms and contentedly blew some impressive spit bubbles, a clear sign her daughter approved of her plan.

Okay, then. First she'd pack up a meal to go and add extra for Conlan as a bribe. After that, she and Phoebe would start their quest.

"Riley, you did a fine job. I haven't had quite this much fun in a damn long time. Did you see Rafferty clock his pet medic?" He smiled at the memory. "I bet Fitzhugh's head is still ringing like a bell."

Banan's cousin sat cross-legged on the ground. "Yeah, it was almost too easy to be fun. Those noble types make me sick."

"When Rafferty gets done with him, he won't be feeling anything but pain." Banan laughed as he scraped the dried blood out from under his nails with his knife. "Or more likely, he won't be feeling anything at all. He'll be dead."

Riley opened a pack of blood and poured it into his glass before topping it off with some whiskey. "Of course, once we snatch your woman, they'll know it wasn't Fitzhugh since they've got him under lock and key."

"True, but as much fun as we've had, I'm ready to be done with it. Once the sun goes down completely, we'll check out Megan's place. As soon as it's safe, we'll grab my daughter and call in our ride for the last time."

Riley belched and scratched his head. "Megan's not going to give up her baby without a fight."

Banan's smile showed off his fangs. "I'm counting on it. And when I'm finished with her, you're welcome to what's left."

Considering how helpful Riley had been, he supposed he should offer to let him have the first chance to enjoy Megan's considerable charms. But that wasn't going to happen. First of all, while Riley didn't seem to mind leftovers, Banan was more fastidious about his fun. But more important, he couldn't afford to leave any witnesses behind.

His cousin had become expendable. He'd leave Riley behind, staging his death as if Megan had managed to take him out before dying herself. Then Banan would torch her house with the accelerant Riley had brought along, which was guaranteed to leave nothing but ashes behind. With luck, once the fire was out, Rafferty and his chancellor buddy wouldn't be able to tell whether or not Phoebe had died along with her mother.

By the time they got some forensic expert to tell them any differently, his daughter would be safely stashed away in the Delaney compound where she belonged. His parents and grandparents would be satisfied he'd done his duty by the family and give him free access to the Delaney fortune.

It was time to set the last details in motion. "I'm going to go down to the creek and wash up. Contact your buddy so he'll be ready to swoop in and pick us up. I want to make sure he's in place before we make our move."

"He'll be here. I promised him extra to make sure he'd stay close by."

"That was real smart of you, Riley. You've thought of everything. I appreciate it."

"Anything for you, cuz. After all, blood is thicker than water." Riley held out his glass of the red stuff as if making a toast and laughed at his own joke.

"That's a funny one, Riley. I'll be back in a few."

Banan let himself out of the tent before he gave in to the urge to punch his cousin on general principles. Although it didn't hurt to pay the hired help the odd compliment, he hated to encourage stupidity.

The only comfort came from knowing that by this time tomorrow, he'd be back among his own kind and living in luxury as he so deserved.

"No, Megan. This isn't a social club." Conlan crossed his arms over his chest and planted himself directly in front of the door. "He's a prisoner, not a guest. He isn't allowed visitors."

"I'm not just any visitor, Conlan Shea. I'm delivering another meal." Megan tried to push past the security officer, but she might as well have been pushing against a stone wall.

"Rafferty said no one in, no one out."

"Fine." Megan turned her back to Conlan. "Can you lift Phoebe out of her carrier, please? I need to change her."

He sighed and pulled Phoebe out of the back carrier and then held her out to Megan. Instead of taking her daughter, Megan picked up the basket and slipped past the now furious chancellor.

"Damn it, Megan, come back here."

"Not until I see Seamus, Conlan."

She kept moving, but glanced back to see how he was doing with Phoebe. She would have laughed at the sight of him holding her daughter out at arm's length, but he was already mad. There was no use in making the situation worse. He caught up with her after only a short distance.

"Okay, okay. I'll take you to Seamus."

"Seriously?"

"Seriously," he said, sounding thoroughly disgruntled. "I hope you'll feel real bad when this costs me my job. Rafferty carries a mean grudge."

"He won't fire you for letting me talk to an inno-cent man."

She injected as much conviction as she could into the statement. It wasn't hard, though, because she believed what she was saying.

A familiar voice spoke up. "You believe I'm innocent?"

She whirled around to find Seamus walking toward her, looking tired but smiling at her. When he held out his arms, she didn't hesitate. It was hard to tell which one of them needed the hug more.

"I've been so worried." She blinked hard, trying not to cry.

"I'm sorry about that," he whispered.

He gently brushed away her tears with his fingertips as he bent his head down and kissed her. She gave herself up to the moment, taking comfort in the strength of his embrace and the promise of Seamus's kiss. Here, wrapped in each other's arms, for a few seconds the world and all of their problems simply ceased to exist. At least until Phoebe let loose with a loud wail. She felt Seamus's mouth turn up in a smile.

"Someone feels left out," he whispered as he eased away.

Conlan immediately handed Phoebe into Seamus's waiting arms. As soon as Seamus cuddled her up to his shoulder, she stopped crying. When he had her settled, he wrapped his free hand around Megan's shoulders and pulled her close. She'd never thought she could trust another man, much less a vampire, but it felt so right for Seamus to offer her and Phoebe the shelter of his arms.

Conlan looked a bit jealous. "One of these days

you're going to have to explain this gift you have for charming females."

"Not all females, Conlan. Just these two."

"Yeah, I see that." The chancellor's expression turned serious. "I hate to break this up, but we need to get moving."

Megan looked from one man to the other. "You're setting Seamus free?"

Seamus carefully eased Phoebe back into her carrier. "We're going to examine the body. Conlan wants to verify what I told him about her injuries. We have to hurry because the longer we delay, the greater the chance someone else will get hurt."

"Can I come?" she asked, but wasn't surprised when he said no.

"It's not safe for you to be seen with me. Whoever is out there could be watching. We don't want to put you at risk by letting them know how much you mean to me."

His words and the heat in his eyes melted her heart. She wanted to tell him about her own feelings for him. But now clearly wasn't the time, and not just because Conlan was still hovering right behind her. She knew Seamus well enough to know he'd want to finish clearing his name before taking that next step with her.

"Okay, I'll go home and wait for you there." She raised up high enough to kiss him again, but kept it simple and sweet. Even so, she flashed her fangs at him. "Don't make me wait too long."

He did a little flashing of his own. "I'll try to hurry. Lock yourself in and stay there unless it's me, Conlan or Rafferty at the door."

His words sent a chill through her. "Do you think

I'm in danger? You really think it could be Banan, don't you?"

Conlan nodded as he led the way down the hall. "We thought of him first off, but computer records show he's been in New Eire since he left the estate. I've sent one of my operatives to verify that in person. We should know for sure soon."

They'd reached the door, but Seamus stopped her from leaving.

"All we know for sure is the killer has been going after females, but I have a bad feeling about this whole situation. It can't be coincidence that both murders were done when I had no alibi. The only vampire I've had a problem with was Rafferty, but he's not behind this. If the killer is targeting me for some reason, that could put you and Phoebe at risk."

"Can't I stay at the clinic with you?"

"We don't want anyone to know that I'm out and about, so my warden here was going to slip me out a secret way." He was clearly unhappy about having to refuse.

Conlan spoke up. "Why don't I follow her home and stay with her until you get there? Rafferty will meet you at the clinic."

Seamus held his hand out to Conlan, who gave it a firm shake. "Let's get this wrapped up."

"Sounds good."

"One more thing, Conlan. I'm sorry if Rafferty comes down hard on you for letting me run loose."

The chancellor didn't look overly concerned. "Either he trusts my judgment or he doesn't. Besides, it wouldn't be the first time I lost a job. I was looking for work when I came here. I can look again."

Despite his nonchalant attitude, there was a definite undercurrent of pain in Conlan's voice. Megan sensed he wouldn't appreciate any questions.

"Thank you, Conlan. I'll feel better knowing you're with me."

"It's nothing," he said.

But they all knew that wasn't true.

In the end, Megan made a show of leaving in a fit of anger, in the hopes that it would throw anyone who might be watching off their trail. Then Conlan let Seamus out of the building through an underground tunnel that resurfaced in a thicket of trees about thirty meters away.

Once they climbed out, Seamus closed his eyes to listen to the night. Other than the usual rustles of small critters and the breeze stirring the leaves overhead, it was quiet. When he looked around, he noticed Conlan was doing the same thing.

"Seems clear. I'll take off for the clinic. If all goes right, I should be able to do a quick examination of the body and take pictures. If I don't catch up with you at Megan's in an hour, come charging to the rescue." Then he added, "But make sure you take Megan and Phoebe someplace safe first."

Conlan smiled. "Man, you've got it bad."

"Jealous?"

"Yeah, maybe I am." He clapped his hand down on Seamus's shoulder. "Don't worry, I'll keep her safe or die trying. See you in a few."

Then he took off at a dead run. Seamus waited a few seconds to see if he picked up on anyone else in the area who might follow Conlan. When all remained still, he headed for the clinic. When he reached the trees across the field, it was hard for him to slow down and proceed with caution. He couldn't shake the feeling that the situation was poised to go from bad to much, much worse.

There was only one vampire who had reason to cause problems like this on Rafferty's estate—excluding Seamus himself—and that was Banan Delaney. According to Conlan, no one had entered through the gates nor had there been any breaks in the electric fence. That didn't mean that the vampire hadn't found some way to go over the fence or maybe even under it.

Once the bastard thought Seamus was out of the way, he would go after Megan again. With the horror of that prospect riding him hard, Seamus took off running for the clinic. He let himself in through the front door and quickly locked the door behind him.

Only a few steps into the waiting room, he came to a screeching halt. He wasn't alone. Another vampire had passed through the room recently. After tasting the air, he relaxed, at least marginally, when he recognized the scent as Rafferty's.

"Okay, where are you?"

The older vampire limped into sight. "About time you got here. I hate to be kept waiting. I've already put the victim in the same room we used last time."

He headed for the examination room to study the victim's injuries. Rafferty followed him.

He got his equipment and then uncovered the body. The injuries looked even worse under the stark overhead lighting. The woman had suffered a lot of pain and violation before she'd died. Seamus clicked on the recorder and did his best to choke back his fury as he started at her head and methodically cataloged the cuts, bruises and worse.

It took a long, long time to describe them all. By the time he was finished even Rafferty looked pale. Seamus forced himself to do a brief summary of the cause of death and then formally signed off.

When he was done, he walked away from the table and out toward the lobby. Rafferty followed close on his heels. Seamus stopped and stared at the furniture scattered around the waiting room, his hands itching to pick up the closest table and destroy something with it.

"Go ahead, because if you don't break something I will. Or maybe we both should." Rafferty picked the table up, testing its weight. "I think it would make good kindling or maybe a whole bunch of toothpicks."

Seamus couldn't help it. He laughed, although it wasn't a happy sound. "Yeah, but it does okay as a table, too. It's not the furniture's fault that someone needs to die."

"So listening to you in there, it was definitely two vampires who did that?" Rafferty's eyes were ice cold.

"It took two to do all that damage. The second one might not be a vampire, but my gut feeling is that both of them are. The kind that like to play with their food."

"When I get my hands on them, I'll do more than play with them. They'll die, and it won't be pleasant."

Seamus shot him a questioning look. "So you're not coming after me for this?"

"Not after I saw your face in there. Any doubts are long gone. Your rage over what was done to her was genuine." He set the table down with exaggerated care, obviously still not quite in control of his emotions. Then he sat down in the nearest chair. "Sit down. I'm too tired to look up at you."

Seamus needed to get back to Megan, but they needed to solve this mess even more. "You want to hear my theory?"

"Sure, because I'm drawing a blank here. If it wasn't you, then it was one of my other friends. I don't like the thought of that any better than when the facts pointed in your direction."

"Both murders were done at times when I wouldn't have an alibi, which makes me think it's someone who wants them pinned on me. The only problem with that theory is that I haven't been here long enough to piss anyone off that badly." He risked a small smile. "Well, except maybe for you."

The older vampire's own smile was a whole lot scarier. "For the record, if I was that mad, you'd be the one who was dead, not two innocent women."

"Duly noted, boss. But there was a vampire here who might think he has good reason to want me dead— Banan Delaney. As Phoebe's father and Megan's ex-lover, he wouldn't like me messing with what he'd see as his property. He might not want Megan anymore, but I'm sure his family feels differently about Phoebe. As a pureblood vampire, she represents their future."

"But why kill these other women?"

"To hide his real target? Remember, he's already tried to kill Megan once. If I hadn't had the antidote in my medical case, she'd have died shortly after Conlan found her. She didn't want anyone to know."

Rafferty's eyebrows snapped down as he flashed his fangs at Seamus. "For future reference, Dr. Fitzhugh, patient-doctor confidentiality be damned if one of my people is threatened. I expect to know about it, and sooner rather than later."

"Knowing what I do about you now, I wouldn't hesitate to tell you. Back then, I had no reason to trust you with her safety."

"Point taken."

Seamus drew a deep breath and launched back into his theory. "I think Banan wants his daughter and knows Megan will fight him on that. If he eliminates Megan from the picture, makes me take the fall for the deaths, he's got a chance at taking his daughter home to his clan. I can't imagine he wants Phoebe for any reason other than a power play within his family. We both know the vampire who ensures there's a next generation carries a lot of clout."

He didn't need to explain that any further to Rafferty. Seamus was the last of his clan. If he never produced an heir, his family name would disappear, and Rafferty wouldn't be taking in strays like Seamus if his own clan was thriving.

"But Conlan insists he dragged Banan off my property himself. I have no reason to doubt that he did exactly that."

"Conlan just told me that he sent someone to make sure that Banan made it all the way to New Eire, but he hasn't heard anything yet. I think Banan came back. It's the only thing that makes sense. Not through the gate, of course, but maybe over the fence some way. I know you've got sensors and stuff, but there has to be some flaw in the system he could have exploited if he was willing to spend enough money."

Rafferty was back on his feet. "Maybe there's another way to find out. I'll call his grandmother. She might not approve of me or what I'm trying to do here, but she won't refuse my call. I have too many friends and too much money for her to risk offending me."

"Won't she be suspicious if you accuse Banan of murder?"

"Give me credit for being more tactful than that. I'll tell her how much I enjoyed his visit and ask if she knows where he can be reached. It seems that he left one of his favorite jackets at my house, and I'd like to return it."

"You really are a sneaky bastard, aren't you? Can you make that call now? The night's not getting any longer, and I need to know Megan's safe."

Rafferty punched in the number of the Delaney estate and asked to be connected to the matriarch of the clan. Seamus waited impatiently for the a few minutes for her to be located. The conversation didn't last long.

When Rafferty disconnected the call, he definitely looked worried. "Seems the lady is not pleased with her grandson. He hasn't been home in a while and is supposedly visiting a distant cousin that she doesn't approve of. Seems Banan's cousin Riley had criminal connections and has been disowned by the family as a whole. No one has seen or heard from either of them in days."

Seamus was already starting for the door. "If he lays a hand on either Megan or Phoebe, he won't live long enough for you to kill him. They're mine."

"Let me warn Conlan that you're on your way." Rafferty was already punching in the numbers. After a few seconds he hung up. "No answer."

"Son of bitch, they're already there."

Rafferty pulled a gun out of the top of his boot and tossed it to Seamus. "Go. Run. I'll only slow you down, but I'll be right behind you after I call in the rest of the security force for backup."

Seamus gave Rafferty a long, hard look at his fangs before snarling, "Call in whoever you want to but warn them not to get in my way. You can have what's left of Banan and his cousin when I finish with them."

Then he ran out into the night.

Chapter 16

Seamus ran full out, not caring who heard him coming. In fact, Banan should know that death was on its way. There was no way Seamus would let the bastard live this time. He wanted a future with Megan. For that to happen, he needed to lay her past to rest, preferably in a shallow grave.

If he left enough of Banan to actually bury.

The urge to go charging in, fangs and gun at the ready, was powerful. Even if it were only Conlan in peril, his predator instincts would be aroused. But with a helpless infant and the woman he loved at risk, those same instincts were at full boil and ready to explode.

By sheer strength of will, he brought himself under control. He needed to know what was waiting for him. Only a fool went in blind, especially when it could endanger the very people he wanted to save. He tested for scents on the air. Vampire. Chancellor—Conlan. Blood. Fresh blood.

Shadow to shadow, step by step, he approached Megan's cottage. Voices, angry but with a spicy hint of fear, carried on the night air. He recognized Megan and Banan, but not the third voice. Conlan's absence from the conversation worried him. Was the chancellor dead? He'd better not be. Banan already had enough to answer for.

He stooped lower, not wanting to draw anyone's attention until the last possible minute. He'd made it within twenty meters of the front door when he spotted a still form lying on the ground just ahead. He froze briefly to make sure no one was watching from the doorway before sprinting forward to verify the body's identity. Conlan. It was too much to hope that he'd managed to take out one of the bad guys.

He felt for a pulse and was relieved to find one. Using his sense of touch, he did a quick check for injuries. The chancellor was bleeding from a shallow gash on the side of his head. Seamus used his own shirt as a bandage to help stanch the bleeding. Conlan was in no immediate danger, so Seamus dragged him farther from the house to remove any potential of him being used as an additional hostage. Hopefully Rafferty and his security forces would find him if Seamus didn't survive his encounter with Banan.

He had a lot to live for now that he had a home and a woman he wanted to share it with, but he would gladly die to save Megan and her daughter. That might be his only advantage against two vampires in bloodlust.

He positioned himself against the house, pressing his ear against the wall to listen. Hearing the filth Banan was spewing out to Megan in a series of threats infuriated him even further. At least the two vampires had yet to lay their hands on her and Phoebe.

From what he could discern, she'd barricaded herself in her bedroom by shoving the furniture in front of the door. The cottage had no windows in the bedrooms, so the only way Banan could get to her was through the barricaded door.

Suddenly Banan stopped shouting threats and started whispering. Seamus could only make out a few words, but one stopped his heart cold.

Fire.

Before he could react, the front door flung open and a vampire charged outside to head straight for a transport parked at the side of the road. Should Seamus go after him or not? Deciding he should to avoid the risk of him returning before he could subdue Banan, Seamus picked up a hefty rock and went on the attack. He reached the vampire just as he stepped off the curb. Leaping high, Seamus hit the bastard on the back of his head, putting all of his strength into swinging the rock. The blow sent the vampire plummeting to the ground, his face hitting the concrete with a satisfying jolt.

Seamus put his knee in the small of the man's back and bent his arm up almost to the point of dislocating his shoulder. The vampire whimpered in pain when Seamus cranked on it even harder as he leaned down near his ear.

"Let me introduce myself. I'm Seamus Fitzhugh, the vampire who is going to kill you. You must be Riley."

"Banan said you were locked up," Riley whimpered.

"Well, he was wrong, wasn't he?" Seamus laughed

nastily, "What's more, boyo, Rafferty O'Day is on his way here. You'll hate meeting him."

That set off a full-blown panic attack as the frantic vampire tried to buck Seamus off his chest. "It was all Banan! He made me help him."

"Don't bother lying to me. I saw what you did to those women. You and your buddy in there deserve everything you're going to get and then some."

If Megan wasn't still at risk, Seamus might have taken the time to teach the stunned vampire a lesson about playing with his food. Instead, he went right for the jugular, ripping into the side of his victim's throat, inflicting as much pain as possible. As tempting as it was to kill him outright, he decided to leave some of the fun for Rafferty. He drained enough blood to weaken the vampire and left him sprawled on the edge of the road.

That left Banan. Wiping the blood off his mouth, Seamus stood up. If he didn't hurry, the other vampire might come looking to see what was keeping his cousin. Seamus yanked Riley's hooded sweatshirt off his body and put it on, hoping he could get close to Banan before he recognized him.

The house had grown ominously quiet. Seamus approached the front door, his heart in his throat. If he'd made the wrong decision in going after Riley first...

But then Banan's voice rang out again. "Go ahead, bitch, and think you're safe. When I get back, we'll see how much you like being toasted. I know you'd rather see Phoebe with her father than dead. Think about that."

Megan's fury burned brightly in every word she uttered. "Phoebe doesn't belong to you, Banan, and never will. Even if you manage to kill me this time,

Seamus Fitzhugh will hunt you down and get her back. And think how many interesting ways a doctor knows for killing animals like you!"

"Yeah, well, your lover isn't here, is he? By the time they put out the fire, I'll be on my way home with the brat. My partner out there will be another unfortunate victim, so Rafferty will think he's found the killer. My parents and grandparents will get their precious heir, and I'll get my inheritance. It's a win-win situation for me."

Megan still had plenty of fight left. "No matter what happens, Banan, you'll be a loser. Do you really think your grandmother doesn't know what a worthless piece of garbage you are? Otherwise, why are they more concerned about the next generation instead of you?"

"Shut up, bitch!" Banan backed up and kicked the door again.

Seamus turned the corner to find Banan standing outside Megan's bedroom. There were huge cracks in the wooden door, and it would have likely shattered if Banan and Riley had attacked it with their combined strength. He shut down that thought. There'd be time later to think about how close he'd come to losing both Megan and Phoebe to this madman.

He eased closer, hoping to sneak up on Banan, but something gave his presence away.

"It took you long enough, Riley. We don't have much time before we have to get out to the pickup zone."

Thanks to the sweatshirt, it took Banan a couple of seconds to realize that he wasn't talking to his cousin. When he recognized Seamus, his eyes went huge and he backed up a couple of steps. That was all the invitation Seamus needed to go on the attack.

"Get ready to die, Banan. Personally, I'm looking forward to watching you bleed out."

At the sound of his voice, Megan called out, "Seamus! I knew you'd come."

"Stay in there, honey, while I take out this trash. Rafferty's on his way with help."

Banan lunged at Seamus. The fight turned brutal quickly. Desperation was driving Delaney, but all of Seamus's protective instincts were running at full bore. He would make this night safe for his females or die trying. The two vampires banged from side to side in the narrow hallway until they finally stumbled into the kitchen.

Banan managed to snag a butcher knife off the counter and slashed at Seamus's chest with it. The blade sliced through his shirt and skin, but he didn't even notice the pain or the blood that immediately soaked through the cloth. Instead, he latched onto Banan's wrist with both of his hands.

Despite Banan's best efforts, Seamus slowly bent the knife around until it was aimed back toward the other man. Lunging forward, he forced the blade up-ward and into Banan's chest. When he yanked it back out, blood came gushing out in pulsing waves. Banan gave up all pretense of fighting as he attempted to stanch the bleeding with his hands.

Seamus wanted to watch his enemy as Banan's life force poured out onto the floor. But now that he was no longer a threat to anyone, Seamus's medical training kicked in. He grabbed the dish towel off the rack and tried to get Banan to let him apply pressure.

"Let me stop the bleeding! You'll be dead in seconds if you don't."

But Banan was too out of his head with pain and fear to listen to reason. He stumbled past Seamus, heading for the front door. By the sounds of things, Rafferty had finally arrived. He could deal with the Delaney heir any way he wanted to. Seamus had more important things to do.

A few seconds later, an agonizing scream rang out, and then there was silence.

Seamus needed to get to Megan and Phoebe, but he was covered in blood, some of his own, some Banan's. He wiped off what he could with the towel and washed some of the rest off at the sink. The gash on his chest was far more serious than he'd realized, so he got out more towels and did his best to close the wound and slow the bleeding.

When he'd done all he could, he ran down the hallway to the bedroom.

"Megan, honey, open the door. It's safe now."

He could only hope he could stay on his feet long enough for her to come out. He had something to say, something important, and he needed to say it now, before it was too late.

Finally, he heard the last piece of furniture slide out of the way and the door opened. Megan peeked out. When she saw him, she started to smile, but then she noticed the blood dripping down onto the floor.

"Seamus! You're hurt."

His vision was going black around the edges, and he couldn't feel his feet. He was surprised to find he could still stand. When Megan reached his side, she wrapped his free arm around her shoulders.

"Come sit down before you fall down."

"No, that's not what I need to do," he told her, standing his ground. "Need to tell you something."

"It can wait until we stop the bleeding."

"No. Waited too long already." He fought the dizziness and the fog.

"Okay, tell me as we walk over to the couch. That'll work, won't it?" She tugged him along a step or two.

"No, listen. Look at me."

"Stubborn man, what could be that important?"

She propped him up against the wall and positioned herself to catch him if he should fall. Bless her.

He smiled or at least he thought he did. Megan only looked more worried, so maybe he wasn't doing it right. No matter. Words were better. Clearer.

"I came here. Life over. Hated Rafferty."

"Yes, I know. We've been over all that."

"Didn't tell you, though."

"Tell me what?"

"Love you. Love Phoebe." He managed to drag his hand up to her face. It left a blood smear on her pretty skin, but she didn't seem to mind. "Want you. With me. Please."

He was pretty sure that it was tears making her eyes sparkle so brightly. On the other hand, she was smiling, so maybe he was wrong about that. None of it mattered, though, because as he slid down the wall to land on the floor, she said the words he'd been hoping to hear.

"I love you, too. Now can we get you some help?"

"Good idea," he managed to whisper.

Then the lights went out.

Megan walked into the clinic and headed straight for the pre-op room. She'd spent a good part of the day there until Rafferty and Joss ran her off with orders to get some sleep. Since her cottage wasn't exactly livable at the moment, she'd commandeered Seamus's bedroom and slept there.

Joss was staying with Phoebe for a while, freeing Megan up to visit the two patients currently housed in the clinic. Rafferty had flown in an outside doctor to care for Seamus and Conlan.

Banan's body and that of his cousin had been returned to the Delaney clan. The family had agreed to accept Rafferty's offer to report the deaths as tragic accidents. They all knew that if the two had survived long enough to stand trial, they'd be facing execution if convicted. No matter how much money the Delaney clan had, they wouldn't be able to buy their way out of this one. The scandal was buried along with their bodies.

Megan wondered if she should be feeling some regret about that, but she wouldn't lie to herself about how she felt. Banan had destroyed any feeling she had for him with his atrocious actions. Someday, Phoebe might have some questions about her father that would be tough to answer. Somehow she and Seamus would find a way to handle them when the time came.

She could already hear the grumbling from inside the makeshift patient ward before she'd gotten halfway across the waiting room. Both males were due to be discharged within the next day, and neither of them took being invalids particularly well. She stopped in the doorway to study their battered faces. Conlan looked the best, but that wasn't saying much. It terrified her to know how close she'd come to losing both of them.

Pasting a bright smile on her face, she knocked on the door frame. "Up for some company?"

Seamus immediately sat up straighter, his handsome

face marred with the yellow-green tinge of fading bruises. He held out his hand in welcome.

"Sure thing." He motioned toward Conlan. "He hasn't stopped complaining since he woke up."

"Yeah, well, he slurps when he feeds." The chancellor glared at Seamus. "I'd rather he snored."

She giggled. "He does."

"Hey!" Seamus protested, even as he tugged her down for a kiss. "I have other redeeming qualities."

Her memory of some of those talents had her blushing. But when he winced as she accidentally bumped his cheek, she was reminded that he'd been willing to die to save her and Phoebe. She tried not to cry, she really did, but the fear was still too fresh, too painful.

"That's it! I'm out of here." Conlan threw back his covers and stalked out of the room, quietly closing the door on his way out.

Seamus scooted to the far side of his bed and tugged her arm, trying to drag her onto the mattress with him. He didn't have to try hard. She so needed the comforting touch of his body next to hers.

He held her close while the tears soaked through his hospital gown. Cuddling next to him, resting her head on his shoulder felt like coming home. She needed to know where they went from here.

"Did you mean it?"

He didn't pretend to not understand. "I might not have been at my most eloquent, but yeah, I meant it. I love you, I love your daughter and I want you both with me."

"Good, because I've already packed our stuff. Rafferty promised to have it all moved into your quarters this evening."

She looked up into his handsome face, so dear to her. What she saw reflected in his eyes chased the last bit of doubt and fear of the future from her soul.

Then he frowned. "I had a long talk with Rafferty about Phoebe and the Delaneys and any potential claim they might have on Phoebe. I've asked him to officially make me part of his clan. He's going to put through the necessary paperwork today, and he'll officiate at our wedding as soon as I'm up and about. Once you two are legally mine, we'll all be part of the O'Day clan."

Bless his heart, always thinking about her and Phoebe even when he was hurt and bleeding. The strength in this man never failed to amaze her. "Are you sure about all of this, Seamus? I don't want to rush you into anything."

His kiss was meant to comfort, but incited at the same time. "Here, and I thought I was the one rushing you. Do we have a deal?"

"If you're sure, then yes, we do, Dr. Fitzhugh."

"Good," he said, his smile looking awfully satisfied. "I hope it's all right that there won't be time to invite your parents or anyone to the ceremony. We need this all laid to rest as soon as possible."

"I have all the family I need right here. I can face anything life throws at me as long as you're there beside me."

His eyes gleamed with satisfaction. "Then, that's where I'll be."

* * * * *

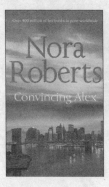

Have Your Say

You've just finished your book.
So what did you think?

We'd love to hear your thoughts on our
'Have your say' online panel
www.millsandboon.co.uk/haveyoursay

- 🌹 Easy to use
- 🌹 Short questionnaire
- 🌹 Chance to win Mills & Boon® goodies

Visit us Online
Tell us what you thought of this book now at
www.millsandboon.co.uk/haveyoursay